MW00584053

BLOOD RUNS DEEP

DOUG SINCLAIR

Storm
PUBLISHING

This is a work of fiction. Names, characters, business, events and incidents are the products of the author's imagination. Any resemblance to actual persons, living or dead, or actual events is purely coincidental.

Copyright © Doug Sinclair, 2024

The moral right of the author has been asserted.

All rights reserved. No part of this book may be reproduced or used in any manner without the prior written permission of the copyright owner.

To request permissions, contact the publisher at rights@stormpublishing.co

Ebook ISBN: 978-1-80508-467-9
Paperback ISBN: 978-1-80508-468-6

Cover design: Blacksheep
Cover images: Shutterstock

Published by Storm Publishing.
For further information, visit:
www.stormpublishing.co

For Maaike, who believed in me when I couldn't. Love you, wife.

ONE

He thought he was ready. They said he was ready.

But the headaches were back. And he was talking to himself again.

Walk away. You'll hurt people. You always do.

Walk. Away.

He clutched the minicab's grubby door handle and considered throwing himself out, as if hitting tarmac at forty miles an hour might hurt less than what waited for him. He couldn't afford to waste money on a taxi at night-shift prices, but the callout had interrupted one of his rare, failed attempts to get drunk in what he liked to call his local, which had left him no other option. He'd told the miserable sod at the wheel to drive slowly and take the scenic route. He preferred the town at night – quiet and empty. But the late hour meant they flew through every junction. Every light stayed green, and he arrived too soon.

He stepped out of the cab into the dark night and crossed to the west side of the road, into the shadows of trees along the verge. Beyond them lay an expanse of farmland that stretched past the town boundary towards the Pentland Hills. He could barely see their massive, brooding heights at this time of the night, no more than vague black shapes far off in the dark, but he wished – not for the first time – he was walking them now, even in these temperatures. Up there lay a place colder and more inhospitable than anywhere here in town, yet he yearned for its bleak and lonely comfort. He promised himself he'd go to the hills again before his fiftieth, before he got too old and worn out for the climb.

A hundred yards further on, trees on both sides of the road flickered with shocking blue flashes from a patrol car parked on the grass verge, like far-off lightning strikes heading his way. He choked down memories of the last time he'd been blinded by blue lights, six months ago.

He pushed the thoughts away. *You can't think about that. Not now.* As the heavy November night settled around him, all sound ceased. He used to enjoy nights like this: peaceful and still, devoid of traffic noise and fumes. Ice in the air made clouds of his breath and cut straight through his clothes. He told himself it was the bitter cold making him shake deep in his guts.

He froze. He'd stopped the cab a hundred yards from his destination, but now found himself afraid to leave the dark shelter under the trees, afraid to commit. What the hell was he thinking? How could he think he was ready? He bent and braced his hands on his knees, breathed long and slow, then stepped out from the shadows.

As well as yellow crime-scene tape this side of the patrol car, he saw more across the opening into the suburb of Murieston. The tapes swayed, slow and lazy on a breeze that skulked across the farmland to the west and through the trees that lined the road.

Six months away hadn't been enough. A few weeks more would have been ideal, but he'd said that a month ago. Besides, would he ever feel ready again?

He wrapped his fingers around a lamp post and rested his

forehead – slick with sweat even in these temperatures – on the freezing metal. Stomach acid and cheap rum burned his throat. He narrowed his world to the small, achievable goal of not throwing up, then straightened and sucked in a great icy breath, imagined it filling him to his fingertips.

It'll come back. Nineteen good years. Six months of recovery.

Panic screamed inside him, but he'd survived hundreds of nights like this and hadn't broken yet.

Give it time. It'll come back.

He wiped the sweat from his forehead with his jacket sleeve, straightened his tie, and tucked away his shirt-tail that never seemed to stay in for long. He forced his feet to move, crept closer to the junction. From the shadows under the trees, he studied the scene. An ambulance sat a few yards beyond a dark crumpled mass on the road, at the entrance to the estate. No details visible, yet. Not from this safe distance.

One step, then one more. You've got this.

Two paramedics worked, heads down, and a uniformed constable watched, a clipboard under one arm, stamping his feet and rubbing his hands together. The white puffs of his breath came short and fast.

Malkie heard the rustling of the hi-vis jackets and occasional brief instructions. They spoke in calm, efficient voices, focused on the poor bastard they fought to save. The strobes on the ambulance roof were brutal as they lit up the dark heap of rags and bloody flesh visible between the two men. Malkie's stomach lurched, and he braced himself to flee, but the constable turned to him.

'DI McCulloch, bloody happy to see you, sir. Terry Munro.'

Malkie flinched at Terry's obvious faith in him. He felt like a fraud, undeserving of Terry's trust, but he reminded himself how many full investigations he'd run without any problems before his enforced leave. Plenty of the residents of Saughton prison owed their free bed and board to him, which had to say something about his capabilities. Before he lost his edge. Before...

He forced what he hoped was a reassuring smile. 'It's DS now, Terry. And call me Malkie at this time of the night, OK?'

'Sorry... boss.'

Terry was less than a year on the job, and this one looked to have him rattled. Shallow breaths and a tremor in his voice; must be a bad one. First responders always got the shitty end of the stick. In Terry's nervous words Malkie found a crevice to dig his fingers into, something to anchor him, save him from a sickening fall that gaped beneath him.

Somebody needed him. Here, now, he had a purpose, a use. This was his world, a job where even in his fragile state he could make a difference. *We do what we can*, as his mum used to say. Before the accident. Before the nightmares started.

The nightmares you brought on yourself.

He shut the thoughts down before they could set him off. He pulled his shirt cuffs down to cover the damage to his wrists from that horrific night, then hauled in a deep breath, held it, released it, and stepped under the tape. 'What do we have, Terry?'

'RTC, sir. I thought you were still... You know?' He grimaced, as if terrified he'd overstepped some mark.

Malkie put the poor man out of his obvious discomfort. 'Let's call it medical leave. And I'm still Malkie, son. How's Marie?'

Terry perked up. 'She's good, sir. Due any time now. Knackered and grumpy, but gorgeous with it. Obviously.'

'Another one? You're going to need more overtime, mate.' He shook Terry's hand, found it icy and trembling. 'Where's Steph?'

'DC Lang's with a witness, sir. Just inside the estate.'

Malkie placed his other hand on the lad's shoulder. 'Terry.

It's Malkie. Keep that "*sir*" shite for when McLeish is around, OK?'

'Aye, boss. Sorry, boss.'

Malkie gave the lad's arm a squeeze. Terry smiled and lifted his clipboard to sign Malkie into the crime scene.

A gaggle of eager spectators clustered behind the scene tape, most with smartphones aimed at the locus. DC Steph Lang stood with a man in pyjamas and slippers and a puffer jacket. A head taller than she was and at least twice her weight, his folded arms and looming posture suggested he was making the classic mistake of patronising her. He'd learn. She spotted Malkie and waved. He lifted his hand in response, then forced himself to turn and look at the victim.

The man lay on his back, a spinal board beside him and a plastic brace around his neck. His face was a ruined, wet mess. Thick layers of dressings swathed his head, blood already saturating the white cotton. His right cheek glistened, black and swollen, his eye bloated and weeping. Both legs had been twisted into ugly angles. The man's fingers stretched and curled as if searching for something. His mouth twitched, but no sound came out. Blood bubbled from between his lips.

Malkie shook his head. 'What a mess.'

The man opened one eye and turned towards him, but his gaze wandered, glassy and distant. His hand lifted from the tarmac and reached out. Malkie froze. He wanted to step forward, hold that hand, give the man a connection to cling to, but his legs refused to move. Tears spilled from the man's open eye and ran into blood smeared across his cheeks. His eye closed, and his hand fell back, and he went still again.

Malkie swore a silent oath to find the fucker who did this, then swore at himself – another rash promise. Would he never learn?

He jumped as Terry Munro spoke behind him. 'Happened

around fifty minutes ago, sir. One witness heard the collision but didn't see the vehicle. DC Lang is with the gentleman now.'

Malkie felt the familiar comfort of procedure and took refuge in his responsibilities. 'Am I the ranking officer, Terry? RTC, you said? And stop bloody calling me sir.'

'Aye, RTC and failure to stop. DC Lang says no way it's accidental. DI McLeish attended, but he didn't stay long.'

Malkie turned toward the ambulance. He didn't want Terry to see his disappointment. Accidental might mean quick and simple, maybe dump the whole thing onto Road Policing. Doubts meant complicated, and he wasn't ready for complicated.

'DS McCulloch? Malkie?' Terry's voice now gentle, something personal coming.

Malkie froze. *Here it comes. Be nice.*

Terry smiled, but it was weak and miserable. 'Good to have you back, boss.'

Is it, Terry? 'Thanks, mate.'

'I'm glad you're on tonight. DS Ballantyne, I don't think she likes me very much.'

'DS Ballantyne doesn't like anyone, Terry, but you didn't hear that from me, right?'

Terry stared at Malkie in mock disapproval, then chuckled to himself.

Malkie walked past evidence markers either side of a long, black streak of burnt tarmac with a slight curve on it, which led towards the mess on the road. The ambulance lamp revealed more than enough detail from where he stood.

'How's it looking, lads?'

One of them didn't react, too intent on getting a line into a blood-slick arm. The other shone a penlight into a swollen eye. He sat back on his heels and glanced up. Malkie hunted for his name – Jim, or John something. He looked tired.

'Hi, Malkie. You OK? You know, after...?'

Malkie twirled a finger to the man to carry on.

'Sorry. You look like I feel, mate. Anyway, got a bloody mess here. Obvious multiple breaks to both legs and right wrist. Severe penetrating wound to the front right temple. Query fractured ribs and internal bleeding, too. Whoever hit this guy really had the foot down. We should get pain relief in soon so we can get him immobilised and loaded. Hope to be on our way in five, ten minutes.'

Malkie turned away and nearly jumped out of his skin. Steph Lang stood inches behind him.

'Fuck's sake, Steph. Don't do that.'

'Sorry.' Her tone suggested she was anything but. She punched him on the arm. 'How are you? I've missed you.'

A sudden lump in his throat threatened to set him off. Unlike many of his colleagues, she meant every word she said, always.

'I'm fine. Stop asking.'

She studied him, seemed to accept his assurance. There was more to say, much more, but later.

Steph stood a half-inch over five feet but exuded an air of effortless intimidation. Despite being short and mousy, her face and her manner seemed always to say, *'Give me an excuse'*. Many of their colleagues practised judo or karate. As the scariest wee bastard in J Division CID, Steph did an Israeli thing called Krav Maga. Whenever they did good cop/bad cop, Malkie had to play the nice guy; she just didn't have it in her.

He took her by the arm and led her away from the medics. 'Why the hell am I here? I'm not due back until tomorrow.'

A twinkle appeared in her eyes, but her voice softened. 'Have you been drinking? You hate the taste of booze. Are you still trying to find something you can stomach enough to get pissed? Like that'll solve anything, mate?'

'I can drink when I need to. I'm not supposed to return to

duty until tomorrow. Anyway, don't change the subject. Why am I here?'

Steph raised an eyebrow but let him off easy. 'Terry attended and called it in. I attended and called it in. McLeish attended and told me to call you, then buggered off again.' She paused for effect. 'He said to work it as accidental.'

'So, we're doing that, right? Accidental?' He held his breath.

'Nope. One enthusiastic witness swears otherwise. Mr Drummond lives in the house at the opening to the estate. He's adamant it was no accident. He found the victim in the road and saw a vehicle's brake lights heading north towards the town centre. Saloon car, light grey or silver.'

Malkie scanned the street and clung to his hope for an easy comeback case. He needed this to be nothing more than some idiot drink-driver, wasn't sure he could handle anything ugly, anything like the too many atrocities he'd seen people inflict on others.

I can do this. I've seen so much worse.

'So, some drunk came pelting down the road too fast, hit someone, shit himself, and scarpered? Can I go home to bed now, Sherlock?'

Steph held his gaze for a second. It was a look he'd learned to respect.

'Mr Drummond heard the vehicle's engine getting hammered, and the sound of a wheel-spin, right before the impact. And I found burnt tyre rubber at the roadside just south of the junction. Looks like the driver floored it from stationary.'

Malkie closed his eyes and pinched the bridge of his nose. One of those peculiar gestures that everybody did but which never helped.

'Suggesting that someone meant to do' – he waved his thumb over his shoulder – 'that?'

'Yep.'

'Suggesting attempted murder.'

'Yep, given the speed the vehicle must have been doing. But there's more.'

Of course there bloody is.

'We found more rubber three metres before the point of collision. Looks like the driver floored it from stationary, but then must have braked again at the last moment, or the victim would be dead already. McLeish suggested accidental in that affectionate way of his that we all find so endearing, and I wasn't about to argue with him. You know what he's like.' She left that hanging, but Malkie ignored it.

He smiled at the irony dripping from her assessment of McLeish's people skills. 'Aye, he's a charmer, isn't he? Any ID? On the victim, I mean? Not McLeish. That would be silly, right?'

She grimaced, familiar with Malkie's so-called sense of humour but never encouraging of it. 'Nope. Just a bunch of keys, and we only got those a minute ago. Paramedics couldn't risk moving him to check his pockets.'

'No wallet? No phone? Did the driver take them?'

'Not enough time. Mr Drummond reached his front door only seconds after the impact. Said the car didn't even stop.'

She called over her shoulder. 'Terry, the victim's effects, please?'

Terry fetched two evidence bags from the back seat of the patrol car, one paper and one plastic. Steph checked the labels stuck across the flaps and handed them to Malkie. He ignored the paper bag – it would contain his jacket and a fair amount of the poor man's blood. The other held two house keys, and a barrel-shaped one, for a desk or a filing cabinet. Plus, a BMW remote-locking fob.

'You tried this yet?'

'Like I said, I've been taking statements. We only have Terry for support, typical Friday night, no backup, everyone's out on shouts or booking in. We've taped off and set up scene access the best we can. SOCOs are busy, too – a couple of idiots stabbed each other in Whitburn.'

Malkie raised the key fob high and pressed the button through the plastic. They heard a beep from somewhere inside the estate and walked to the junction. Another press, another beep, and the indicators on a gleaming black BMW blinked on a drive fifty yards away. He took comfort from this small result but avoided Steph's gaze, not ready to let her in. Not even his partner. Not yet.

'OK, so some curtain-twitcher heard a vehicle getting thrashed, then the collision.'

'Yep.'

'And we have fresh tyre rubber?'

'Yep. In two places. Looks like hard acceleration followed by braking, like I said, but Road Policing will confirm that.'

'And – possibly – only yards from the suspected victim's home?'

'Yep. So, RTC? Like McLeish said?'

He scowled at her. He loved her to bits, but the wee shite knew him too well; even after what he'd been through, with his nerves as shredded as they were, he'd never take an easy way out.

'Accidental, my arse. This is attempted murder. And McLeish, as usual, is a prick.'

Malkie had made another in a long history of promises to complete strangers. Could he dare to hope he could deliver justice for the broken and bloodied man lying in the road? Might that allow him to believe he could atone for whatever it was he did – or didn't do – that night six months ago, when his life fell apart?

Could this be a promise he'd manage to keep, unlike so many before?

Or might it finish him?

TWO

Malkie forgot about the black BMW when they found the house door ajar and the lock damaged.

Steph produced two pairs of latex gloves and shoe covers without needing to be asked. He struggled to pull his gloves on over damp palms and fingers. He couldn't stop shaking, and he hadn't drunk nearly enough to blame it on that.

She pulled a pepper spray and her baton from somewhere under her jacket. 'First sign of trouble, you go get Terry, OK?'

'It's not like you to be nervous.'

'I'm not. It's you I'm worried about.'

He shrugged – she had a point. Wouldn't be the first time he'd let her loose on a deserving knuckle-dragger and stood well back.

She stopped before stepping to the door. 'We touch nothing and mind our feet, aye?'

'Yes, Steph. I think I remember how this crime-scene stuff works, but thanks for that.'

She sighed and pushed open the door.

A carpeted hallway, with doors at the end and in either wall, and the foot of a staircase on the right. A console table stood on one side, coats and scarves on hooks, polished black and brown brogues in neat rows underneath, unopened mail stacked on the shelf. Malkie heard nothing and stepped inside, was happy to feel hard concrete under the carpet, no creaky wood. He indicated the envelopes to Steph – addressed to a Mr Robin Wilkie.

Through one door was a dining room. On a table sat three stacks of manila files full of papers with coloured tabs. One folder lay open, with what looked like legal papers spilled out.

Opposite they found a kitchen. It looked expensive, with brushed chrome, gleaming wood, and a marble worktop. Bare counters, no clutter. A row of knives hung from a magnetic strip, ranging from a small paring knife to a large carver.

The second largest space was empty. Malkie glanced at Steph, and she nodded her acknowledgement.

Back in the hallway, she pointed up the staircase then crept up, placing her feet at the sides of the treads. Malkie moved through to the living room. A massive leather corner sofa filled one corner, a huge glass coffee table before it. Magazines and remote controls sat on the table, lined up in a neat row. Two patio doors led to a garden. A massive TV hung on the wall with two speakers either side and on the wall opposite, behind the sofa. High-end gear, with the wiring hidden in the walls.

Not short of cash, Mr Wilkie.

The only thing approaching clutter was a stack of shelves, every square inch stuffed with photo frames. Family photos showing holidays in sunny locations. A graduation photo which Malkie had to assume was of the man fighting for his life outside, though any attempt at comparison was futile in his present condition. He saw no siblings, only a handsome and fit-looking young man with his parents, the father tall and solid and dependable, the mother capable-looking and ageing with grace, always with one hand on her son's shoulder or arm. He resisted a sudden urge to think back to his own mum, couldn't afford to set himself off. The largest photo showed a crowd of young people in a beach bar under a garish neon sign that read 'The Copa Banana'. Every one of the laughing twenty-somethings held aloft shot glasses and beer bottles. One man appeared in every picture, and the difference between the handsome, smiling face of Robin Wilkie in print and the swollen black mess outside had Malkie choking back a surge of anger. He knew nothing about the man yet, but he reaffirmed to himself his earlier promise. He'd never learn.

Steph called from upstairs. 'Up here, Malkie.'

He checked the patio doors – locked with the key on the inside – then headed upstairs.

At the top of the stairs was a bathroom, all ocean-blue mosaic and seashells. A single toothbrush lay beside toothpaste, floss, and interdentals, on a glass shelf above the sink. On another shelf sat aftershave, moisturiser, and hair gel.

Two other doors led into bedrooms. The first contained boxes and plastic crates and a huge exercise bike that looked straight out of a swanky gym.

Steph waited at the entrance to the main bedroom. It had been ransacked.

Drawers hung open and clothing lay strewn across polished wooden floorboards. The mattress lay shifted sideways under a mess of loose sheets She pointed towards a built-in wardrobe. On the floor inside sat a safe. In front of it lay the missing knife from the kitchen, the tip broken off. Malkie crouched closer, found scratches on the paintwork next to the lock, a circular slot, kinked at random points around its circumference. He could just make out a fragment of steel lodged deep in the groove.

He recalled the keys in the evidence bag. The barrel-shaped one could be a fit for the lock, but he couldn't confirm that until the SOCOs signed off on the safe.

No doubt now though. Robin Wilkie's accident was no accident.

They returned downstairs; Malkie didn't want an arse-kicking later for poking about without a paper onesie.

'Steph, did McLeish OK a SOCO callout?'

'Aye.'

'Who's the on-call Scene Manager tonight?'

'Josh Lamb.'

'Good, he owes me. Ask him to send his lot up here ASAP. Tell him McLeish OK'd it verbally and I'll make sure he logs it tomorrow. Work this as RTC serious injury for now. Do not – repeat, do not – let Road Policing take this. I'll argue it with them later. And get more bloody uniforms here. Put PC Terry Munro on the door. You and I can carry on interviewing those concerned citizens, until we get reinforcements to continue the door-to-doors, OK?'

Steph grinned at him.

'What?'

'Good to have you back, boss.' She punched him on the arm again.

Malkie returned to the lounge so she wouldn't see the affectionate smile he couldn't keep off his face. He fished out his personal mobile, took a wide shot of the photo shelves, and a close-up of The Copa Banana. He'd get a hammering if McLeish found out he'd taken crime-scene photos on his own phone, but he wanted something to keep Robin Wilkie real, more than just a name in the case notes.

Terry stood outside the front door. Poor sod: it was bloody freezing, and the lad had a long, boring shift ahead of him. If the SOCOs took a while, he'd also have several irate neighbours demanding to get their cars off their drives.

Jim – or was it John? – loaded up Mr Wilkie, then handed Malkie the paperwork, his expression grim.

'St John's A&E is ready for him, but it's not looking good.'

Malkie sighed and signed the form. He touched the man's elbow, the briefest recognition of shared compassion.

'Thanks, Jim.' No reaction to the name – he got that right, at least. 'Do what you can, eh? Save me some paperwork?'

Jim managed a smile as he climbed into the passenger seat, and the ambulance drove off. A brief blast of the siren as it pulled away threatened to waken ugly memories in Malkie's mind, but he ignored them; this wasn't about him or his many failings.

'Right. Let's start the door-to-doors. Keep us busy until Josh's lot arrive.'

Fifteen minutes in, Steph shouted his name. He excused himself from a short, intense woman called Cynthia who asked more questions than she answered. Steph stood with a different man in a dressing gown and woolly cardigan who clutched a steaming mug. Malkie caught a whiff of hot chocolate and hunger twisted his stomach.

He nodded at Mr Cocoa and smiled, then turned to Steph. 'You called in more support?'

'Yes, boss. A couple of uniforms just left the station. Should be here in minutes.'

'OK, what do we have?' He turned back to Mr Cocoa, who opened his mouth but shut it again, his eyes drawn to the ground.

Malkie looked down, swore under his breath, and yanked the bright blue plastic covers off his shoes.

Steph, ever the professional, soldiered on. 'Same as we got from Mr Drummond. Engine noise, tyres, collision, didn't stop. But Mr Neville here got to his window as the vehicle passed by. Silver-coloured saloon, partial registration. SK12 then U or V but he missed the last two letters. And a white oval on the side.'

As they walked back towards Wilkie's house, Malkie thought aloud. 'At this time of night? Minicab?'

Steph continued. 'Aye, and even that partial reg match

15

might be enough, cross-ref'd with taxi firms. But let's start with a general vehicle search, shall we?'

'Why? It's a no-brainer.'

'Really? No other cars on the roads ever have signage on them, do they?'

Fair point. She's always got a point. 'Fine. Call it in, then.'

She fixed him with one of her looks. 'I'm just about to. OK?'

'Good, we've got bugger-all else.'

She made a show of looking at her watch.

He deserved what was coming but couldn't be bothered. He needed to keep moving. Stopping meant time wasted. Time that might allow his thoughts to go where he couldn't bear them to. Steph, as always, showed him no mercy.

'The collision occurred at 1:45. It's now 3:15. That's ninety minutes elapsed, and we have the victim's name and address and a partial ID on the suspect vehicle. Not enough for you?'

He resisted a petulant response. No point. She couldn't see a line without taking a dirty great leap over it – her unique way of showing she cared.

'You know the job. Collect evidence. Work the evidence, document, cross-ref. Dull and methodical, remember? After what you went through, you need to ease back into things, or...' She didn't finish.

'Or what, Steph?'

She held his eye contact but stayed quiet.

'That therapist they made me see threatened to block my return to work. Bloody "expert" thinks...'

Shutters slammed down as half-memories crashed against walls in his mind. Flames. Screams he might never stop hearing. For six months, he'd worked to drag dark, elusive fragments into some kind of clarity, without success. Now would be the worst time to succeed. He closed his eyes. His fingertips lifted to his chest, to the thin cotton of his shirt that covered the permanent reminder of his utter inadequacy. His personal and indelible badge of disgrace for whatever he did – or failed to do – that night. The Police Scotland-mandated therapist had tried to coax the memories out of him and into daylight, dig out the guilt that never stopped eating at him. But did he want to remember? Would it heal him? Or would it break him?

He forced his eyes open again but his vision flicked straight to the flashing blue on top of Terry's patrol car, and he had to turn his gaze down to the grey road surface. When he looked up again Steph stood, arms folded, patient, her lips set hard, but her eyes soft. He nearly lost it again. He swallowed tears he'd denied himself throughout the past six brutal months.

Nearly six months. One hundred and seventy-nine days. How much longer?

She gave him a second. 'Better?'

'Aye. Sorry.'

'Take all the time you need.'

A second patrol car appeared. Two uniforms got out. PC Julie – what was her surname again? – headed for the crowd of spectators. PC Davie Semple approached Malkie and Steph.

'Welcome back, boss.'

All three looked at each other, the air thick with unfinished business. Semple waited in obvious discomfort.

Malkie did him a favour and spoke first. 'Morning, Davie. Is that Julie with you?'

Semple glanced once more at Steph, but she'd turned away to dial her phone.

'Aye, Julie Faulds. Where do you want us?'

'Door-to-doors, plus sixty yards of street and that private residence to babysit.' He pointed at PC Terry. 'Now the victim's away to hospital, we need all these fine citizens interviewed before they decide the show's over and go back to their beds. RTC about 1:45, light grey or silver saloon car, possibly a mini-cab, last seen heading north, back towards the town centre.'

Davie went to fetch Julie. Malkie followed Steph. She ended her call.

'SOCOs are on their way. They found ten bags of amphetamines on one of the mouth-breathers. Didn't take them long. They'll be here pronto, this time of morning.'

'Good. I want to know what's in that bloody safe.'

THREE

Walter Callahan woke with his heart hammering in his chest and his blood pounding in his ears.

Unconscious one second, on his feet the next, scanning the room, checking the corners, reaching for his weapon – the one that hadn't been there for eleven years.

He remembered screaming. Impacts. Rage. But nothing clear, nothing concrete. Everything lurched around him. He staggered back to the sofa, crossed his arms, and folded forward into himself to stop himself shaking. Dread in his bones dragged at him, whispered to him. Familiar and eager.

An ache tightened at the base of his neck, and he headed for the bathroom cabinet. But even as bottles clattered into the sink, he wondered why he bothered. No medication worked. No damned therapy, no talking, no stupid sharing, no point.

It was back, and he never saw it coming.

He found his pills and returned to the living room. Falling onto the sofa he scanned the mess on the coffee table for something to wash them down. A bottle of cheap whisky, a couple of mouthfuls left. He popped two capsules from a foil and swallowed them, dropped the box on the table. His unit doctor always warned against mixing them with alcohol but what the hell did they know?

He stretched out and closed his eyes, slowed his breathing, drifted off. The edge of a grassy cliff, hot sun on his face, the muffled roar of breakers crashing and foaming on a rocky shore, birds calling to him as they wheeled and dipped on a warm and salty breeze. He went through his routine, focused down into his core mantra – full control, his choice. Roll left and drop into oblivion or roll right, away from the fall to solid ground and sanity.

He imagined leaning right towards safety, but something made him pitch left. His guts sank as he dropped towards wave-battered rocks that waited far below. He landed hard. Lay frozen for long seconds, face down, eyes screwed shut. Anchored himself to the hard wooden floor under the carpet. No waves. No rocks. Just a floor. When his head stopped spinning, he looked up.

And saw the smashed TV screen.

The remote control lay below amidst slivers of glass. A nightmare. They still came most nights. Wouldn't be the first time he'd trashed the place. But this was different. Usually, he remembered nothing more than scraps of ugly memories. This time he could taste it, lingering on him, staining him. He loathed it. But God help him, he'd missed it, too.

Violence.

He rubbed his face with his fingertips – no cuts, no bleeding – and ran his tongue around his teeth. Found none missing or loose. He checked his cheeks and knuckles, no bruising, no scrapes. No blood on his jeans, or his shirt. Nothing. No evidence he'd hurt anyone. Not this time. How many people had suffered at his hands?

Still, something nagged at him. Not just guttering flickers of the same sickening dreams. More like a memory of reality. But the images refused to form, they remained fleeting and elusive, tormenting him.

The spider web of cracks on the TV screen called to him as if it knew him and knew the things he'd done. He scrambled across the floor, fell over the table, sent the bottle and glasses and meds flying, and gazed into the centre of the radiating fractures. His vision narrowed, drawn to where the whole ruined mess came together. As if the worst of it – the worst of himself? – lurked there, waiting to be let loose.

A memory slammed into him, this one vivid and true – no dream, this. Blood. Shattered glass. He searched the smashed screen for traces of red. Prayed he wouldn't find any.

Nothing.

Relief flooded through him, and he sagged back against the sofa, exhausted. The pain flanked his scalp now, creeping forward. If it reached the front of his skull and took root and made him do those things again, they'd come for him. They tried to kill him the last time.

No matter who got in his way, what damage he did, they would never get him again.

He stretched out again, pulled a blanket over himself. Tucked a cushion under his head. Closed his eyes. Pictured the cliff-top in his mind. Sun and birds and a warm, salty breeze.

But sleep came nowhere near him.

It was back.

FOUR

Malkie tried a second mouthful of his coffee. Still crap.

'I hope this place does better burgers than coffee. Why the hell isn't there a Costa open somewhere?'

Steph sighed. 'Only drive-throughs at this hour and I wanted out of the car.'

He checked his mobile for the third time in ten minutes. 'How long does it take? That bloody computer is quick enough to chase me for my timesheets, but we have to wait an hour for a simple registration lookup?'

'A partial registration. We don't even have the make or model.'

If they had limited the search to local minicab firms as Malkie wanted, they might have got a hit already, but Steph requested a wider search, and he couldn't afford extra scrutiny from her. Not now.

He pushed his coffee away. 'I'm getting a tea. Has to be better than this pish. You want a muffin?'

'No, but you go ahead. Knock yourself out.' She glanced at his waistline, her disapproval plain, the same unspoken but judgemental expression his mother always did so well.

At the thought of his mother, memories slammed into him. Screams and flames and acrid, choking smoke. As always, none of them came anywhere near clear or coherent. He grabbed the table edge to stop the world pitching around him, screwed his eyes shut, pushed the images down, forced himself into the present.

'Malkie? What's wrong?'

He opened his eyes, dragged himself back to the moment. 'Just a flashback. They're starting to ease off, though.'

'You want to talk?'

He stared at her but found no words.

She stood. 'Sit down, I'll get the teas.' He sat, watched her step away – was she worried about him as a friend or keeping an eye on a colleague she needed to rely on? A bit of both, knowing her. Steph grew up in a sink estate where benefit fraud counted as a career choice. She was adopted by her uncle when her mother overdosed in Cornton Vale while doing two years for Assault. She grew up surrounded by career criminals, but somehow resisted – loathed, in fact – the lifestyle choices of her peers. On her seventeenth birthday, she joined the police as a parting 'fuck you' to her nominal family. Malkie took three years to learn that much and considered himself lucky she stuck with him despite himself. While most DCs cycled through various teams, he and Steph became a regular double act. His moods slid off her, and her no-nonsense manner that irritated so many colleagues, he found refreshing. He suffered the lash of her tongue often but preferred that to the corporate shite spouted by too many Police Scotland career-junkies. He bitched at her, and she bitched right back. Made for each other. She'd been assigned to DS Pamela Ballantyne, McLeish's golden girl, in Malkie's absence. He couldn't begin to guess how they got through that without bloodshed.

She returned to the table with teas and two muffins, pushed

one of each across the table to him, picked a chunk out of hers and chewed it without looking at him.

'Talk to me,' she said while pretending to dig out a stubborn chocolate chip.

'About what? Whether I should even be back at work?'

'Oh, stop that. We both know the best thing for you is to be out here, doing what you're good at.'

He held his hands up in mock surrender. 'They still hit me sometimes. Flashbacks.'

He caught her momentary glance at his wrists. He lowered his hands, planted them on the table. Steph reached forward, pulled his jacket cuffs down over his burns and rested her hands on his arms for a second. 'Try to get something out, anything. I won't go running to McLeish. Promise it'll stay between you and me and these muffins.'

He checked his mobile again, still nothing, no escape there. Would it kill him to let a small part of it out? The harsh fluorescent lights and orange plastic chairs and the faint smell of bleach from the mopped floor of this burger bar reminded him of the mortuary at St John's, where he'd had to identify his mum's body. That had nearly broken him. He hadn't talked about it with anyone beyond feeding the Police Scotland therapist enough to get her off his back. But maybe now...

'It was the day after Mum's birthday.'

He swallowed, braced himself for his first confession, the first admission of his abject failure. He realised he was scratching at his wrists and laced his fingers together.

'It started in her bedroom. By the time I got there, the fire had already taken hold, spread outside the bedroom, but no emergency services had arrived yet. I found Dad on the hallway floor. Mum had been ill, bed-ridden for weeks before that. When Dad opened the bedroom door, a backdraft blew him back against the wall. He broke both hips. I started to pull him out, but a ceiling beam fell in on us. Hit me in the chest. That's how I got burned.' Steph didn't glance at his wrists again so Malkie refused to look at them, too.

Ugly fragments strobed across his mind. A horror show he'd failed to piece together for six months, orange and red and yellow. Murderous black smoke creeping along a ceiling. Heat and fumes stinging his eyes and his lungs. Dad on the floor, reaching for her bedroom, choking, screaming words Malkie couldn't understand. Images hammered into him, tormented him, dangled only bits of the story. He stopped, looked at Steph, swallowed a lump of shame in his throat.

'I must have got us out to the front of the house. The next thing I remember is blue lights and sirens and people running across the lawn. Someone took Dad from me. He looked awful. I thought I was going to watch him die. The house was too far gone to save.'

He swallowed. 'They wouldn't let me go back in for Mum.'

Tears pressed at his eyes, demanded release, but he refused to indulge his self-pity. He reminded himself, again – one hundred and seventy-nine days without tears, six months of denying himself any kind of comfort. He knew what a bad sign counting the days was, but the habit had him now.

'What else, Malkie?' She read him as easily as a charge sheet. The tenderness in her voice nearly broke him, but he wiped his eyes on his jacket sleeve and straightened in his chair, heaved in a huge, stabilising breath, let it out in a long, shivering sigh.

He ached to confess to her, and only to her, the worst of it, but he could get no more out. Not now. He lowered his head, stared at the table. Shame flooded him like a contagion with no cure.

Steph said nothing, just sipped her tea. She was one of few people Malkie knew who never felt a need to barge in with ill-considered pop psychology and useless, trite advice. She took a breath to speak again, and he begged her, silently, not to dig any deeper for now.

She nodded at his hand. 'How bad is it?'

He'd been rubbing his chest through his shirt and dropped his hand like a wee boy told to stop picking a scab. But he was happy to change the subject.

'Doctors said I was lucky. Cracked ribs and "localised third-degree burns," they said.'

He remembered how 'localised third-degree burns' hurt like a bastard when they slathered on jellies and ointments and surgical gauze that felt like sandpaper soaked in vinegar. Three nurses had struggled to hold him down.

'It stung a bit.'

Steph shook her head, a knowing twinkle in her eyes. 'And your dad?'

Malkie looked away. 'Still in hospital.'

'But how is he?'

Malkie closed his eyes, couldn't answer, couldn't meet her gaze.

'When did you last see him, Malkie?'

No words would come. Shame welded his lips closed.

'This week? Last week? Last month?'

'How can I face him, Steph? He's lost everything, and that's my fault.'

'Oh, Malkie. Really? First, he didn't lose *everything*.' She let that hang for a moment. 'Second, you did what you could, didn't you? How do you make any of that your fault? No, don't look away. Answer me.'

She reached across the table and rested her hand on his. Her fingers were warm and soft – why did that surprise him? That small contact, that small bridge to another soul he could believe really cared, threatened to set him off again. He looked up at her. His throat thickened with denial of the tears he craved, constricting the words he longed to get out, to confess to her.

She let him off. For now. 'Try the tea. Like you said, has to be better than the coffee, right?'

He emptied six sachets of sugar in and stirred it, watched the steaming liquid eddy around inside the cup. This was the first time he'd relived the events in any detail, not counting the dreams that ripped him, sweating and suffocating, from sleep most nights. The world continued to turn. He tasted ashes but managed to keep breathing through them.

She sat back in her chair. 'You still looking to move out to Harperrig? You and your dad?'

He breathed again. 'Aye. The cabin is all we own now apart from a plot of ashes in the Livingston Village. Needs work, and it's isolated, but it's far enough away from this bloody place.' He nodded outside the window at the dark and near-deserted avenue between the town's two largest shopping centres. A woman sat against a wall, head down, legs splayed, an empty bottle in one hand and her handbag in another, the contents spilled onto the ground.

Malkie closed his eyes. *Stop the world. We want to get off.*

Steph leaned forward, elbows on the table, her eyes bright. 'Hello? Planet Earth to Malkie? I was saying, you grew up in the old Livi Village, didn't you? What was it like back then?'

'Steady. I've only just turned forty-five.'

She cracked an evil grin and scrunched her eyes at him; she'd played him again.

He cast his mind back, dragged ugly memories into the light. Even he struggled, now, to believe the stories his mind told him.

Well, Steph, I became a copper to get out of a gang that wanted me to run drugs and hurt people. Oh, and let's not forget the delightful Sandra Morton, a toxic, wee bitch who swore she loved me then tried to have me stabbed. Twice. Happy days.

'It was pretty dull, really.'

Again, that knowing smile that she never bothered to hide.

Steph's phone rang. They both jumped. She let it ring four times, her eyes locked on his, before she answered.

'DC Lang.'

She listened for a minute, hung up, then waited. When it pinged, she studied the display.

'Let's see. Blah, blah, yadda, yadda, ah! Four hundred and eighty-three cars registered as minicabs across West Lothian. I know, I know – a girl can change her mind, can't she? A hundred and sixty-eight of them grey or silver. Ah good, they're sorted in reg order. Hang on.' She sat silent, her eyes scanning the screen, her forefinger scrolling the display.

Malkie's patience ran out in seconds. 'Well?'

Steph looked up from her phone, considered him.

'You're sure you're alright?'

'Yes, for fuck's sake. Let's do something.'

He waited. She studied him so long his temper broke.

'Spit it out, Steph, or—'

'Don't go off on one, OK? One of the minicabs belongs to your old pals the Fielding Family. You going to behave, Malkie?'

He felt his guts sink, and sighed. 'That I can't promise, Steph.'

FIVE

Malkie wanted Steph to drive straight to the Fieldings' family home. He wanted to get out of the town centre before it woke up, before the onslaught of noise and traffic that frayed his nerves so much these days. Lowlifes like the Fieldings had to be their first call for something like this. He knew their sort, had suffered at the hands of their like before escaping his old stamping grounds. But Steph insisted they head to the minicab depot first. The Fieldings had garage facilities on-site, and could – could, she stressed – already be sanitising the car. If the car was even theirs, she reminded him. Malkie agreed, but with ill grace. With luck, they'd find the car up on a ramp and getting hosed down, but equally, it could already be at the bottom of a reservoir.

'Are we going to have a problem, Malkie? Even Jacob Fielding has been legit for a while now, hasn't he?'

He stared at her, incredulous. 'Is "legit" a relative term now? You think their kind ever go straight?'

'I'm just saying even a family like that wouldn't let anything like this touch them. They know we'd be all over them.'

'As we are now.' He didn't bother to keep the 'I rest my case' out of his voice.

'OK, forget it. We check the depot first, find out if they even have a car missing. By the book, aye?'

Second lecture in eight hours. He had the sense to change the subject. 'Fine. By the way, we call him *"The Jakey"*. Because he hates it.'

'Aye, I heard that. Jakey as in a wino or a tramp? He's worth millions, isn't he?'

'You've never met him, have you?'

'No, I've only seen his mug shots. Why?'

'You'll see.'

Fielding Minicabs sat in the Houston Industrial Estate, to the north-east of the town centre. At this time of day, the main commuter road through town would be filling with traffic heading for the motorway. Steph must have noticed a spike in Malkie's stress levels because she took the slower route through the housing estates. He didn't thank her; clumsy sentiment would only embarrass them both.

He stared out the window in silence, and she didn't give him the satisfaction of asking more about The Jakey. When they arrived, he couldn't get out of the car fast enough.

Corrugated iron fencing surrounded the minicab depot, which consisted of two garage bays and a grubby-looking office. Malkie saw no cars on the ramps. He turned back to find Steph examining him.

'Is it too much to expect clean shoes and a shave and a decent suit? And when did you last brush your hair? You want people to treat you like an adult or not?'

Malkie opened his mouth to protest but shut it again. His personal care had suffered through the past six months, and with his car-crash finances – something even she mustn't find out about – his salary barely stretched to hot food these days, let alone a new wardrobe. *I'll get my suit cleaned, maybe start shaving on Mondays, again. Anything to get some peace.*

Inside the office, a lump of a man sat wedged in a swivel chair, his eyes glued to a TV suspended from the ceiling. He took a bite from a bacon roll and ketchup dripped down the front of his 'Whitburn 6k Fun Run 1996' T-shirt.

Steph flashed her ID while Malkie marvelled at the irony of it all.

'Morning, sir. Are you in charge here?'

The man nodded but didn't speak, too engrossed in news coverage of a fatal stabbing in Greenock docks the previous night, some deckhand from an Eastern European freight ship. It had been looping every half hour on most news channels all morning, reporters whining about a lack of police briefings, as if nothing else had happened in the world today. Your typical concerned citizen did enjoy a good murder story.

Steph cleared her throat, loud and insistent. 'And your name is?'

The man stopped chewing when he saw her ID. His eyes widened and he swallowed his mouthful. 'Derek. Derek Woodburn.'

'Mr Woodburn, we're investigating an incident which occurred early this morning, involving a vehicle we believe may be registered to this company. Can we talk to the proprietor, Mr Fielding?'

She smiled, yet her neutral tone managed to convey a threat of imminent violence.

Woodburn's eyes bulged. 'Which one?'

She frowned. 'What do you mean?'

'Jake or Liam?'

She sighed. 'Which one runs this business?'

'Liam. But he's not here.'

'*You* can assist us, then.' She grabbed a used envelope from

Woodburn's desk, scribbled on it, and slapped it back down in front of him. 'Whose car is this?'

Malkie wandered around the side of the desk, feigning boredom, scanning the mass of papers strewn across the surface. Woodburn's head turned left and right, as if unsure which copper to watch.

Steph placed her hands on the desk and leaned forward. 'Mr Woodburn?'

Woodburn swallowed. He looked about to capitulate, but seemed to have a brainwave. 'Don't you need a warrant or something?'

Malkie replied more quickly than he meant to. 'Correct, Mr Woodburn. We can't force you to co-operate without a warrant. But if you don't, we'll need to go all the way to Kirknewton to ask Mr Fielding personally.'

Steph swore under her breath. She leaned across his desk, stared at him for long seconds, her eyes cold. 'I'm hoping you'll choose to assist us voluntarily.'

The bacon roll wobbled in his fingers, but he found some inner reserve of backbone.

'No, I don't think I should show you anything without a warrant. Or Mr Fielding's permission.'

Malkie clapped his hands together. 'Fine. We'll go and ask him, then.'

Steph turned and walked out the door without further comment.

Malkie flashed a grin at Woodburn, then followed her.

Outside, Steph waited in the car. She stared forward as he got in, her eyes ablaze.

She held a finger up between them. 'Not a word. Not one word.' She slammed the car into gear and took off.

He'd got what he wanted, but at what price? He settled in for a short, uncomfortable, and silent journey.

SIX

They drove in silence. Early morning rain saturated the landscape, a typical central Scotland morning when even the air felt soaked through, and you had to take it on faith that the sun lurked somewhere above the heavy grey slab of cloud that stretched from the open northern horizon to the hulking, brooding mass of the Pentland Hills to the south.

Malkie knew these roads and these views. Livingston had grown since his childhood but hadn't yet encroached on the semi-rural land that lapped at the feet of the hills. He recalled his dad's stories where ghosts of nineteenth-century shale miners haunted ruined slum villages. Even more ancient ghosts of cattlemen forced complaining livestock over the old Drovers Road to the markets of West Linton and beyond. Convoys laden with hides and salted beef walked across boggy fields, at mortal risk from reivers who lurked there to slaughter the drovers and lead away their valuable cattle. Malkie grew up in the old Livingston Village after it was swallowed by roundabouts and estates built in the sixties and seventies to house the overflow from Glasgow. 'Plague of The Townies', his dad called it.

As he took in the familiar sights on his way to the Fieldings, he wished he were alone and could drive past their house, to hide in the cabin. Once a family getaway, now fallen into disrepair, both Malkie's and his dad's recovery depended on it.

It sat behind Harperrig Reservoir, nestled against boggy approaches to the Pentlands. It used to be his regular refuge from screw-ups that – even at school age – he seemed to attract like a shit-magnet. He'd needed it most after learning too late how toxic wee Sandra Morton and her family could be when crossed. She took a fancy to him in high school, and pressured him to join her brother's gang, The Livi Bad Boys, one of a dozen local gangs that spent most weekends tearing lumps out of each other. When she suggested he participate in the family's pharmaceutical enterprises, she took his refusal as a rejection, and he nearly paid a lethal price. Surgeons at St John's had assured his parents that both stabbings had been intended to finish him. Now, every trip to the town centre risked a chance meeting that might reopen scabs he knew would never heal. The worst of her brothers, the one who'd tried to kill him, William, had been released from Saughton a year ago, but word was that Sandra had grown up and told both brothers not to risk finishing the job. So far, there had been no sign William meant to disobey her, but crowded spaces never failed to have Malkie wishing he had eyes in the back of his head.

Because of the fire, the cabin was now all he had left. His dad owned a charred plot of land but was otherwise penniless, although he didn't know it yet. A once-canny old man, he'd taken equity release through some dodgy financial advisor. He'd planned to build a conservatory, and – of all things – had bought a boat, a lifetime dream of his. The boat turned out to be a knackered old money pit, and his builder bled him dry then disappeared leaving a bad job half done. His dad's insurer used the bodged and undeclared building work to void his policy. Bankruptcy was now the obvious option, but he'd lose everything, and that might finish him. Instead, Malkie had sold his own flat to pay his dad's debts until they could sell the remaining patch of ashes.

The cabin needed a huge amount of work and the land it stood on was sodden, good only for keeping people away. But, quiet and isolated at the end of a narrow road beside a peat-blackened stream that trickled down from the hills, it was remote and – the main consideration – mortgage-free.

Necessary renovations were costing a fraction of the price of a new home, but still threatened to wipe Malkie out. Police Scotland showed zero tolerance for his kind of financial expo-sure, so he couldn't let his dad or McLeish – not even Steph – learn the true reason he'd had to change his address, or how skint he was. Dad couldn't handle the shame and McLeish would crucify him with enthusiasm.

'We're here. Wake up,' Steph barked at him at the turn-off for the private estate where he found himself both relishing and dreading a clash with the Fieldings.

They owned a huge villa near Kirknewton, three floors high and eighty feet wide, with immaculate lawns and thick stands of trees on all sides. As Steph parked, Malkie peered into the open doors of a triple garage, saw a sleek silver Aston Martin and a white Land Rover. The Aston's plates started 'LɪAM'. The Land Rover had standard plates and was filthy. Street grime stained the white bodywork, and a greasy film caked the windows. In the third bay sat a massive Ducati motorbike with gleaming black bodywork and huge chrome exhausts.

Jake and Liam Fielding built their wealth on the blood, sweat, and broken legs of countless poor souls they'd screwed over, to build a stinking, fat fortune of the filthiest lucre imagin-able. Every copper in Livingston CID dreamed of nailing them – Malkie more than most, given their past clashes.

He got out and stretched. He hadn't slept since the previous morning and had eaten only a muffin. Steph waited for him to nod his readiness, then moved to ring the doorbell.

Malkie braced himself. *Deep breath, old boy. You're already on warnings, and these bastards know how to push your buttons.*

As if she read his mind, Steph's finger stopped short of the button.

'For the benefit of this junior officer, we're here only to get permission to examine the minicab logbooks. Right?'

Malkie feigned innocence. 'Absolutely, Steph.'

She turned back to the door.

'Even when the owner of said minicab firm is a homophobic, sociopathic shitbag I wouldn't piss on if he was on fire.'

Her shoulders slumped, but she pressed the button. The door opened. A pale young woman appeared, her face bruised and swollen from what looked like a recent impact.

'Good morning, er...' Malkie checked her left hand. 'Miss?'

'Mrs,' she replied, in a small, quiet voice.

He produced his warrant card. The woman muttered something inaudible and closed the door.

Malkie sighed. 'Poor woman probably walks into cupboards all the time.' He judged her to be in her late thirties and The Jakey had no daughters, which meant she had to be Liam's wife. Amanda, if he recalled correctly. Being shackled to a Fielding seemed to have eroded her, robbed her, bled years from her life.

Steph's eyes raged as she jabbed the doorbell again.

The door opened, and Liam Fielding stepped out. The Jakey's son and only remaining family. A vicious bastard and proud of it. An over-muscled and under-educated middle-aged school bully, and the one man Malkie couldn't be trusted around, even before his mum's death had filled him with so much fury and grief he ached to take out on someone.

Red-eyed, pale, and unshaven, Fielding glared at Malkie with recognition and loathing. But something else, too. Fear. As if a copper was the last person on earth he wanted to see right now.

Could it be more obvious? He's up to his filthy neck in this. Somehow.

A telephone rang inside the house. Fielding ignored it.

'What...' He swallowed. 'What do you want?'

Malkie flashed his warrant card although Fielding needed no reminder.

'We need to discuss an incident which occurred early this morning. Possibly involving a grey Vauxhall Astra owned by you. I mean, owned by your company.'

Fielding's eyes betrayed him; he was thinking on his feet.

Malkie gave him no time. 'Mr Fielding?'

'I'm on my way out.'

'We'll only need a minute. And besides, your phone is ringing.'

Fielding looked about to slam the door shut but stepped back.

'Thank you.' Malkie beamed at him.

Inside, a hallway led ahead to a lounge and a staircase climbed on the right. The decor aimed for stately home grandeur but missed. Reproduction antiques sat next to IKEA's best. A signed photo of a football team, draped with a filthy football scarf, hung beside an original oil landscape, tastefully framed in blue wood.

The phone continued to ring.

In a kitchen to the left, the woman Malkie assumed was Amanda Fielding sat at a breakfast bar, chewing her thumbnail. Before her sat a half-full bottle of vodka and a glass, a battered old paperback, and a spectacles case. She stared at Malkie with an expression he found himself desperate to read – she had something to say but the bruises on her face had her mouth sealed shut.

And so it started. Despite knowing nothing about her, he

37

saw a woman in trouble, and the same kinds of stupid promises that had caused him so much grief before lodged in his conscience before he could refuse them. The misery in her eyes tugged on his over-developed sense of chivalry, but there was more; he recognised another person stuck in a personal hell. He remained certain that his was of his own making, somehow. But he couldn't imagine how she could deserve such suffering.

Fuck's sake. Here I go again.

Fielding placed himself in the doorway. 'Well? I was on my way out.'

Malkie dragged his eyes from the woman. 'Yes, you said. Where to?'

Fielding looked from Malkie to Steph and back again. Again, that cornered look, as if he wanted to be anywhere but here.

'Personal matter. What do you want? We've got three silver Astras.'

'We need your permission to examine your vehicle logbooks, hopefully exclude them from our enquiries.'

The phone continued to ring. Fielding's head tilted towards the noise, but he kept his eyes on Malkie.

'Mr Fielding, are you OK? Please, answer that if you need to. We can wait.'

'I'm fine. You can see them, but I want to be there. Wait outside.'

Fielding gestured to the young woman. She picked up her bottle and her book and shuffled towards him. As she passed, Malkie almost recoiled at the desperation in her eyes as they met his. He'd have taken her into protective custody on the spot given any justifiable excuse.

Fielding reached out to grab her arm but she raised the neck of the upturned bottle in her fist, white-knuckled and trembling. She glared at Liam with eyes that promised murder. Furious breaths heaved in and out of her. Fielding stepped forward, nose to nose. She backed up against the wall and looked both terrified and furious, ready to smash the bottle into his sneering face but afraid to. She sagged, humiliation spilling from her eyes, then ran up the stairs. She sobbed once before disappearing down a hallway. Fielding glared at Malkie and Steph, dared them to comment, then followed her.

'That man is worse than an animal.' Steph sighed. 'Although I wouldn't want to get on *her* bad side either.'

'I only said grey.'

'What?'

'I said a grey Astra. He said silver.'

'That's thin, Malkie. Let's reserve judgement, shall we? But if we do get something on him, let me make the arrest.'

The quiet violence in her voice chilled even Malkie.

She gestured towards the outside. As they turned to leave, an older man appeared from the living room, his face haggard, his nose stained with an alcoholic's spider veins. Sparse grey hair lay plastered to his head and nicotine stained his whiskers yellow. With a stooped posture, he leaned on a walking stick as he shambled toward them, his left leg slack and weak, lurching sideways with every step. He pulled cigarettes from a cardigan pocket, the packet blank but for an ink stamp. Even with his millions, the tight old bastard wore manky rags and smoked cheap, knock-off fags.

Only when he reached them did Jake Fielding, The Jakey, look up.

'Who the fuck are you? Pigs, right?'

As the old man leaned forward to study them both, Malkie gagged on his breath, felt it pollute his lungs.

Jake ran a small empire of strip bars, lap-dancing dives, private security, warehouse storage, and haulage. A master of screwing people over for money and for fun.

Keep it professional.

'Good morning, Jakey.'

'Don't fucking call me that. What are you doing in my house? Where's my son?'

'Mr Fielding, I'll ask you to moderate your language. Your son is upstairs.'

Jake lit his cigarette, took a long drag, then blew it into Malkie's face.

'I know you. You're the Pig that attacked my son last New Year. In that queer nightclub. All those perverts and you arrest the only straight guy in the place.'

Malkie took a deep breath, reminded himself Steph was watching. The Jakey wanted a reaction, had poured all his bigoted poison into the accusation, but Malkie held firm to his professionalism. *Don't throw away your pension. Not because of a rancid old fucker like him.*

'Your son was questioned in connection with an incident in The Libertine nightclub during which seventeen people were hospitalised.'

Jake sneered at him, revealing dirty yellow teeth. 'Shite, man. Those freaks attacked my son first. It was self-defence. Fucking disgrace, it was. Liam was never charged because you had nothing on him.'

He pushed past and staggered up the stairs, muttering more abuse between racking, rattling coughs.

Malkie opened his fists, found deep crescents gouged into his palms from his fingernails. Steph spread her fingers at her sides, took a breath, and even Malkie recoiled at the cold, hard loathing in her eyes. 'If I ever meet that... man when I'm off duty...'

'You and me both, Steph. But for now, take a look around outside, would you? I know we don't have a warrant, but have a wee wander, stretch your legs, aye?'

She tore her eyes from the old man's hunched back retreating up the stairs. Her anger not yet spent, she turned on

Malkie, harsher than even he was used to from her. 'What are *you* going to do?'

'I'll wait right here. Don't worry, I won't get into trouble. Go get some air, knock the heads off some rhododendrons or something.'

After a warning glare, she left. Steph rarely lost her cool; had working under DS Ballantyne been even worse than he'd expected?

Malkie stepped into the kitchen. He pulled a CID contact card from his pocket, and a pen. Instinct told him Amanda Fielding wouldn't call a station number. After a futile argument with his better judgement, he scribbled his personal number on the back and slipped it inside the spectacles case she'd left behind.

On his way out, he recalled the look in her eyes, the violence she'd barely contained. *You know nothing about her so don't get involved.* He turned to get the damned thing back, but Steph reappeared on the front step.

'Out here, quick.'

With no way to retrieve his card without Steph seeing, he followed her and prayed he hadn't made things much, much worse for himself.

Steph led him around the ivy-clad corner of the property. On the other side of an immaculate lawn sat a cottage. A gravelled track ran around the lawn to its front door. Under a carport sat a silver-coloured saloon car with a white oval on the side. Malkie recognised an Astra when he saw one, and he knew Steph would too.

Malkie suppressed the thrill that always accompanied a possible lead; even an animal like Fielding wouldn't be stupid enough to park it in plain view on his property. Would he?

Steph nudged him. 'Well?'

She headed across the lawn. He followed, focused on her calm stride ahead of him. She could take down someone twice her size without breaking a sweat, but even so a knot in his gut refused to loosen.

Moisture seeped into his shoe from grass wet with morning dew. Why couldn't he get something as simple as a shoe repair done, like an adult would?

'Malkie? Some urgency here?'

He caught up and they approached the cottage.

SEVEN

Curtains masked every window in the front of the cottage. Somebody valued their privacy.

The plate on the rear of the Astra matched the one they were looking for. At the front, they found the bonnet and front grill dented and a damning bullseye-smash on the windscreen, the glass a mess of blood. Peering closer, Malkie spotted strands of blond hair and tasted bile as Wilkie's ruined face flashed across his mind.

Right behind your own house, Liam? Even you're not that stupid.

Malkie and Steph shared a look. She'd be thinking the same thing – what kind of person smashes into a pedestrian then drives home and parks outside his own house? Any sensible person would wipe the car down and dump it, report it stolen. Or take it to a friendly garage for sanitising, just like the one the Fieldings owned.

They walked the perimeter of the building, found the back windows curtained too, and another door. Steph took up a position at a back corner to cover the back door, and Malkie returned to the front.

Liam Fielding appeared at the side of the main house. He stared in their direction then returned to the front. Seconds later, the Aston Martin roared away up the drive.

Steph commented from her position, 'OK, I admit that looked dodgy.' She pulled her phone out.

'Damn right it did. Flag the reg for ANPR. There are more cameras than people in town these days, so we'll nab him later. We'll never catch him in that thing, anyway.'

Before Steph could make the call, the cottage door opened.

A man appeared on the step, thin and wiry and looking like he'd slept a week in the same clothes. He scanned the lawns like a man eager not to find anything there.

He spotted Malkie and tensed.

Malkie strolled towards him, fishing in his jacket pocket for his warrant card. Steph backed up behind the corner of the cottage.

'Good morning, sir. That your car?'

The man glanced at the car, then back. Malkie expected to see someone who knows he's collared but instead got a confused frown.

'It's a pool car,' the man said, his eyes still scanning the grounds and the main house.

Malkie pocketed his warrant card. 'A pool car. You work for Fielding Minicabs, then. And your name is?'

The man took a step backwards and stiffened as if coiled to bolt.

'Walter Callahan. And yes, I work for the Fieldings.'

Steph stepped out and angled away from the wall to cover as much of an escape route as possible.

The man followed Malkie's glance, spotted her, and adjusted his stance to keep both in his field of vision.

'OK, Mr Callahan. We only want to talk, mate. Don't make this difficult, eh?'

'What do you want to know?'

His confusion looked genuine. Malkie needed to test him, and his own instincts.

'We need to eliminate this vehicle from our enquiries into an incident last night.'

Steph looked at him, confusion in her expression; the mess on the front of the car left no doubt it was the suspect vehicle.

'I wasn't driving last night. I got home before dark and played cards until late.' Still no sign the man felt anything but confusion.

'In that case, we won't need to trouble you for long. Can I have the keys for a minute, please?'

Callahan turned as if to re-enter the house, but then bolted for the carport, and left Malkie grabbing at fresh air. Callahan stopped at the car, stared at the damage, and again Malkie saw confusion, a bewildered panic that he doubted any man could fake. It lasted only seconds before the man's shock gave way to sick dread as if some terrible fear had become reality.

Malkie caught up with him and reached out a hand. 'Let's go inside and talk, mate. OK?'

Steph crept closer behind Callahan.

Callahan gaped at Malkie, his eyes wild with what looked like appalled recognition.

'It's back.'

Malkie stopped, recoiled from something he recognised only too well; this man carried demons, too. As merciless and unrelenting as Malkie's? He'd bet his pension on it.

Callahan bolted towards the tree line, away from Steph but past Malkie. Malkie, thrown by Callahan's cryptic comment and his own visceral reaction, grabbed for him but Callahan punched him in the sternum and he went down, winded.

Steph checked Malkie was conscious then ran after Callahan, who was already deep into the surrounding trees.

When the pain in his chest eased enough for him to breathe again, Malkie struggled to his feet. He elbowed the door of the cottage open. It revealed a small living room, gloomy behind heavy orange curtains. The room reminded him of Robin Wilkie's home, but instead of minimalist and chic, Callahan's place was simply bare. A bookshelf stood in one corner, filled with large-format glossy hardbacks arranged in height order. The furniture – sofa and armchair, coffee table, TV cabinet with the doors open, two shelving units – all stood at perfect right-angles to each other.

On the carpet in front of the TV cabinet lay an empty whisky bottle and a pillbox, the foils spilled onto the floor.

A door opened into a kitchen, also pristine and sterile. Another opened into a bedroom. The bed was made to perfection, hospital corners, wrinkle-free sheets.

A small adjoining bathroom looked more like a hospital theatre. An odour of bleach hung in the air. On the wall a bathroom cabinet, the door open, pill bottles lying in the sink below. He fished out his notebook and scribbled down the names on the prescription labels.

The back door was locked. The kitchen was spartan and severe like the rest of the house, with nothing on the worktops, everything spotless and gleaming.

He returned to the living room, and from the kitchen door he saw the shattered TV screen and the remote control on the floor beside a box of capsules. He tilted his head to read the label, recognised the name, and wished he didn't.

'Lost him,' Steph said from the open front door, her breathing laboured. Losing Callahan would piss her off more than she'd admit.

Malkie joined her outside. 'OK, usual background checks and local Veterans Welfare organisations. This place isn't a home, it's a barracks for one. His bookshelves are full of SAS memoirs, Special Forces picture books, stuff like that.'

'So he's a soldier. Or was.'

'Aye, but his meds say he's not a happy ex-soldier.' Callahan's appalled words ran through his mind. *It's back.* 'Seraxo-nine is a PTSD medication. A serious one.'

'I know.'

Malkie stared at her. 'And how the hell would you know that?'

She didn't answer, and Malkie decided not to push his luck.

EIGHT

Callahan had expected better from the small, skinny one. The big guy was a physical disgrace – slovenly, unfit, shirt hanging out – but the female had looked dangerous, her posture and her stance practised, more disciplined. She'd had more training than your average copper.

His escape and evasion training meant he lost her after only a hundred yards. But now he had stopped, the shakes started.

All the signs were there, even after all this time. *It* wasn't done with him yet.

Blackouts were nothing new, but this was different. The state of the car damned him, but he remembered nothing about how it happened. Not one memory of driving after dark last night.

Over eleven hard years, he'd gone longer and longer between episodes, eight months since the last. He choked back memories of the one night, nine years ago, that nearly broke him. Over the years since that shameful incident, he'd retrained himself until he could reduce his dosage by the smallest of steps, and he'd recently dared to hope the worst might be over. His constant hunger to hurt people remained but he controlled it by running himself to exhaustion every weekend, pounding the steep and wild slopes of the Pentland Hills until he collapsed. Somehow, he always found the will to stagger home rather than let cold and exhaustion finish him. It wiped him out every time, but he'd stopped waking up on the floor with skinned knuckles and someone else's blood on him.

He owed Jake for helping him to fight it. The cottage was ideal – rent-free and isolated. Four nights a week driving Jake's minicabs allowed him to save for some kind of far-off retirement. Maybe a wee place on the west coast, miles from anyone. Away from anyone he couldn't bear to hurt. He'd hurt so many people.

But *It* was back. And he feared it. Now more than ever.

This wasn't bruises and scratches. This was the car he'd been driving, smashed and bloody, and parked outside his home.

But it made no sense.

Not once in civvy life had he killed anyone, and he devoured the local news for days after every blackout to make sure of that. Some of those he'd put in hospital deserved it and others hadn't, but even at his worst, he'd never killed. Right now, his clothes carried no stains, bloody or otherwise. His hands bore no damage, no outward signs of violence. None of which could negate the damning evidence on the car. The car he was supposed to have killed someone with.

But he never drove after drinking. Locked up at home was the only place he risked any surrender of self-control. He allowed himself occasional night drives when his dreams wouldn't let him sleep, but never after drinking. What the hell could have got him out driving that late, after most of a bottle of Scotch?

He and Jake and Liam played poker until late. Jake looked comatose but Liam remained wide awake. He remembered nothing past eleven, yet his car bore plenty of evidence that said otherwise. An old adage sprang to mind, something about razors – the simplest explanation was usually the truth. Which suggested he'd driven somewhere so drunk he couldn't remember doing it, and had hit someone.

He rejected the notion. On his night-time drives, when memories and regrets kept him far from sleep, he always drove away from town, straight up the narrow and winding Kirknewton road and out the A70, past the Pentlands then south through sparsely populated countryside toward Carnwath. He took that route because he knew nobody would be walking the road at that hour. He would never drive in any other direction, for just that reason.

A crazy idea popped into his head. Liam took a pool car out last night too, and he was the last man conscious. He and Liam would never be mates – the man was a thug and a bigot. Callahan put up with Liam treating him like shit because they both knew he wouldn't retaliate and risk his rent-free refuge.

Could Liam have driven into town, hit someone, then swapped cars? It was a stretch, but more credible than Callahan driving such a distance and smashing into someone but retaining no memory of it. But if that were the case, why did he wake up this morning sweating and reeling from images of shattered glass and blood?

The world pitched around him. He needed his meds. If *It* really was back, he was a danger to himself and others without them.

From deep in the undergrowth, he watched the two police officers in discussion. The man pulled the front door closed and took up a waiting stance. The woman stepped away, dialling her mobile.

He pulled the spare key from under a rock behind the cottage, unlocked the back door, and slipped inside. In the living room, he saw that the front door stood open a few inches, and the male officer stood facing away. No sign of the woman. He'd need to watch his six in case she came in behind him.

In the bedroom, he grabbed his kitbag and stuffed in handfuls of clothing and his wallet from the bedside table. No question of taking his phone – he'd buy a burner. His meds were nowhere in sight until he remembered knocking them onto the floor beside the TV.

As he crept across the living room, the scruff outside straightened and twisted towards the open door. He mouthed a silent plea to the man.

Turn away. Turn the hell away. I can't afford to hurt a copper.

The man stretched his arms and arched his back, then rubbed his chest through his shirt. When he looked down at his hand he snatched it away, then lifted his head, closed his eyes, and let out a long, trembling sigh.

Walter dived behind the sofa. He needed those meds but couldn't risk being spotted. And where was that woman?

At a stretch, he managed to reach a foil strip on the carpet with only two bubbles filled, but he couldn't risk crawling closer to the copper to grab more.

He lifted his jacket from the sofa, hefted his kitbag, and slipped through to the kitchen. The police officer didn't look back.

With one last look at his meds lying on the carpet, so close and yet so out of reach, he slipped outside. No sign of the wee woman. After two hundred yards, he stopped to check for sounds of pursuit but heard nothing.

First, he'd empty his account. Then find somewhere to hole up and pull himself together.

The trouble was, without meds he might not last the day – not without hurting someone else.

NINE

When backup arrived to secure the cottage, Malkie and Steph detoured past the station to the minicab depot.

Derek Woodburn was ready for them this time. He pushed a shabby notebook forward on his desk. 'Mr Fielding said I can let you see the logbook.'

Malkie marvelled at Woodburn's ability to turn complete capitulation into a generous gesture of co-operation.

'That's good.' Malkie leaned over the desk. 'Means I won't have to drag your sorry arse to the station for questioning.'

Malkie turned the logbook around on the desk and opened it to the previous night, saw smudged columns of blue ink: passenger names; addresses; driver initials; pick-up and drop-off times. He searched for Fielding or Callahan's initials but found nothing.

'Where do you log which drivers take which cars out?'

'We don't. They're all privately owned. They pay us a circuit fee for the booking system and radios, but they're responsible for their own vehicles.'

'What about pool cars? The car we're interested in is registered to the company, not private.'

Woodburn's eyes narrowed. 'So?'

Malkie looked him in the eye. 'You looking for a trip to my office, pal?'

Steph appeared beside him and Malkie didn't need to look to know she'd be giving Woodburn her trademark 'give me an excuse' stare.

Woodburn glanced from Malkie to Steph and back again. He swallowed. His fingers tapped on the desk.

'Only the family use pool cars outside of business hours,' he said in a plaintive whine. 'Liam, Callahan, Amanda. Jake used to but not anymore. He's got a knackered leg. His own Range Rover is adapted for him but he struggles in a pool car.'

Malkie straightened. 'OK, so show me the registration documents for your pool cars.'

Woodburn swivelled his chair around to a filing cabinet, pulled a manila folder from a drawer. Malkie checked each of five documents in the folder and found a match.

'Who had this one last night? A silver-grey Astra automatic.' He placed the book on the desk and pointed to the registration.

'I don't know.'

Malkie turned to Steph. 'DC Lang, call the custody suite, please. See if there's any accommodation free. Overnight.'

Steph played along, stepped away from the desk and pretended to dial a number.

Woodburn folded. 'I don't bloody know. Liam and Callahan both took cars out last night, but I don't know who took which car. We don't log family loans.'

Malkie smiled. 'So, Liam Fielding and Walter Callahan both took pool cars out last night, yes?'

Woodburn turned pale and squirmed. One simply did not grass one's career-criminal employer up to the Pigs. 'Yes...' Dread edged his answer.

'And are both back here this morning?'

'No, just one.'

'And who returned the other car?'

Woodburn thought for a second then grinned with obvious relief. 'Had to be Liam.'

'How can you be so sure?'

'Because he always leaves his Aston here when he takes a pool car to the Armadale speedway races. He never parks his own car there. When I got here this morning, there were four pool cars and no Aston.'

Woodburn sagged, his relief evident.

'So, Callahan took the only pool car that isn't here now?'

An unpleasant gleam appeared in Woodburn's eyes. He scanned the registration documents on his desk, picked out one. 'Silver Astra, 2010 reg, petrol engine.'

He stabbed the paper with his finger, then sat back, looking relieved. 'Callahan had that motor. That's the only one that wasn't here when I arrived this morning. What's that wee prick done now, then?'

Malkie sighed. 'What do you mean by that?'

Woodburn seemed almost desperate to talk now. 'The guy's a bloody psycho. Scares the shit out of me.'

Malkie nodded and lifted one eyebrow, invited Woodburn to continue.

'He never talks to the rest of us. Comes in, hands in his sheets then buggers off again. No chat, no coffee, nothing.'

'Hardly psychotic behaviour.'

'That's not it.' Woodburn leaned forward and licked his lips.

Malkie perched his arse on the front edge of the desk, leaned in, grinned at Woodburn. 'Tell me.'

'Couple of years ago, another driver – Fat Frankie Mitchell – decided he didn't like him. Callahan's like a bloody robot most of the time, doesn't react. Just ignores him and carries on signing his sheets. Frankie went at him for ages, insulting him, poking him in the chest, sticking his face in front of Callahan. Then he pushed him so hard he fell over a chair. That's when Callahan went ballistic. Would you believe he stabbed Frankie in the ear with a biro? He's still deaf in that ear today. Broke his arm and three ribs as well, but that pen sticking out of his ear was the best bit.'

Malkie counted to five. 'I don't remember this getting reported?'

'Nah, Frankie didn't press charges, scared Callahan would finish the job if he grassed on him. Anyway, next shift, Callahan clocked in as if nothing had happened, and I wasn't about to say anything.'

'So, why are you telling me all this now?'

'Because that lunatic scares me. He's done time before, you know? What is it you want him for?'

'I didn't say we wanted him personally. I asked about vehicles.'

'Aye, right.' Woodburn smirked.

Malkie had to suppress an urge to slap the smugness out of him. 'Where can we find Liam now?'

'No idea. He called me and told me to let you see the shift logs, but I haven't seen him.'

'OK, so I'll have his mobile number, please?'

Woodburn didn't hesitate, seemed happy he'd covered his own arse. He pressed a key on his mobile and read off Fielding's number. Malkie punched it into his own phone and saved it.

'Thanks for your help, Mr Woodburn. We'll be in touch if we need anything further.'

Outside, he dialled Fielding's number, got voicemail, and left a message requesting a call-back.

Steph stood next to her car, finishing a phone conversation of her own. 'SOCOs are nearly finished at Robin Wilkie's house, then they'll head for Kirknewton.'

Malkie stretched, stiff from an interrupted night off and not enough sleep. 'Couple of hours, then. Good, I'm hungry.'

Steph grinned, never a good sign. 'McLeish wants us in the CID Suite.'

Malkie groaned. Apart from an obligatory, and mutually uncomfortable, return-to-work interview, he'd managed to avoid any contact with the man for the past six months.

And he'd bet his pension the bastard wasn't just concerned for his mental well-being.

TEN

Steph showed Malkie the small kindness of taking the longer scenic route back to the station. As they passed St John's hospital on the Cousland Road, an ambulance pulled out at a junction, mercifully silent and unhurried. Still, Malkie failed to cover a miserable sigh at an ugly memory – Dad on a stretcher, feeble and in agony yet fighting to crawl back on broken hips into the flames. He sensed Steph turn to stare at him.

'I'm fine, woman. Stop doing that.'

She said nothing, but Malkie knew he'd just moved himself up her to-do list.

He leaned his head against the glass and closed his eyes in case she tried to start a conversation. Even a small helping of McLeish might ruin the rest of his day. He couldn't stomach a dose of her well-intentioned but brutal gob as well.

As Steph swiped her ID at the barrier to the station car park, she turned to him.

'You ready for this? You know what he's like.'

Malkie sighed. He knew, all right.

Malkie had been Gavin McLeish's boss before Malkie got himself dumped down to DS and created the very DI vacancy

McLeish had stepped into. Their last shout in their old roles had been to a swanky hotel in Linlithgow. A London boy band, The All Boys, came to town for a gig on the shore of Linlithgow Loch. Their minder made the mistake of calling one of McLeish's unprofessional acquaintances for a party-pack of recreational pharmaceuticals and a side order of teenage girls. McLeish saw an easy chance to raise his profile and pushed through a rush-job for a warrant.

Malkie attended partly to stop McLeish screwing up and getting them both put on report, but more to get out from behind his desk for a change. At the hotel, McLeish, true to form, barged past Malkie into the boy band's suite, eager for glory and his photo in the newspapers. He ran into a fifteen-year-old girl trying to find a good vein in an arm scaly with scabs. She lashed out. Malkie, right behind McLeish, made a grab for her but got a handful of used needles in his wrist.

During the enquiry that followed, management rebuked McLeish for only a minor breach of protocol. Malkie could have reported him, but he couldn't be bothered getting dragged into an official dispute.

After an agonising wait, his Hep C and HIV test results came back clear. McLeish managed a few appreciative words, in private, and only once. Malkie had hoped for at least grudging respect but learned that McLeish would never get past the fact that Malkie would forever hold a marker over him.

The boy band drones saw their careers evaporate, breaking thousands of teenage hearts in the process. McLeish got his photo in the newspapers – even the big nationals – and a nudge up the greasy pole. What didn't get reported was why a DI left the office to attend a simple drugs bust in the first place. A rumour surfaced that McLeish set the whole thing up himself. It wouldn't have been the first time his reckless pursuit of excellence had earned someone else an arse kicking.

'Come on. Get it over with.' Steph grinned at Malkie, already half out of the car.

Malkie banished the memories, sighed, and got out. When they reached the CID room, he'd hoped to spend a quiet hour typing in his notes over a mug of decent tea and a cheese roll. But McLeish appeared within seconds.

'DS McCulloch, a minute please?'

Heads turned at the mention of his name. Some looked surprised to see him back. Some smiled and nodded. DS Pamela – never Pam – Ballantyne looked him up and down, a smirk on her lips. She wandered over.

'Welcome back DS McCulloch. Still getting a lot of mileage out of that suit, I see.'

Malkie opened his mouth, but Steph flashed him a warning look. He grabbed his jacket and followed McLeish past his usual desk and into a glass-walled office.

Fuck's sake, his own office; he'll be unbearable. 'You had a promotion I haven't heard about, sir?'

Only a raise of a single perfectly groomed eyebrow suggested Malkie's jibe had penetrated McLeish's practised professional veneer. 'DCI Spalding is off sick, not expected back for a few weeks. I'm acting DCI until he returns.'

And the shite just keeps coming.

McLeish removed his jacket and arranged it on the back of what he obviously now considered to be his chair. He picked something off the lapels then sat, smoothed down his tie, and straightened the gold links in his shirt cuffs. For good measure he ran his fingers through his thick, bottle-dyed, black hair as he glanced at Malkie's own thinning mop of salt and pepper. If the man spent half the time on his people skills that he did on his wardrobe and fighting the ageing processes, he might be only half a prick.

'Sit.' He lifted a manila file from the table, opened it, and studied the first page. Another file, a blue one, lay underneath, with one corner of an A4 sheet sticking out an inch. 'What do you have on the Murieston RTA?'

'Aye, it's good to be back, sir. Thanks for asking.'

McLeish ignored him, continued studying the contents of the folder.

Malkie reached forward, under the papers in McLeish's hands, and pulled the protruding page out. McLeish had highlighted one name with a ruler-straight green stripe. 'Who is D F Browne?'

McLeish snatched the folder up and placed it to one side.

'Murieston. RTA.'

Malkie enjoyed McLeish's irritation but knew not to push his luck.

'RTC. It wasn't accidental, and we've identified the car and a suspect.'

McLeish couldn't hide his disappointment, or his surprise.

'Really? The collision occurred less than twenty-four hours ago. How the hell did you manage that so fast?'

Malkie ignored the implication that quick results were a cause for surprise. 'Usual legwork plus a bit of luck.'

McLeish placed his pen on the desk and sat back, amused. 'Tell me. I have to hear this.'

'A witness saw a car leave the scene of the incident, got a partial registration, and saw signage on the door. Partial reg lookup cross-ref'd against local minicab firms turned up a match. The vehicle wasn't at the minicab premises, so we visited the owner at home. Found the car parked on his property. Reg and model matched, front grill and bonnet staved in and bloody.'

McLeish stared at him. 'So, why not accidental? You found skid marks from hard braking, didn't you?'

'Aye, but three separate witnesses said they heard an engine getting thrashed and wheel-spins before the collision, and we found fresh tyre gouges in the grass verge twenty yards up the road.'

McLeish couldn't hide his grudging appreciation. 'OK fine. Keep this one, but run it as accidental for now, don't labour it. So, you have this man in custody?'

Here it comes. 'No. We lost him.'

McLeish stared at him. Malkie sighed – this couldn't end well.

'He came out of the property while we were examining the vehicle. We tried to apprehend him, but he was too fast. Steph went after him, but even she lost him. SOCOs are there now to take the car in for examination.'

McLeish kept on staring, but picked up his pen again, held it between two fingers and tapped it on his thumb.

'I'm waiting for a call back from the owner of the minicab firm. He and the suspect live at the same property in Kirknewton.'

A small frown creased McLeish's forehead. 'And the suspect's name is?'

'Walter Callahan, works for Fielding Minicabs. Owned by Jake and Liam Fielding.'

The pen stopped tapping. Malkie suppressed a smile. *Touched a nerve there.*

'You're familiar with the Fieldings, of course?'

McLeish didn't answer. He put his pen down, leaned his elbows on the desk, steepled his fingers and smiled.

'How are you, after your recent unpleasantness?'

Malkie's lip curled up, disgust overriding what little capacity for tact he still clung to.

'Unpleasantness?'

McLeish's smile faded. 'I mean I need to be sure you're OK out there. I'm juggling significant crossover between two high-value cases I need to manage with care. I need everyone focused.'

'Is that why I was called out on my last weekend to a possible attempted murder without a DI? Who's leading on this one? You?'

'Malkie, I'm swamped, got my hands full.' He glanced at the blue folder again. 'You're accredited to lead, and DC Lang is competent to assist. You don't need another SIO on this one.'

'Aye, I think every copper in J Division is aware I know the SIO role pretty well. But when the Wilkie incident turned dodgy, there should have been at least a DI in attendance for more than two minutes. You know that. You being a full DI. Unlike myself.'

'Oh, for God's sake, Malkie. Let it go, will you? I got a step up and you got out of a job you hated. We both gained from it.'

Malkie bit down on a career-limiting response.

McLeish looked relieved. 'I was busy on another case all weekend. It was unfortunate timing that the Wilkie incident occurred last night.'

Malkie leaned forward. 'What case?'

McLeish blinked. 'Another case.'

'All weekend?'

McLeish dropped his pen again and sighed.

Malkie waited. McLeish crumbled.

'Look, I was at a cross-departmental briefing at the Gartcosh campus on Saturday, then—'

'You and someone called D F Browne?'

What's he not telling me? What's in that blue folder?

McLeish closed his eyes and sighed. 'I was on-call for SIO for anything you—'

'Couldn't be trusted with?'

'Oh, shut up, Malkie. A simple RTA sounded ideal for a return to work, so I told DC Lang to call you out.'

He had to admit, for once McLeish was right on the money. 'I can live with that. I don't like it, but I see the sense. Thanks, Gavin.'

McLeish let the 'Gavin' go, but his narrowed eyes made clear he wasn't finished, yet. 'You still planning to move into that cabin? Bit remote, isn't it? What's your response time going to be when that road out past the reservoir is snowed in?'

Been checking up on me? Slippery sod.

'All checked out, already,' he lied. 'Ten-minute walk to the Colzium turn-off on the A70, even in deep snow, and there's verge parking there.' He held McLeish's gaze. 'Any other concerns about developments in my personal life, sir?'

McLeish shut his mouth, straightened in his chair, and opened Malkie's file again.

'Did I get it wrong, Malkie? Is it still too soon for you?'

A silence hung between them until McLeish seemed happy he'd reasserted his authority. He sat back. The pen started tapping again.

'So, Callahan?'

'Ex-army, I think. Drives a cab for the Fieldings, lives in a cottage on their property. Steph's checking him out now, but we didn't find a single photo of him to circulate.'

'So, do you think the Fieldings are involved, or just Callahan?'

'Funny you should say that.'

Again the pen stopped tapping. Malkie's shite detector went into overdrive.

'We only went to Kirknewton to get permission to see the logbook. But Fielding junior looked like he was stressed out before we even got there. Frantic, in fact. We found the suspect car parked right outside Callahan's home. When Liam spotted us, he tore away in his Aston, so I want a chat with him too. Something odd going on there.'

McLeish studied him, then seemed to come to a decision. 'Malkie, I'm going to trust you here.'

Fuck's sake. First-name terms, again.

'I have the Fieldings under scrutiny for reasons I can't go

into right now. I need you to handle them with care. Don't go in heavy-handed. Be discreet.'

Malkie opened his mouth to demand an explanation, but McLeish cut him off.

'And don't ask me why. For now, I have to insist.'

Malkie inhaled, slow and deep, before he dared speak 'You insist?'

'I do.'

'Officially?'

'Yes. Officially.'

'No chance I'll get that in writing, I suppose?' Malkie stood without waiting to be dismissed. 'I told Josh Lamb to send the SOCOs to Callahan's home when they're finished at Robin Wilkie's house. You did OK a crime scene callout, right?'

McLeish glared at him. 'Yes. Now kindly piss off.'

Malkie stopped in the doorway. 'Gartcosh? That's Serious Crime and Forensics. You and this D F Browne moving up in the world, sir?'

'Close the door on your way out.'

Malkie left the door wide open and made it to his desk without punching something. He closed his eyes and slowed his breathing.

Steph appeared beside him. 'Return to work interview went well, then?'

Malkie threw his phone onto his desk. Heads turned, again. Some grinned, some winced. A few shook their heads, their disapproval obvious.

DS Ballantyne sauntered over. She took an obvious look at her watch. 'Ten minutes. Must be a record, even for you. You fit for work now? I mean, as fit as you ever are? Should I start a sweepstake on how long you'll last?'

Malkie leaned close, made her back up. He smiled, as if delighted to be chatting with her.

'Fuck you very much for the welcome back, Pammy. Put me down for six months, will you?'

Steph stood, faced Ballantyne. 'You can put me down for five years plus.' She added a prudent 'Ma'am', but only as an afterthought. The irritation and the challenge in her tone drew surprised looks from several colleagues, any kind of emotional reaction from Steph being cause for attention. Something had her in no mood to tolerate nonsense, even from a senior officer.

Ballantyne's smile vanished. She glared at Steph, then turned and strode back to her desk, but took her time about it. Several faces grinned at Malkie behind her back, but only briefly, then bent to their paperwork again.

Steph turned to Malkie and leaned close. 'Damn it, that was bloody stupid of me, and you need to be careful too, mate; why did you let her get to you? She can be dangerous.'

Malkie squeezed his fingers into his eyes. He feared a long drop into a sea of shit without a life jacket.

'It's not her. McLeish just asked me, in fact, he bloody ordered me, to lay off the Fieldings. He's up to something he doesn't want me poking about in.'

He stared back at McLeish, installed in DCI Spalding's office.

'Something stinks, Steph.'

ELEVEN

By the time Malkie took a calming lungful of fresh air and returned to the CID room via the canteen, Steph had the case file open on her screen. He bit off a chunk of cheese roll so he could talk with his mouth full. He knew she hated it when he did that.

'What have we got so far, partner?'

Perched on the front of her office chair, she wore an expression Malkie knew well – she was starting to enjoy herself. 'Lab has Wilkie's safe. I asked them to prioritise it and they complained, but based on Callahan's violent reputation, I asked them again and used different words.'

He chuckled and perched his arse on the edge of her desk.

She frowned, but let it go. 'The sliver of steel came from the broken knife, no-brainer there. Prints on the safe but none on the knife. Wiped clean by someone wearing leather gloves, they think.'

'Have the scene photos come through yet?'

'Aye, all uploaded. And the initial Road Policing report, too.'

'Good, I want to see those photos. Got a hunch.'

'Go for it, Columbo,' she muttered.

At his own desk Malkie managed to log into the system without screwing up his password. He opened the case file, selected the photographic evidence, zoomed close into the high-res shots of Wilkie's photos. Wilkie had aged better than Malkie could ever hope to. He'd matured and filled out, become fitter and better groomed with the years. His clothes looked expensive. No way Robin Wilkie bought his shirts in the same supermarkets as Malkie.

Something caught his eye on the top row. He zoomed in, lost more detail but got what he wanted.

'Did we find anything in Wilkie's house to suggest he was married?'

Steph rolled her chair over to his desk. 'No, why?'

Malkie pointed to Wilkie's left hand. On his fourth finger was the unmistakable glint of a ring. 'Call the hospital. Ask if they took a wedding band off him.'

'What are you going to do?'

He ignored an urge to tell her to mind her own business, knew how that would end. 'I need a shower and a change of clothes. Can you drop me off at my digs?'

She studied him for longer than he liked. 'Fine. I need a couple of hours at home, too. You want me to pick you up later?'

'No, I'll drive myself in. But thanks.'

He suspected she'd prefer to escort him back to station, but he needed time alone, space to breathe, gather his thoughts. It had been a long night, more than he was ready for. It had done him good getting into the job again, but six months of inactivity, hiding even from himself, had left him feeling like a brittle and shamed pariah. He now found himself battered and hounded by the very urban world he used to navigate so complacently, before he learned just how fragile life can be.

As they drove out of the car park, he wound his window down, the air in the car suddenly thick and stale. He watched an old couple strolling arm-in-arm, huddling into each other, like his mum and dad never would again. At a bus stop on the Howden South Road, people waited. Some looked busy and serious, hunched over mobile phones, others bored and miserable. Were they – he wondered – completely oblivious to the ugly fallibility of people like him, who they trusted to protect them? He slowed his breathing and counted, in and out. He pondered the peace he imagined lay in the simple mundanity of ordinary people's lives. But every stop and start at one of Livingston's many roundabouts, every scream of a car horn or roar of a thrashed engine, every choking, hot blast of exhaust from stationary buses hammered at him, allowed him no peace to think, no time to breathe and settle and formulate a path through his car-crash of a life.

He raised the window again and closed his eyes.

They arrived at his temporary accommodation on the St Ninian's Road in the historic and wealthy town of Linlithgow. Steph let out a low whistle.

'How can you afford a bungalow right on Linlithgow Loch? You been selling rude photos of yourself to old ladies on the internet again?'

'You're funny. I had a rare stroke of luck. Heard about an old dear who'd had a bad tenant and was scared to rent out anymore. When she found out I was a copper she almost begged me to take the place. I get a huge discount and she knows it's looked after. We agreed on a three-month lease, though she tried to talk me into a year. Should be long enough for the cabin to be fit to move into.'

'Stroke of luck, that.'

'About time something went right for me.'

He didn't need to look at her to know she'd be radiating disapproval; self-pity ranked high on the list of things she accepted from no one.

When she drove off, he shambled up the footpath that

bisected an immaculate rockery garden, to the front door, desperate for sleep and a temporary reprieve from the ugly thoughts that never seemed far from his mind these days. When he'd stepped out of the taxi thirteen hours earlier, his self-confidence had crumbled. Something had taken root deep inside him over the preceding months. Something rotten and damning. It refused to let him forget his failure to protect the two people who'd always tried their hardest to save the best of him from the rest of him. And in return, he'd left one dead and the other wishing he was.

Five envelopes lay on the hall carpet, all bills. He dumped them on a side table; he'd decide which ones to pay later. He gazed at the pitiful story the living room told, his entire life packed into a pathetic few boxes, unopened a month after moving in. Great first step towards a new start?

Bollocks. You're running away. Again.

He dropped himself into his favourite armchair, all leather and brass studs, facing out a picture window, across the loch to the palace. Its brickwork stained and weathered, its windows black and unglazed; still, it formed a solid and imposing sight when the floodlights came on every night.

A number '3' flashed at him from his dad's ancient answering machine, one of the few objects saved from the fire, and miraculous in its refusal to pack up and die despite the damage done to it by the flames. Three messages. Odd. Only Steph had this number.

And his dad.

It had been a week since his last call, something Malkie was ashamed to admit was a relief. He'd robbed his father of everything, then left him to languish for months in a burns unit with nothing but excruciating pain to distract him from the ruin of his life. Too many times, Malkie had made it as far as the entrance to St John's but had to turn around again, terrified, sick, and ashamed, appalled at himself for fearing to face the man whose grief exceeded his own by far.

He headed for the kitchen. On a worktop sat three bottles, covered in dust: rum, gin, and some syrupy, peach-flavoured rubbish. He'd got it years ago from Monty, the owner of the only pub Malkie ever spent time failing to get pissed in. Monty had promised it was sweet enough for even Malkie to stomach, but it tasted rotten, like every other alcoholic drink he'd ever tried.

He opened the peach one, wrapped his mouth around the neck, tipped it back and counted off three huge swallows, then thumped his fist on the worktop as it burned his mouth and throat and down into his stomach.

'Fuck, fuck, fuck.'

The wave of blessed relief he always hoped for failed to materialise. What worked for pissheads drinking alone in bad movies continued to elude him. He dropped into his armchair and glared at the machine, blinking, relentless, and pitiless. Then he bolted for the bathroom and threw up.

It had only been a matter of time. His dad would never stop caring for him, even after being let down so badly. He'd know Malkie had suffered too. Despite losing almost everything, the old man never once, in the past month of unanswered telephone messages, voiced anything but worry and love. But as much as Malkie owed him at least the comfort of shared grief, his inner martyr rejected any chance of solace for his own battered soul. He ached to talk to him, to ask what he remembered, desperate for any sliver of recollection that might cleanse the corrosive culpability he clung to. Until now, he'd felt no right to accept that comfort, but the promises he'd made to Robin Wilkie and Amanda Fielding had gifted him some small spark of purpose, and with that a shred of hope for himself.

He slumped into his armchair, promised himself he'd return the calls as soon as he'd had a nap, just a half hour, then he'd face them with a clearer head.

. . .

He was yanked from sleep by the phone shrieking at him, the noise harsh and grating, amplified by the large, empty room devoid of furnishings or curtains. He checked his watch; he'd slept for over five hours. Dusk had fallen and turned the sky a dull, miserable grey. As he rubbed wakefulness back into his face he let the phone ring, waited for the answering machine to kick in. His own voice droned out a clumsy recorded message, then a beep announced unwanted message number four.

A woman's voice, small and breathless, struggling to form words through heaving sobs.

'Mr McCulloch, you have to help me. He's going to kill me.'

He recognised the voice and knew another of his stupid promises was about to bite him on the arse.

Malkie reached for the phone, but he couldn't complete the move. He'd learned too many times that charging in on impulse was the surest way to end up on people's shit lists, again.

He gave himself an attitude-check, knew he'd already ignored his own danger-signs, his hopeless, idiotic compulsion to protect any woman in distress. Why had he really left her his personal number? Did he burn to nail a Fielding where so many had failed before, or was his motive less professional, more venal? Poor judgement had landed him neck-deep in shit before.

He listened, immobilised by dread, while she breathed down the phone, sniffling and sobbing. When she disconnected a wave of shame sluiced through him. By leaving his card, rightly or stupidly, he'd made her a promise, which he'd just refused to honour.

He sat in his armchair and stabbed the answering machine replay button. Before he could skip through to listen again to Amanda's message, his father's voice stopped him.

'Malcolm? Are you there, Malcolm?' His voice sounded

weak and scratchy, laboured. 'I was hoping we could meet up at the weekend. It's been a while, son.'

Malkie winced. His last remaining close relative. His last family tie since his mother...

'I'm out of bed now. In a wheelchair, but it's wonderful after staring at the same room for twenty-two weeks.'

Malkie cringed at his total failure to support his own father through the nightmare he knew, somehow, he had partly inflicted on the man.

A long, hopeful pause from his dad. Unrewarded.

'Anyway, it would be lovely to see you, son. I miss you. Doctor says I should be back on my feet soon, so I was thinking we could go out on the *Goose*? I haven't seen her since... Is she still in the water? Do you get out on her much?'

Another pause, unrewarded by any response.

'Malcolm, we need to talk, son. Please. I have things I need to tell you.'

I know, Dad. You still love me. Even after... Soon. I promise.

More silence, as if the old man clung to hope his son would answer.

'Well, bye then.' And with a click, he was gone.

Malkie slumped back in his chair, squeezed his fingers into his eyes.

Soon? When?

Another beep, another message, from before Steph dropped him off.

'Mr McCulloch? It's Amanda Fielding here. I found your card. Thank you. I appreciate that.'

She sounded calm compared to the call he'd just listened to live, but there was still an edge. Apart from her animal of a husband – images of her battered face flashed crossed his mind – what could have her so rattled?

'I'd like to meet you if that's OK. Somewhere quiet. Maybe I can buy you a coffee?' She paused for long seconds before continuing. 'I need help.' He heard her exhale, her breath quivering, fearful, and hesitant. 'I heard Walter Callahan killed someone last night. I may have information you can use.'

The sound of a door opening in the background and a male voice barked at her, 'Who's that?' Then the line went dead.

As Malkie turned this over in his head, the machine announced the last of the original three messages.

Fast, heavy breathing for several seconds and a faint sobbing whimper in the background, then the line went dead. Liam Fielding. He'd redialled her last call, found out she'd reached out to a Pig and, of all people, one he loathed.

To hell with the evidence. It couldn't be more obvious – Fielding was up to his neck in all of this, somehow. And she might know how.

The message from only minutes ago played again.

'Mr McCulloch, you have to help me. He's going to kill me.'

TWELVE

Only as he sped along the main road out of Livingston did Malkie consider this might be his worst idea ever.

Whatever Fielding was doing to Amanda right now was his fault.

Instead of calling for backup as he should have, he'd pocketed the answering machine microcassette and charged out the door without a single, balancing, rational thought entering his head. Besides, how would he explain Amanda calling his home number? He'd done it for her protection, but that wasn't working out well so far.

Was this really about nailing Fielding? Was rescuing Amanda in a fit of ridiculous middle-aged chivalry no more than an excuse? Did she even need rescuing? The look she'd shot at her husband in the house had shaken Malkie. And that bottle she wanted to brain him with; was she less of a victim than he'd rushed to assume? Didn't matter. He'd offered his help. His mother died terrified and in hideous pain -- he was damned if he'd ever again let anyone down so completely. He caught himself scratching his chest through his shirt, clawing at his burn scars.

At the narrow and twisting north end of the Kirknewton road he took a bend too fast and narrowly missed a minibus coming the other way. He lifted his foot and let the speed wash off the car, only to see lights flash and the barriers lower across the level crossing at the southern outskirts of town.

He only had to wait a few minutes, but his mind tormented him with what might be happening during that short delay. Amanda Fielding could be curled up in a corner as he waited, battered and bleeding and hating him for ignoring her calls. His fingers drummed on the steering wheel as he fought to ignore memories of the woman he'd let down so badly six months ago. Why hadn't his dad got to her sooner, before the fire got out of control? No, none of it was his father's fault. But still, why the delay?

A train thundered through the crossing and shocked him back to the present. The barriers lifted, and once past the homes and primary school of Kirknewton, he stamped on the accelerator. At the turn-off for the Fielding property he longed to drive straight on, west out on the Lanark Road past wide, flat farmland and Forestry Commission plantations, toward the hulking mass of the Pentland Hills and the isolation of the cabin. But his mind echoed with her sobbing voice. *He's going to kill me.*

In minutes, he sped through the massive iron gateway of the Fielding property, up to the house, and slammed on the brakes, his tyres gouging the gravel to the hardcore underneath.

As he reached for the brass knocker on the front door, he heard muffled voices inside. Sounded like father and son ripping into each other. The furious shouting suggested Liam was on the attack, Jake managing only occasional interruptions between coughing fits.

His need to see Amanda Fielding safe and at least carrying no new bruises overrode his curiosity. He banged on the door knocker and stepped back.

Liam Fielding appeared, breathing hard, his chest heaving, his eyes wild.

'What now, Pig?' He looked over Malkie's shoulder. 'Where's your wee dyke sidekick?'

If Steph was here – if he'd followed protocol – she'd have had the bastard. But he stood here alone, harassing the same man for a second time, off-procedure and out of control. He'd get crucified. And without Steph's combat skills, Fielding could break him in two without breaking a sweat.

Only now did he think it through. Without a formal and recorded report of danger, he had no official authority to force entry. He came up with an excuse so lame he cringed to use it.

'I think I left my notebook here. That's all. Shall we dial down the testosterone a bit, aye?'

Fielding stared at him in disbelief. His breathing eased but his fingers flexed and closed at his sides as if they wanted to wrap themselves around Malkie's neck.

'Mr Fielding?'

From his position on the doorstep, Fielding leaned over Malkie. 'Warrant.'

Malkie sighed. 'You serious?'

Fielding's eyes burned with naked hatred.

Malkie thought fast. He was losing what little grip he had on the conversation. 'I was only in your kitchen. It'll take me a minute to check?'

Fielding seemed to exhaust his scant reserves of patience. 'Show me a warrant, or fuck off, McCulloch.'

He turned to go back inside.

'Mr Fielding, your demeanour this morning gave me cause for concern. I may need to question you further. On the record.' Last gasp – he had nothing else.

A devious gleam burned in Fielding's eyes. 'What, like last New Year?'

Damn it, here we go.

Ugly images flashed through Malkie's head – New Year, The Libertine nightclub, seventeen people hospitalised, Fielding at the bar, pissing himself with laughter as paramedics fought to save lives and uniforms dragged Fielding's boys out to waiting vans.

'You bastards had nothing on me. Gave me a kicking and banged me up all night, then had to let me go first thing in the morning. Because you knew you had nothing. I was at the bar the whole night. The fight kicked off on the dance floor, and about a million people filmed it.'

Fielding stepped down onto the gravel, stuck his face right into Malkie's. 'You got your arse booted for that, didn't you?'

The man didn't know the half of it. Malkie only dodged suspension because McLeish vouched for him so he could consider his previous debt paid in full.

Malkie stood his ground, held his stare. 'If I believe you may be withholding information pertinent to an ongoing investigation, I'm obliged to request a formal interview.'

He looked from one of Fielding's murderous eyes to the other, felt the man's breath on his face, smelled stale whisky.

Malkie expected another 'fuck off', but Fielding calmed, leaned on the doorframe, his fury drained by a visible effort of self-control.

'Just catch that bastard Callahan. My family's not safe while he's out there.'

Malkie snorted his disgust. 'And you're worried about their well-being? I get that – your father looks frail these days, and I gather your wife's a bit accident-prone, yes?'

Fielding's smile disappeared. 'Accident-prone? She's not the victim she wants people to think, McCulloch. Vicious wee bitch with a big mouth, she is. Needs reminding sometimes.'

'Reminding of what?'

'Not to have such a big mouth.'

Malkie resisted an urge to punch him. 'OK, so why is your family in danger because Mr Callahan *may* be implicated in a motoring incident?'

Fielding glared at him but didn't take the bait. 'You know he's hurt people before, right?'

Oh, you really want me to nail Callahan for this, don't you?

'Yes, I know that, and yes, I'm sure you must be concerned for your family.' Malkie took his chance. 'So, where is your father? Your wife? They're OK after this morning, I hope?'

'They're fine. My dad's in his den, sleeping.'

'Can I talk to them?'

Something like panic flashed across Fielding's face. 'No. They've both had a rough day.'

'I'm going to have to insist.' His meagre credibility had crumbled, but he wasn't leaving without seeing Amanda.

Fielding smiled. 'Not happening, Pig. You piss me off, I'll call your boss, say you've been harassing me. Again.'

He made a show of looking around. 'And your wee dyke pal isn't here to back you up. Your word against mine, copper.'

Malkie held his breath – forced his hands to stay by his sides. *One more word about Steph, and I'll have you, fucker.*

Fielding continued, his confidence growing. 'I can get my brief here, and he's itching to crucify you, interview room or court. Your call, McCulloch. Or what is it the other Pigs call you? McFuckup?'

Malkie had nothing. Steph once admitted to him that DI Pammy had called him Defective Sergeant Malkie McFuckup just once, following the Boy Band debacle. The name had stuck. Today, it was bang on. He stepped away, his mind rummaging for a decent parting shot. 'I'll be back tomorrow, with Detective Constable Lang. Be home.'

Without a formal reason to compel Fielding to let him in, he had no choice. He backed up towards his car. Amanda had begged him for help, and he couldn't even check she was OK. He scanned the upstairs windows, hoped to catch a glimpse of her, but saw nothing. Why hadn't he logged the call and brought Steph?

Fielding wasn't finished. 'I hear you had a death in the family?'

Walk away.

'Bad year, mate. Harassment charge for picking on me then losing your mum like that.'

Bloody walk away.

'Terrible accident. Must really burn you up, eh?'

Malkie's temper maxed out. 'What the fuck are you trying to say?'

Fielding shrugged, feigned innocence, and said no more.

Malkie lunged. He slammed Fielding back against the door, clamped one hand around his throat.

Fielding nodded over Malkie's shoulder. Jake stood behind him, one hand on his stick, the other holding a mobile phone, the lens pointed at Malkie, a yellow, gap-toothed grin plastered on his leering face.

Malkie released Fielding's throat but placed one hand on his chest and leaned close.

'You and me. We're due a reckoning. We both know you caused that shit at The Libertine. But I noticed you stayed out of it, safe at the bar. Does Daddy know you were scared of a wee fight, that night?'

It was a desperate dig, but it hit something in Fielding. His grin disappeared and he glanced at his father, a look of sick dread draining all his previous fury.

Malkie returned to his car and drove off. He punched the dashboard, bruised his knuckles, swore. Another classic Malkie McCulloch fuck-up. Steph would freak if she found out.

But he'd touched a nerve with his comment about the nightclub. Was The Jakey's big, bad son not the hard man everyone thought he was? Was there something there Malkie could use? Something to persuade McLeish to let him go after them, despite his warning? A chance to salvage something from this bloody car-crash of a day, maybe force Fielding to lay off his wife?

Time for another look at The Libertine case files.

THIRTEEN

Callahan risked a bus into Edinburgh, paid in cash and wore a baseball cap pulled low over his face. He tried to empty his bank account, but a cashier in a pressed and spotless waistcoat and her condescending supervisor allowed him to withdraw only three grand in cash from the sixty he knew was in there.

He bought three burner phones from different shops and on different networks, all with cash. He bought new combat trousers and a jacket, and even managed to obtain a used Fairbairn Sykes combat knife in great condition from a private dealer in Leith. Finally, on the high street, a bottle of Cardhu eighteen-year-old single malt, and he smiled as he looked forward to opening it.

Now he stood in a manky toilet in a Bathgate pub, staring into a cracked and grimy mirror. Without the bags under his eyes and the grey flecks in his eyebrows and hair, the man who returned his gaze could have been thirty years old, blue-helmeted and rolling into Srebrenica, not yet brutalised by atrocities he was made to watch but could do nothing about. An age had passed since those horrific tours, and yet in some ways he feared he was frozen in time, incapable of change despite so many hard years of trying.

He shook his head, banished memories he couldn't bear to look at, staggered out the side door. An alleyway led to a park strewn with used needles and empty Buckie bottles, the preferred tonic wine of drunks and students since alcohol became a primary food group. On the other side lay Bernard's house. Bernard, after Jake, was his oldest friend. A friend he hadn't visited in four years.

Bernard's sheltered housing was a squalid wee box in a terrace, a council-sanctioned ghetto for screw-ups and invalids, as he liked to describe it. The gate hung off its hinges and the lawn grass stood two-feet high. He punched the same combination he last used four years ago into the key safe. The panel popped open. He removed the key and unlocked the door.

The house was dark except for a light flickering under the bedroom door. He heard a football match in progress, and recalled evenings spent with Bernard, shouting at the TV and getting pissed on Scotch.

Another door opened into a combined living room and kitchen. The place was immaculate. Bernard always ran a tight outfit, and his carers obviously knew it.

Callahan crept to the bedroom door. He eased it open and peered into the gloom.

A voice growled, low and menacing. 'Stop there or I'll fucking knife you.'

'With no hands? That would be impressive.'

Bernard Robertson lay half-elevated in bed. He'd got fatter and his hair was thinner. His eyes gleamed in the darkness, reflecting the TV. Even with no hands and no legs beneath his knees, he was ready to have a go.

Callahan reached for the lamp beside the bed and switched it on.

Bernard cracked a delighted grin. 'Walter. Good God.

What brings you to my lavish abode?' He spotted Callahan's kitbag and his smile disappeared. 'What's up, mate?'

Callahan felt some of the tension drain from him. Here was one man he could talk to, the only person who might understand.

He pulled the bottle from his pocket. 'First, a drink.'

Bernard's eyes lit up. 'Is that Cardhu? The eighteen-year-old one?'

'Of course it bloody is. Wouldn't bring you anything less, would I?'

Callahan fetched two glasses from the kitchen, pulled up Bernard's wheelchair, and poured them each a dram. He placed Bernard's glass between his stumps, made sure his grip was as good as it could be, then they toasted each other without words, eyes locked in bitter, shared memories, and sipped the soft, warm, golden liquid.

Despite the four-year absence, Bernard gave Callahan time to get to the point of the visit. Eventually, Bernard asked the question.

'Is it back, Walter?'

Callahan forced words past a sudden dryness in his mouth. 'The Dog? Aye.'

'Fuck's sake man, you're not depressed, you're—'

Callahan's expression shut Bernard down. As always, a conversation for another time. 'And yours?'

'Been good for two years now. How bad is it this time? As bad as...?'

Callahan swallowed. Shame clogged his throat. 'Worse.'

Bernard lifted his glass. 'Ach, it'll pass, always does. How the hell can you afford Cardhu?'

Callahan relaxed. Bernard would shelter him. He could rest here, catch his breath.

'So, what have you been up to? You still living at Jake's place?'

'Aye. Driving minicabs for my rent.'

'You two are still buddies then?'

Something in Bernard's tone jarred on him. 'Of course we are. Why would you ask that?'

'Steady, mate. I was only asking. It's been a long time since we came home, that's all.'

Callahan studied Bernard's eyes, looked for something more, found nothing. Either his question was genuine, or Bernard was a better liar than he'd realised. He shook his head, banished the thoughts. What was happening to him? This was Bernard, for pity's sake.

'I drive his cabs and do some extra jobs on the side. Nothing heavy. He's straight these days.'

Bernard snorted. 'Aye, right.'

Callahan's temper broke before he could catch it. 'Oh, don't start, Bernard. I work for the guy. I live there. We play poker twice a week. I think I know him better than you.'

Bernard took another sip. 'Oh, that's good.' He held his glass up to the light, admired the golden glow. 'So. Has it happened again?'

Callahan couldn't answer immediately. He rubbed his eyes with his fingers, took a long drink, relished the burn down his throat, the heat in his stomach.

'When I woke up this morning, I found two coppers outside the house. The front of my car was all staved in and covered in blood. Someone must have seen me or the car. Only happened last night but they came for me this morning.'

Bernard shook his head. 'No, no, no. Your episodes wouldn't come on while you're driving. You only ever kick off when someone gets in your face first. Ninety-nine times out of a hundred you only go apeshit in self-defence. Well, except—'

'I know. You think I don't remember every bloody day what I did to her? Her of all people?'

Callahan choked down tears, couldn't afford to let himself

break down. Not now.

'But I decided, a while ago...' He paused, dreaded his mate's reaction. 'I stopped my meds three months ago.'

Bernard stared at him for what seemed ages. 'You. Fucking. Idiot.'

Walter stared into his glass, couldn't argue. 'I've been on Seraxonine for more than ten years. One morning I woke up feeling good, felt like maybe I could try weaning myself off them. I went on half doses. A day turned into a week, then a month, and I've been off them for a few weeks now.'

'And?'

'It feels good, mate. Felt good. I don't sleep any better and I still get the urges, but I think I have it under control. I'm running again, and I'm enjoying stupid wee things like a quiet pint by myself or falling asleep on the sofa without double-locking the doors and hiding the keys. I still jump when someone slams a door, but I'm learning to handle that, too.'

Walter waved his hand at Bernard's legs. 'You learned to handle that. So, why not me?'

Bernard stared at him. 'Mate, my missing legs make it less likely I'll hurt someone, not more. Don't you think I feel like hurting people? Don't you think I'd love to meet that idiot Markham and mess him up? Did you hear he made Major? Markham, a fucking Major.'

Bernard raised his whisky but fumbled and soaked his pyjamas. 'And now I've wasted eighteen-year-old Cardhu. Not on, Walter. Not on.'

Callahan said nothing, didn't want Bernard going off about Markham again. Not now.

Bernard calmed down with obvious effort. 'Walter, running someone over in a car isn't your style. You'd never get behind the wheel of a car pissed.'

'I must have. It was my car. I was drinking and playing poker with Jake and Liam until late. After they left, I must have gone for a drive. And it looks like I hit someone, it triggered a blackout and I drove home without even realising.'

Bernard mulled this over. 'I don't think so, Walter. Every time I've seen you lose it, someone's asked for it. True, you over-react, and you've hospitalised people, but I never once saw you start any trouble. Remember that dickhead in Musselburgh, the Friday race night? He pushed you hard, but you walked away. Prick yelled abuse at you all the way to the door. You could have ruined him without even breathing hard, but you walked right out of the place. You still think you could run someone over and not remember a thing about it?'

Bernard had a knack of seeing straight to the centre of matters. He would have made a cracking officer, but he'd enjoyed the rush of bomb-disposal too much. They'd both suffered for their career choices. He waited, hoped Bernard might find the centre of this knot, help him to unpick it.

Bernard stared into the remains of his Cardhu, pursed his lips as his mind worked.

'OK, you know you messed up. Stay here tonight. Tomorrow, you call the outreach centre. You ask them to let you try again, if they'll let you. But stay here tonight, get some sleep.'

'I need meds, had to leave mine behind when I left, only managed to grab a couple. I really need them. I'm not going inside again. I'll die in there.'

Bernard shushed him. 'Fine. You've got a dose for the morning, so calm down. There's a doss bag and blankets in the cupboard beside the sofa. You're safe here.'

Bernard held his glass out between his stumps. 'Where's that bottle? Let's get rat-arsed.'

Callahan stared at him. Waited.

'Walter, I'll sort you out. In the morning, OK?'

Callahan reached for the Cardhu. 'Thanks, Bernard. I owe you.'

'Yes, mate. You do. We'll talk about that in the morning, too.'

FOURTEEN

Halfway back to the station, Malkie spotted the Ducati.

It hung back until the traffic built up, then moved closer. The massive bike looked like a tank under the rider – too short and wiry to be Fielding so it had to be one of the McGuire brothers, the wee skinny one, Robbie. No chance of stopping at his digs for a change of clothes and to brush his teeth, couldn't risk leading one of Fielding's crew to his temporary address. A few random turns failed to shake him off. Steph would come running if he called her but explaining why Fielding wanted him followed would lead to questions he didn't fancy answering.

He pulled over without indicating. A Mondeo screeched past him, horn blaring. The bike turned into a side street. After five long minutes, he moved away again and the bike reappeared, again three cars back. He took the scenic route back to the station via Dedridge and the Livi FC football ground. The bike followed. At the lights where he waited to turn into the Howden South Road, he jumped out of the car and ran back towards the bike.

The rider pulled a wheel-burning turn and sped off.

'Aye, fuck off. Tell your prick of a boss to send someone bigger next time.'

He made it back to his car in time to miss another green light and spent forty-five seconds imagining furious eyes boring into him from behind. At the station he parked behind the building, out of sight of the front gate. Upstairs in the CID room he crossed to the windows and peered down through the blinds. No sign of the Ducati or either of the McGuires. He turned back to find faces watching him, but none showed any surprise at his behaviour. Some scowled. Others raised their eyebrows, amused. He suspected another booting was imminent from McLeish for his absence all afternoon.

Steph slouched at her desk, almost horizontal in her seat, typing at arm's length, bored. He sneaked up behind her, but she spoke first.

'I know how much you enjoy entering stuff into this damned computer, but I wanted it done before McLeish asks.' She smiled up at him. 'You can do tomorrow's updates. We've got something in from Forensics.' She leaned forward, pointed to her screen. 'Most of the safe contents were unremarkable, but they found an SD card in a plastic bag under a rubber mat.'

Malkie's eyebrows lifted. 'That explains the bungled burglary, then. What's on it?'

She shook her head. 'Encrypted. It's in the Techies' work stack, but would you believe there's a backlog?'

'When is there not?'

'I called your old pal, William Loudon. He was in a bad mood as usual but said for you he'd hurry it up.'

Malkie and William went way back. So, although careful never to push his luck, Malkie could rely on William to cut a few corners.

He wanted to play her Amanda's messages but knew he shouldn't. It would end nowhere good.

She stared at him, suspicious. She did him the small favour of lowering her voice. 'What?'

He laid his phone on her desk, span it in a slow circle with his finger, couldn't make eye contact.

'What have you done now? Please tell me you didn't go out there again?'

He couldn't maintain eye contact, busied himself gathering her pens into a neat bundle for no good reason.

'Oh, Malkie. Why?'

His next words sounded beyond pathetic. 'Amanda Fielding called me. Left a message. Said she has something on Callahan.'

Her expression softened, her irritation edged out by curiosity.

'Let me hear this message, then.' She nodded towards his mobile. He groaned inside, pulled the microcassette from his pocket, and placed it on the desk.

She stared at it, confused at first, then appalled as the penny dropped. 'Your dad's old answering machine. You gave her your bloody home number?'

He nodded.

She sat back, rubbed her eyes with her fingers.

'It was when you asked me to look around outside the house, wasn't it?'

Worse was yet to come. 'I left one of my cards for her. In the kitchen. In her spectacle case.'

'And if her pig of a husband finds it? Can you imagine how he'll kick off?'

He took a deep breath and got the rest out. 'There were three messages. The first one she sounded OK, only a bit tense, which was understandable, her calling a copper. The second was...'

He swallowed. Steph stared at him open-mouthed as if dreading what else was coming.

'The second was silence, probably Fielding calling her last

dialled number. Then she called again and said he was going to kill her.'

Steph deflated, beaten. 'Oh, Malkie, what were you thinking? Even by your standards—'

'Aye, all right. I fucked up but it's fixable.' *Unless your stupidity has already got her killed.*

'How, Malkie? How the hell do we keep this from McLeish?'

He stared at her, stunned – she wanted to protect him, despite the professional risk to herself. He didn't deserve her.

'What?' she asked.

'What do you mean, what?' He scowled at her.

'Don't sit there and stare at me like a bloody doe-eyed teenager. This is bad, mate.' She sighed. 'OK, why do you think she's still safe? And don't leave anything out, you idiot.'

He considered pulling rank on her for the 'idiot', but as usual she had a point.

'I heard shouting inside the house, but not Amanda – male voices. When Fielding answered the door—'

'Which Fielding?'

'Liam. He got right in my face, bloody raging, like he wanted to rip my head off. When I asked if Jake and Amanda were OK, he said his dad was asleep but he said just about nothing about Amanda.'

'And that proves what? That he doesn't care where his own wife is? Or maybe he's beaten her senseless?'

'Fuck's sake. Don't say that.'

Steph studied him, fidgeted with a pen. 'So, you think she's run away from him?'

'I think so. Something I said spooked him. Funny thing...'

'What?' Steph prompted him.

'See, he tried to push my buttons, get a rise out of me, like he was desperate to deflect the conversation.'

Her eyes flashed. 'But you kept your cool, right?'

'Of course I did. But then I mentioned The Libertine at New Year...' He hesitated – the thought of Liam Fielding, scared... 'It was weird. He changed in a second.'

'The Libertine.' She said it with an air of unwelcome recognition. 'You were lucky to get away with a reprimand for that.'

'Aye. He had it coming though, standing at the bar watching his crew do all that damage. Made sure we couldn't touch him for it. Slippery bastard.'

Something scratched on Malkie's mind. 'Now I think about it, it was when I mentioned him staying at the bar, that was when he looked sick.'

'Worried people think he was too chicken to get stuck in himself?'

'Could be. His dad would kill him for being scared of a fight.'

Steph stood, lifted her jacket from the back of her chair. 'Get some sleep. You look rotten.'

Malkie opened his mouth to say something sentimental, to thank her for never quite giving up on him, but she spoke over him.

'I don't want this biting me on the backside. Your backside is your problem.'

He chose to hear affection in her parting abuse and smiled.

He looked out the window, scanned the car park and the Howden Road. No sign of the Ducati, but he imagined eyes on him from the darkness outside. If Fielding sent mini-McGuire to find his wife, then Malkie wanted her in custody quick. Enemy of his enemy, all that shite.

He could find no doubt in his own mind that the woman he'd met in that kitchen was genuinely terrified. And besides, he'd as good as promised her...

He headed for the vending machines. A sandwich and a couple of hours trawling the video archives, then home to bed.

His eyes felt dry and gritty, and he had a headache building.

FIFTEEN

'McCulloch. Wake up. Morning briefing, if you'd care to honour us with your attendance?'

'Yes, sir. At once, sir.'

McLeish continued towards the far end of the room where the rest of the squad waited. They must have all filed past him, asleep at his desk. Great start to his comeback.

His back muscles spasmed from slouching in his crappy office chair. He stood, stretched, grunted as his neck creaked. He'd removed his tie and unbuttoned his top two shirt buttons at some point, and now his fingers fumbled with urgency to cover the mess underneath.

He grabbed his can of fruit juice and joined his colleagues. Most of their faces turned to enjoy his rude awakening. Several grinned, their enjoyment plain. Some smiled with pained sympathy while others scowled and shook their heads, their disapproval obvious.

McLeish stood at one end of the CID Suite beside an old friend of Malkie's from their cadet days at Tulliallan, DI Susan Thompson. McLeish, probably relishing his temporary DCI role, made no effort to check that Thompson was OK with him taking the lead. Malkie knew that Thompson's acceptance of McLeish's assumed authority would be feigned, and that McLeish had just added himself to what she liked to call her 'lists'. He'd spent enough time on her lists himself.

McLeish cleared his throat. The few faces still staring in obvious glee at Malkie turned away.

'I'm meeting Detective Superintendent Whittaker at nine, so I'll keep this brief.'

Malkie heard a low, happy, sigh. McLeish couldn't have missed it but let it go.

'Blackburn stabbings. Update.'

DC Rab Lundy stood, as McLeish always insisted.

Lundy, experienced but – like Malkie – happy to remain at a junior Detective rank even in his mid-forties, was industrious and effective, but with a refreshing rough edge and without the smugness and air of superiority that often accompanied such traits in others. Malkie liked him.

'Two wastes of oxygen—'

Thompson, his DI, growled, 'Rab...'

'Sorry, boss. Two victims. One Todd Hamilton, twenty-two, resident of Blackburn, the other Jordan Middleton, twenty-eight, no fixed abode. Two weapons found, a six-inch hunting knife and a kitchen bread knife. Both had the prints of one and blood type of the other, more to be confirmed when DNA matches come back. Looks very like one waste of... I mean, like each victim killed the other. Ten bags of pills and a large wad of cash found on one, a few twenties on the other. My guess, a purchase of recreational pharmaceuticals went arse over tit. Sir.'

McLeish scowled at him, then nodded for him to sit.

'McCulloch. Murieston.'

Malkie stood. Heads turned. Some smiled, others looked like they wanted nothing more than to see him make a complete prick of himself. DC Louisa Gooch – no fan of McLeish, either – winked at him and grinned.

'RTC. Non-fatal, so far. Initially thought accidental but that's no longer the case.'

'Here we go.' Sounded like DS 'don't call me Pam' Ballantyne. Several loud chuckles applauded her cutting wit.

'Witness statements and initial investigations led to a minicab found at a Kirknewton address, the bonnet and windscreen severely damaged and with copious forensic evidence plastered all over it.'

He glanced at McLeish to gauge how far he could go this morning. Not far.

'Suspect escaped into woods behind the property. His details and an old mug shot are being circulated through the usual channels. Forensics have attended both scenes and Kirknewton.'

McLeish stood. 'That'll do, McCulloch. Thank you.'

Despite considering he'd delivered a fairly decent briefing, he caught numerous smirks and scowls as he returned to his seat. Thompson did the bare minimum to hide her amusement, which cheered him up.

McLeish covered the usual items of other daily business, then wrapped up the briefing. On his way to his office he stopped beside Malkie.

'My office.'

Steph frowned at him as if asking what the hell he'd done wrong now.

McLeish took his time. Hung his jacket up. Smoothed his shirt sleeves down and adjusted his heavy gold links. Then he folded his arms and loomed over Malkie for long, long seconds.

'I've had a complaint, Malkie.'

Malkie studied McLeish's polished burgundy brogues, then made an obvious act of studying the man from head to feet.

'Do you wear heel lifts?'

McLeish sat behind his desk, not impressed.

'Liam Fielding called me. Said you went back to Kirknewton yesterday. Said he felt threatened.'

Threatened. Not attacked. What the hell is Fielding up to?

McLeish sat forward, rested his elbows on the table, knitted his fingers together. 'He wants you charged with harassment. He dragged up that incident last New Year again. The nightclub. We discussed this, didn't we, Malkie?'

For the second time in two days, McLeish was ringing alarms in his head. 'No, Gavin, we didn't discuss it. You told me to lay off the Fieldings, no explanation. That's not a discussion.'

McLeish bristled at Malkie's over-familiarity but didn't give him the satisfaction of any further reaction. 'So, why were you out there again? Was I not clear enough? You want it in writing?'

Malkie took a deep breath. He needed to walk a thin line. If Fielding had reported their fight, McLeish would have led with that. Why would Fielding withhold that priceless nugget of information? 'I got a call from Amanda, his wife.'

'Oh, I know who she is.'

'What do you mean?'

McLeish sighed, as if losing patience with the disappointment before him. 'Amanda Fielding has had four separate formal cautions for breach of the peace, nearly got done for assault and battery the last time. She keeps attacking Liam Fielding's girlfriends. But none of them ever press charges.'

Malkie hated hearing this, and that worried him. A gleam appeared in McLeish's eyes as Malkie fumbled for a response.

'She told me she was in danger, said Fielding was going to hurt her.' He stopped there, prayed McLeish wouldn't dig any deeper.

McLeish held Malkie with a calculating gaze, then seemed to come to a decision. 'So, you wanted to check up on her? I can accept that.'

Malkie didn't relax. Backing down didn't mean McLeish

was OK with his explanation, only that he'd accepted it. Not the same thing.

'Did you see her at the property?'

'No. Fielding made it clear he wasn't about to fetch her.'

'Did you ask to look inside?'

'I'm not a complete amateur. Sir.'

McLeish flashed him a warning look.

Malkie held McLeish's gaze before continuing. 'He asked if I had a warrant. I didn't.'

McLeish chewed on his thoughts for a moment then stood. 'OK, I'll call the house, ask to speak to her. If they give me the run-around, I'll send a uniform out there, OK?'

Malkie searched McLeish's eyes for the catch. Was he getting a rare break, a rare concession from McLeish? Time to get out while he was ahead?

'Fine. I need to see if William Loudon's got anything off the memory card from Robin Wilkie's safe.'

McLeish held the door open. Malkie stopped halfway through. 'How is Mr Wilkie? The paramedics weren't optimistic.'

'He's in an induced coma in St John's.'

'With a uniform on the door, aye?'

McLeish stared at him.

Malkie's temper broke. 'Why the hell not? This wasn't accidental. Someone drove at him deliberately. And he's got no protection?'

McLeish held a hand up. 'We don't know that yet and until we do, we can't spare a uniform twenty-four seven. He's in a secure room under constant observation. The nurses have an alarm button. Hospital security have been alerted in case anyone tries to visit him.'

Malkie stared at him in disgust, then returned to his desk before his mouth could make things worse. He dropped into his seat, kicked his shoes off, rested his forehead on the desk, and closed his eyes.

Was Amanda Fielding the fragile damsel he'd assumed? He logged in to the Police Scotland system but couldn't bring himself to run a search on her. Liam Fielding was the issue here. However much she'd been forced to defend herself against her pig of a husband, she was the victim in their brutal and abusive marriage.

He opened the folder of archived videos he'd extracted last night and started from the beginning again.

The sight of Liam Fielding queuing to enter an iconic gay nightclub like The Libertine should seem ridiculous to Malkie, but he'd seen first-hand the damage Liam and his goons had caused once they got inside.

He and four sidekicks arrived at 23:07 and queued for fifteen minutes to get in. Two of them he recognised as the McGuire brothers. Mitch, tall and bulky, the other shorter and lean: Robbie, the one that tailed him on the Ducati. Fielding looked bored but the others messed around with each other like overexcited children. Word was that Fielding allowed his employees to indulge in pharmaceutical recreation but never touched anything stronger than alcohol himself.

The Libertine was the most popular gay nightclub in Livingston. Malkie knew the head bouncer and liked him. Big Tam sported a thick moustache, black leathers, and a permanent *You'll do* pout. Fights broke out most weekends, but Tam and his crew were as hard as they came, and they made sure few incidents ever escalated to a shout for uniforms to attend.

When Fielding and his pack moved inside, Malkie switched to the foyer camera. They accepted a stamp on the wrist from a tall, elegant young man whom Malkie later identified as Alexander in a glittering ball gown with a tiara perched on permed blond hair. Malkie had held his hand while they strapped him onto an ambulance trolley. Two hours later Alexander had lain in an induced coma with a machine breathing for him. *You never did remember to find out how he is now, did you?*

Malkie forced himself back to his PC screen; he had the rest of his life to indulge in flogging himself.

Inside the club, Fielding's crew took up a position at one end of the bar. Fielding scanned the ceiling until he found a CCTV camera. The man was an animal, but no idiot. He wanted himself on video to prove he took no direct part in the coming events. They ordered beers and shots and formed a circle, necked their shots, and ordered more.

They spent a few minutes watching the dance floor, then Fielding whispered to the larger McGuire, who headed into the throng, his eager mates close behind him.

With his playthings wound up and set in motion, Fielding leaned on the bar and waited for the entertainment to kick off. Malkie paused the bar camera, then opened the two dance floor cameras in new windows, synced them to the same time, then ran all three together.

As the four prowled the dance floor, a young man in a waist-coat and flat cap approached Fielding, leaned close to talk to him, rested a hand on his arm. Fielding threw the man off as if scalded. The young man recoiled. Fielding glanced up at a camera as if to remind himself why he'd chosen that spot – far from his jacked-up buddies and any accusation of his own involvement. He spat a few aggressive words at the young man, who stumbled backwards, then hurried away.

On the dance floor, the McGuire brothers high-fived each other, then all four turned and piled into one dancer each. Starting back-to-back, the Amphetamine Musketeers and their violence radiated outwards, laying into one innocent reveller after another.

At the bar Fielding watched the carnage begin, and smiled up at the bar camera as if goading him personally from so many months ago. Malkie had to swallow a surge of exactly the kind of revulsion he imagined Fielding intended.

Fielding's reaction to Malkie's mention of the nightclub footage made sense now. He'd allowed a homosexual man to come on to him, to get close enough to lean all over him and he'd done nothing, just to keep his hands clean. His dad, the legendary Jakey, would break his fingers for less.

Malkie filed this thought away. As he logged off, McLeish's words came back to him. Amanda. Four cautions.

Do I want to know? Do I need to know? Self-defence isn't Assault and Battery. Certainly, nowhere near Attempted Murder.

He shut down his terminal and headed for his car. The first of the rising sun tinged the view to the east. The old rhyme ran through his head. 'Red sky in the morning...'

Fuck that. Superstitious bollocks.

His thoughts wandered to his dad, who always woke early, ate breakfast, and read the morning papers with Mum. How did he fill his mornings now, without her? Malkie glanced at his watch: nearly nine. Home, shower, shave, grow something like a backbone, and drive to the hospital, show his dad the respect of facing him. Time to clear out some emotional clutter, make space for him to function like the half-competent copper he used to be.

He drove out of the car park with something like a smile on his face.

SIXTEEN

Callahan woke on Bernard's sofa, more exhausted than before he'd fallen asleep. He'd lost count of the times he'd woken in a sweat reeling from nightmares too real not to come from genuine memories. Memories he dreaded might return to him and damn him. Some man's face smacking into a window, the glass shattering and buckling inwards, the man's eyes furious, his mouth spewing rage and hate but making no noise.

By the time he handed Bernard his coffee, he was in no mood for small talk.

'What's this going to cost me, then?'

'What do you need?'

'Meds for a week or two, stabilise me so I can sort this mess out. You were on Seraxonine too, weren't you?'

'Aye, until two years ago. Until I dealt with it.'

'Unlike me, you mean?'

Bernard stared at him. 'I got help.'

Callahan ignored the well-intentioned but stinging dig. 'You got any Muzzle then?'

Bernard stared for a second as if sizing up a job applicant. 'Can't get Muzzle anymore. Norrie had to stop cooking.'

Callahan stared at him in disbelief.

Bernard held up his stumps as if to protest his sincerity. 'When you last asked for some, only you and Pedro Stevenson were still using it, and Pedro popped his clogs three days after he got his last batch. Norrie got sloppy, bought cheap coke. Pedro got the first lot of that and died puking and shitting himself. Norrie tried to sell more but word was out and Jake kettled him for trying to offload some on him. He stopped cooking after that.'

Callahan recalled Jake's favoured way of persuading strays to return to his fold. Kettling, he called it, long before the term was coined during the miners' strikes in the eighties. Dripping boiling water on people. It hurt like hell and was plausibly deniable – anyone can trip over while making a brew and scald themselves. The part of Callahan he called The Dog roused itself and slavered – the excuse he hid his culpability behind, a fraying knot of long-suppressed fury. He'd stood by, appalled, but did nothing as men and women were held down, thrashing and screaming, while Jake 're-educated' them. The Dog lapped it up, every time.

The Dog? Hypocrite. He had lapped it up.

He shook himself. Why did his mind keep going to places he worked so hard to close off? He needed meds. Today. Tomorrow might be too late.

'Bernard, what the hell am I going to do? This is bad. I'm getting worse. I've blacked out an entire night and killed a man from inside my bloody car. This wasn't some idiot in my face asking for it. Self-defence won't cut it this time. I'm not going inside again. I'll kill myself first, mate.'

Bernard leaned forward, touched Callahan's arm with a stump. 'Walter, breathe. We'll fix this.'

Callahan looked at him. 'Can you contact Norrie? He might have something left, no?'

'I told you, he stopped cooking years ago.' Bernard stared at him, his eyes heavy with sympathy that triggered a stab of resentment in Callahan. He settled back in his chair, stared out the window.

Bernard broke the bitter silence first. 'You remember playing British Bulldog in Bastion? Remember me hanging on to you as you dragged me over the line?'

Callahan smiled. 'Aye, I remember, Bernard. Not many good memories of those tours.'

'For some stupid reason, British Bulldog always pops into my head when I drop my guard and notice all over again that I've got bugger-all left in the hands department.' He held his stumps up. 'You know why this happened?'

Callahan dreaded where this might go. Bernard never discussed his disability, refused to be defined by it. 'I was there, mate. Remember? I saw you shamble up to that crossroads in your crappy bomb suit and I saw that IED go off in your face.'

Bernard didn't break eye contact as he continued. 'And why did I come home in this state?'

Callahan realised now where this was going. Was Bernard's help going to carry too high a price?

'Tell me, Bernard. What was it that took your hands and legs? Enlighten me.'

Bernard's expression showed he hadn't missed Callahan's warning tone. 'I'm in this state, old friend, because of that fucker James Markham.'

Callahan's guts turned over. Bernard's price might be too high for him to stomach.

'I told him I needed R&R that day, Walter. I didn't see Bastion for seven weeks, and I was doing ten jobs a day, sometimes fifteen. He spent every day safe behind the wheel of his Jackal while I was sleepwalking from one shitshow to the next. I actually started wishing those bastards would nail me so I could bloody sleep.'

'Bernard, we've talked about this. Yes, Markham was an

incompetent prick like every other rich, entitled *Rupert* we had to take orders from. But that's the whole point – he'll never answer for it. He retired a Major and his dad's a Brigadier.'

Bernard stared at him until the penny dropped.

Callahan's stomach sank. 'Christ, Bernard. No.'

'I don't want him dead. Just hurt him. Make the bastard suffer, make him piss himself. Bring me a photo. That's all. Do that for me and I'll get you the last good batch of Muzzle Norrie ever made.'

Callahan stared at him for long seconds. How little did he know this man he'd trusted for so long? 'No. You're asking too much. I agree Markham deserves to suffer for what he did to you. But that's...'

Bernard waited, stubborn.

'Bernard, you're better than this. You make me do this, you're as bad as he was.'

'No, Walter, I'm already no better than him.' He stopped, swallowed, took a moment before continuing, to push past something Callahan was missing. 'That bastard took my hands and my legs. I'm a useless lump of meat now. Remember my brother? He visited me when I came home. Stayed an hour, looked at me twice. His kids wouldn't stay in the same room. So I'm sorry if your lofty moral code can't stomach an animal like me, but I want to see that piece of shit crying and pissing himself and thinking his last moments have come.'

Bernard fell back into his pillows, covered his eyes with the remains of his forearm, looked ready to cry.

'Walter, I want to help you. But...'

Bernard lowered his arm and Walter saw nothing but desperation in his eyes. A broken man clutching at his last chance to silence a rage that had eaten at him from the inside out, every day and month and year since his spirit was murdered that brutal, hot day in a Musa Qala backstreet.

'I need to see that man suffer. I need to see him as fucked up as he made me. You remember what he used to call you?'

Callahan sighed. How low would Bernard stoop?

'Of course I do. He called me Jake's Bitch. Not likely to forget, am I?'

Callahan stared at his last remaining friend other than Jake. Should he have seen this coming? Hiding away in the cottage, he'd turned his back on a world that made no sense to him anymore. But all that time spent sucking his thumb, he'd been failing his oldest friend even more profoundly than the cold, uncaring world had failed them both.

Was torturing a disgrace like Markham justified in return for more meds to stop him from killing again? What alternative did he have? Break into a pharmacy, hope the police didn't arrive before he found the right pills? Threaten a nurse at the outreach centre, the only place that had ever tried to help him?

'I'm not killing him, Bernard.'

Bernard raised his head, a mixture of weariness and hope in his eyes. 'Fine. I've got his address. He lives on his own. You get me pictures and I'll get you Norrie's last safe batch. Markham might even have a stash if he was using it too.'

Callahan had no intention of going through with it; as much as he'd enjoy hurting the man, he couldn't risk setting a foot on that path.

He'd worry later about lying to his oldest friend.

'OK, but I'm not killing him, and you give me Norrie's address first so I can ask him myself.'

'Fine, but you're wasting your time. There's an old Insta-matic camera in that cupboard.'

Callahan stared at him, feared his disgust must be obvious, but Bernard didn't see it or didn't care.

He grabbed a pen and notebook from Bernard's side table and wrote down the number of the burner phone.

'If you get any calls about me, tell them I let myself in but you sent me packing and told me not to contact you again. Then call me on that number.'

He fetched the camera from the closet. 'Where does Norrie live?'

Bernard grinned. 'Front of that notebook in your hand. Under "N" for Norrie.'

'You're a right arsehole sometimes, Bernie.'

SEVENTEEN

Malkie made it home without another sighting of the Ducati. When safe behind his front door he let out a shuddering breath. The morning rush-hour traffic had seemed to come at him from all directions. A sustained assault on his senses. A barrage of noise and fumes. Vehicles appearing out of nowhere. Horns blaring and furious faces yelling words he didn't need to hear to understand. He crossed to the front windows and peered down at the street, scanned left and right, saw no bike.

Despite feeling like an idiot he checked both door locks and the chain. For good measure, he propped his dad's golf-club bag against the door too.

Was this ridiculous? Why would Fielding send one of his goons after him? Did he expect Amanda to come running to a copper? Did McGuire leg it when Malkie drove into the station car park?

He forced himself to take a reality check. Twenty-four hours on the job after six months away and he'd already assaulted Fielding, suffered two warnings from McLeish, and pissed Steph off, twice. He'd already given McLeish enough to take to Professional Standards if he chose to.

McLeish's cryptic orders picked away at his mind. One warning he could believe was to keep Malkie and Fielding apart, but a second so quickly after his solo visit to Kirknewton – it smelled rotten.

McLeish was protecting something. Could it be his big secret case with the Glasgow lot? And D F Browne, whoever that was? Some big score McLeish hoped would raise his profile and launch him on his way to full DCI? Something he didn't want Malkie screwing up?

Malkie recalled how much he and Steph turning up yesterday morning had rattled the younger Fielding, but it seemed excessive to send a McGuire after him. Was Fielding on McLeish's radar, a suspect in his big task-force case? Did the arrogant prick want to be the man to finally bring the Fieldings down? And was Liam so intent on finding his wife because she knew more than was good for her? Could she confirm his involvement in Wilkie's attack?

Malkie set his phone alarm for an hour, pulled his tie off and unbuttoned his shirt, then settled into his armchair and closed his eyes. He tried to sleep, imagined himself and his dad on a porch at the front of the cabin. Two rocking chairs, a table, a coffee pot, and two steaming mugs. But despite himself, he spent the hour chewing over the Wilkie case, getting nowhere except frustrated, then the landline rang. After four rings he remembered he'd taken the microcassette out of his dad's old, battered, and smoke-blackened answering machine. He'd never bought himself an answering machine. He already hated that trouble could find him via his work voicemail, so he refused to risk bad news waiting for him when he was home and wanted to shut the world out. But his dad's battered old relic was the only thing salvaged from the fire intact enough to remind him of the home he grew up in. He'd also discovered the joys of call-screening, although it made it easy to ignore calls he knew he should take, as well as those that deserved to be ignored.

It might be his dad again. He was tempted to answer, could do with hearing a familiar voice, but Dad deserved their next conversation to be face-to-face.

Could it be Amanda Fielding, his best chance to make progress? Could she shine a light on her long-suffered husband's obvious complicity? Despite McLeish's warnings, he wouldn't allow himself to be sidelined. He'd as good as promised her his protection. As soon as he'd seen her bruises nothing on earth could have stopped him leaving his card.

The phone stopped ringing but was followed by a knock at his front door.

He crossed to a window and scanned the road. No sign of the Ducati. But there were plenty of places to park around here, and even the smaller of the McGuire brothers could mess him up without breaking a sweat. A look through the front bay window gave no decent view: his visitor was standing too close to the door.

He crept down the hallway, peered through the spyglass.

Amanda stood outside, staring straight at him. How the hell did she get his address?

He reached for the latch but then snatched his hand away. Was it time to minimise the damage he was doing to himself? Only last night he'd feared he'd earned her a beating or worse at Fielding's hands, but she looked fine. Did he now have a second chance to do something right by not screwing up again?

The letter box clattered.

A CID contact card came through the door and fell to the floor. He knew without looking that it had his home phone number scribbled on the other side.

This woman might help him nail Fielding, yet he hesitated to open the door, to give credence to his own suspicions. None of his theories held any real basis in fact, and his hunches had blown up in his face often enough before. If Liam was up to his neck in all of this, she might know how, but then, was she involved too? Her fear had sounded genuine on the phone and her heavy hint through the letter box suggested she was desperate, but that look she'd given Liam, and those previous cautions, all for violence...

He applied his standard litmus test to the situation – what would Steph do? She'd take the woman straight to the station, get her placed in protective custody. But he doubted Mrs Fielding would agree to that; nowhere would be safe for her if word got out she was talking to the filth.

On top of practical factors, he couldn't ignore less worthy reasons to let her in. A part of him he wasn't proud of longed to take the attractive woman into his protection. He had felt a momentary sense of connection the previous morning, a recognition of two souls suffering their own private hells. Had she felt it too? Whatever it might have been, he knew nothing could come of it, but it had been so long since...

'Mr McCulloch? I'm not leaving.'

He swore again. With one reckless act only one day back on the job, he'd compromised himself. Again. His card lay on the floor, accusing him of breaking his word. He was being lectured by a piece of cardboard. Steph would be so proud of him.

Fielding's behaviour and his wife's appearance here all supported his gut feeling – she'd escaped, and her husband had reason to fear that. Malkie needed to find out what she knew. Could she be a useful ally? Did they both have something to gain from taking Fielding down? But then, what did Malkie really know about her? Why didn't he read her file when he'd had the chance? His head spun. He needed sleep. Indecision rattled inside him. Mrs Fielding piled on the pressure by rapping his door knocker – a slow, insistent demand for his surrender.

He unlatched the bottom lock. She stopped knocking. He took several long seconds to unlatch the top lock, then remove the chain and move the golf clubs, all the time wishing he'd left earlier for the hospital.

She stood scowling on the front step, in biker leathers, holding a glossy black crash helmet.

She must have followed me from the Fielding house then waited all night to follow me home from the station.

She scowled at him. 'Something amusing you?'

Malkie recovered. 'No, Mrs Fielding, sorry. The Ducati, I assume? That's a big bike for a girl your size, isn't it?'

She turned a look on him, disappointment in her eyes, as if reconsidering an earlier opinion of him. 'And that's a misogynistic comment from a boy your age, isn't it? I needed to follow you to some place I could talk to you.'

They stared at each other, their mutual discomfort growing almost tangible as the seconds passed.

Mrs Chalmers from next door appeared in her front garden and fussed over some rose bushes without a single tool in her hands. Malkie allowed Mrs Fielding to enter, then pushed the door closed.

She picked up Malkie's card again, shot him a look that dared him to take it off her.

He indicated the door to the lounge. 'Please. Take a seat.'

Despite the obvious idiocy of his actions, Malkie locked himself in with the desperate wife of a Person of Interest in a live investigation. Before he followed her in he buttoned up his shirt collar and re-tightened his tie knot to hide the ugly reminders of the last time he'd let someone down.

EIGHTEEN

Callahan gazed up at the top floor of a grubby tower block where – Bernard claimed – Norrie lived.

He found himself reluctant to enter the building. If he'd blacked out so completely on Sunday night, how dangerous was he right now? What might he do if Norrie Wallace refused to give him what he needed or tried to give him bad pills? But staying off meds much longer might prove even more dangerous.

He couldn't think straight, and losing it now – killing a second person in two days – would be the end of him. Frustration overcame his dread, and he stepped inside the dark entrance.

On the third floor he passed three kids in jeans and trainers that probably cost more than he earned in a night. They'd forced open a window. One spat at someone on the ground outside, then they laughed and fist-bumped each other. They sized him up as he passed, but either didn't fancy their chances or doubted he had anything worth nicking.

On the fourth floor he heard a woman scream garbled words

at someone. She cried out as if in pain, then fell silent. Callahan continued climbing.

Unlike the other doors on the top floor, Norrie's was steel skinned, no window, serious security.

He rapped on the door. Heard nothing.

He peered through the letter box, saw a cluttered hallway, one door either side and what looked like a living room at the end. Little light penetrated the gloom, thick curtains drawn across the one visible window, but he could make out a floor eight inches deep in newspapers, pizza boxes, and lager cans.

A man who had to be Norrie appeared at the end of the hallway. His manky dressing gown, too small for him, hung open, revealing boxer shorts, emaciated arms, and a sunken chest, all covered in loose skin hanging on a stooped skeleton. His gut, somehow both flaccid and bloated at the same time, hung over skinny white legs.

'Who's there?' Norrie shouted.

Callahan put his mouth to the opening. 'I'm a friend of Bernard Robertson. We served four tours together.'

Norrie turned away. He shouted again as if he had only one volume setting. 'Never heard of him. Fuck off.'

Callahan took a deep breath – was nothing easy anymore? 'I need Muzzle, Norrie.'

Norrie stopped, turned again. 'I've got no idea what you're talking about.' He wobbled for a second, had to brace himself against one wall.

'Bernard gave me a bottle of Cardhu for you. The eighteen-year-old stuff. Said you'd appreciate it.'

Norrie looked up, a feral gleam in his eyes. He approached the door. Callahan heard bolts retract around the frame. The man didn't skimp on home security, which might mean he was still cooking after all.

The door swung inwards, and Callahan gagged on a stale stench of refuse and sweat and rancid food.

Norrie looked him up and down. 'Where's the Cardhu, then?'

Callahan clamped a hand around Norrie's scrawny neck, pushed him inside, and kicked the door shut behind him.

'I lied, genius. Get inside and shut up.'

Norrie shuffled into his living room. Walter had to suppress an urge to hurt the man. He could do it. An animal like Norrie deserved no better. He'd be doing humanity a favour. But he recognised the long slippery slope before him, a fast-track back to someone he'd worked hard to bury, someone he couldn't allow to get out.

Norrie folded himself into a manky armchair. 'What did you say your name was?'

'Callahan.'

Fear glittered in Norrie's rodent eyes. A tremor crept into his voice. 'Walter Callahan? Jake's...' He caught himself. 'Man?'

Callahan stared at him. Norrie cowered even deeper in his chair, his slack, wet lips trembling.

The floor lay thick with rubbish. Trenches in the refuse snaked from his armchair to a kitchen and a bathroom, each room as filthy as the next. In the kitchen, food-crusted dishes covered the worktops and scummy water filled the sink. In the bathroom, a yellow film coated the floor and the toilet. A mass of glass tubes and flasks, burners, and rubber hoses filled the bath.

The evidence confirmed Bernard's claim – Norrie hadn't cooked a batch for some time. Callahan hadn't tasted real panic for twenty years, but it flooded him now. A frantic knot in his guts, a sensation of losing control, of events escaping him. Without meds, he was an IED on legs, ready to go off in the face of any idiot who got in his way, said the wrong thing, or only looked at him too long.

He tried again to remember what he'd done to the poor man he'd run over in his car but got nothing. If he wasn't even feeling the warning signs anymore, he could go AWOL any time.

He sat on the edge of the bath, willed his nerves to stop screaming before he could risk facing Norrie without hurting him. He spotted a plastic zip-lock bag holding three capsules, and his heart quickened. He grabbed it and charged into the living room.

'What's this?'

Norrie's gaze snapped up and his eyes widened. He dropped a roll-up, spilled tobacco into his lap, his bony fingers shaking. His eyes narrowed, greedy and calculating. Would this sorry excuse for a man risk trying to score some cash and send Callahan off with a bag of magic that would ensure no come-back? But the stories about Norrie's bad batch were as well-known as Callahan's reputation. Norrie's eyes dulled again. 'It's nothing. Mixture went wrong. You don't want that.'

Callahan threw them in Norrie's face. Norrie looked up at him, miserable.

'You must have some good stuff left? Give me something or I swear I'll hurt you, Norrie.'

He meant it as a hollow threat but realised he wanted the man to give him an excuse. Norrie whined, pulled his arms and legs in as if they could protect him. Tears glistened in his eyes and he whimpered. The sight fuelled Callahan's rage, threatened to overcome him, let *It* loose. This wasn't a man, it was a whipped animal, no use to anyone. Who would miss him?

No. He was stronger than this.

He pushed the heel of his hand into one temple, rubbed and dug at it, used pain to drag himself away from losing control and making his situation even worse.

Norrie whined even louder. 'Honest, mate. I haven't cooked for years. Not after...' He tailed off, held his arms out to show leathery blotches and scarring where Jake had kettled him.

A sick knot twisted Callahan's guts. He'd worked hard at

forgetting the kind of man Jake used to be. He sat on the sofa, cradled his head in his hands. If the pounding at the back of his head moved to the front, behind his eyes, he'd lose it and resurface only to find Norrie a bloody mess on the floor.

He ran through his routine. Cliff-top, sun on his face. Roll away from the edge. Breathe.

When he opened his eyes, Norrie stared at him with a mixture of relief and, he was surprised to see, sympathy.

'Never gets better, does it?'

Norrie had suffered, too. It explained how he'd formulated Muzzle to be so much more effective than standard meds. Seraxonine took the edge off, but only someone with personal experience could cook it with other junk to numb the rage they'd all brought home with them.

Callahan stood, his fury spent. The thing inside him whispered dark promises. One day, soon, it would slip its leash and let loose all hell. But for now he held it in check, told himself he could contain it.

'Don't give me that shite, Norrie. You got any prescription meds? Anything?'

'I stopped taking them last year. I keep hoping I'll top myself but...' Norrie picked at some crusted stain on his dressing gown. He spoke without looking up. 'How is Bernie?'

Callahan examined the room, the ankle-high garbage and cigarette packets and empty bottles.

'He's happy as a pig in shit, Norrie.'

NINETEEN

'Are you moving in or packing to leave?'

Malkie gazed around the room, at taped-up boxes. 'Leaving. Soon, I hope.'

'Can I stay here until you move out?'

'What? God no. That's not happening.'

Amanda Fielding looked at him as if explaining the simplest of concepts to a child. 'I've got nowhere else to go. I came here because you offered me your help.' She changed in an instant, stepped close, looked up into his face, her eyes frantic. He felt her heat, caught a waft of her perfume, spicy and sweet and excruciating.

His stomach lurched. A frightened and vulnerable woman, alone with him in his home – what was he thinking?

'I'll take you to Livingston police station. For your own safety,' he said as she looked at him in alarm.

'I'm not going to the police.' She sat in his one armchair and folded her arms, as immovable as the most stubborn child.

Malkie pulled a packing box in front of the armchair and sat, arms on knees.

He fixed her with a look, aimed for both stern and sympathetic. She unzipped her leather jacket, revealed a tight white top and a gold chain that hung down and rested between the top curves of her cleavage. Her skin looked soft, her complexion fair and unblemished.

He tore his eyes away. Raised them to hers. 'What exactly do you think I can do for you, Mrs Fielding?'

She glared at him.

'Sorry. Miss?'

'Amanda Bayne. Call me Amanda. Don't ever call me Fielding.'

'OK, Amanda. What else do you think I can do for you?'

She stared at him as if he were talking nonsense again. 'You offered to help me. Protect me.'

And there it was. He'd made her a promise. He detected panic in her voice.

'OK, I'll help you, Mrs... Amanda. But you can't stay here.'

'Why not? I'll sleep on the floor. This is the last place he'll think to look for me.'

'Who?' He needed to hear it from her.

'You know who. Liam. He's an animal. His dad too, but I didn't marry his dad.' She looked down at her hands as if embarrassed. Tears welled on her eyelashes. She wiped them away, harsh and angry.

Any doubts Malkie harboured about her motives evaporated; nobody could fake this. Could they? He ached to reach for her, comfort her, but also feared how much he wanted to. It had been years since he'd looked twice at a woman. Even before the fire, intimacy was a bitter and dangerous thing to him. Long and painful years of teenage friendships he could never get the hang of had mirrored a similar absence of school romances. Though scruffy even at school age, he'd never been bad looking, as far as he knew, but the few girls ever to look at him twice had been too pretty or clever or funny to be seen with Malkie-no-mates. His first, and so far only, real relationship, in his late teens, ended with a Morton-brother blade in his guts. Twice. He'd hoped he might – in time – try again with someone less toxic but he never did find the right woman. Or the right time. Or the right words when they mattered. Now, his burns made any serious relationship impossible. Attractive women like Amanda were now a closed door to him; one look at the mess under his shirt would likely stop any woman in her tracks.

He pushed the thoughts down. Returned to the moment.

'Let me take you to—'

'I told you, I'm not going to a police station.' Her eyes widened, fearful.

'It'll be fine. I'll have DC Lang – you met her yesterday – and my DI talk to you, get you into a shelter.'

Even as he said the words, he doubted she'd accept that either, but his top priority had to be to get her out of here. His behaviour over the past twenty-four hours could bring Steph to his door, and if she found Amanda here, nothing would save him.

Amanda studied his face, chewed on a fingernail as she'd done yesterday morning. 'You get me through today and tonight, I'll think about it tomorrow.'

'OK, deal.' It was enough, for now. He couldn't let her stay alone all afternoon in his rented house, so he'd sort out something today, and worry about tomorrow, tomorrow.

Malkie braced himself for what came next, tried not to get his hopes up.

'So, what do you think you have on Walter Callahan?'

Fear flashed in her eyes again. Malkie held his hands out towards her, a halfway connection, reassurance.

'Don't panic. I'm a police officer, you can trust me.'

Her expression showed how little that meant to her. He shrugged, pulled a rueful smile.

'OK, fair point. But I stuck my neck out giving you my home phone number. If you can't trust me...'

She considered this. Malkie waited. She could have no idea why he cared so much about protecting her, but he wasn't desperate enough just yet to use his own neuroses as leverage.

'Trust you?'

He saw raw desperation in her now. She took a huge risk walking out on the Fieldings. Turning snitch on top of that could be the end of her.

Malkie dug deep – they both had too much to lose. He could end up on McLeish's shit-list, but she could end up dead at the bottom of a reservoir. 'Amanda, I let someone down six months ago. It was... unforgivable.' He paused, swallowed, bit down on bitter and unacceptable self-pity. 'I let someone get hurt. Badly. So now, you, here...'

He stared at the floor, chose his next words not for effect, but for the truth in them. 'I can't mess up again. That's all.'

Then don't. Get it right, this time.

He regretted the words even as they came out. What the hell was he thinking? Unburdening himself to a Person of Interest in an active investigation? Worse, as she struggled to trust him, he found himself drawn to her. He'd hoped she'd refuse his help so he could do the right thing and hand her over to McLeish.

She seemed to come to a decision, but not a happy one. 'I don't know anything specific...'

Malkie's heart sank. If he'd stuck his neck out for nothing...

'But something is going bad between Liam and Jake. Family business. They've been fighting. Vicious. And Liam's treating me even worse than usual.'

'Like leaving doors open for you to walk into?'

A bleakness fell across her eyes again. 'Yes, his temper's been rotten the last few weeks. He's scared of his dad, so he takes it out on me.'

One day, Malkie would nail Liam Fielding to a wall by his balls. 'Could it be because of that nightclub incident? Jake won't have liked finding out his son even went inside a gay nightclub.'

'No, they fought about that, but it passed. I think Liam's building some new business he's keeping from Jake. I've seen a man at the house late at night, after dark. Big guy, overcoat, smart. Looked like a right arrogant bastard. I hated him. I think Jake's not happy his precious son is going it on his own. He's always treated Liam like he couldn't run a raffle.'

'You think Jake's trying to knacker Liam's big new deal, get him back on the leash, but Liam's standing up to him, wants to prove himself? Could the hit-and-run have been Callahan doing Liam or Jake's dirty work and he went too far?'

'Could be. He does a lot of dodgy jobs for them, and he's got a hell of a temper when he's pushed.'

'Aye, I hear he's lethal with a ballpoint pen.'

'What?'

'Nothing. Forget it. This man you saw – did you hear what they talked about? Did he come by car? Did you get the registration?'

'No, they met in the trees behind the house, so I'm guessing he parked on the Kirknewton Road.'

'Are you sure he was a big guy? No chance he was closer to five foot eight, slim, fair-haired?' Wilkie's ruined face flashed across Malkie's mind – blood and dirt and matted blond hair.

She stared at him; it was no random question. 'No, he was over six foot, I'm sure. Big, stocky man, and I'm sure he had dark hair.'

She slid down in the armchair, closed her eyes, sighed.

Malkie's mouth turned dry – was this all she had? At least even this minimal information reinforced his own guesswork. Liam Fielding was into something so big it was causing a family split. No wonder Acting DCI McLeish had warned Malkie off – it had to be connected to his secret case. And he wanted Malkie nowhere near it because – no getting away from it – he hadn't covered himself in glory in recent years. After the incident in The Libertine, the slightest sniff of Malkie anywhere near the Fieldings should already have had their rabid solicitor Simon Fraser complaining to the Procurator Fiscal. No wonder McLeish wanted Wilkie's hit-and-run wrapped up and Malkie shunted off to muggings and the local amphetamine mob, as far as possible from whatever juicy side project he was keeping to himself.

All of this also meant he couldn't take Amanda to the station. If even half of this were true, once she got into the system Malkie's investigations would flag on McLeish's radar and Malkie would get moved on, away from the Fieldings, away from Amanda, and he wasn't ready to let her down, couldn't believe she was complicit in her husband's crime.

She couldn't stay here, and he couldn't hide her at the cabin; the roof was more holes than tiles and the electricity and water weren't yet reconnected.

That left only one other option. He stood, clapped his hands together.

'I know a place you can stay. It's a bit cramped, but no one knows the address except me. You're not claustrophobic, are you?'

TWENTY

The last person Callahan wanted to rely on right now was Jake, but needs must...

'Aye, I've got some, Walter.'

Callahan released his breath, allowed the tension to melt out of him. Enough to let him think straight again.

'Can you bring it to me?'

'No chance, mate. You're all over the TV. Come for it yourself, after dark.'

Jake never stuck his neck out for anyone, happy to help a pal as long as it carried no risk to him. Nothing had changed since Bastion.

'Tonight? If Liam's home, warn me. I know there's trouble between you two, something you don't want to let me in on. What's the boy got himself into now, Jake?'

No answer. What could have Big Bad Jake lost for words?

'Jake, you there?'

'Liam's been away all day. Amanda's run off. Took the Ducati. Bitch has got him all fucked up again. He's raging.'

'What the hell has she run off for? Like we don't have enough of a mess to clean up?'

'We, Walter?'

Callahan's blood ran cold. Jake's friendship had always been negotiable, but two words changed even that.

'So, what does that mean? I'm on my own?'

'No. I wouldn't do that to you.'

I wish I could believe that, Jake.

'I'm too old for all this, Walter. I get caught helping you, they'll nail me for aiding and abetting. I can't risk that. Liam needs me.'

Callahan recognised shite when he heard it. He'd rather Jake showed him the respect of a simple 'Sorry, not up for it.'

Time to part ways. He'd lied to himself too long. Should he hand himself in to those two coppers? With the right brief, he might get away with temporary insanity. Brave and patriotic warrior returned from the wars and abandoned by the very country he fought to defend. Could a few years in a secure unit be any worse than eleven years of self-seclusion at the mercy of Jake's charity?

No, not yet – he wasn't ready. His mind still reeled, and he could find no clarity, no balance. He needed to move forward on his own terms. If they found him before he got stable again, he'd lash out and hurt more people, give them more justification to put him away again.

'Walter? You there?'

He snapped back to the present. 'I'm here. Can you leave it behind the cottage? I don't want to come to the house.'

'Then I don't see you until this is all sorted?'

'Fine. I'll not bother you again.' He hoped this last barb would stick, but he knew how thick-skinned Jake could be.

'I've got one box left. I'll leave it on the kitchen window-ledge.'

Callahan heard nothing for long seconds. If Jake was waiting for gratitude...

'Walter, what did you do?'

Callahan's head span. Damning fragments of memories, of glass and blood, battled with two certainties – he never blacked out before an incident, and he always remembered afterwards. Always.

'I don't know. You saw the state of my car. But I don't remember driving anywhere. My head's all messed up.'

'Fuck's sake, Walter. Again? You need to turn yourself in. You need treatment, mate.'

Something in Jake's tone snagged on Callahan's frantic thoughts, but the line went dead before he could pin it down.

TWENTY-ONE

Amanda looked appalled. 'You're kidding, right?'

Malkie studied the boat. Thirty feet of chipped and curling teak, salt-crusted aluminium, and stained fibreglass. Six months of rain and seawater had left her in a shocking state.

'What's wrong with her? She's cramped, but she's safe.'

Amanda stared down into the water, caught her glasses as they slipped down her nose. 'How deep is this? What if it sinks while I'm asleep?'

'Amanda, she was in perfect condition when my dad bought her nine months ago. She's fine.' The truth was that the boat's annual lift-out and hull-check was overdue, but he needed her inside before someone saw them. 'She's registered in Dad's name. No one will find you here.'

She looked unconvinced. Then she smiled. 'The *Droopy Goose*?'

Malkie laughed, fond memories adding to his relief. Her smile was a good sign. 'Mum and Dad wanted to take me cruising the Scottish coastline, some day.'

As usual, the mere mention of his parents dragged his mood

down – one he'd allowed to die, the other he'd saved, then neglected for six months.

'I heard what happened. From Liam. Sorry, Mr McCulloch.' She touched his arm.

He tensed to pull back, afraid of his own shabby feelings, but he needed to encourage whatever delicate trust might be building. He patted her hand, returned her smile. 'Thanks. Call me Malkie, aye?'

He invited her to board the *Droopy Goose*. As she took his hand to step up onto the deck he caught another waft of her perfume. And underneath that, her hair, her skin. Her.

He closed his eyes as her scent filled him and spread a tight, hot, shameful ache he hadn't felt for years.

Grow up. Act like the professional you're supposed to be.

He stepped up behind her, rummaged in his jacket pocket, pulled out the key with the amusing plastic anchor his dad had attached to it, and unlocked the hatch. He pulled out the wooden partition, slid the hatch open, and climbed down into the cramped cabin. He was relieved to find it clean and tidy from the last time he'd hidden here, the last time Steph decided he needed a talking-to. He found an envelope on the floor and stuffed it in his pocket.

Amanda appeared at the hatch, peered down, frowned. She straightened and looked towards the marina gates as if debating her options, but then climbed down the ladder backwards. Malkie looked everywhere except at her until she stood at the bottom step and turned towards him.

They stood for a moment, awkward. Malkie broke the silence first. 'There's a small cabin at the front, you can have that. I'll be OK in here. Unless you'd like me to leave you on your own, for some privacy?'

Her alarmed look told him how much she dreaded that prospect. He held his hands out, to reassure her. 'OK, don't worry. You take the front cabin and I'll sit here through tonight at least, OK?'

'*Forward*,' she said.

'Aye. Forward.'

She smiled. 'I did some sailing on holiday last year. Liam spent two weeks clubbing all night and sleeping by the pool all day. I went sailing. He forced me to go on his rotten holiday, then ignored me for two weeks. But then, sometimes being ignored isn't so bad. Better than...'

Her smile disappeared.

Malkie touched her arm, hoped she'd find the gentle gesture reassuring. 'Go *forward*, see if it's OK.'

She went through to the cabin. He emptied the bag of shopping he'd bought on the way: toiletries, clothes, groceries, enough for a day, two at the most, until he decided what to do with her. She'd left the Ducati in the garage behind the rented house, and they'd driven to Port Edgar in his car. She'd fallen asleep on his rolled-up jacket, propped against the window. He'd taken his time, happy that she trusted him enough to sleep until they stopped at the supermarket outside South Queensferry. She bought white wine and soda, and a bag of ice, said she needed to unwind.

He filled the kettle with bottled water and switched it on. Nothing happened. He tried the light switch. Nothing. With an unpleasant feeling of inevitability, he pulled the envelope from his pocket and opened it. The harbour manager had disconnected his electricity. Non-payment of berthing fees. Six months. Since the accident.

'And the shite just keeps coming.'

'What?'

Amanda returned from the forward cabin. She'd changed into leggings and a T-shirt he'd bought her from the supermarket. He'd had so little experience with women's bodies – and

127

even then, only dead ones – that he'd misjudged her size. The thin cotton swamped her.

He waved the letter he'd found on the floor. 'I'll need to pop up to the marina office later.'

She slid in behind the small table. He sat beside her but left a clear space between them.

'You're safe here. This time of the year the weather's shite so there's only a few lunatics down here at the weekends. Nobody but me knows about this boat, not even DC Lang.'

She looked unhappy but said nothing, so he continued. 'I need to go to work—'

She opened her mouth to complain, but he held a hand up.

'I have to. I need to find Callahan, sort out those Fielding bastards. We both know you crossed a line today, Amanda. They won't let that go.'

She stared at him, sullen, but didn't argue.

'Plus, it'll look dodgy if I call in sick on my second day back on the job. I'll get the electricity switched on. There's a TV in that cupboard, crap reception but there's some DVDs. Stay on the boat, don't even walk to South Queensferry, OK?'

She nodded but couldn't have looked less happy.

'I'll be as quick as I can. Don't make any phone calls, either.'

He climbed the stairs, replaced the wooden partition. As he pulled the roof-hatch closed, she said, 'Thanks, Malkie,' in a quiet and miserable voice. She looked small and lost. He wanted nothing more than to climb inside again, shut the world out and spend the day hiding with her. But he also considered that she might need some space, and time to think things through.

With an effort, he headed for the marina offices, braced himself for a difficult conversation with the harbour master.

Twenty minutes later he'd settled the berthing fees and paid six months in advance. While rummaging for his dad's credit card he found the ridiculous plastic anchor. He'd meant to leave the keys with Amanda. As tempting as it was to return to her, Steph would expect him at the station. He hooked it onto his own keys.

Halfway to his car, his mobile rang. Steph.

'Malkie. Where are you?'

'Love you too, Steph. I'm on my way in. Be there in forty minutes.'

'Forty minutes? You live twenty minutes away. Where the hell are you?'

Malkie thought fast, needed something convincing, anything to stop her getting nosy.

'Malkie? Tell me you're not out at Kirknewton again.' She sounded menacing now.

He wanted to tell her to mind her own business, but he didn't enjoy a wealth of professional support. He went for a bare-faced lie instead.

'I'm at the hospital, with my dad.' He felt a soul-sucking certainty that his words would haunt him later. He held his breath, waited for her reaction.

'OK, sorry, Malkie.'

She sounded embarrassed, which was a first. Shame flooded him.

'I don't want you screwing up again. McLeish is asking me about you, and—'

'I bloody knew it. He's got you watching me, hasn't he?'

'Will you shut your trap for a minute?'

He waited, breathing hard, pacing the marina car park until she continued.

'I said I wouldn't tell him everything. I never said he wasn't asking. So, wind your neck in and remember who you're talking to.'

'OK, sorry. I'm tense. Tired.'

'It's OK. You're overweight, under-achieving, and generally a disgrace, but I keep the faith you're saveable.' Her unique way of telling him she was on his side. 'You need to get back here to the station. Someone identified Callahan, and William Loudon's found something juicy on the memory card.'

'He's cracked it? That quick? Clever old William.'

'No, he said he might never crack the security, but it's not what's *in* it, it's what's *on* it that's interesting.' He could swear Steph was grinning now. 'Don't go off on one, OK? We still like Callahan for this, right?'

'Spit it out, Steph, or—'

'Liam Fielding's prints are all over it.'

'Well, smack me in the face with a wet fish.'

'Quite,' she said, and hung up.

TWENTY-TWO

Malkie met Louisa Gooch, youngest DC in the team and his favourite unofficial protégée, leaving the CID room. 'Ah, Gucci, got a wee job for you.'

A delighted grin lit up her face – he hadn't yet managed to upset her like he had so many other colleagues.

'Hello, boss. Good to have you back.' She leaned closer and grinned. 'Well done. At morning briefing, I mean. This wee job, is it urgent? I'm on my way out for lunch.'

'This afternoon is fine. I need you to check the internal directories, see if you can find someone called D F Browne? With an "E". Might not be one of us, but somebody connected to law enforcement somehow. Thanks, Lou.'

'For you, I'll start ignoring it, immediately.'

'Funny woman.' He scowled at her but couldn't keep a smile from his eyes. She grinned and pushed through the doors to the stairwell. Malkie chuckled to himself. *I'll be calling you ma'am in five years' time, Lou.*

Inside, Steph sat at her PC, but looked far from bored now. One elbow on the desk, chin propped on her fingers, eyes fixed on the screen, she was enjoying this one. He laid a hand on her shoulder, and she jumped.

'Touché.' He grinned at her.

'What?'

'Nothing. Forget it. What's happening?'

'It's been an eventful morning, actually.' She glanced at her watch and then at him.

Malkie sat at his desk. She rolled her chair to see between their monitors and pulled out her notebook, despite having the case notes on her screen.

'OK. Mr Robin Wilkie. Hit-and-run victim.'

'Right. Wilkie. Hit-and-run. With you so far.'

She glared at him. But she saw his look and shrugged to concede the point.

'He's stable but in an induced coma. Doctors say he might survive, but he'll never walk again.'

Malkie recalled the mess on the road at Murieston, and how he'd frozen, incapable of providing Robin Wilkie the smallest of comforts. Ashamed of his failure to even touch the man's desperate, fumbling fingers, he renewed his vow to Wilkie and to himself. And to let Steph arrest Fielding when the time came.

She continued. 'Neither the ambulance crew nor the doctors found a wedding ring on him. He's in high dependency at St John's.'

Same hospital Dad's in. For six months.

'Malkie. Pay attention. Callahan's picture went up on the website yesterday and we got a call from a whisky shop on North Bridge in Edinburgh. He bought a bottle of something expensive. Techies are trying to track him on city centre CCTV, but he kept his face down so it'll take some time.'

Malkie drummed his fingers on the desk. He wanted the good stuff, but she was making him wait, testing him for any fixation on Fielding. She glanced at his fidgeting hand, and he knew he'd blown it.

'Initial tests confirm Wilkie's blood type matches that on Callahan's car. And Callahan's prints are all over the inside of the car – he's on file for three previous assaults. And get this – the second one got him stuck in a secure psych ward for seven months. I requested his service record but there are whole pages redacted, for operational reasons, I was told. Loads of Liam Fielding's prints too, he's on file for The Libertine incident. Some of Jake's too. And a few partials from someone else.'

She paused. Malkie had to nod at her to continue.

'They're too smudged to be admissible, barely two edge patterns, but when I pushed them, the techies admitted – off the record – that the fragment matches the same area of Amanda Fielding's. She's on file for assaults on several female acquaintances of her darling husband.'

She looked to Malkie for a reaction.

He returned her stare. 'Noted. Carry on.'

She held his gaze for long, uncomfortable seconds before continuing.

'The prints on the steering wheel and door handles are smudged. SOCOs think Callahan was wearing gloves, wrong kind of smudging to suggest he wiped everything down.'

'You mean the driver was wearing gloves.'

She frowned. 'And your point is?'

'You said "Callahan". The car sitting outside his house doesn't prove he did it. That's confirmation bias right there, partner.'

Steph took a long, slow drink from her water bottle.

'We've searched every box, file, shelf, and drawer in both Callahan's and Wilkie's places. Nothing of note.'

She looked at him, invited his comments.

Malkie glared at her. 'Pushing your luck, Detective *Constable* Lang.'

She smirked but continued. 'William says he can't get into the memory card. Without the encryption key he says no computer we can afford has any chance of cracking it. Then he went off on one about MI5 and the NSA and I kind of switched off. But Fielding junior's dabs are unambiguous. Thumb and forefinger.'

Malkie sighed. Frustrating not to get the contents yet, but those prints were a bonus. 'OK, let's put together what we know.'

Steph turned a new page in her notebook. Their wee hit-and-run didn't warrant a whiteboard. He only noticed now that McLeish had commandeered the biggest whiteboard in the CID room, moved it into DCI Spalding's office with its blank side facing out. Malkie soaked in the familiar surroundings, the comfort of routine. The jagged anxiety that had grown like an ulcer in his guts over the past six months eased off, now he had a job to focus on.

'Some as-yet unidentified suspect tried to kill Robin Wilkie with a motor vehicle.'

Steph sighed but joined in. 'Callahan's prints are full and clear on everything but the steering wheel, so they corroborate other apparent indications of his involvement but, granted, Liam and Jake and another, possibly Amanda Fielding, need to be considered too. Happy now? But no arguing that car was found outside Callahan's cottage.'

'Aye, but remember the look on his face? If it was Callahan, I'm positive he doesn't remember doing it.'

'OK, fair point, he did seem confused, and his Seraxo-nine indicates PTSD, and he's served in the Falklands, Northern Ireland, Bosnia, Iraq twice, Sierra Leone, Afghanistan – the man's a full-on war junkie. His doctor said he's been on those meds since returning to the UK, ten years ago. He also said he needs his meds or – quote – all hell could break loose.'

Malkie picked at his trousers. Another thought nagged at him. 'There's another possibility.'

She waited.

'Do we know for certain that Fielding and Callahan returned the same cars they booked out?'

She surprised him. 'Fair point.'

He waited for the other shoe to fall.

'But McLeish thinks his behaviour and his mental issues make him the strongest suspect by a long way. He's SIO and acting DCI – I know, I know – and he'll not approve resources to pursue multiple leads. We're to concentrate on Callahan.'

Malkie recalled Amanda's report of trouble between Fielding and his dad, and the secret meetings behind the house. That might persuade Steph of Fielding's involvement, if only he could admit he'd spoken to Amanda.

What the hell are you doing? You're playing with fire, and you know it.

'Fine, but I want it recorded that I mooted it.'

'Mooted?'

'Aye, mooted. Did you check the date on his pills?'

'His last prescription was issued on 10 October, 120 tablets, two months' supply at two a day. There were seventy-eight left in the packet.'

'So, he's been off his meds for, what, four weeks? Did his doctor OK that?'

'Three weeks. And no, he simply didn't show up one day. They called him and he said he was doing OK, that he'd be in touch if he felt the need. They'll call us if he contacts them.'

'Get Legal to pressure the army for those redacted pages, aye? Can you take a drive to that whisky shop, see what the owner remembers about Callahan's alleged visit yesterday?'

'Nope. I'm interviewing three ex-services doctors in Edinburgh. See if I can find out if he was treated anywhere.'

Malkie dreaded the thought of driving into city traffic, but he swore at himself. Could this be a chance for him to beat at least one lingering neurosis from that night?

'Fine. I'll do the whisky shop.'

Steph studied him for a second, then nodded and turned back to her monitor. As she pecked two-fingered at her keyboard, his phone trilled, a text alert. He unlocked the screen, saw an unrecognised number, but braced himself for trouble when he read the text.

> Someone's outside.

He swore under his breath. Steph looked up. 'What is it?'

Malkie failed to think of anything convincing. 'Nothing. Personal. I need to take this.'

In the stairwell he dialled the number on his personal mobile, braced himself for an unpleasant conversation. It had to be Amanda, bringing new meaning to 'Don't call me at the office.'

She answered after one ring and sounded frantic. 'Malkie, there's someone walking up and down the pontoons. He was looking in the windows. I had to hide in the head.'

'The what?'

'The toilet.'

He took a breath. 'Older guy, bad dye-job, blue water-proofs? White badge on a cord round his neck? Walkie-talkie?'

'Yes?' She sounded sheepish.

'That's Derek, the harbour master. He tours the marina twice a day. I haven't been there for seven months, and he's a nosy bastard.'

She was quiet for a moment, then, 'Sorry.'

She sounded so miserable that his irritation drained out of him.

'Amanda, you need to get a grip. You texted my work mobile. Your number's now logged against mine. I can explain that – we give out contact cards all the time – but if you turn into a MisPer ' – *or end up dead* – 'we'll trace your calls, and that'll lead to a network mast in South Queensferry, maybe even narrow it down to the marina.'

'What's a misper?'

'A missing person. Liam will be looking for you, but he'll keep quiet about it. But is there anyone else who might report you missing? Friends, relatives, anyone?'

She took a few seconds to respond. 'No.'

Malkie had never heard one small word carry so much pain. He considered concocting an excuse to disappear for the day, drive straight to the marina. Be there for her, whatever that might mean.

'You need to stay off the phone. Stay inside the boat, keep the curtains drawn. I can't worry about you at the same time I'm working this case. I need to concentrate, or I'll let something slip, drop us both in it. You understand?'

'I understand. But you need to understand something, too. Imagine living in constant fear of another punch, or the next kick, or another cigarette burn. Imagine having no one you can turn to. Imagine a life locked up with a man who's told you he'll kill you if you ever cross him. A man who's good at finding other people.'

Malkie could find no words. Shame filled him. Every slap of water on the *Droopy Goose*'s hull could be a footstep on the deck. Every car motor at the marina gates could be one of the McGuire brothers. Inside that boat she was blind and cornered, and every random noise could be her pig of a husband coming to get her.

'OK, I get the point. But what can I do? If you know a safer place for you, please go, and don't tell me where. Text me when you're safe. Or let me bring you in, get you into protection. I need you, to work this case.' *And what else, you idiot?* 'But I need to know you're safe, too.'

She paused for a long time. He wondered if she'd disconnected.

'Amanda?'

'I've got nowhere else to go. My parents live up north, but I'm not welcome there. You better not be late. I'm scared enough here in daylight. You leave me here on my own after dark, I'll freak, Malkie. I know I will.'

'Amanda, breathe. I'll be there before dark, I promise. You fancy a takeaway? What do you like? Chinese, Indian?' He didn't care what she wanted, but he needed to anchor her frantic mind on something safe and mundane.

'I'm not hungry. Feel sick. Bring what you like.' She hung up.

The best he could do for her now was his job. He barged back into the CID room, grabbed his jacket from his chair, tried to flee before Steph could start on him again.

'Malkie. Sit.'

Damn it. He sat.

'Talk to me.'

He sighed, looked toward the stairwell and escape, but he knew he'd have to give her more, sometime. She cared too much to go easy on him. He checked no one else sat within earshot, leaned forward, elbows on knees, took a breath, and began talking before he could change his mind again.

'The fire started in her bedroom—'

'You told me that, already.'

He glared at her. The woman was bloody merciless.

At the thought of revealing more, he choked on bile, burning and bitter. Second time she'd offered him a hearing, a confessional he could trust to be non-judgemental, but he couldn't get his words past a rotten taste of complicity, like ashes clogging his throat.

He stood.

'Look, Steph. I need some air, bit stuffy in here, you know? Let's talk later.'

She looked up at him, and he had to persuade himself he saw compassion in her eyes, not pity.

'Aye. Later.'

He fled. The challenge of a drive into the noise and smells and crowds of Edinburgh might be distraction enough to stop him overthinking for a few hours.

He felt a bastard of a headache building, right behind his eyes.

TWENTY-THREE

At two o'clock Woodburn took his usual lunchtime stroll for pastries and coffee to get him through a long, strenuous afternoon behind his desk. Callahan looked through the office window, saw no idle drivers.

A silver Astra with a faulty meter sat beside the garage roller-doors. He switched the plates with another knackered old Astra, then headed for the office to get the keys. Luckily Liam liked all his cars to look the same.

The door wasn't locked. Woodburn always was an idiot. Callahan eased it open. The squeak of the hinges sounded deafening in the silence. As he searched the wall hooks for the key to the Astra, an arm clamped around his neck and pain exploded in his lower back. A voice hissed in his ear.

'Your turn, you fuckin' psycho.'

Callahan clutched at the man's arm, but another burst of agony slammed into him. He threw his head back, felt his skull connect with a crunch.

Fat Frankie, the man he'd deafened in one ear, staggered back, clutching the mess where his nose should be. In one hand he clutched three pens, now dripping with blood.

Rage exploded in Callahan. He launched himself at Frankie, who went down hard. His head slammed against the steel floor. One solid punch and Frankie went slack.

Callahan took the pens from Frankie's hand and placed the nibs on his closed right eyelid. Then pushed down into the thin skin, pressed on the eyeball underneath. Before he could slam the heel of his other hand down, the desk phone rang.

The harsh squeal broke through the black fog in his head, enough to penetrate his fury. He pressed two fingers to Frankie's neck, found a steady pulse, confirmed his airway was clear and rolled him onto his side. Whatever he'd done last night, whatever charges he was already facing, murdering Frankie could only sink him deeper. He waited for the phone to go silent, then dialled 999 and said only 'Ambulance'. He laid the handset on the desk and grabbed a first-aid box and a roll of electrical tape from a shelf – his wound would likely take a beating in the coming days.

He found the keys to the Astra and drove out of the industrial estate, his back in agony and his mind rattled. Someone like Fat Frankie getting the drop on him should never happen.

As he drove, his back burned, and hot blood ran into his waistband.

He pulled off the A70 onto a farm road to check the injury. Frankie's fat fists had left only enough of the pens exposed to allow shallow penetration, but infection could yet kill him. Twisting to reach the wound sent shards of agony slicing through him but he managed to drench the bloody holes with bottled water and slather on antiseptic cream with a sell-by date over a year past. He pressed dressings on and bound his waist with the tape. It would hurt like hell coming off, but he needed it secure so he could operate unhindered.

He reclined the seat and closed his eyes. Three hours until dark, and his last safe chance at getting more meds.

If that failed, he would have to risk trusting Jake.

TWENTY-FOUR

The drive into Edinburgh went more smoothly than Malkie had feared. He took comfort from the fact that he'd navigated busy city traffic and hadn't lost his nerve.

The whisky shop owner, Mr Armitage, was a short, round man who wiped his nose every few seconds, and explained how Callahan's manner had sent him scurrying to the Police Scotland website.

Armitage confirmed Callahan's mug shot and added some comments regarding how shifty he looked. He'd bought an expensive single malt and left nearly five pounds change in his haste to leave. Malkie bagged the banknotes that Armitage had set aside, untouched. Armitage also claimed Callahan never looked up, and that the security camera caught only the top of a baseball cap and what looked like an army kitbag. Malkie viewed the tape but saw nothing usable.

Unless the techies found something on city centre cameras, Malkie was no closer to finding him, and he had a feeling Callahan would be good at not being found.

He walked to North Bridge, stared west across the glass roof of Waverley Train Station to the gardens beyond, savoured a momentary lull in the noise of the traffic. To the north lay Princes Street, lined with shops huddled under modernised storefronts and a few surviving Victorian New Town facades, sprinkled with distant shoppers, wrapped in thick coats despite the November sun. Old Town tenements crowded the steep slopes to the south of the frosted grass and trees of the gardens. The castle watched over it all, perched high on Castle Rock, magnificent and solid and dependable. Life buzzed around Malkie – traffic, laughter, voices in multiple languages. He envied their ignorance of the ugliness he had to face too often, the atrocities even the best of people could commit when pushed hard enough. If he could rewind his life, take a different path, do something less damaging, would he? But then, wasn't his job a privilege, an opportunity to change what he could, do some good? Wasn't that what he signed up for?

Don't kid yourself – you were running away from your own mess, even at that age. What were you thinking? The Livi Bad Boys, the Morton family, and Sandra, their precious and vicious wee girl, of all people.

He shut down that memory, loathed hearing her name even in the privacy of his own mind. He closed his eyes and let the sounds of the city wash over him, tried to recall better times when the noise and bustle and traffic fumes didn't choke him with creeping and suffocating dread.

A passing engine dropped gear and roared, and a two-tone horn blasted at him from out of nowhere. Images slammed into him, memories he couldn't fight off. Blue strobe lights, flames and smoke, a fire crew and paramedics, his dad thrashing and screaming and sobbing.

He staggered back against the painted concrete parapet of the bridge. His nerves screamed. His breath heaved, ragged and desperate. Clammy sweat beaded his forehead. His head swam. He saw it all again, as clear and brutal as the night it happened. Wet, muddy grass. Blue strobes. The acrid stink of wood smoke.

He threw up. Two women had stopped to ask if he was OK, but they jumped away now. He stood, waited for the world to stop pitching and spinning.

'I'm sorry. I'm so, so, sorry.'

One of the women said, 'No problem, pal,' as she stared in dismay at her shoes. They left him, oblivious to the fact that his apology wasn't meant for them.

He forced his feet to move, back to his car, sidestepping tourists, their attention everywhere but in front of themselves. He couldn't begrudge them their distractions. He loved to look for the good in people, but that brought to his mind the kind and gentle person he'd avoided for six months. In this instant, as he floundered, adrift and drowning in his own inadequacy, he needed his dad. If he could summon the courage to face the old man, might they, together, work through the inevitable discomfort and recriminations to begin the process of healing each other?

If anyone could help him find a way to see past this...

He drove back towards Livingston, towards St John's. He needed the rock his dad had always been more than he feared facing him.

He wanted to check on Wilkie too, ideally to ask about Fielding's prints on the memory card, but he doubted he'd have regained consciousness yet. Was Wilkie bad news himself, involved in Fielding business? Did Jake send Callahan to scare Wilkie, scupper his own son's deal, retrieve the SD card, and it all went to shit? He still believed Callahan remembered nothing yesterday morning, his reactions too convincing to be faked. And although blackouts were a common symptom of PTSD, could someone erase several hours of conscious activity like driving?

His headache flared again. He opened a window, hoped to flush the pain away with fresh air, but thoughts of Amanda, alone at Port Edgar, whispered to him and wouldn't let his mind settle.

At the hospital he headed for Wilkie first – he didn't expect to spend long watching a man in a coma. Wilkie lay in a single room in the High Dependency Unit. His legs, cased in plaster, hung from wires, and a breathing tube protruded from his mouth. Bandages covered his head but left his face exposed, swollen and purple but now clean and free of gore. Rage surged in Malkie, rage and renewed determination. Could resolving one injustice atone for another? He could hope. A window filled one side of Wilkie's room, and the nurse's station sat outside that. He cursed McLeish for the absence of a uniform presence. A young nurse sat behind the desk, working through a pile of forms. He looked up.

'Can I help you?' His badge read Colin.

Malkie flashed his warrant card, then pointed into the room. 'Robin Wilkie. How is he?'

Colin stood, and they both stepped up to the window.

'Not great. He's stable but could go either way. He's in an induced coma, not breathing for himself, but his brain function looks OK.'

'Will he wake up?'

'Like I said, could go either way.'

Malkie wondered if Wilkie felt anything. Was he aware of his agony but unable to move, unable to communicate? What did an induced coma do to a person? He considered entering the room, but what could he say to the man, even if he thought Wilkie might hear him?

'You have instructions not to admit anyone who can't show you police ID, aye?'

Colin nodded, but his eyes stayed on Wilkie.

'And any visitors, you notify us right away?'

'Aye, we know the routine.'

Malkie's anger flared. 'Routine? Mate, someone drove a car

at this man, tried to kill him. There's no routine here, pal. You'll watch this guy twenty-four seven like he's one of your own, got it?'

Colin nodded. 'Sorry. Just a figure of speech.'

Malkie looked at the earnest apology on Colin's face and hated himself.

'You're all right, son. But keep a close eye on him, please. Someone wanted this guy dead.'

Colin turned to him, his hands held out as if to fend off a threat he'd only now recognised. 'You mean someone might come here for him? To finish the job?'

'Hang on, calm yourself. It's not like in the movies. The guy I think did this, he isn't going to risk coming here with all these cameras everywhere. You must have an alarm button. Hit that the second you feel threatened. Security will come running and they'll call us, OK?'

Colin chewed his lower lip, stared at Wilkie through the window. He had more to say.

'Sit down, son.'

Colin sat at his desk. He opened his mouth then closed it and opened it again.

'There was a man here last night. Late, after eleven. I went to the loo – I was away less than a minute, I promise.'

Malkie closed his mouth and Colin relaxed again.

'I found the guy standing at the window. His cheeks were wet, and he didn't even hear me walk up behind him.'

Malkie perked up. A mystery visitor might shed some light on how Wilkie got himself on the wrong side of the Fieldings.

'Did you get his name?'

'No. Said he was a friend. But I think he was more than a friend, if you get me.'

Malkie did. Although Mr Wilkie's personal life remained a closed book for now, his photo collection suggested one possibility: the mystery visitor had to be Wilkie's partner and would be in one of those pictures.

'What did this guy look like?'

'Early forties, medium height, fit. I didn't get a good look at his face – he was standing up against the glass and he walked away when I asked for his name. He had a hoodie on, pulled down over his forehead. I think he and Mr Wilkie aren't out, you know?'

Or he knows Liam, too, and he's scared shitless.

"Are you on shift again tomorrow evening?"

Colin nodded, but didn't look happy about it.

"Good. I doubt the guy will come back during daytime, too many people around." Malkie pulled out one of his CID contact cards, laid it on the desk. 'If he shows up again, you call me, OK?'

Colin nodded and shoved the card in his trouser pocket.

Malkie left before he freaked the lad out anymore.

He found his dad two floors up, in a room with three other patients. The old man sat at a window, dozing in a wheelchair, early afternoon sun on his face, a newspaper and pen on his knee.

Malkie watched the man whose life he'd destroyed, the man whose phone calls professed non-negotiable love, despite it all. He'd lost weight. The consequences of Malkie's failure had exacted a heavy toll, must have hurt him beyond measure. Malkie wanted to leave, try again at the weekend. But would the time ever be right?

He pushed open the door, his heart in his throat. His dad's eyes remained closed, squeezed tight against the sun blazing hot through the window. Malkie realised only now how much he'd missed the old sod. He savoured these quiet moments before daring to move forward.

'Tommy, you old bugger. You've got a visitor.' The man in the bed opposite – stocky, tattoos on both arms, more gaps than teeth in his mouth, and a grin you couldn't wipe off with an orbital sander.

His dad turned, saw Malkie. A trembling smile touched his lips and tears spilled from his eyes.

'Malcolm,' he managed, then broke down and sobbed. Malkie knelt before the wheelchair, wanted to take the frail old man's hands, but feared he didn't yet deserve to offer even that small comfort. He pushed one hand forward a little, and cold, trembling fingers clamped around his. Malkie pulled up another chair and took both of his dad's hands in his own. They felt thin and knotty, but as strong as he remembered.

Neither spoke for a while. Malkie's dad wiped his eyes on his pyjama sleeve, blew his nose on his handkerchief. When he'd restored his composure, he smiled.

Malkie could find no words except, 'I'm sorry, Dad.'

'No, Malcolm.'

Malkie stared at him, confused.

'We're not doing this. I've done a lot of thinking, lying here.'

Six months. I know.

'Maybe one day, but not now. Do you remember your Aunt Rebecca? Auntie Becky?'

'Bit random, Dad?'

'Your mother hated her. Some stupid argument they had years ago, went too far, feelings got hurt, words were said that they couldn't take back. Remember?'

'Aye, I remember how awkward family events were. We couldn't wait for Becky to leave. Which never took long. And her side of the family pretty much never showed their faces south of Dundee until Mum's funeral. Bloody vultures.'

Dad smiled, ever tolerant of Malkie's negativity.

'Remember your mother fell down those stairs, banged her head and the doctors said we might lose her? I called Rebecca. Took me two hours to make that call. I was terrified your mother would hate me, but I hoped they'd see sense before it was too late.'

Memories tugged his lips into a wry smile. 'Mum said she wasn't dead yet, then told Becky she wasn't getting a penny when her time did come.'

Malkie's dad grinned. 'They didn't say a word to each other for a year after that. But you know what your mother told me? She said I didn't have the right not to warn Rebecca, had to give her the choice, wasn't my decision to make. What was it she used to say? *"We do what we have to"*?'

'She said *"We do what we can"*, Dad.'

His dad stared at him, a smile on his lips and affection shining from his eyes.

Would these be the only words they'd ever say about that night? He'd never wash the stain from his conscience, but could he learn to live with it, in time?

His phone rang, Steph's name on the display. Dad's eyes clouded over, so he rejected the call and switched it to silent.

He stood. His father looked distraught.

'Come on. Let's have a coffee and a bun and a seat in the sun.'

Three nurses watched them leave. Their scowls stated loud and clear that his visit was long overdue, but Malkie ignored them.

They were all each other had now, Aunt Becky's rotten lot aside. He chose to believe better times waited for his dad.

Maybe even for himself.

TWENTY-FIVE

Callahan found a pharmacy in a scruffy Bathgate housing scheme, the kind of neighbourhood where people were nosy but also minded their own business. A short lane led behind a parade of shops, the pharmacy near one end. He parked nearby and waited. Three lads sat on a wall stuffing chips and cheap cider down their throats and menacing passing pedestrians. They strutted like hard men, legs wide, baseball caps low over their faces, big men in skinny jeans hanging off their backsides, and hoodies.

Callahan's headache eased a little, but he needed the mouth-breathers to wander away so he could get in there and get himself well again.

In the pharmacy at Kirknewton, he knew exactly which drawer held his meds. But there was no guarantee he'd find them here. The pills he'd taken since leaving the cottage had settled his nerves but the possibility of leaving here empty-handed ate at him. And the longer he had to wait, the worse it got.

He leaned back on the headrest, closed his eyes, considered

running through his cliff-top routine, but decided he'd had a bellyful of that bollocks.

He looked across again. One boy finished his chips and let the greasy newspaper fall at his feet. Rage boiled inside Callahan, the boy's casual ignorance worse than if he'd screwed it up and chucked it over a garden fence. A tour in Basra would teach wee shites like them a lesson they'd not forget.

He could hurt them. Wastes of oxygen, like Norrie Wallace – who would miss them?

His fingers gripped the door handle without him knowing, his other hand resting on the scabbard of his knife on the passenger seat, an inch of the blade exposed. It glowed a dull orange in the light of a nearby streetlamp, itching to be put to work.

Reality crashed into him – a simple beating might end with three more fatalities. His hit-and-run might yet turn out to have been accidental, but this wouldn't be. If he got banged up inside with hundreds of hard cases all desperate to climb the shit heap, he'd be inside for life. He'd hurt so many other inmates that no parole board would give him another chance. He'd spend the rest of his days expecting a shank in his liver, or a mug of scalding sugared water in his face.

Only one thing could suppress the rage and restore clarity. It hurt like hell, but it caused no permanent damage, and it worked.

In the glove compartment he found a sheaf of log sheets fastened with a paperclip. He removed the clip, straightened out one pin, and inserted it under his left thumbnail. With a shuddering breath he rammed the metal deep into the tender tissue under his nail. Agony shot up his hand, excruciating even for him, and he gasped. When he could breathe again, he confirmed the metal was deep, embedded nearly to the root. Blood dripped onto his trousers. He rested his forefinger on the protruding loop of metal and watched the boys again.

Every few seconds he imagined piling into them with his steel out, then jabbed the pin so hard that fire lanced into his hand. Fury grunted and hissed through his teeth, but the pain eclipsed the blackness, banished it, reaffirmed his mastery of the ugly thing at his core. His previous record was twenty-two. If these idiots didn't disappear soon, he might beat that. It would prove nothing but would scratch the itch in a way that hurt only himself.

He made it to fourteen, then the alpha-dickhead chucked his empty cider bottle into a garden and all three wandered away. After ten minutes he eased the car door open and climbed out. The wound in his back burned. He slid the paperclip out from under his fingernail, sent one last white-hot needle up his thumb. When the pain subsided, he eased the door closed and crossed to the parade of shops.

No lights shone inside the pharmacy. An alarm box hung on a wall inside the door, but no blinking LEDs indicated it was operational.

He melted into the shadows and crept behind the buildings. Crouched against a chain-link fence backing onto gardens and pebble-dashed terraced boxes, he scanned the roofs of the shops. He spotted his way in, a skylight. The woodwork looked shabby – every chance it would have no alarm sensors.

He tested the dressing across his back, confirmed the tape remained stuck fast.

He hopped up onto a wheelie bin and prised loose a section of guttering. The creak of splitting plastic sounded deafening. He laid the broken guttering inside the next section along, then grabbed the exposed edge of the roofline, took a deep breath, and pulled himself up. With his feet braced against the brick-work, he pulled with his arms and pushed with his legs and stepped up onto the slates. His wounds burned but the tape held.

He watched the gardens for a few minutes. TV screens

flickered in some windows, but no curtains twitched. Thoughts of his own home, in Kirknewton, troubled him for a second, but he dismissed them. That was a life he'd never return to.

He crawled up the roof on all fours, spreading the load, and reached the skylight. No wires or magnetic contacts, so he slipped his blade in and prised it open. The sound of rotten wood splitting and cracking made him wince and he scanned the nearby houses again.

Even with the skylight lifted the opening was small, but he'd always been a skinny wee runt. The bigger problem was that it opened too high above the floor for him to return this way unless he found a handy stepladder.

He sat on the edge, his legs dangling inside. He'd be happier sticking his head in a bear-trap, but he couldn't function much longer without meds.

He lowered himself through the opening, hung for a moment, listened and watched. He spotted an infrared sensor high on one wall but saw no sign it was live. He heard no alarm, saw no flashing LEDs on the alarm control panel. He dropped to his feet and crouched, silent.

A wide space of cupboards and shelves and drawers confronted him. He scanned the alphabetically ordered labels until he found 'S' and yanked on the handle.

Locked.

A cold wash of dread flooded him. He cast his eyes around for a toolbox, pulled drawers open in a kitchen area. Cutlery clattered to the floor. He pushed the blade of a dinner knife into the gap at the top of the 'S' drawer and pushed down. The metal snapped. He scoured the kitchen again, found a screw-driver, jammed it into the drawer, found it would only insert a half-inch, the steel shaft of the tool thicker than the cutlery knife. He could almost sense the capsules, lurking in the dark drawer, so close. As he slammed the knife against the screw-driver handle again and again, rage built in him. They were *his* meds. He needed them. He wasn't stealing; they'd been prescribed to him. He was entitled to them.

As he inserted the blade of his Fairbairn Sykes, prepared to sacrifice even that to get at his meds, he heard a heavy click behind him, and the street door swung inwards.

TWENTY-SIX

By the time Malkie returned to the station, McLeish was raging.

'Where the hell have you been? Steph's been calling you all afternoon. We've had Liam Fielding waiting in interview room two for more than an hour. She wanted to wait, but I told her to start without you. Fielding's lawyer was threatening harassment. Again.'

McLeish had a point. All three should have agreed an interview approach before engaging with the enemy but Malkie had gone missing on only the second full day of a case. *Thin ice, mate. Thin ice.*

'I had some urgent personal business.'

He left it at that, knew it would only push McLeish's buttons harder, but he refused to apologise.

McLeish stabbed a finger at him. 'You. Do not. Go in there. Understood? Let Steph handle it.'

Malkie opened his mouth to protest but saw the sense in McLeish's order. His feet always had an infamous affinity with his mouth. Steph would maintain the necessary neutrality. Her reactions at the Fielding house had showed she loathed them too, but she would stash that away somewhere, for later. Her

non-negotiable sense of professionalism was one of her annoy-
ingly few faults.

Also, he couldn't trust himself not to let something slip
about Amanda.

He grabbed a cup of what passed for coffee from the
vending machine and took a seat in the gloomy monitoring
room. Only TV coppers sat in dark, neon-tinged rooms
watching through one-way mirrors, like professional voyeurs.
Ordinary coppers watched on a monitor beside a keyboard, on
an otherwise bare desk. The interview would be recorded
centrally, but he could watch and listen. He logged on and
brought up interview room two. A window opened showing
Steph on one side of the table, a manila file in front of her,
Fielding and his brief, Simon Fraser, on the other. Fraser's arrogance was legendary. He specialised in disrupting interviews
with pointless questions he knew the answers to and arguing
subtleties of legal process to the point of pedantry. The fact that
he couldn't be reprimanded for simply doing his job was only
one reason Malkie despised the man.

The tedious preliminaries had been dispensed with, and
Steph started on the good stuff.

'Mr Fielding, I've advised you in pre-interview disclosure
that evidence has been discovered indicating a direct relationship between yourself and a Mr Robin Wilkie, recently injured
in—'

Fraser didn't disappoint, interrupting her first question.

'No, Detective Constable Lang, you've established a
circumstantial link between a vehicle used by a company which
happens to be owned by my client, and a road traffic incident
which may yet prove to have been accidental. Fielding Minicabs currently engages the services of twenty-three self-
employed drivers. Any one of these drivers might borrow a pool
car for personal purposes outside of working hours without my
client's permission or knowledge. No direct connection has

been indicated between my client and either the alleged victim or any specific vehicle that may have been involved in said incident.'

Malkie leaned forward, impatient, his fingers drumming on the desk.

'Agreed, Mr Fraser, but the particular vehicle in question was discovered on the Fielding family's property in Kirknewton.'

'Parked beside a property occupied solely by Walter Callahan, no relation to my client.'

'Also agreed, but I attended the property the morning after the incident, and your client's erratic behaviour gave myself and my colleague cause for concern. Sufficient concern to—'

'May I see evidence of your qualification as a certified Police Scotland psychologist, DC Lang?'

Steph opened her mouth, but Fraser talked over her. 'You were accompanied by DS Malcom McCulloch that morning, were you not?'

Malkie sighed. *Here it comes.*

'That's correct, Mr—'

'A CID officer reprimanded on three previous occasions and, in fact, demoted following the third, and found guilty of harassment of my client.'

'A complaint which resulted in no formal action being taken, Mr—'

'Actually, I believe an official reprimand was initiated against Detective Sergeant McCulloch but was withdrawn without any explanation to my client?'

Steph paused. Bad move, show of weakness, but who could blame her? What could she say?

'Returning to the link between your client and the victim—'

'The alleged link, yes.' Fraser nodded, magnanimous in his complacency.

No mention, yet, of the memory card, so Steph had omitted

it from pre-disclosure. Risky. While it was common practice to spring key evidence late in the interview, it risked later accusations of lying by omission, something Fraser wouldn't fail to make use of.

'Mr Fielding, can you think of any other way in which you might have come into contact with Mr Wilkie? Might he have booked one of your minicabs?'

Fielding stared at her. Malkie expected his usual arrogant smirk, confident that Fraser charged exorbitant rates for a good reason. Instead, he saw a troubled man, a man wondering where this was going. Fielding's leg started to bounce. Fraser touched his knee. Fielding looked at him, confused, then regained his composure, but then continued to stare at Steph with dread. Was he afraid his big deal had been rumbled, or that Fraser would ask Jake about it? Was Wilkie involved? Was it so heavy he feared a spell banged up in a cell in Addiewell?

Go for it, Steph. Bastard's ready to buckle.

Fraser intervened. 'My client can't be expected to remember the name of every client who has booked his company's minicabs. It has been stated twice that Mr Fielding has no recollection of any encounter with Mr Wilkie.'

'I appreciate that, Mr—'

'I suggest you reveal whatever you've withheld from pre-interview disclosure so my client can respond to your concerns fully, and in possession of all relevant information.'

Fraser was gearing up to end this. They'd been at it less than twenty minutes and based on what Steph had other than the memory card, Malkie was impressed she'd kept them talking this long.

'Mr Fielding, during a search of Mr Wilkie's home...'

Steph paused. Malkie spotted it, too. Fielding was no stranger to a police interview, but Steph's words rattled him. A momentary tightening of his musculature, a stiffening of his posture. When he rubbed his nose with his fingers, Malkie knew Steph would nail him. He settled in to enjoy the show.

'During a search of Mr Wilkie's home, we discovered physical evidence linking you directly to Mr Wilkie.'

She paused for effect. 'Care to comment, Mr Fielding?'

Fraser frowned. Had Fielding withheld critical information from his own brief? That would piss off the smug bastard.

Steph continued, her professional demeanour worthy of a BAFTA. 'Mr Fielding? Can you explain why we found your fingerprints on a memory card locked in Mr Wilkie's safe?'

Fraser stood. 'I request a client conference.'

Fielding stared at Steph, hatred glittering in his eyes.

She stared him down.

Fielding buckled and surged to his feet. His chair toppled backwards.

Oh yes, well played, Steph.

Steph maintained unwavering eye contact with Fielding, one eyebrow raised in question. 'Interview suspended at 17:17, Mr Simon Fraser has requested a conference with his client.'

She stopped the recording devices and the video window turned black. She came through, nodded towards the now-blank screen.

'What do you think?'

'Bastard was twitching before you even mentioned Wilkie's house, or his prints. He's lied to his own brief, too. Guilty as hell.'

'That's why McLeish didn't let me wait to discuss strategy with you.' She shook her head, disappointment in her eyes. 'Where were you? I called you. Repeatedly.'

'I went to St John's. Checked in on Wilkie, then...' Why did he fear his next words so much? 'I went to face my dad.'

'Again?'

'Eh?'

'You said you were there this morning.'

Lying to Steph. What was he thinking?

'Ah, no, this morning was just a quick resupply visit. I went back again when he was out of bed. We had a late lunch.'

Well done. Lie upon lie, to the one person who always has your back. Well done.

'Good for you. Let me guess – long clumsy silences, lots of foot-shuffling and picking fluff off trousers?'

That's what he'd expected, and the opposite of what he got. 'Actually, it was OK. I think we might be all right, in time.'

She smiled. 'That's brilliant. Happy for you, boss.'

Before he could compound his sins, she stood. 'I'm going out for some air. I can handle the second half of the interview, yeah?'

'Aye, Steph. Message received and understood.'

Five minutes later, she popped her head through the doorway again and grinned. 'This should be good.' She ducked away again.

He hadn't closed the video window. It sprang to life with an audio-click and Steph's voice.

'Interview recommenced at 17:36.'

He sat forward but his eagerness crumbled, replaced by a sick feeling in his guts. Fielding looked too confident considering Steph's bombshell.

'So, Mr Fielding, would you like to—'

'My client will not be answering any further questions, and I'm terminating this interview, Detective Constable Lang.'

Steph was silent for several seconds. 'On what grounds, Mr Fraser?'

'On the grounds that further evidence has surfaced of harassment of my client which casts serious doubt on the professional objectivity of your colleague, Detective Sergeant Malcolm McCulloch.'

Fraser pulled something from his pocket, pressed a button on the side and placed it on the table.

Malkie knew without needing a close-up. Jake's battered and knackered old brick of a phone. The screen lit with a freeze-frame of video.

'My client apologises that he didn't disclose this prior to the interview. He's under significant stress at the moment.'

Malkie's stomach sank. He lowered his head to the desk and banged it twice on the hard, unforgiving wood.

TWENTY-SEVEN

A fast bleeping sounded and two police officers stepped through the street door – a young lad and an older woman. Their torches slashed through the gloom as they scanned the shop area. She was taller and stockier than her colleague and looked meaner. A seasoned old copper teaching a newbie the ropes. Both held their batons extended.

An elderly man in a cardigan and pyjamas opened a plastic cabinet behind them and punched buttons. The beeps stopped. Ceiling lights flared into life, brutal and blinding.

The uniforms spotted Callahan and advanced, their batons raised. The young lad glanced at his partner.

'Jen? Maybe call for backup?'

Jen sneered at him. 'You serious, Pete? There's two of us and one of him.'

Pete swallowed, then moved left to flank Callahan. Jen moved towards the open hatchway through the counter.

'Let's not do anything stupid, pal. There's no other way out.'

Callahan turned the hilt of his knife in his hand, but he resisted the urge, slipped it into its scabbard. If he went AWOL with steel in his hand, these people were dead.

He backed up, scanned the room for an exit. As expected, the skylight was too high to reach. His headache surged forward. Deep inside him The Dog smelled violence and stirred. He banged the heel of his hand against his temple, backed away, holding his other hand out, a warning to stay away. There was no coming back from killing a copper, no sympathetic hearing, no diminished responsibility. He'd get a cell for life in Saughton, and he'd die in there.

He looked Officer Jen in the eye. 'I'm warning you. *It*'ll hurt you. *It* wants me to hurt you.'

Nothing happened for several seconds. No rush, no more words. The coppers looked at each other, uncertainty in their eyes, Callahan's behaviour promising their worst psych-case nightmare come true. Jen lowered her baton. The young lad, Pete, looked ready to puke.

She held her free hand out, low, palm down.

'Look, pal. We don't want trouble. Calm down and we'll take you somewhere safe, have a cup of tea and a chat, OK?'

She hid her baton behind her leg, took a step forward.

Pete found his voice. 'Should I call for backup, Jen?'

Jen glared at him. 'And do what until they arrive? Lock the front door and hope he doesn't get to that skylight? You muppet. There's two of us against one skinny wee runt.'

She launched herself through the gap in the counter.

Callahan sidestepped her with ease. She crashed into the wall of steel drawers but got one hand on his collar as she flew past. He bolted for the front door, but her grip was solid. His top half yanked backwards. Somehow, she turned him in mid-air. He landed on his front and his face slammed into the floor.

She jumped on his back. Pete hit the ground beside her and yanked a pair of handcuffs from his belt. He tried to clamp one bracelet around one of Callahan's wrists, but they were both about to learn how powerful a skinny wee runt like Callahan could be.

Jen grunted as she struggled to stay on top of him. Pete held on to his wrist but couldn't slap the bracelets on.

Jen shifted position, and her knee dug into Callahan's wound. He screamed as agony exploded across his back. Black spots swam in his vision and his head span as he tumbled to the edge of passing out. The rage in his mind bloomed again. It sang in him, joyous and furious and hateful. It filled him and goaded him, but he held it off, clung to the steel at the core of him and rejected the snapping of hungry jaws ringing in his ears.

Desperation galvanised him. He twisted, unbalanced Jen enough to reach around and land a backhand on her face. She fell away, blood pouring from her nose.

Pete extended one leg over to pin him down. Callahan grabbed his balls and squeezed. The lad screamed and fell sideways, clutching his groin. He scurried away backwards, his boot heels squeaking on the vinyl floor.

Callahan lurched to his feet. Waves of agony sliced through him. He made for the front door, but Jen got a hand on him.

'No chance, you wee prick.' She caught his trouser leg in one fist and slammed the other into the blood-soaked area of his back.

He fell again, the pain too much, washing over him, dragging him towards a blackout. His vision clouded and pressure battered at his skull, the animal inside him rabid and slavering and tearing at his failing willpower.

He lost it then, gave in to it, set it loose for everything he'd suffered the past two days. He'd warned them to walk away, and they didn't listen. They deserved what was coming.

He turned on Jen, slammed the toe of his boot into her ribs, heard them crack. She screamed and clutched her side, let go of him. Her baton fell from her fingers. He snatched it from the floor and threw himself on top of her, stuck his face in hers, raged at her. 'I warned you, you stupid bitch! I bloody warned you!'

He raised his hand, held the thick steel baton high, savoured a feeling he'd missed – the taste of carnage.

'Officers down, officers down. Fuck's sake, where is it?' Pete, his voice frantic. He sat against a wall, one hand clutching his groin, the other fumbling for the orange button on the AirWave hanging from his shoulder.

'Officers down. Moss Bridge Pharmacy. Urgent backup required.'

For the second time in one day, cold hard reality pierced Callahan's blind fury. He slid sideways off Jen and gestured at her, moaning, her breath rattling.

'Take care of your colleague, son. Check her breathing, make sure her tongue isn't blocking her airway. I don't want a dead copper on my sheet.'

Pete stared at him, vacant.

'Now, son. Get her into the recovery position, or she'll choke.'

Pete crawled to the fallen woman, turned her onto her side and examined her. 'Her pulse is OK.'

Her chest rose and fell, shallow but even – she was out, but breathing.

Callahan stood, staggered to the door.

Pete called after him. 'You'll go down for this, you fucking psycho.'

'Aye. Very probably, son.'

TWENTY-EIGHT

Malkie waited, aware of the amount of shit about to hit him.

He felt beaten, saw now he'd taken on more than he was ready for. It should have done him good to return to the job. But he was carrying too much anger, still reeling from six months of nightmares and flashbacks and guilt he needed to find a peg to hang on.

Should he have excused himself from the case when the Fieldings became involved? Steph had shown him the respect of letting him decide for himself, and he'd screwed that up, too. Or should McLeish have moved him to another case? Was the man so obsessed with his own career-making secret project that even his self-serving judgment had failed him?

None of this excused Malkie's latest and greatest screw-up. He switched the lights off and waited in the darkened room for McLeish to announce his fate. He held out hope for nothing worse than more leave, spend a week with his dad, at least fix that. He'd felt more alive and awake the past couple of days than he could remember since that horrific night, but his breakdown today had shown how brittle his budding positivity was. He had Amanda hidden on his dad's boat, for fuck's sake.

Worse, he'd promised her his protection completely off-proto-col. Hell, it damned-near amounted to perverting the course of justice.

He needed to bring her in. Was his judgement so skewed he should never have trusted her in the first place? Was he emotionally fit to look after himself, let alone her? Despite his foolish promise, under suspension he'd be useless to her, and he was certain to be ordered to stay away from the Fieldings, which would include her. Of all the fallout from this, his latest screw-up, betraying her would hurt the most.

He slumped in his chair and waited.

When Steph stepped into the room, he braced himself for the mother of all arse-kickings. She sat, studied him, her expression confused and disbelieving. Nothing like the fury he expected.

He took two seconds to lose patience. 'Well? Professional Standards, right?'

She stared at him, combed her fingers through her hair, scratched her scalp as if unsure where to start. 'You' – she pointed at him – 'are a jammy bastard.'

Malkie didn't need to feign shock; Steph never used language like that.

She smiled, shook her head as if struggling to believe her own next words. 'Fielding isn't pressing an assault charge. Not even harassment. Fraser is livid.'

This made no sense. Fielding hated Malkie as much as he detested Fielding.

'McLeish wants you out of here. Now. You're to take a few days. He spoke to Fraser off the record. Fielding looked less smug than I'd expected, to be honest. McLeish wants you out of here before I can continue the interview.'

'But the bastard's prints are on a memory card we found locked in Wilkie's safe. That minor fact hasn't gone away, has it? What's McLeish playing at, Steph?'

She held his gaze for a second, either for his language or to let him know he was on thin ice.

Malkie dragged his temper back under control. 'There's something McLeish isn't telling us. You know it, I know you do. Regardless of my stupidity, those prints drop that bastard right in it. I told you, didn't I? Something stinks, Steph.'

She sat back, didn't deny it. 'You're to take time off. Go work on that cabin of yours, anything, but don't be here. And stay away from the Fieldings. And Robin Wilkie. McLeish will continue as SIO, but he's allowing me to lead under his supervision. And he's lending me Rab Lundy for a week. I know he's as rough round the edges as you are, but I think we'll bumble along OK.'

Malkie sighed, gave up. Some battles weren't worth fighting. He stood. 'OK, I'll disappear for a few days. There's a roof I need to work on. Me and Dad.'

She stood too and nodded her approval. 'Sounds good. Spend time fixing a few things up, aye?'

He smiled at the depth of wisdom that few, possibly only he, knew lurked under her usual menacing demeanour. There was more to come. 'What?'

'You said the fire started in your mum's bedroom, but what caused it?'

He swallowed, choked back an urge to tell her she was asking too much, but she deserved better from him.

'It was a stupid bloody candle. You know, one of those big fat scented ones? Must have fallen onto the floor or her bedclothes or something.' His memory flashed back to Liam Fielding's comment about a terrible accident, and his words stuck in his throat. Was Fielding suggesting it was deliberate, that someone started the fire? Was it nothing to do with the stupid candle? No, he'd read the Fire Investigation report and it said a candle started it. Fielding was only baiting him.

Steph's eyes demanded he continue, pleaded with him to

trust her. He braced himself to confess what he'd told no other soul – the stupid, thoughtless act of his that had sealed his mum's agonising death. The theory he'd settled on to explain the guilt he couldn't bring himself to let go.

'I gave her that candle, Steph. For her birthday. It was me that brought the damned thing into their house. Into my old mum's own bedroom. Me.'

He swallowed again, waited, expected her to be incredulous, disgusted, appalled by his idiotic actions. Perhaps he wanted her to react that way.

Steph stepped forward, close. She stared up and into his eyes, drilled into him in a way that demanded his attention.

'I bought my mum's husband a hedge trimmer for his birthday.'

This surprised him – she rarely discussed her family.

'Your stepdad?'

'My mum's husband. Point is, he hasn't lopped off any of his fingers yet, but I live in hope. Thing is, if he did, it would be his fault, not mine.'

Malkie's secret shame crumbled, pathetic and feeble when exposed to the harsh examination of a full-on Steph. As human as it was to feel responsible for bringing the instrument of his mum's death into her home, Steph's words challenged him, confronted him with how tenuous his claim on the blame was.

Something snagged at his mind. 'Hang on. Your lot live in a council tower block. Not a lot of gardens twenty floors up, are there?'

She grinned. 'Correct, boss. Made it up. But you get the point.'

Malkie chuckled despite the shitshow today had turned into, but something insidious whispered in his mind, promised further ugly revelations to come.

Is that it? Could that be the limit of my complicity? Then why can't I stop feeling so shitty? What am I still not remembering?

'Malkie.'

Steph's irritated tone wrenched him from his thoughts.

'You need to get out of here before McLeish changes his mind.'

He felt her eyes on him until he left the CID room and stepped into the stairwell.

He descended to the ground floor but couldn't walk out the front door. He had to know. He continued to the basement server room. Lizzie Baxter from IT Support sat stuffing a sandwich into her mouth, her eyes fixed on a magazine. Something to do with women on roller skates, armoured up to their armpits.

'Hiya, Lizzie. How's things?'

She jumped then relaxed when she saw it was him. 'Malkie. About time, old man. What can I do to you?'

Malkie smiled. He'd always liked Lizzie – no-shite sense of humour and a tongue that could flay the skin off you. 'Well... See... There's an interview in progress but I've upset McLeish again.'

Lizzie grinned. She made no secret of her feelings towards McLeish either.

Malkie grinned back. 'Can I watch from down here?'

Lizzie took a few moments. The request was unusual, but she and Malkie went back a few years. 'That PC is a secure build and networked, but your access will be logged.'

'Thanks, Lizzie. I owe you.'

She returned to her magazine. The details of what went on in the building didn't interest her. She fixed computers when idiots pulled plugs out or spilled coffee on keyboards and called in the external supplier for anything more complex, but she'd never expressed the slightest interest in what went on upstairs.

He logged on to the feed from interview room two. Steph

and Fielding and Fraser sat as before, but McLeish's stocky figure had joined them. Lizzie looked over as the audio began. He apologised and turned the volume down.

He listened as Steph worked hard on damage limitation. 'I will continue the investigation into Mr Wilkie's attempted murder, under Detective Inspector McLeish's supervision.'

Fraser nodded, magnanimous as ever. 'That is satisfactory, Detective Constable Lang. My client has no desire to suffer further harassment by DS McCulloch. He wishes only to assist your investigation in any way possible.'

The formal unpleasantries dispensed with, Steph continued.

'Mr Fielding, can you explain how your prints were found on a memory card locked in Mr Wilkie's safe, considering you claim to recall no prior contact with Mr Wilkie?'

After a small nod from Fraser, Fielding spoke in a controlled monotone. He'd never win any acting awards. 'I think Callahan stole it from my office at home, but I don't know how it got into Mr Wilkie's safe. Maybe Callahan gave it to Wilkie then wanted it back for some reason. That's my guess.'

Steph stared at him. She could smell shite as well as Malkie could, but what did she have to challenge it? If only he'd shared what he knew...

'And why do you believe Mr Callahan stole your memory card?'

Fielding glanced at his brief, who continued to stare at Steph. 'I found him in my office at home three weeks ago, said he was looking for something to write on, but I checked my CDs and memory cards and found there was one missing. He said he didn't take it. I couldn't prove anything, so I had to let it go.'

'Do you know what's on the missing memory card?'

'Aye.' He made her ask.

'And that is?' If she felt any irritation, her voice betrayed none of it.

'Copies of background checks I ran on him. I asked a mate who knows someone at the army veterans' association. I can't remember their names now, though. Sorry.' He grinned. 'The guy sent me Callahan's psychological evaluations. I saved them in case he ever turned violent again. I'm guessing he found out and stole them.'

Fraser sighed. Steph gave him a chance to comment but – strangely for him – he remained silent.

'So, Mr Fielding, you admit to committing a breach of 2016 GDPR legislation, then?'

Fielding's grin disappeared. He turned to Fraser, who stepped in without hesitation.

'My client sought only relevant hearsay or anecdotal information on Mr Callahan. He could not have expected a full, official dossier. He regrets not thinking to report this at the time but will – of course – do so in future now that he understands data protection legislation more fully.'

Steph didn't hesitate for a second.

'How did the memory card end up in Mr Wilkie's safe, Mr Fielding? We've found no connection between Mr Callahan and Mr Wilkie. Are you aware of a connection?'

'No. But he must have got it from that bloody psycho. Must have known the guy already.'

Fraser touched Fielding's arm – his client was in danger of padding his role.

'Can you confirm the make of the memory card?'

'No. Don't remember.'

'Can you confirm the capacity of the memory card?'

'No. Don't remember.'

'Can you confirm the password you used to encrypt the memory card?'

'Peachpit 1997.'

Steph stared at him.

'All one word, capital P.' He smiled. The Peach Pit was a lap-dancing dive in a side street off Leith Walk in Edinburgh, one of several the Fieldings owned on both sides of central Scotland.

Malkie itched to call William Loudon at the lab, but he was supposed to be long gone, not eavesdropping from the basement.

The physical evidence from Callahan's vehicle trumped Liam's prints on the memory card, so Fraser would have his client out of there today. And McLeish – for reasons he wasn't sharing – had listened to Fielding's ridiculous story without asking a single challenging question.

He needed to scarper without running into Steph or McLeish.

'Thanks, Lizzie. You're a pal.'

He tapped the side of his nose and grinned. 'You ain't seen me, right, doll?'

She looked up, tried to look stern. 'You know I have HR on speed-dial, Malkie?' But she couldn't help herself and cracked a grin. 'Piss off before I grass you up to McLeish.'

He ran up the back stairs to the car park. Amanda would be waiting for him, and he hated how much that mattered to him.

He headed for Port Edgar.

It was time to ruin the poor woman's life.

TWENTY-NINE

Callahan eased Bernard's bedroom door open. Bernard's eyes glowed, eager and feral, in the gloom. Only one thing he wanted to hear – no luck with Norrie, leaving only one other option. Callahan would love to see Markham weep and beg and piss himself, but he couldn't risk losing control. Putting aside the hit-and-run he still remembered nothing about, he'd stopped short of blinding Fat Frankie, and the police officers in the pharmacy were arguably self-defence, so none would suffer long-term damage. Everything so far a decent brief could weave into a story of a brave ex-squaddie, dumped by the army, left to rot, hiding from a world that had no more use for him. With his psych record and the right journalists on board, he could argue for medical help, get the treatment he needed eleven years ago.

But if he risked doing Markham, he might lose it completely, go too far and earn himself life without parole. That couldn't be allowed to happen. He deserved little, but more than that.

'Where's your stash, Bernard?'

Bernard's gaze faltered. Disappointed, but afraid now, too.

Callahan picked up the bottle of Cardhu, removed the

screw-top and dropped it on the floor, took a long swallow from it. 'I'm not doing Markham for you, so don't make me ask a second time.'

'I told you, mate, I stopped taking them two years ago. And I haven't had any Muzzle for years before that. Honest, no lie.'

Callahan stared. And waited. Eventually, Bernard buckled.

'Markham might have some?' His voice was small and pathetic, the pleading of a man seeing his last chance at revenge slip away.

Callahan's arm lashed out and the bottle smashed against a wall. Whisky rained down on the bedclothes. He roared at his old friend, all self-control blasted away in a blinding detonation of rage. 'Tell me where your stash is, or I swear...'

Bernard wiped whisky from his eyes and his hair.

The broken neck of the bottle landed at Callahan's feet, and he fought an urge to use it on Bernard, open the man's throat, give The Dog what it craved, but he'd been there before...

Instead, he picked up Bernard's ex-service lighter. His conscience shrank from the sight of their regimental insignia, but he flicked open the top and thumbed the wheel. Sparks flared into a guttering yellow flame. Bernard's eyes switched from the flame to his bedsheets, soaked with Cardhu.

'Christ, Walter. It's me, mate.'

'I need it, Bernard.' His voice came out low and guttural, a growl that promised violence.

Bernard crumbled. 'In the wardrobe, in my kitbag, you fucking lunatic.'

Callahan closed the lighter, clutched it in his fist, relieved and sorry at the same time. The Dog screamed at him. *He lied to us.*

Us? There was only himself. What the hell was happening to him?

He fumbled in the cupboard, desperation making him care-less. He found the kitbag and inside, a small plastic bag, containing six capsules. He braced his hands on the shelf, fought to control his breathing, tasted bile.

'Six? You'd have sent me after Markham, knowing what I might do to him, for six Muzzles?'

'What? There should be loads there. I swear, mate.' Bernard's voice rose to a hysterical pitch, his words tripping over each other.

'I'm getting a serious headache, Bernard.' The pounding in his skull intensified.

The colour drained from Bernard's face. 'Walter. Mate. For fuck's sake...'

Callahan stepped forward. Bernard's whining grated on him. He opened his hand, stared at the lighter, with the same engraving as his own, back at the cottage. They all brought souvenirs home with them: trinkets and tattoos and broken souls.

He laid the lighter down on the table and backed away, couldn't look at his old friend.

What the hell was happening to him?

He could find no words, the apology he wanted to offer his old friend choked off by his shame. He left.

In the car, he examined the bag. Six Muzzles, three days, nowhere near enough. And were they even the real thing? They looked right, yellow and blue capsules, no markings.

He drove south out the Whitburn Road, turned down a farm lane, and stopped on a grass verge beside a field. He pointed the car at the majestic and serene Pentland Hills so they'd be the last thing he ever saw if Bernard's meagre stash was bad.

He pulled a bottle of water from his kitbag and tipped two pills into his hand. What day was today? Tuesday? Wednesday? Two a day gave him until Thursday or Friday. Not enough. And how old were they? Did they come from Norrie's bad batch? What choice did he have? He swallowed them, drank half the water, then forced himself to relax and wait. He gazed at the hills where he'd come so close, so many times, to ending his miserable existence. He could clamber up there right now, open his wrists, let his hot, red blood drain away into the frosty, green turf. But no – he wasn't nearly beaten yet.

The dashboard clock ticked past five minutes. He dared to believe these capsules were OK. A wave of relief washed over him but faded again. Only two days to get more. Two days to find out why he'd run down a complete stranger he could swear he'd never met. Not nearly long enough, but the idea of going for Jake's stash set alarms screaming in his head.

He rolled down the window a few inches, reclined the seat, and closed his eyes. He dozed for a while until his phone beeped. A text message from Jake. 'Waiting now. Come between nine and ten.'

Not any random time after dark. A one-hour window. To make sure Liam wasn't home, or to ensure he was? Would there be more than meds waiting for him?

His alleged actions on Sunday night made no sense. He couldn't reconcile what he was supposed to have done with any of his previous episodes. Nothing made sense. Something was missing.

He saw no other choice. First, sleep. Then he'd head for Kirknewton.

Early. On his terms, not Jake's.

THIRTY

Malkie couldn't bring himself to get out of the car at Port Edgar. Could he do this? *Are those partial prints in the car yours, and why are they there? Oh, and I'm turning you over to my boss to protect myself.*

His phone rang. Steph. The last person he deserved to talk to right now, but it would delay his conversation with Amanda. He hit the call button. 'Steph.'

'You OK? I saw you leave after I finished with Fielding. But that was after the second session.'

He waited for it.

'Where were you?'

And there it was. He'd pushed her into a place where even her support was becoming conditional.

'Malkie, please tell me you were in the canteen, drowning your sorrows in crap coffee?'

He rummaged for any excuse credible enough to let her back off but found nothing. Any more screw-ups, McLeish would make sure Steph suffered too.

'I logged on to listen to the rest of the interview. I needed to hear what Fielding had to say.'

He heard her sigh, more obviously than necessary. 'Malkie, you're on leave. Don't put me in a difficult position.'

'Steph, I will never see you held responsible for my stupidity. I owe you that much.'

She'd see through his weasel-words, but would she bother to argue?

'OK. I'll keep you informed. Don't go getting us both another kicking from McLeish, OK?'

'Yes, Steph.'

'I'm trusting you.'

'Yes, Steph.'

'Oh, grow up.' She disconnected.

His fondness for her made him smile, until reality intruded. *Amanda.*

He'd encouraged her to trust him, and now he was about to betray yet another undeserving victim of his habitual misguided best intentions. It had to be the right thing to do. She'd be safer in a shelter, and he could forget his creeping fear that she was in some way complicit. Despite the evidence pointing at Callahan, and despite his unshakeable conviction that Liam Fielding was neck-deep in culpability too.

His phone chimed. A text from Steph.

> Would you believe Fielding's password didn't work?

Radio Four announced the seven o'clock news. Time to act. If he allowed the situation to drag on, he'd risk handing his career to McLeish on a plate. That would dump himself and his dad in financial shit, and the old man didn't deserve that.

He climbed out of the car, took a breath, had to fight a ridiculous feeling that the majestic road bridges towering over Port Edgar glared down at him in immense and appalled disappointment.

A glimmer of light in one of the *Droopy Goose*'s portholes

179

caught his eye, the curtain open a few inches. Before he could stop himself, he peered inside.

Amanda stood, her back to him, her posture leaving no doubt she was having one hell of an argument with someone on her phone.

He opened the hatch. Amanda dropped her phone like it had scalded her.

'Seriously, Amanda? After all I told you?' She picked it up from the floor, then sat like a scolded child.

'Who was that?' As he heard his own words, he regretted the question; his protection entitled him to nothing.

Her expression suggested she felt the same. 'Marjorie, a schoolfriend. I needed to hear a friendly voice.'

He stared at her. 'Marjorie.'

She laid her phone on the table, folded her arms, another defensive tell. 'Yes, Marjorie. I trust her, I'm not an idiot, Malkie.'

No, you aren't, are you, Mrs Fielding?

He closed the hatch, then turned to her and forced a smile. 'I'm sorry. I'm worried for you, OK?'

She returned his smile. Her obvious relief – perhaps even affection? – couldn't be fake and still feel this real, could it?

Stop this. She has to go. Tomorrow.

'I'm sorry, too.' She didn't look like she convinced even herself. 'Any news? Any contact from Liam?'

He couldn't bear to tell her he had nothing. Fear glittered in her eyes but even in such a vulnerable state, he wanted what he had no decent right to. Shame forced his gaze to his feet. She sighed, as if she'd read his mind.

'Malkie? Tell me. I can handle it.'

OK, Amanda. I'm going to lie to you all evening then betray you in the morning. 'We interviewed him today.'

She brightened. He continued before she rallied too much.

'But we couldn't arrest him.'

'Why?' Her voice was hoarse.

Here we go – lie number one. 'Not enough evidence to hold him. It happens.'

Her eyes moistened and she nibbled on her thumbnail, a habit he found endearing, as inappropriate as that was.

'And Callahan?'

'No, but we'll find him.'

'Did you question Jake?'

'On what basis? Beyond his official statement, we have no evidence he's involved. I only know what you've told me, but how do I explain our conversation to my boss?'

He was on a greasier slope than he'd realised.

She sat beside him, leaned forward, her forehead on her folded arms, close enough that he felt her heat. She sighed. A long, desolate expression of the pain he both wanted and dreaded to believe was real and tearing her up inside. He stood, grabbed the kettle. 'Coffee?'

She lifted her head, stared at him with a smile that failed to convince.

Malkie took his time, dragged it out, pretended to spill coffee on the worktop and took an age to clean it up.

He placed two steaming mugs on the table and sat beside her.

'What's up, Malkie? And don't lie to me.'

He stirred his coffee for too long. She turned towards him. Her knee touched his, and his resolve crumbled. The urge to place a comforting hand on hers was overwhelming. Conscious of the space she must need right now, he found the strength to move away a few inches, enough to put a sliver of space between them.

Tomorrow. He'd let her have one more night free from fear before ripping the heart out of her. Later, when he'd nailed her husband and moved on to other cases, if she still welcomed his comfort, then to hell with professional ethics.

'We got a lead. A nurse saw someone visiting Robin Wilkie last night. His boyfriend, we think.' *We? Steph knows none of this.*

'And what did he say?'

'I haven't spoken to him. The nurse will call me if he comes back. He might know why Callahan or Liam, maybe even Jake, has it in for Wilkie.'

She frowned. 'You still think Liam's involved?'

Up to his filthy neck in it. 'Aye. Somehow. He and Callahan aren't exactly besties, are they?'

'No. They work together for Jake, but there's no love lost. Liam treats Callahan like shit and Callahan takes it because he needs the cottage.'

'Could Liam be using Callahan to clean up his mess?'

She twisted in her seat and peered out of a porthole.

Malkie couldn't help it. He imagined reaching for her, pulling her to him. He felt heat fill him, tighten him, demanding and insistent and wrong.

She straightened up. 'You think this man Wilkie had something on Liam, and Jake sent Callahan to deal with him?'

Malkie cleared his throat, pushed away his shame, before he could answer. 'Could be. From what I've seen it's all but evident either Liam or Callahan is responsible, maybe both, but Jake's in there too, somehow. Callahan had a pool car, but no obvious link to Wilkie. Liam does though, and he had a pool car out too. And Jake would do anything to protect his precious family reputation.'

'I use those cars too, sometimes.' She stared at him, and he struggled to read her expression.

What's your point, Amanda? Are you testing me? Playing me? Fuck's sake, you're not involved, are you?

She turned back to the porthole. 'What does Liam have to do with Wilkie? I've never heard of him before.'

Oh, I so want to believe you.

'We found a memory card in Robin Wilkie's house with Liam's prints on it.'

She looked intrigued, but said nothing, just listened.

'So, we have a definite link between Liam and Wilkie, but nothing linking Callahan except the car, and believe it or not, technically that's only circumstantial. Yesterday morning Liam looked shit even before I mentioned the incident, then he scarpered without an explanation. But when Callahan came out of his house, he looked confused when he saw us. Even when he saw the car, I'm convinced he remembered none of it.'

'So? He's a nutjob.'

Malkie took a deep breath. 'Or he wasn't driving that car.'

Her eyes demanded he continue.

'What if Liam was at the wheel and hit Wilkie, then switched cars? Perfect mug to frame, a nutjob with PTSD? I know it's far-fetched, but Liam was freaked out and Callahan wasn't. Not at first.'

She shifted in her seat and her knee, again, rested against his thigh.

Christ. Not again.

She chewed her lip, pondered. He lost himself in her face, her eyes glittering with hope, her skin smooth and unblemished, her lips a delicate pink, her teeth perfect and even. What would her lips taste of? Would they be warm? If he—

She grabbed his hand, her eyes alight. Heat and blood flooded his crotch again, fired up a surge of hunger as shameful as it was unbearable. He closed his eyes and swallowed, coughed to cover his reaction.

'Hang on, you said Wilkie had a boyfriend. Liam hates gay people. Hates them. Remember that nightclub?'

'Aye, The Libertine. I was there.'

'Yes, I know. I locked myself in my room all that day. So, Wilkie is gay. Liam hates gay men, like psychotically. His dad's the same. Maybe Wilkie has nothing to do with Liam's secret

183

deal or that man I saw him with? Maybe Wilkie works at the club? He could have something on Liam... CCTV of that night?' Her eyes sparkled now. 'I bet this Wilkie guy has video of Liam getting his hands dirty.' She snapped her fingers. 'The memory card.'

Her theory had legs. Even if Wilkie was just a punter but knew the management, it wouldn't be hard to get a copy of a security video. Was Wilkie blackmailing Liam? Did Liam get his knuckles bloody that night after all, somewhere he thought was off camera? Did the memory card contain a wee movie that might nail the bastard? It was thin, but he wanted it to be true so bad he could taste it.

She removed her hand from his, plucked at her lower lip with her fingers, deep in thought.

Malkie's mobile rang. He escaped out onto the deck to take the call, relieved to flee from temptation. His screen showed an unknown number – never a good sign.

'Mr McCulloch? It's Colin Prendergast. At St John's. The hospital.'

He breathed, again. 'I know what St John's is. What's up, Colin?'

'That guy's been back, Mr McCulloch.'

Malkie resisted an urge to promise Colin a lollipop. 'You said he's been there. Past tense.'

'Yes. I told him I'd let him stay longer if he came back at nine. That'll give you time to get here, aye?'

He heard desperation in the lad's voice, couldn't blame him after their earlier conversation. 'Good thinking, Colin. I'll be there before nine, OK?'

A relieved sigh. 'Thanks, Mr McCulloch.' He hung up.

Malkie stood with his elbows on the roof of the cabin, tapped the mobile against his lips. Wilkie's house had turned up nothing indicating a partner or family, except maybe a wedding ring on Wilkie's hand in a photograph. Liam's memory card was a dead end for now. He suspected Callahan would be good at not being found. Wilkie's secret boyfriend might be his only lead.

He returned below. 'Amanda, I have to go.'

Fear darkened her face. 'No. I—'

'I have to. Wilkie's boyfriend is expected back at St John's. He might be able to ID Liam or Callahan.'

She stared down into her lap like a sulky wee girl. 'I'm losing the plot here, Malkie.' Her eyes glistened.

Despite himself, he put one hand to her face, rested his fingers on the soft downy skin of her neck, stroked her cheek with his thumb. This time, she cupped his hand in her own and leaned into his palm, screwed her eyes shut. Tears spilled and ran down over his fingers. He couldn't stop himself remembering the last woman who cried into his hands – Sandra Morton, twenty-five years ago. Long ago but still raw and bitter in his mind. Her heartbreak had turned to venom when he tried to escape his own mess, and she'd set her rabid pair of brothers on him. Could he ever trust a woman's tears again?

Did Mum cry? Alone in that room? While she was dying?

He chased away his own inner scourge. Amanda was different. She couldn't be faking this, and he was right to give her the protection he'd promised. She deserved peace, kindness, safety. She did seem to want to draw closer to him, and he wanted to offer her all the comfort she might want. He craved her affection in return, and after so long on his own, his defences had crumbled long ago.

He needed to go to the hospital, and he needed to stay here with her.

He eased his fingers from her grip and climbed out onto deck before he could change his mind.

THIRTY-ONE

Callahan found the cottage deserted, yellow crime-scene tape stretched across both front and back doors. From the darkness between the trees, he spotted a white box on a window ledge. Jake had delivered, if only to get rid of him.

He skirted the tree line to the side of the main house, then sprinted low and quiet to behind the garage. Through a window, he saw Jake's Range Rover but no Aston or Ducati. Jake was home but Liam was out, which suited him. The missing Ducati suggested Amanda was away, too.

He found a spot from where he could watch both properties. Stretched out on a bed of damp leaves, he pulled his parka hood over his head for warmth and to hide his ashen-white face.

Thirty minutes, he'd give it. He used to spend hours on recce like this, shifting only inches every five minutes to stave off cramps, but the last few days had shredded his nerves and he couldn't calm himself. He willed himself into the zone, motionless but alert and focused. But he couldn't find it. The first time since Helmand he needed his old talents, and he couldn't think straight for needing to get his hands on that box.

With his chest tight and his guts churning, he made a move for the window ledge.

Adrenaline burned in him, made every small sound a threat, every step forward a point of no return. His heartbeat pounded in his ears. He feared sudden violence from any direction but couldn't drag his eyes from the box on the window ledge, under a broken roof slate.

Despite his mounting crisis, he hesitated. Why the roof slate? No wind tonight, or rain. Had Jake booby-trapped it? Or alarmed it? His vision narrowed. The pounding in his ears surged, an overwhelming roar of rushing blood that thundered through his head like all hell breaking loose.

He lifted the roof slate. Nothing happened. Disgusted by his own fear, he threw it into the trees and grabbed the box before he could overthink it anymore.

The box was too light. Empty.

Something slammed into him from behind. His face smashed into the wall, but he twisted his head enough to avoid losing teeth. The impact winded him, stunned him, and Robbie McGuire's nasal whine buzzed in his ear.

'Message from the family, psycho. You're not...'

He slammed a fist into Callahan's right kidney.

'Fucking...'

Another punch, harder.

'Welcome, you mental bastard.'

Before a third punch could land, Callahan jabbed his elbow up and backwards. It slammed into flesh. He heard teeth snap off.

McGuire staggered back, clutching his mouth. Callahan swung a roundhouse kick at his head, slammed his steel toecap into his ear. McGuire went down.

Only then did he notice Robbie's more vicious and unstable brother, Mitch, and two others. One was Fat Frankie, his nose dressed, his bruised eyes furious. The other was Paul, a bouncer from Liam's strip bar, The Peach Pit. Even with an axe to grind, Fat Frankie was no real danger, but Paul was handy, a competition level kickboxer.

Mitch hissed at his brother. 'Robbie, you OK?'

Robbie tried to push himself up but flopped to the ground. His eyes rolled up white and he moaned.

Mitch barked at the other two. 'What you waiting for? Fuckin' do him. But don't kill him.'

He grabbed his brother's jacket collar and dragged him away, his eyes locked on Callahan.

Frankie and Paul squared up, but their eyes showed they'd not liked how he'd dealt with Robbie. They separated, presented two angles of attack, but neither moved closer, neither willing to make the first move. Callahan stood, his posture relaxed, ignored the agony in his back, flexed his fingers open and closed, eager for violence. A too-familiar growl started between his ears, but he dismissed it, cleared his mind, recalled Mitch's command, 'don't kill him.' Callahan, too, meant to finish this long before risking more death.

Mitch looked up from his brother and screamed at them. 'Will you pathetic wee lassies get that scrawny shite?'

Paul and Frankie shared one last worried look, then Frankie feinted a rush, as Paul dived at Callahan's legs.

Callahan rolled to the side and both men grabbed at empty air. Paul recovered first, launched himself again, aimed a rugby tackle at waist height.

Callahan rolled with the impact, wedged one foot in Paul's gut and launched him backwards over his head. He completed his reverse roll onto his feet as Paul landed on his back with a grunt, then dropped onto the man and slammed an elbow into his gut.

Paul clutched his stomach and agony hissed between his clenched teeth.

Callahan grinned. They'd asked for this, and that gave him the right to enjoy himself.

He turned to Fat Frankie, but an arm snared his neck from behind and more pain exploded in his back.

Mitch McGuire spoke, low and vicious. 'If my brother dies, you die.'

More blows slammed into him, felt like steel crowbars hammering at his now-bleeding wounds.

Rage exploded behind Callahan's eyes, but he refused to give in to it. He wanted it, yearned to kill the bastard. But something – maybe Bernard's Muzzles – anchored him, enabled him to contain the rage that surged up his throat.

He twisted his head a quarter turn and pushed his chin into the inside crook of Mitch's arm. The ape had such huge muscles Callahan easily found a gap between them to release the pressure on his throat. With a sideways push of his hips, he cleared space to lash back with his elbow, heard Mitch grunt. He rammed the heel of his other hand down and into Mitch's groin. The man's arm flew from his neck, and Callahan span to face him. His right hand jabbed hard, and Mitch staggered backwards, clutching at both groin and throat.

Mitch writhed on the ground. Callahan hadn't punched hard enough to collapse the man's airway, only enough to put him down for a few minutes.

Frankie was long gone, stumbling across the lawn towards the main house.

Mitch's wheezing stopped.

Too hard. He'd gone too far, again. Glassy, sightless eyes, a livid purple hollow where his throat had caved in, a chest that seconds ago had been heaving to draw breath, now still.

Sickening dread dropped into Callahan's guts, and as adrenaline drained from his system, exhaustion fell on him. He dropped to the sodden ground, one hand clutching at his wound, his back warm and wet.

As he fought to stop the world from pitching around him, Robbie McGuire moaned and clutched his ear, his eyes sluggish and vague. His lips moved but nothing intelligible came out.

Callahan grabbed him by the collar, screamed into his face. 'What the hell is going on, Robbie? Tell me or I swear I'll finish you.'

Robbie continued babbling, muttering low whining noises. His fingers probed his ear and came out bloody.

Callahan sat back to ease the pull on his wound. He felt blood soak his right thigh. From the lawn he heard voices, Frankie whining and a furious Jake swearing. Callahan heaved himself to his feet and staggered towards the trees but stopped. Could he reach the car conscious, let alone drive himself to safety to fix himself up?

He remembered a first-aid kit in the bathroom, pulled the spare key from his pocket and opened the door. As he ducked under the police tape, he spotted the empty box on the ground.

Seraxonine. Six months' supply issued two months ago.

Where are they, Jake?

He locked himself in then stuffed a tea towel under the tape to staunch his reopened wound and sat in a chair to one side of a window. His head swam. Fatigue and shock begged him to lie down and close his eyes. He pushed the towel deep, forced more agony from the wound, yanked himself back to consciousness.

Jake and Frankie appeared around the side of the cottage, and Callahan eased the window open an inch to watch and listen.

THIRTY-TWO

When Malkie arrived at the hospital, Colin Prendergast was in a flap.

'Mr McCulloch. Glad you're here. I nearly called in sick tonight. That guy should be here in fifteen minutes, but he might turn up early, eh? I wasn't—'

'Colin. Breathe.'

The nurse stopped, calmed himself. 'Sorry, Mr McCulloch.'

'Call me Malkie, son.'

'I'm nervous, you know? That guy looked rough.'

Malkie steered Colin to his seat behind the nurse station, sat him down, perched himself on the desk. 'What did he look like? You said he kept his face hidden, but did you get a look at him tonight?'

'Aye, he seemed shy. Like lost, you know? They're defo an item.'

'What makes you so sure?'

'It was the tears on the guy's face, Mr McCulloch. His cheeks were soaked, and you can't fake that.'

'Fair enough. You said he was fit?'

'Aye, looked like he could take care of himself.'

'And you told this man to stay away until nine, aye? Are there any other staff on duty tonight?'

Colin brightened, happy to be on more solid ground. 'Just me and Fiona, but she's got exams tomorrow, so I told her to take a long break and I'll buzz if I need her.'

Malkie reappraised the nervous young man sitting bolt upright in front of him. 'Not bad, Colin. I'm impressed.'

'And I told security I'm scared because Mr Wilkie's accident was no accident. They promised to get here quick if I hit the panic button.'

'Good work, Colin. Try to relax now. You mustn't seem nervous when this guy appears, OK?'

Colin relaxed. 'Time for a meds round. That'll keep my mind busy.'

'Good lad. Is Mr Wilkie in the same room?'

'Aye, room eight. I figured you can sit in the bathroom with the lights off, to wait.'

He laid a hand on Colin's shoulder and gave it a squeeze. 'You did good, Colin. Appreciate it, son.'

Colin didn't look convinced as he turned to the medication trolley.

In room eight, Wilkie looked much the same as the previous day – swathed in bandages, tubes sticking out of him everywhere. Machines blinked and pinged and traced various erratic threads that tied him to life.

Malkie switched off every light except a single Anglepoise above the bed. Wilkie's room and the bathroom fell into darkness. From the shadow of the bathroom, he had a clear view of Wilkie's bedside.

His mobile rang. He switched the damned thing off without looking at the screen.

. . .

Bang on nine, shadows flitted across the window from the corridor outside. Malkie braced himself. He'd report this to Steph in the morning, if only to cover his arse. But first, he needed something for himself, and for Amanda. Something to prove he wasn't risking everything for nothing.

He heard the door to Wilkie's room open and close, then a moment of silence. A man stepped to the bedside. As Colin had said, the man wore a hoodie pulled down over his forehead and moved like someone who worked out.

A chill started in Malkie's guts. What the hell was he thinking? Alone, with no backup, and about to confront a younger and almost certainly fitter bloke who seemed determined not to identify himself.

No, this wasn't fear. This was something else.

The man leaned over the battered husk in the bed, touched his forehead to Wilkie's own, and rested his fingertips on Wilkie's cheek. Tears dropped onto swollen and bruised eyelids that didn't react. Malkie noticed two gold rings on the man's left hand. Two wedding rings. It couldn't be...

His breath froze in his chest. Recognition slammed into him, winded him.

He stepped out of the bathroom.

'Hello, Liam,' he said, and then everything went to shit.

THIRTY-THREE

Callahan took some satisfaction from watching Jake take one look at the scene and going ballistic.

Paul's head snapped up. He stopped retching onto the grass and stood, with difficulty. Robbie got to his feet but leaned on Frankie, his eyes glassy, his knees unlocking and locking, ready to fold under him. Paul stepped to Robbie's side, stared at Jake as if expecting the worst.

Jake put two fingers to Mitch's neck and swore under his breath. He ran a hand through his thin grey hair and stared at the sky as if looking for divine guidance.

A tattoo of expletives belted out of him as he landed kick after kick on Mitch's corpse.

'Stupid. Useless. Fuckin'. Bastard.'

Robbie looked too terrified to protect his dead brother's dignity.

Callahan choked on bile; two men now dead at his hands.

Jake bent over, clutched his knees, coughed and hacked until he gobbed a mouthful into a handkerchief from his pocket. He stared at the three men, his face scarlet and murder in his eyes.

'I should kettle every bloody one of you.'

Frankie looked ready to throw up. Paul's mouth clamped shut into a thin, hard line.

Callahan had seen Jake lose it this badly only once before. He'd learned that day never to come between a man like him and a fifteen-year-old Iraqi girl trapped in a cellar.

Jake aimed the torch beam straight into Paul's eyes, then switched to Frankie.

'You, arsehole, get him' – he pointed the torch at Robbie – 'up to the house, put him in the kitchen. Second thoughts – put him in the garage. Moron's bleedin' everywhere.'

Frankie looked relieved to be dismissed. He shouldered Robbie's arm and dragged the man, stumbling, away towards the house.

Jake turned to Paul. His eyes lost some of their rage, but danger glittered in them still.

'I expect better from you, Paul.'

Callahan felt fresh heat spread down his back. He pushed harder on the tea towel. Agony forced a hiss of air through his teeth, until he bit down on the noise. Sweat dripped from his forehead and soaked his shirt. He needed to clean and re-dress the wound or he might not see tomorrow. Exhaustion whispered to him – lie down, in his own bed, finish his good Scotch, and sleep.

Jake's voice yanked him back to the present. He peered through the window to see him standing over Mitch again, hands on his hips, studying the body and surrounding ground.

Paul waited, looked ready to puke.

'Did any of you geniuses even hurt him?'

Paul nodded. 'Aye, Mr Fielding. Robbie battered his face into the wall, and Mitch punched him where Frankie said he stabbed him.'

'Show me where.'

195

Paul looked confused, moved one hand to his own back before getting the idea.

Jake stared at him, incredulous, as Paul stepped to the window. Callahan leaned sideways and melted into the darkness.

Paul pointed to the wall off to the left. Jake studied it, nodded, then tracked backwards, scanning the ground.

'OK, there's some of his blood there. The Pigs don't need much these days. Did *you* bleed anywhere?'

'No, Mr Fielding. Just winded.'

'Good. Right, listen. Liam asked you to watch the grounds in case Callahan showed his face. You were to warn him. Nothing more than that, got it?'

Paul nodded as if his life depended on getting it.

'Mitch went to do a circuit of the grounds, right?'

Paul nodded.

'When he stayed away too long, you came down here and found him like this, and no one else. Repeat that back to me.'

Paul did.

'Where did Robbie go down?'

Paul pointed. Jake examined the ground, shone the torch into the grass. Eventually, he stood and nodded to himself.

'OK. Leave Mitch where he is. You got a blade on you?'

Paul produced a kitchen knife, a screwdriver, and a chisel, all unbloodied. He had the decency to look sheepish. Jake snatched the screwdriver from him and approached the door. Callahan slid to his right so he could watch.

Jake rattled the door handle and panic shot through Callahan – had he locked it? The door held. He released his breath.

Jake worked at the doorframe with the screwdriver but didn't go as far as forcing the lock. He stepped back, studied his handiwork, crisscrossed the clearing, his hands gesturing as if working up a feasible story, locking it in. Paul stood, mute, throughout.

Jake nodded. 'Right, find that pillbox, and come up to the garage. I'll sort those other useless pricks out. If Robbie can't keep the same story straight, we're all fucked.'

Paul turned to look for the box. Jake headed back towards the house.

Before he knew what he was doing, Callahan grabbed the phone mounted on the wall, couldn't risk using his mobile with its backlit screen. He punched the quick dial for Jake's mobile. He'd set the landline to withhold his number years ago and congratulated himself on that small measure of foresight.

Jake's phone rang, a piercing shriek in the quiet of the night. He pulled his phone out, read the display, swore under his breath.

'No number. It's him, I know it.' He pressed a button, and the call connected.

'Hello, Jake. Thanks for the welcome-home party. Sorry I couldn't stay.'

Jake span on the spot, stared into the dark shadows between the trees, then backed up next to Paul.

'You think this was me? I left the pills like we agreed, mate. It must have been Liam. I don't know what the hell's going on in his head anymore, and I'm cleaning up his mess again.'

Jake shuffled from one foot to the other, his hand flexing and clutching his walking stick. 'Walter, I'll make this right, mate. The lad's been all over the place recently. You and me go back too far. We can fix this, even after what you did on Sunday.'

Callahan watched Jake fret before asking, 'What did happen on Sunday, mate?'

'You tell me. We played poker, watched the boxing, drank too much Grouse, then you passed out on the sofa. Liam and me went to

197

bed and I heard you drive off later, which I thought was weird, you driving after a drink. Next thing I know, the Pigs are at my door harassing Liam again, and I find out you've run someone over in one of our cars. It's you that's got some explaining to do, don't you think?'

Something in his tone rang off-key, something he wasn't saying.

'Why can't I remember, Jake?' He took a breath, wasn't sure what answer he wanted to his next question. 'Did you spike my drink?'

A long silence answered the question before Jake replied. 'I gave you a wee sweetie, aye, to help you relax.'

Callahan nearly slammed his fist into the wall. 'Damn it, Jake. We've talked about this before. What was it?'

'Ach, nothing heavy. You needed something.'

Callahan struggled to hold his temper – he needed answers. 'What time did you go back to the house?'

'About eleven. I was in bed when...'

A pause. 'When what, Jake?'

'I told you. You drove away out of the estate. When you came home, your car was all over the place. Since when did you drive that drunk, man?'

The world lurched. The Dog stirred. Callahan hung up.

Jake called his name into his mobile, then stuffed it back in his pocket. His eyes scanned the tree line, then he hobbled away towards the main house.

Callahan fetched his medic kit from the bathroom and tried the wall-cabinet again, in case he and the police had missed some Seraxonine, but he found none.

He peeled his shirt off, then took his time removing the tape, made it hurt, punishment for his stupidity. Blood seeped from a broken crust. He cleaned it, rough and furious, soaked it in antiseptic, and slapped on clean dressings and fresh tape.

Jake had the meds he needed but had betrayed him.

He turned on us. Kill him.

He shook his head, refused to allow his conscience the salve of blaming *It*.

He had work to do. He needed Jake's meds, and he needed to know what kind of 'wee sweetie' had turned his Sunday night so bad.

THIRTY-FOUR

Malkie and Liam Fielding stood beside their cars on a shingle beach west of South Queensferry. Malkie gazed across the brooding, black mass of the Forth Estuary to the lights of Fife and wondered how the hell he should handle this.

'So, what now, Liam?'

'What do you mean, what now?'

'I mean, what now? Even you must realise this changes things. Even you're not that stupid.'

'Fuck you, McCulloch.'

'Well, that's progress, at least.'

Fielding looked at him, confusion battling with anger in his eyes.

Malkie shrugged. 'I prefer that to McFuckup.'

Fielding deflated, leaned back against the front of Malkie's car. He lifted his beer, downed half the bottle, then lifted his face to the sky and closed his eyes. Moisture leaked from his eyes. Malkie gave his mouth a rest, waited until Liam broke the silence.

'How's your lip?'

Malkie touched it with his fingertips. It had stopped bleeding. 'I'll live. Did you have to bloody belt me?'

'You surprised me, what do you expect?'

'I should charge you with assaulting a police officer.'

'Aye, but then you'd have to explain why you were there. You're off the case, remember?'

'Aye. No need to rub it in.'

They stood in silence, Malkie not sure where to start – *Don't screw this up.*

Fielding sighed. 'Fine, I admit I care about Robin, OK?'

'I saw that. So, at least show him the respect of accepting you're in love with him, Liam.'

Fielding exploded. 'I'm not gay, McCulloch. You say that again, I'll fuckin' kill you.'

Malkie held his hands up, placatory. 'OK, fine. You're not gay.'

Fielding's eyes locked onto Malkie's, dared him to step over a line.

It took only seconds for Malkie's inner idiot to win. 'You're just in an intimate relationship with a homosexual man, I get that.'

Fielding stomped away to the waterside. Malkie congratulated himself on another fine deployment of his legendary absence of tact. He gave Liam a few seconds, then approached him.

They stared across the water together. Fielding's breathing slowed. He let out a long sigh and squeezed his fingers into his eyes.

'Why did we come to this dump, anyway?'

Malkie swept his hand across the scene before them, as if the answer was self-evident. 'This is my favourite place. I come here when I'm struggling. Which is all the bloody time these days.'

Fielding's expression softened and his shoulders loosened.

Malkie gestured over his shoulder. 'There used to be a chain across the entrance to this wee beach, probably ordered by the toffs up at Hopetoun House, too many riffraff leaving Buckie bottles and needles around. But someone kicked the poles down years ago and the chain got mashed into the mud. You can hardly see it now.'

Fielding's lip curled. 'I know how it feels.'

He noticed Malkie staring at him and set his face hard again.

The lights of Rosyth twinkled like will-o'-the-wisps on the dark, choppy water of the Forth. Waves lapped at the small stretch of shingle shore, rhythmic and soothing.

Malkie tried to twist the top off his beer bottle, failed, and hurt his hand. Fielding took it from him, prised it off with a key, and returned it.

'So that's how you do it.' Malkie took a swig from his bottle, hated it, but didn't let on. 'My dad used to bring me here at the weekends. We got hot pies and cold milk from the bakery and drove here for lunch.' He smiled, lost for a moment in better times.

Liam sighed. 'Mine took me to dog fights. And boxing matches. We had pies too, but he made me drink lager, said milk is for poofs.'

As Amanda had claimed, there was tension there, but was it nothing to do with family business after all? Bigoted pig of a father and a gay son. Did Jake know? Did the old bastard send Callahan to scare Wilkie off, but Callahan went too far? Was that what Amanda heard them fighting about? Or was she already aware of Wilkie and how much she could hurt her bastard of a husband by—

He shut down his line of thinking, took another drag from his bottle, nearly gagged.

'I hate beer.'

'Nobody likes beer at first. Same with fags.'

Malkie glanced at him.

Fielding shrugged. 'Cigarettes.'

Both men smiled, but only for seconds.

'Do you think your dad knows about you and Wilkie?'

'If he knows, he'd have said something by now. And he's not going to hear about it. Is he?'

They stared across the water again, in a strange parody of companionable silence. Malkie's mind worked hard. Was Liam lying now? Or showing a scrap of trust? There could be no doubt he was guilty as hell somehow, but this new information complicated everything.

Malkie pointed out over the Forth. 'There used to be a passenger ferry sailed from Grangemouth to Holland.'

'Belgium.'

'Aye, that's it. Was impressive, something that massive, turning on the spot and lumbering away out to sea. I always expected it to get stuck under the bridges, but I watched it from above one time, and it came nowhere near. Funny how things look so different from a different perspective, eh?'

Fielding turned on him. 'Oh, fuck off, McCulloch. You think I'm a moron? Enough with the amateur psychiatry. Ask me what you want to ask.'

Malkie suppressed a comment that might have ended the conversation, let Liam continue.

'You want to know about me and Robin, right?'

'Aye, now I know what you meant to each other.'

'Mean.'

Malkie stared, confused. 'Eh?'

'What we mean to each other. Not meant.'

'Fair point. Sorry.'

Fielding stared at him as if searching for any sign he was taking the piss but seemed to accept the apology at face value.

'I'm not gay. Disgusting perverts. The way they fuck around, spreading diseases.'

Malkie took a breath. Was Liam just parroting his father's poison, the bigotry he'd had hammered into him since before he could even think for himself? 'Liam, HIV isn't a death sentence these days. Some people live long, long lives with HIV. And straight people spread diseases, too. As for fucking around, I suspect homosexual men are just as monogamous as hetero-sexual men.' *Do you even know what monogamous means, Liam?*

'Will you ever accept you're gay, Liam?'

Fielding grabbed a handful of Malkie's jacket in one hand and pulled the other back, ready to slam his bottle into Malkie's face.

'I'm not. Fuckin'. Gay.'

His eyes glittered with hate. Spit flew from his lips.

Malkie raised his hands in surrender. 'Fine, you're not gay. Got it.'

Fielding let go of him and stepped away. His shoulders heaved until he got his breathing under control.

In a quiet voice he said, 'I'm not a pervert.'

Malkie straightened his jacket and tucked his tie in. 'Whatever you say. Tell me what's on that memory card, then. Why did Wilkie have it?'

Fielding heaved in a breath, and the look on his face stopped Malkie dead. He'd expected denial, feigned ignorance, barefaced lies. He saw pain. No doubting it – Fielding knew Wilkie had the memory card, and it was his fault his partner now lay comatose in hospital. But why?

Malkie waited, willed Fielding to unburden himself, but defiance replaced the self-loathing in the man's eyes.

'I told you – copies of Callahan's psychiatric reports.'

'How did Mr Wilkie get them?'

Malkie watched him try to come up with something, but neither Fielding was ever the sharpest knife in the cutlery drawer.

'Liam?'

He gave up. 'I've got no idea, McCulloch.'

Malkie's shite detector went into overdrive. 'Is Wilkie involved in your business dealings? Is that how you met him? Did you ask your dad to sort someone out and you didn't know that person was Robin? Is that it? Is it your fault Wilkie's in the state he's in?'

Before Malkie could talk sense into his own inner idiot, he went for the big one.

'Was it you? Did you run down your own partner? Did Jake send you to hurt someone based on half-arsed intel and you didn't know it was your own bloody lover? Was that what I saw in you yesterday morning?'

Tears spilled from Fielding's eyes. He wiped them on his wrist, folded his arms and bowed his head.

Malkie recognised self-loathing when he saw it, but any possibility of shared empathy between the two men stopped there. It was obvious that Fielding was neck-deep in Robin Wilkie's attempted murder, regardless of fingerprints or Callahan's reputation or manufactured alibis. Self-loathing implied guilt. Fielding drove that car, there could be no doubt about that. At best, Jake sent him to hurt someone, and he failed to recognise his own lover until it was too late. But his culpability didn't stop at the point of that realisation.

'Talk to me, man.'

Liam sounded broken. 'It's my fault Robin got hurt. Is that what you want to hear?'

Malkie reeled inside. A confession. Qualified, but a confession nonetheless.

'I bloody knew it. But why, Liam? Tell me the rest. How, exactly, did it happen?'

Fielding's eyes burned into Malkie's, racked with self-hatred and – hopefully – desperation to unburden himself.

Tell me, Liam. I know what it's like, trapped in a mess of your own making and hurting like hell to escape. I know.

For a second, he thought Fielding might crumble, but the man closed in on himself again, clutched his chest, his voice weak and weary.

'I can't tell you.' His voice tailed off, thick with grief. His breath heaved in and out of him, shuddering and laboured. When his crisis passed, Malkie tried again.

'Is it something to do with the arguments between you and your dad?'

As he said the words, he cursed his own stupidity.

Liam's head lifted, his eyes blazing. 'How do you know about that? You've heard from that wee skank, haven't you? Where is she?'

Malkie waited him out.

'How do you know it wasn't her? Maybe she found out about Robin and did it to get at me. You know she's hurt people before, aye?'

Despite the huge backwards step, Malkie let Fielding play this out. 'You think she'd go that far?'

'Wouldn't put anything past that bitch. She's not as sweet as she makes out. Where's my fuckin' wife, McCulloch?'

Malkie turned on his heel, walked towards his car emptying his beer onto the ground. 'She called me, but I have no idea where she is. Shouldn't *you* know?'

Fielding said nothing.

Malkie stopped, turned back, raised one eyebrow, queried his sudden silence.

Fielding considered him. 'Why aren't you after Callahan? It's bloody obvious he did it. Why are you trying to nail me for it?'

Malkie pulled his keys from his pocket, dangled them on one finger, his other on the car door, a silent threat to end the conversation.

Fielding stared at the keys as if hypnotised, then he looked at Malkie with realisation in his eyes. 'You really don't think he did it.' His tone was incredulous.

Malkie leaned against his car. 'Why would Callahan run down Wilkie? There's only circumstantial evidence for that, and nothing resembling a motive except your dodgy story about psychiatric reports. No one's identified him. You both had pool cars out that night, and us finding the damaged one right outside his cottage was convenient but doesn't prove he parked it there. He makes one hell of a stooge, doesn't he? A loner with PTSD and a reputation for violence?'

Fielding was incredulous. 'Where is this shite coming from? I told you – I left my Aston at the yard and took a pool car to the Armadale speedway. I can't park a ninety-grand car there. Yesterday morning my Aston was at home and my pool car was back in the yard. So, it had to be Callahan.'

Malkie smiled. 'Funny, that's pretty much word for word what Derek Woodburn said.'

Fielding raged at the sky. 'For fuck's sake, it's the same story because it's true. You've got such a hard-on to nail me you're making something out of nothing. I parked my Aston at the yard, took a pool car to Armadale, drove it back to the yard, then I drove home in my own car. And that's it!' his last words screamed in Malkie's face.

Malkie smiled. 'You have quite a temper, don't you, Liam?'

Fielding's eyes turned devious. 'Not as bad as yours, McFuckup, and I've got that on video.'

Malkie ignored the bait. 'You know what? You're right. I am going to bloody nail you. I know you're up to your rotten neck in this, but how? Tell me, Liam. Save us both a lot of shite.'

Fielding stared. His jaw clenched. Tendons tightened in his neck. His fingers clutched at air at his sides.

Malkie hoped Fielding might snap, spill his guts, let something slip, but a phone shrieked and both men jumped.

Fielding held his mobile to his ear, his eyes locked on Malkie's.

'He's what? Aw, for fuck's sake. I'll come home.' He pocketed the phone, glared at Malkie.

'What's happened?'

As Fielding headed for his car, he yelled at Malkie. 'Do your bloody job and catch that psycho.'

The Aston's engine roared, then it wheel-spun and fishtailed away towards South Queensferry.

Malkie chewed over his options. Try to follow the Aston or stay away? Every scrap of him wanted to see what had rattled the man, but Steph's warnings played on a loop between his ears.

Follow? Or stay away?

Sod it, Amanda needed him.

THIRTY-FIVE

Callahan only realised he'd passed out when he fell off his chair.

He'd dragged the chair to a front window to watch the main house. Twice he'd drifted off. Blood loss and exhaustion threatened to leave him oblivious and defenceless. With a mug of coffee so strong it caught at his throat, he swallowed two more of Bernard's Muzzles.

He dug out his binoculars– original army-issue Avimos still in perfect working order – and set them on the window-ledge.

As he fought to stay awake, his mind tormented him with questions he had no answers to. Jake or Liam must have sent him into Livingston that night. He could see no other explanation. For eleven years, his trips into town had consisted of driving to the depot, working, then getting the hell out again before dark. He never breathed easy until dual carriageways and roundabouts fell away in his rear-view mirror and the hulking, brooding mass of the Pentlands stretched ahead of him.

But now two people had died at his hands in three days: the hit-and-run victim – whoever that was – and Mitch McGuire. And that kick to Robbie's head might yet kill him, too.

He heard the low, throaty growl of Liam's Aston turn into the estate and charge down the drive. Headlights slashed across the lawn then away again as the car fish-tailed to a stop in front of the house. Looked like Liam had heard about tonight's events, and he might think to check inside the cottage.

Callahan downed the rest of his coffee and set the mug on the floor. His Avimos brought the interior of Jake's lounge into sharp view. Best binoculars ever made, good gear and looked after. Liam entered the living room, stood before Jake. An argument erupted, Liam losing the plot, Jake slouched in his battered old armchair.

He itched to hear them, but he couldn't risk moving closer – every security floodlight along the roofline blazed tonight.

Liam stood over his dad, raging. Jake jabbed a thumb over his shoulder, towards the cottage. Liam threw his arms up then squeezed his fingers into his eyes. He grabbed a bottle from a drinks cabinet – a chrome and diamanté monstrosity that reflected the family to perfection – then dumped himself in another chair, opened the bottle and took several long swallows.

Jake spoke. Liam held out the bottle as if to say 'What, this?' then took another long swallow.

More inaudible words, then Liam sagged as if beaten. Liam spoke again and Jake surged forward in his chair. Liam held his hands up, and Jake relaxed again.

Jake waved one hand as if to dismiss a matter, heaved himself to his feet, grabbed his stick, walked to the French doors, and stared out the window. For a moment, Callahan feared his Avimo's lenses would reflect the security lights, but the brilliant white beams illuminated only the thirty feet of lawn closest to the house.

Liam stared at his father's back for a minute then left the room. Jake took a mobile phone from his pocket and dialled a number. He sipped his drink, stared out through the doors.

After a few exchanges, Jake looked at the phone, held it to his ear, looked at it again, then threw it across the room, slammed it against the wall.

What's your precious son done to get you so rattled, Jake?

THIRTY-SIX

Malkie grabbed the door handle and, for the fifth time, let it go again.

His phone buzzed in his pocket, third time in thirty minutes. He ignored it, again, couldn't imagine any call he'd want to take right now.

The takeaway food on the passenger seat would be cold soon and Amanda must be hungry. Poor, desperate, terrified Amanda. The porthole curtains on the *Droopy Goose* glowed soft and warm in a mist shrouding the pontoons. He hated how strongly those lights drew him.

He should call Steph, share what info he could, but she would take only seconds to realise there was more he wasn't telling her. He couldn't mention Fielding and Wilkie either. He shouldn't have been anywhere near Wilkie, or his mystery visitor he'd said nothing about to the case team. Which – as of five hours ago – didn't include him.

If the truth got out, he'd say he visited Wilkie out of nothing more than professional concern. Feeble, but not disprovable. No one knew he had Amanda stashed on the boat, and he had to hope she had the sense not to show her face in South Queensferry.

Every way he spun it, the situation could only get worse if he confessed all to Steph, though he loathed himself for shutting her out. He needed to capitalise on this information, to find something worth taking to her, and Callahan was now his only hope. If he had anything to do with Wilkie's attack, Fielding or his dad had to have put him up to it. Was he guilty of nothing more than a damaged mind and shite taste in mates?

Fielding's and McLeish's comments intruded. Could he trust Amanda? Was she playing an angle of her own, not as fragile as she appeared? Did she hate her husband enough to punish him for years of abuse? He shook his head, chased away the thoughts. He'd seen her as no one else had – raw and exposed, her broken dignity laid bare. She couldn't fake that, could she? But then, that phone call she'd made...

He shook himself. Every other line of reasoning led to Liam Fielding: the state they found him in yesterday morning, his direct – and intimate – link to Wilkie, and his cryptic confession that Wilkie's current trauma was his fault.

But how, damn it?

Did he run down his own lover without realising who he was? Or did Jake send an unstable and violent Callahan to scare Wilkie off, or to retrieve the memory card? Either way, Liam Fielding had dragged Wilkie onto his family's radar, and he was culpable.

Malkie grabbed the door handle for the sixth time and told himself to grow the hell up. He owed Amanda a duty of care. She'd put her safety in his hands. The last people who depended on him – one was dead, the other left alone in a hospital room for far too long. Life with his dad might be fixable, but Malkie could never undo his negligence. He wasn't sure he'd survive Amanda becoming one more stain on his conscience.

He lifted the takeaway bag and threw the door open, slammed it shut, locked it, and strode down the pontoons like a man determined to face at least one responsibility head-on. He just hoped he didn't find her on the phone, again.

When he slid the hatch back, Amanda leapt up from the couch, confused, her eyes bleary. Her phone lay on the cushion beside her.

'Jesus, Malkie. Warn me next time. What happened to your mouth?'

'Nothing. Shoplifter.' He descended into the cabin, slid the hatch closed, and made an obvious show of pushing in the latch. 'You're safe here, Amanda.'

She rubbed her eyes, yawned, then stared at him in alarm. 'No. I fell asleep. Anyone could have got in here.' Tears welled in her eyes. He reached for her without thinking. She folded herself into him, her arms clutched between them as if holding her heart together. She sobbed, buried her face in his shirt, her chest heaving against his.

There's no way she's faking this. I know what fake tears feel like.

He gathered her into him, and she responded, slipped her arms inside his jacket and pulled herself into him. He lowered his face to her hair, breathed her in, nearly gasped in a sudden, excruciating craving for her. Heat flooded him, and shame; none of this could be right.

He broke, eased away from him, lifted her chin with his fingers.

'You're safe here, Amanda.'

She sniffed, wiped her nose on the back of her hand. He tore a sheet from a kitchen roll and handed it to her, then steered her backwards, sat her on the couch, took his jacket off and laid it across his lap as he sat beside her.

She blew her nose – a loud, wet snort. Then sneezed.

Malkie smiled. 'Bless you.'

She smiled, her cheeks wet with tears. 'Thank you.'

He squeezed her arm, smiled with affection he didn't need to force.

She bowed her head. 'So much for the big brave wife of hard man Liam Fielding, eh?'

The smiles disappeared, the moment soured. Malkie ignored thoughts of her cautions for assault, had no time for them. Amanda fidgeted with her tissue, folding it over and over. When she headed for the toilet, Malkie noticed her phone left on the seat beside him. He couldn't help himself. He pressed the button to wake it. *What the hell am I expecting to see?* He angled it to read the display, saw nothing of interest, and certainly nothing from any Marjorie.

'What are you doing?' Amanda's eyes flashed with anger, but he saw worse there, too. Disappointment, confusion, fear of the very betrayal he intended for her.

'Sorry. I thought I heard it buzz.' He placed it on the table, couldn't hold her gaze. He clapped his hands together, reached for the takeaway bags. 'You hungry?'

She stared at him for longer than he thought he could bear, but eventually came to some kind of decision. 'Did you get Chicken Chasni?'

He grinned. 'I bloody love Chicken Chasni.'

She pulled two plates from a cupboard. He pulled foil trays and spoons from the bags and pulled off the lids. Aromatic steam filled the cabin. He stuck one spoon in the rice and handed her another.

'Dig in.'

She smiled – grateful, maybe even fond, but hesitant, too. He'd have to work hard to recover from his appalling breach of her trust.

He pressed the button on the radio behind the couch. Soft, sultry music played. He read the DAB display. Smooch FM.

'You like your curry a bit cheesy?'

She laughed, nearly spat a mouthful at him. 'Shut up, it relaxes me.'

They ate in an uneasy silence. A conversation would have to follow, but for now they seemed to enjoy an illusion of normality, the comfort of companionship.

He pulled a bottle of Pinot from the other bag, twisted the top off and filled two plastic beakers. He'd prefer Coke but sharing a bottle of wine felt more grown-up.

Malkie raised his beaker. 'Here's to just deserts.'

Her smile disappeared.

Idiot. Nothing spoiled a girl's appetite quicker than a reminder of her vicious and abusive husband.

She put her drink down, untouched.

You. Fucking. Moron.

He carried on eating, but the silence had changed, each mouthful now a countdown to an ugly conversation.

Amanda managed another few mouthfuls, then pushed her tray away and turned to face him.

He pretended not to notice, poked at bits of chicken with his spoon. When he pushed his food away, her eyes locked onto his. No anger, no impatience, only misery and a determination to hear the worst.

He sipped his wine once, grimaced, didn't bother to hide his distaste.

She leaned into him, wrapped her arms around his, rested her cheek on his shoulder.

Damn it. Here we go again...

'Tell me.' Her voice was small and fearful.

He couldn't make her wait any longer. 'I met Robin Wilkie's boyfriend.'

Her grip on his arm tightened then relaxed again. Hope. A straw to clutch at.

How would she react? Would she go off on one? Or might

the revelation trigger some memory she didn't realise might be relevant?

'Robin Wilkie's boyfriend is—'

He choked on the words, struggled despite having seen it himself. How ridiculous would it sound to the man's own brutalised wife?

'It's Liam, Amanda.'

He waited, not sure what to expect.

'Ah. Right.'

This threw him. 'Eh?'

She sat up. 'That holiday he took me on? He got arrested at a beach bar by the local police. They found him blind drunk and ranting about perverts and deviants.'

He saw where this was going. 'The Copa Banana?'

She stared at him. Her eyes demanded an explanation.

'Robin Wilkie has a photo of himself and his chums at The Copa Banana. I'd bet my pension that's where Liam met him.'

'Or he knew Wilkie already, and they arranged to meet there.'

This hadn't occurred to him. How long had Liam been hiding his secret? Or hiding from it?

'When did you realise, Amanda?' *Or did you always know? And did you want Liam punished?*

Her eyes fell; he'd touched a nerve.

'He was never a considerate lover, selfish, always desperate to get himself off, then go back to ignoring me. And it was always' – she swallowed, took a breath – 'cruel. Like he wanted to fuck me but hated me for it.'

Fresh tears filled her eyes. He took her hand. It was soft and warm, and she clasped his fingers. They were crossing a line and she must know it. If she wanted to share such intimacy with him, she must feel safe, must trust him.

'About a year ago he started doing other things to me. Things I begged him not to. Things that hurt.'

She couldn't say more. Shame bowed her head. Her tears dropped onto both their hands. She wept, quiet and ashamed. Malkie couldn't speak. Fury flooded him. A rare and precious soul like Amanda, and Fielding could only abuse her and brutalise her, punish her for his own shame. Considering the weight of Liam's secret and his fear of its discovery by his bigoted pig of a father, Malkie had almost felt sorry for him. Not now. Even if her suffering did offer a motive for involvement in Robin Wilkie's attack – *No. She couldn't have* – who could blame her for wanting to punish Liam for years of abuse?

'Listen, Amanda. Even if Liam finds you, he won't touch you, not now. He knows if he hurts you, I'll leak his secret. And then I'll kill him.'

She smiled. A weak smile, but it stopped her tears. 'But he'll report you for harassing him again and hiding me. Won't that hurt you?'

It would, more than she knew. 'Nah, I'll be fine. They won't sack an experienced and gifted CID all-star like me.'

She smiled – she obviously knew shite when she heard it.

'I've heard Liam's side. Now I need to find Callahan. I think one of them went to retrieve that memory card, and either Callahan went psycho, or Liam didn't realise who he was driving at until it was too late. It would explain the state he's been in, running over his own boyfriend. But he won't tell me what's on the memory card and we can't hack into it. He claims it's psychiatric reports on Callahan from some army doctor.'

'The LESOC,' she said.

'The what?'

'Lothians Ex-Services Outreach Centre. Somewhere called Airngath Hill? Our postie stopped delivering to the cottage after she met Walter on a bad day. She leaves the mail at the house now. I saw letters from the LESOC every month. I was nosy, so I looked them up.'

'You'd make a brilliant detective, you know that?'

He smiled at her. Fondness welled in him, so intense it hurt.

He thumbed the power button on his phone to look up the LESOC. The screen stayed black, except for an empty battery symbol.

He opened a drawer under the hob, hunted for a charger, dumping junk on the worktop as he rummaged.

Amanda stood, moved beside him, picked through the clutter. He found the charger and turned around. She held a wooden frame, her eyes locked on the photo, her face ashen. He knew what she held, and a shitty feeling washed over him.

A newspaper cutting showed Malkie and McLeish, celebrating the infamous arrest of the All Boys. Amanda's trembling finger rested on McLeish.

'Who's this?'

'My boss, McLeish. Why?'

She stared at him, appalled.

'That's the man Liam's been meeting.'

THIRTY-SEVEN

Callahan waited an hour after the last light went dark, then crept around the tree line to the garage and along the back of the building, hugging the wall to avoid triggering the floodlights. He found the French door with the faulty lock, the one Paul was supposed to have fixed months ago. A shove with his blade forced the mechanism. The door swung in, noiseless on well-oiled hinges. He closed it behind him but left it unlatched. He crossed the room on the balls of his feet, his senses buzzing, peered around the doorframe, down the hallway. No lights, all quiet.

He crept upstairs. The woodwork was exquisite, expensive, no danger of creaky treads, but he hugged the wall. At the top, hallways ran left and right. Jake and Liam slept at opposite ends of the house. He turned right and crept to Jake's bedroom. No lights under the door, no sound from inside.

He pushed down on the door handle. The door swung open.

Sloppy, Jake.

He stepped onto the deep pile of the bedroom carpet, eased

the door closed and locked it, winced at the heavy click as it engaged.

Jake lay under a single thin sheet, despite the chill air wafting in through an open window. He slept like a child, curled up and foetal. So much for the criminal legend that was Jake Fielding.

Callahan crossed to the massive bathroom. He sneered in disgust; all the marble and gold plate in the world couldn't elevate a man like Jake beyond the lout he'd always be.

In a wall cabinet he found enough medicines to fill a pharmacy. Jars and tubes and boxes crowded the shelves, but no Seraxonine.

The world pitched around him. Nausea set his head spinning. He clutched at the sink, locked his knees to stop himself collapsing to the floor.

Back in the bedroom, Jake slept on. Callahan grabbed a pair of socks from the floor and tucked them into a ball. He stepped up onto the mattress, then dropped to his knees on Jake's chest, stuffed the socks into the old man's gaping mouth, and pinned his arms to his sides. His other hand clamped on Jake's throat, enough to hurt without choking him.

Jake's eyes snapped opened, terrified, confused. He thrashed and jerked but had no strength in his thin, old arms. When he realised who was sitting on top of him, he froze.

'Where's the meds, Jake?' He tightened his grip. Jake's eyes bulged as he struggled, too feeble to break free. Callahan eased off and Jake sucked oxygen in through his nostrils, wheezing and snorting.

'I'm going to take the socks out. You shout, I hurt you.' He pulled the socks out.

'You fuckin' maniac, Walter. What—'

Callahan slapped him. 'Try again.'

Jake's eyes flared then turned feral – nobody laid a hand on Jake Fielding. 'I sold them to Bernie Robertson.'

Callahan punched him, hard enough to hurt like hell without breaking his few remaining teeth. 'One last chance, Jake. And forget Norrie Wallace, I've seen him, too.'

'Stop hitting me, you fucking psycho.'

He struggled, but he was pinned. He gave up, went limp. 'I gave them to Liam and told him to make sure you got them.'

The second punch snapped a tooth off.

Jake's mouth gaped in agony. Blood spilled from his gum. 'Fuck's sake, Walter. It's the truth.'

Callahan felt the familiar ache build at the back of his head. If it moved forward Jake might die, right here. He couldn't afford that, couldn't risk adding another death to his tally.

'The box was empty.'

Jake said nothing, too busy probing his gums for gaps.

'You going to tell me Liam arranged that welcoming party, too?'

Jake's eyes feigned surprise, which looked nothing but wrong. 'I didn't know, I swear. I told him to leave the pills and stay away. If he told the boys to hurt you, he's even lying to *me* now. When I found out, I cleaned up after him like all the other times, and that's all. He's my flesh and blood but if I knew he'd pull this stupid stunt I would have stopped him. We're mates, aren't we?'

Callahan's fury surged, demanded retribution. 'Was it your boys?'

'Aye, they told me after you got away. I told Liam he was a bloody idiot, told him not to try anything that stupid again. Are you OK, mate? Did they hurt you?'

Callahan's temper snapped, bloomed into a hunger for Jake's blood. The edge of his blade could open his scrawny neck in a second.

Do it. Bleed him.

He grabbed hold of *It*, muzzled it, beat it down. He had to

222

get a grip. He'd open his own throat before letting them put him away again.

He lowered his face to Jake's. 'Why use that screwdriver on the back door, then?'

Realisation dawned on him. 'You were still there? You were fuckin' watching?'

Callahan stared at him, gave him nothing.

Jake screamed. 'Liam—'

Callahan stuffed the socks back into Jake's mouth. Jake thrashed under him, found surprising strength from a deep instinct to save his own skin, until a right-hand upper cut silenced him.

Callahan listened, heard nothing for long moments, then the door handle rattled.

'Dad?' Liam's voice, more irritated than worried, then an impact on the door.

Callahan leapt off the bed and crossed to the window, cast his gaze once more around the room, desperate for any insight into the hiding place of Jake's pills.

Another impact and the hinges loosened in the frame. On the third, the door burst inwards. Liam's eyes swung from Callahan, halfway out the window, to his father looking more dead than unconscious.

Callahan slipped through the window, slid down the roof tiles of the lower storey and dropped to the ground. His wound complained, but he sprinted away across the lawn with his headache screaming like a vice around his brain.

He staggered back to the cottage and downed the last two of Bernard's Muzzles. At his discharge medical, a bored MO had warned him never to overdose, and his heart hammered at his ribs now, but he ignored it, couldn't afford to come down. Not yet. He fled his home for the third time in three days, before Liam came looking for him.

He had only one chance left now.

THIRTY-EIGHT

After a long, sleepless night under a single sheet on the saloon sofa, Malkie left without hearing a sound from Amanda in the forward cabin. He considered waking her with a coffee, but then he might not leave for another hour, and he had work to do.

The Lothians Ex-Services Outreach Centre sat behind thick stands of trees on the north slope of Airngath Hill. Malkie rounded a bend in the wooded drive and a two-storey mock-baronial stately pile appeared. Even this early, lights burned in most of the windows. Bowling-green-perfect lawns surrounded the property, interrupted only by the approach drive edged with whitewashed boulders. A flagpole soared fifty feet and a saltire flapped, slow and lazy, in the chilly November breeze. The place exuded discipline and order, but flowerbeds and bark chippings softened the severity of it all. Ducks floated on the surface of a small pond. They watched him, looked bored but curious, as he drove up.

Five minutes trawling the internet last night had revealed the sorry tale behind it. The house once belonged to some toff whose only son returned from Iraq blinded and minus his legs.

The boy opened his wrists a month after coming home and his mother – also a military widow – fell apart. She gifted the property, with a life-time granny-flat clause for herself, to a charitable trust, and the LESOC was born.

The poor woman passed away in her sleep before seeing the centre open its doors to do the good she'd intended.

Malkie parked beside a liveried minibus and climbed wide stone steps through a glass door that slid into the wall as he approached.

A hallway opened out inside, a staircase on the left, plush carpet, polished brass carpet rods and a gleaming mahogany handrail. Ahead, a lounge bar and dining room. The place reeked of money, but also a sense of long, dependable tradition, of solidity and permanence. As swanky as any country club hotel, he could imagine traumatised young war-fodder being wheeled in here and feeling safe.

'Can I help you, young man?'

He jumped. A small woman, all tweed twinset and blue rinse, looked up at him over the rims of half-moon spectacles. She appeared every inch a formidable lady but laugh lines framing her eyes suggested a kind soul. Malkie took an immediate liking to her.

'Sir?' she repeated with a patient twinkle in her eyes.

He flashed his warrant card but snapped it closed as she glanced at it – officially, he had no justifiable cause to be here.

'I'd like to talk to someone in management, please, regarding a patient of yours.'

She crinkled her nose and nodded towards an office.

'Let's see if *I* can help you, shall we?'

He followed her like a wee boy promised a sweetie by his auntie.

She seated herself behind a huge antique desk, her posture immaculate. Malkie took the chair opposite and felt like a slob. He closed his jacket over his paunch and straightened his tie.

'Sorry, I didn't catch your name, madam?'

She looked at him over her reading glasses and grinned.

'That's because you didn't ask, Detective Sergeant McCulloch.' She nodded at his warrant card, still clutched in his hand.

Damn it.

'May I ask which of our patients you wish to discuss?'

'A Mr Walter Callahan.'

He couldn't miss her reaction. There was a connection there, something personal, and painful.

'Are you familiar with Mr Callahan?'

She stared at him for several long seconds. As he considered asking again, her composure returned, but her cheery demeanour had gone, replaced by a distracted civility. 'Mr Freeman should be available soon. Would you like to wait in the lounge?' She smiled again, the epitome of grace and hospitality.

'And Mr Freeman is?'

'Mr Freeman is our therapist. He gives us two days a week, gratis. A level of generosity one finds to be all too rare, these days.'

'Perfect, thank you, Mrs—'

'Dame Helen Reid. Founder and director of this establishment.'

You. Idiot.

She gestured for him to precede her out of the office, then led him to a lounge. He half expected some bloke in a uniform to chase a scruff like him out, but she indicated a rather massive armchair, and he sat.

She left, and Malkie released a breath. He'd rather go twenty minutes with a pissed-off Steph than take on Dame Helen Reid again.

As he waited, he watched two nurses help a young woman out of a wheelchair on the lawn behind the house. She faced to the left and away, so he couldn't see her face, but the early morning sun set her blonde hair aglow, like a halo of gold. From what he could see of her face, Malkie guessed her to be in her thirties but she stooped like someone three times as old.

The nurses took an elbow each, but only fingertips, reassurance more than physical support. The woman took a hesitant step forward, then four more, each shakier than the last, before she turned back towards her chair.

The right side of her face was a mass of burns, her eye milky-white and striated and only half-covered by a ruined eyelid.

She spotted him watching her. He expected her to turn away, but she didn't. She laboured her way back, every step seeming to trigger new agony, and fell into her chair, exhausted.

When she looked his way again, he waved and smiled, hoped it communicated his admiration. She smiled back, a huge, lopsided grin, the right side of her face stiff and scarred. Despite the carnage inflicted on her features, her teeth were perfect.

He wiped his eyes on his jacket sleeve.

His phone pinged a reminder, and he found a text from Louisa Gooch.

> David Browne – Fettes, Edinburgh, HR. PC
> Donald Brown – Glenrothes. Diane Browne –
> Gartcosh – not one of us, no department listed.
> You're welcome.

Gartcosh. Organised Crime? Or Forensics? Customs & Excise?

Before he could send Louisa a thank you, a man strode through the door. He looked like a college tutor: corduroy trousers and a polo shirt. 'Detective Sergeant McCulloch?' His voice was rich and deep. Soft, but resonant with the tone of a man used to being listened to.

Malkie stood, offered his hand, didn't bother with his warrant card. 'Mr Freeman?'

Freeman shook his hand, then sat and gestured for Malkie to do the same.

'I have to admit to some confusion, Detective McCulloch. We had a young lady here yesterday, a Detective Constable Lang, asking about Mr Callahan. Are you from the same team as she?'

Damn it, Steph. You're too bloody efficient sometimes.

'Ah. Yes. I didn't see DC Lang yesterday. There's some urgency to find Mr Callahan, so—'

'DC Lang claimed to be acting investigating officer. I queried this, her being only a Detective Constable. She said her DS had been reassigned but offered no explanation as to why. DS McCulloch, who, exactly, is in charge of this case?'

Malkie saw two ways he could play this. Appeal to the man's better nature, apologise and assure him no other officers would make the same mistake. Or put his Tulliallan cadet training to use, dominate the situation, assert. Freeman had to be a compassionate man, consulting free twice a week, but Malkie also detected a vein of propriety ran through him, a respect for process.

He leaned forward. 'Mr Freeman, DC Lang and I are at a critical stage in a serious investigation. Mr Callahan is wanted for questioning in relation to a potential fatality. I'd prefer not to have to waste time obtaining a warrant to see his medical records?'

He stared at Freeman, at his hands resting relaxed on the arms of the chair and his legs crossed at a lazy angle. *Wrong call?*

Freeman stood. 'Detective Sergeant McCulloch. We gave a copy of Mr Callahan's file to Detective Constable Lang yesterday. She arrived with the necessary paperwork prepared in advance, and we were happy to assist.'

Malkie's guts sank to his arse. *Yep, wrong call.*

'I'll call your colleague and request she provide you with a copy of the file.'

Malkie stood. 'That won't be necessary, Mr Freeman. I can—'

Freeman interrupted him, his soft voice carrying an edge now. 'No, Detective Sergeant McCulloch. I insist.'

He turned and walked out.

THIRTY-NINE

Callahan woke, aching and stiff, to the dull grey haze of a November dawn, his heart hammering like it meant to burst out of his chest.

He jolted upright in the car seat. His back muscles spasmed and his wound burned. He reached behind him, found the dressings dry.

Recollection slammed into him. Markham. Victorian country manse secluded behind eight-foot walls and surrounded by wheat fields and woodland, the grey expanse of the Forth Estuary at Black Ness visible just below the northern horizon.

Money. Privilege. Entitlement. Everything he despised. Everything he and Bernard and Norrie and their like could only dream of.

Captain – Major, for God's sake – James Markham.

Bernard's deal.

His head reeled and he fumbled in his pocket for Bernard's capsules, but he'd taken the last of them seven hours ago. No more meds unless Markham had some. No choice now. Circumstances drove him here, made a victim of him.

He'd exhausted every other option. What choice was left to him?

Markham was fair game. The man was a disgrace, his military career a sham. Three token tours spent safe behind the wheel of an armoured Jackal or sweating over paperwork, hiding behind twenty-foot razor-wire fences and armed guards. He'd gone straight into officer training, no son of the Top Brass expected to slum it with the rabble. Callahan had to claw his way up the ranks until he hit what he called The Class Ceiling. Markham strutted in, displayed complete ignorance of the realities of modern warfare, and made a grade A prick of himself, a complete *Rupert*, as the ranks called his type.

Whether Markham had meds or Muzzle or nothing, Callahan would waste no sympathy finding out.

If Norrie or Jake had come through for him, he could do this with a clear head, the damned Dog leashed and muzzled. But they'd both let him down, so his head was a mess. He'd killed twice in three days on half his recommended dosage. No telling what he might do in his present state.

We're not going back.

We? I. I'm never going back.

He forced his focus to the mission in hand. His first problem was familiarity. He'd always been an ugly wee man and Markham would recognise him or his voice in a heartbeat. He checked his gear – gloves, balaclava, reliable old Fairbairn Sykes scabbarded on his thigh and just itching to be set loose. *No. Not that.* As long as he didn't speak out loud, kept to whispers, he'd get through this without doing too much damage to Markham.

The Dog whispered to him. *Enough, get in there.*

He pulled on his gloves and balaclava. His fingers brushed the hilt of his knife, and he drew comfort from its cold, hard dependability, its simple and unambiguous purpose.

He scanned the visible windows and doors, saw no movement. He clambered over seven-foot wrought-iron gates set into the wall. The garden was neat and well-tended, but he could see signs of neglect creeping in from the corners.

He heard music from behind the house, sprinted across the lawn to where a gravel path led to another gate, overgrown with ivy and roses.

In the morning chill, James Markham sat in the rear garden swaddled in a quilted jacket. A mug steamed on a patio table and a radio droned out easy-listening rubbish. Markham sat hunched forward, folded into himself, his chin on his chest.

He looked broken too.

Callahan suppressed a pang of empathy, bludgeoned it with memories of horrific, hot days thousands of miles from home, Markham hiding in his armoured car while his squad waded soul-deep in blood and dirt. No, Markham was fair game, and Callahan needed relief from the pain chewing at the back of his head. Besides, he could search the house quicker with Markham out of commission.

Out of commission, he reminded himself. *Not dead.*

Callahan waited. Markham barely moved except to sip his drink. A telephone rang, unanswered, inside the house for over a minute, which suggested Markham lived alone, as Bernard had said. When his mug ran dry, he stood and wandered towards the house. Callahan followed him in. He'd forgotten how small the man was, five foot six and scrawny, which only compounded his platoon reputation as a useless wee weasel.

The kitchen further confirmed Markham lived alone. Dirty dishes filled the sink and food packaging spilled out of an open bin. The table lay covered in junk, with one clear space where a plate and cutlery sat, caked in dried food. The air hung heavy, rank and sweltering. He touched a radiator and found it burning.

Markham stood at a worktop, his back to the door. Callahan lifted a pair of leather dog leashes from behind the door and a hemp shopping bag from the floor. He crept across the kitchen and looped the leashes around Markham's neck and yanked them tight. Markham's hands clutched at the leather. A kick to the back of the knees and a controlled chokehold rendered him slack and still. The Dog bayed at Callahan to gut the man, but he ignored it.

Apart from the leashes, he saw no other signs of a family pet – no food or water bowl, no collar hanging from the same peg on the door. He scouted the hallway, heard nothing. A pile of unopened mail sat on a console table, all addressed only to Markham. Bernard's intel proved right – the man was a recluse. Callahan returned to the kitchen, pushed the table to one side and man-handled Markham into a chair. He found nylon clothesline in a cupboard and secured Markham's wrists and ankles to the chair, then tied the leash off with only a few inches of slack, wedged a rolled-up dishcloth between his teeth, and pulled the bag over his head.

With Markham's sight safely blocked, Callahan pulled off his balaclava. The air inside the house, heavy and humid, clogged his breathing. His heart hammered in his chest. While he waited for Markham to regain consciousness, he repeated to himself, over and over: *Two dead already. No more.*

Callahan had applied his chokehold with trained precision, and Markham took only minutes to waken. His head snapped up and swung from side to side, listening, his breathing rapid and frantic through his nose.

Callahan allowed confusion and fear to work on the man, then leaned forward and whispered, quiet and low.

'Got any Muzzle, Markham?'

Markham's head snapped up. He whimpered and tried to talk but gagged on the cloth in his mouth.

'Shut it. I'm going to ask again, and you're going to nod or shake your head. If I hear even a whimper, I'm going to hurt you. Then I'm going to ask you again. Then I'll hurt you again.

Copy?' He almost choked on the ugly threats he hoped he could never follow through on.

Markham sobbed, his shoulders shuddering, his neck tugging on the leather garrotte.

'If I don't get what I want, I'll end you, but I'll make that take hours. Now, nod if you have any Muzzle.'

Markham thrashed and bucked and sobbed through his gag.

Callahan slapped him.

Markham screamed muffled words, turned his head as if expecting a second blow.

This pitiful excuse for a man was a symptom of all that went wrong in Helmand, the shambles that left men like himself and Bernard sweating and screaming through sleepless nights for years, long after mustering out. Bernard claimed he'd recovered by himself, but some hadn't even tried, had chosen death by drink, or ended up doing time for violent crimes. Crippled by rage and the discovery that they were considered no longer useful, embarrassing remnants of wars-for-profit waged by people like Markham – the privileged, the entitled, the elite.

His fist slammed into Markham's gut before he knew his hand had moved.

That's for Bernard Robertson.

Markham grunted, winded. He retched, sucked in air, and gagged.

Callahan reeled. *What the hell's happening to me?*

Markham screamed again. Callahan spotted a radio on the worktop, tuned it to a hard rock station and cranked it up, not that he expected visitors to be common out here. Markham listened, then lost it. He thrashed and yanked at his bonds, coughed and choked as the leather noose bit into his neck.

Callahan eased the leather off. This mustn't end with Markham at his feet, butchered and lifeless, another avoidable atrocity.

The Dog surged within him, and he was tired. He needed

to finish this quickly. He clamped his hand on Markham's throat until the man's screams choked off.

'Nod if you have some Muzzle, or I swear I'll end you, right now.'

Markham's head snapped up. A cold knot formed in Callahan's gut. He'd raised his voice.

Even through the gag, Markham's single word was recognisable.

'Callahan?'

FORTY

When Freeman disappeared upstairs, Malkie left the lounge.

Dame Helen Reid sat at her desk, head down over a pile of paperwork. He cleared his throat, risked one last attempt to avert disaster.

She looked up, studied him, removed her spectacles.

'You've upset our Dr Freeman, Mr McCulloch. What exactly do you want with Mr Callahan?'

She failed to hide her specific and personal interest – he might yet save this. He gestured to the chair he'd occupied earlier. 'May I?'

She smiled.

He sat, ran his fingers through his hair, took a moment to gather his thoughts.

'Mr Callahan is a suspect in the hit-and-run of a young man, Robin Wilkie. Mr Wilkie is in a critical condition in St John's hospital. I've excused myself from the case because of previous history I have with another Person of Interest, a Mr Liam Fielding—'

She held one hand up. 'Liam Fielding? Father's name Jacob?'

'Aye, that's them.'

'Thank you. Please continue.'

He'd got her attention, and she didn't bother to hide it. She could hardly have a high opinion of Liam and his loving father, so it might be worth sticking his neck out.

'Mr Callahan lives with, and works for, the Fieldings, drives a minicab for them. Thing is, Miss Reid, I don't think he even remembers the evening of the incident. I know he suffers from PTSD – I found his Seraxonine. I did wonder if perhaps he ran down Mr Wilkie then had a blackout, but I've researched depression and PTSD and I've not heard of someone blacking out an entire sequence of events like that – a drive into Murieston, running someone over badly enough to nearly kill them, driving home, parking the car, then going to bed. It doesn't happen that way.'

His voice had turned ragged with anger. This was all conjecture, but he couldn't ignore it for the sake of an easy arrest. He took a breath. Dame Reid stared at him so long he had to fill the silence.

'I know how it feels to have a miserable, black cloud clog up my head for days at a time, turning everything upside down so nothing makes sense. Makes me hear the worst in every little comment people say to me and flogs me with every screw-up I've ever made. I have my own Big Black Dog, Miss Reid, and I bloody hate the bastard.'

I can't believe I'm going to say this out loud.

'I think Mr Callahan is being framed for someone else's crime. Liam Fielding's, in fact.'

There. If you've still got a problem with me now, I'm humped.

She lifted her phone, dialled a number. 'Mr Freeman, please hold off on calling Detective Constable Lang, would you? I'd like to discuss it first.' She listened and nodded. 'I'm afraid I feel a need to insist. Thank you, Mr Freeman.'

She hung up. Left her hand on the phone handset, tapped her fingers as she chewed over her next comment. 'I know all about the Fielding family from Mr Callahan. If there exists even a tenuous possibility of their involvement, then I find myself confident in doubting even partial culpability on Mr Callahan's part.'

He had to admire her. Why use five words when twenty would do? Yet, he understood exactly what she had said, and what she hadn't said. 'You believe me?'

'We build exceedingly close relationships with our patients. In many cases, closer than they are to their own families. They feel comfortable revealing to us under the reassurance of patient confidentiality information they wouldn't tell their own mothers. Mr Callahan was rude and unpleasant, even intimidating at times, but...'

She considered her next words for several long seconds.

'That man had the strongest will, and the most non-negotiable self-control of any man I've ever met. Except for a few unpleasant occasions when...' She paused as if her words had caught in her throat. 'Mr Callahan never struck me as the kind of man who would allow such an incident to occur and remain unaware of it. If you are convinced that he has no recollection of the incident involving Mr Wilkie—'

'I am.'

'Then I would, as you suggest, give serious consideration to the possibility of his having been at worst only indirectly involved.'

He smiled at her. 'Thank you, Miss Reid. You've been more helpful than I had a right to expect.'

'As long as you get that man where he needs to be, you're welcome, DS McCulloch. If that's a cell for life in Saughton or Addiewell, then so be it, but if professional care can help him where we couldn't... where I couldn't... Please do your best to make that happen. Too many redeemable men have been thrown into prison and come out more broken than when they came home. Thirteen per cent of ex-service personnel commit violent acts after returning home. Mr Callahan was one of those. We enrolled him in an intensive residential programme. I had hope for him, but...'

She drifted again. For only a second, but Malkie saw pain flare deep in her eyes. She leaned forward over the desk. 'And get him medicated as quickly as possible. Without it, I fear for his safety and for that of others. He's never accepted he has PTSD. Many don't. They find life on civvy street intolerable, so they lie to army doctors, say they're fine. So they can go back on more tours, back to the life they know, where they know what they are, to routine and discipline and not feeling like monsters loathed by the society they went out there to protect in the first place.'

Malkie stared at her. He'd thought human behaviour couldn't appal him any more than he'd seen in his job. 'That's bloody disgraceful. Is coming home to that kind of abuse common?'

She took a breath. 'Yes. It is. Mr Callahan chooses to believe he's simply been depressed for eleven years. Denial is quite common. It can also arise from a refusal to believe oneself so weak as to succumb to a cliché like PTSD.

'So, Mr Callahan – Walter – has never had the treatment he needs. Help him, DS McCulloch. Please help him.'

She turned to her computer. He considered trying again, but her posture told him he was dismissed.

Back outside, the woman with the burns sat by the pond, throwing seeds to squabbling ducks. For no clear reason, he needed to meet her. He'd still never looked up the name of the poor bastard whose hand he'd held in The Libertine.

She looked up as his feet crunched on the gravel and flashed a lopsided smile.

'Morning, miss.' He showed her his warrant card and she frowned. 'Nothing to worry about. Just wanted to say hello.'

She studied him. 'You don't look like a policeman.' Her voice was scratchy and raw.

He studied himself. Scuffed shoes, shirt hanging out over a belt too low on his hips, jacket worn to a dirty shine.

'I'm undercover.'

She laughed, then wiped her disfigured mouth with a tissue. 'Even a split lip? That's commitment.'

He touched his mouth, felt crusted blood. 'Drunk student.'

'Undercover.' Her eyes twinkled. 'So, what are you disguised as?' A conspiratorial grin lit up her ruined face.

He looked around the lawns and under her wheelchair, leaned close. 'Well, obviously I'm a dirty old man.'

She laughed, and it broke his heart. The job often tempted him to believe in a god, and a devil dragging fuckers like the Fieldings to unending misery on the end of hot, pointed objects. But the reality was people like this young lady enduring lives defined by wheelchairs and pain, while mouth-breathers like the Fieldings flourished.

'You've been hurt too?' She nodded at his hand. He'd been scratching his chest again.

'A house fire.' He looked away.

'Can I see?'

This blindsided him. Despite his revulsion for the mess under his shirt, the concern on her devastated face was impossible to refuse.

'It's not pretty.' He despised how obscene his comment sounded, compared to the atrocities inflicted on her. He surprised himself, didn't settle for exposing only his wrists. He found courage to unbutton his shirt, show her what he had the gall to call the worst of it, but he looked away, couldn't handle her reaction to his self-pity.

'That must have been awful for you.'

He searched her eyes for sarcasm, found none.

Her eyes brimmed. 'The healing hurts most, doesn't it?' She reached out a scarred hand to him.

His eyes burned. He didn't feel anywhere near deserving enough to take her hand, but he couldn't refuse. Her skin, although streaked and rutted with burn damage, was soft.

Does it, Dad? Does it hurt more when we're healing?

He ached to release his own tears, to acknowledge such bravery in the face of her far greater trauma, but he didn't yet feel any right to such self-indulgence.

'I'm Deborah Fleming. Known by my mates as Flight Lieuy Mad Bitch Debbie.'

'Malkie McCulloch. Known to my colleagues as Defective Sergeant McFuckup.'

'Lovely to meet you, Malkie.'

She raised her arm to salute him but screamed and snatched it back. She sobbed, folded forward in her wheelchair.

Malkie couldn't breathe. Shame flooded him. She didn't deserve this. *Why am I so damned sure I do?*

Malkie backed away, horrified. 'I'm sorry. I...'

Deborah looked mortified, which only shamed him more. 'No, don't you apologise.'

He started to turn away but stopped himself; she deserved more. 'It was lovely to meet you too. You're probably the bravest person called Deborah I've met today.'

Through her tears, she managed to laugh.

'And you're the nicest dirty old man I've ever met, Mr McCulloch.'

He returned to his car, found Dame Helen Reid standing on the top step of the LESOC entrance, a cigarette in one hand, the other tucked under her elbow. 'That girl died three times. Her parents can't look at her, and she was told she'd never ride her horse again. She disagreed. She's one of the loneliest people I've ever known, yet she refuses to surrender to self-pity, refuses

241

to give up on herself. She deserves more happiness than I fear I'll ever be able to give her and I think I shall always regret that. Very deeply. She's a remarkable woman.'

'What happened to her? If that's not a rude question?'

'Deborah went where she was ordered to go and did what she was ordered to do, things I don't think I could ever do. Then her country disowned her when she became an embarrassing victim of cutbacks in helicopter maintenance budgets. An utter, fucking disgrace, Mr McCulloch. Pardon my language.'

Malkie could find no words.

Dame Helen unfolded her arms, handed him a slip of paper.

'Find Mr Callahan quickly, DS McCulloch. For everyone's sake.'

Written on the paper were a name and address:

ATO Bernard Robertson
7 West Pilton Square
Bathgate

Malkie smiled at her, but she remained impassive and stern. Despite himself, he had a way forward again.

FORTY-ONE

Callahan staggered back. He'd spoken out loud.

Idiot.

No point in trying to bluff his way out. Even after eleven years, there was no doubting the recognition in Markham's tone.

Walter cursed his stupidity, paced between Markham and the outside door, smacked the heel of his hand against his forehead.

The Dog howled in him. *He knows you. Finish him.*

'Shut up. Shut up!' He raged at *It*, his words hissing through clenched teeth as he fought to leash *It*.

He gripped the edge of the table, lowered his head, counted off until he felt self-control seep back into him. He stood, breathed, pulled the bag from Markham's head.

Markham blinked in the sunlight blazing in through the windows, then his eyes darkened as he saw his guess confirmed. He froze, swallowed.

Callahan placed another chair backwards before Markham and sat. He drew his knife and tapped its gleaming edge on his arm.

He expected Markham's eyes to betray fear but saw resignation instead. He pulled out the tea towel.

Markham worked saliva into his mouth and spat. 'Christ's sake. Murdered by a grunt. What will the neighbours think?'

Callahan stared at him. Where was the whining weasel he remembered? 'I'm not going to kill you, Markham.'

He's seen your face.

Markham's eyes glittered, not with hope but with defiance. 'You will follow orders, or I'll see you in a cell for life.'

Callahan frowned. This made no sense.

Markham sighed as if struggling to communicate with a child. 'It's not difficult. Kill me or I'll see you banged up in Saughton. Then I'll pay big, ugly bastards to hurt you. Regularly.'

'You want me to kill you?'

'Might as well be you as anyone else. Christ knows *I'm* not man enough.' He nodded down and behind at his bound hands. 'How about it, *Bitch*? You up to the job?'

Callahan swallowed as much resentment as he could stomach. He'd forgotten what Jake used to call him. He lifted Markham's jacket sleeves with the point of his blade, found multiple slashes across both wrists, all healed but – he suspected – never stitched. As if the man wanted every scar to remain an ugly reminder of his failure to see a job through.

Callahan rested his forehead on his hands as weariness overcame him. 'I'm not going to kill you, Markham.'

Markham raged. 'Follow orders, Lance Corporal Callahan. Bitch. You will kill me, right here, right now.'

Callahan stood, staggered back. Even after so many years, an entitled prick like Markham barking orders had him jumping to obey. He held his blade out, stared at it horrified, afraid he might follow the order.

'That's right, bitch. End me. Do me a favour. Do us all a favour. End me.'

Markham's commands rose to a scream and hammered into him, demanded obedience. The Dog slavered and snapped. *He wants it. He wants us to kill him. Can't you see?*

Heat flooded Callahan's veins even as ice churned his guts. The vice tightened around his neck, reached up into his head. His fingers clutched the hilt of his blade. He believed in the man's hunger for an end, to stop the nightmares he – like too many others – knew only so well. Hadn't he been trying to do the same all these years? Running himself to exhaustion along the Pentlands, pushing far beyond his expectation to survive the return journey? Hoping he'd succumb to the whispering urges of fatigue and exposure, lie down on top of West Cairn Hill, and let sleep take him. But he never ran quite far enough to finish the job.

Bernard Robertson.

Norrie Wallace.

Pedro Stevenson.

Had every one of them spent the last eleven years committing slow suicide?

No. Not all. Jake came home unchanged. Helmand only forged his sick heart into something colder and crueller. Callahan had recognised Jake's basic character from their first tour together, but he ignored it on returning home in the face of his offer of safe shelter in the cottage. He wondered now if dying in the gorse and scrub high on the hills on a clear, freezing night would have been better than the life – the capitulation – he'd settled for.

Markham wasn't yet beaten. 'You're a joke, Callahan. Even before you were RTU'd and had to crawl back up Fielding's arse.'

The word hammered into Callahan. RTU'd. Returned To Unit. Rejected. Discarded. Disgraced. Picked from so many and given a chance to become one of so few, then rejected at the last, without explanation.

Callahan remembered, would never forget. But something in Markham's words caught on his thoughts.

'What do you know, Markham? I was told no regulars could ever know about it. What are you not telling me?'

A vicious gleam appeared deep in Markham's eyes. He leaned forward until the leash tightened around his neck.

'It was me that had you RTU'd, you idiot. One word from my father and you got dumped back where you belonged – Jake's Bitch, slumming it with the rest of the grunts. Did you know those selectors fought to keep you? Said you were the best they'd seen in years. But my father was higher up the food chain than them.'

Callahan reeled. He hadn't failed, all those years ago. He'd earned that cap-badge, and a door to more should have opened for him. But Markham had slammed it shut in his face, ripped away the one thing that would have made him more than just another squaddie, more than just more meat for the grinder.

His headache flared, surged forward, stabbed at the back of his eyes. Rage erupted through him, set him ablaze. Some guttering spark of self-preservation made him throw his blade away down the hallway. Then he launched himself at the trussed and helpless Markham, slammed his fist into the man's face.

Markham screamed. Or laughed. The Dog raged too loud in Callahan's head for him to know which.

Markham spat blood into Callahan's face. 'Do it, bitch. Do us both a favour, you worthless, piece-of-shit grunt.'

Callahan lashed out again, desperate to stop the poison pouring from Markham's swollen and bleeding lips.

Weeping inside, Callahan watched himself hammer at Markham. He screamed at himself to stop, but The Dog was loose and gorging itself on eleven years of buried fury.

FORTY-TWO

Malkie reached Bernard Robertson's house in thirty minutes, desperate for a way out of this growing mess. He studied the dismal, ugly street. Overgrown and garbage-strewn gardens, manky windows, not one car unscarred or newer than ten years old. Residents who lived lives of dreary brutality he couldn't begin to imagine. What would they make of him and his middle-class problems?

Through the glass in the front door he saw a massive TV, and the foot of a hospital bed in a room at the end of a short hallway. He rang a doorbell on the wall beside a grubby key safe and heard a voice yell from inside. He bent to the letter box, pushed his fingers through, and shouted.

'Bernard Robertson?'

There was a pause before he heard the voice again.

'Who wants to know?'

'Detective Sergeant Malcolm McCulloch, from Police Scotland. I'd like a word, please?'

No response for several seconds, then, 'Bollocks.'

Malkie sighed. *Why does it always have to be like this?*

'I'm looking for an ATO Bernard Robertson. I need to talk to you about an old mate of yours.'

Silence.

'It concerns Walter Callahan, Mr Robertson.'

More silence. Then, 'Come to the bedroom window, show me your warrant card.'

Malkie swore under his breath. At the rear of the building he stepped over a low wooden fence, saw the top edge of the TV through a window. He leaned on the window ledge and pushed up on his toes, peered through grimy glass.

Robertson sat in the bed. No hands, stumps for wrists. He leaned forward, peered out. Malkie slapped his warrant card on the glass.

'Fine. Code is two-zero-zero-seven.'

Malkie returned to the front of the house, punched the number into the key safe and let himself in. He left the key on a wooden shelf inside the door.

Bernard Robertson lay under a thin woollen blanket. Looked like no legs below the knees, either. Malkie felt guilty for standing in front of the man.

'Can I sit down?'

Bernard nodded but looked irritated.

Malkie sat in a wheelchair, the only other seat, showed Robertson his warrant card again.

Robertson cast an obvious frown at the wheelchair, then Malkie's ID. 'So?'

'What does it stand for? ATO?'

Robertson scowled at him. 'Ammunition Technical Officer. IED Disposal.'

Malkie smiled. 'Ah, bomb disposal. I suppose that explains...' He trailed off.

'You think? But I'm not an ATO.'

Malkie frowned. 'Eh?'

'I'm full EOD. Or was.' He held up his stumps.

'What's EOD?'

Robertson sighed. 'Explosive Ordnance Disposal. Step up from ATO.'

'Fascinating. Can we talk about Walter Callahan?'

'Depends. What do you want him for?'

'A young man is in a critical condition following a hit-and-run on Sunday night, and forensic evidence has implicated Mr Callahan. When did you last see him?'

'Yesterday. He came to visit me the night before, asked to stay for a while, said he was in trouble.'

'What kind of trouble? What did he want from you?'

Robertson didn't answer immediately. He glanced at an open cupboard door, then snapped his eyes away again.

'He said he'd had an incident – that'll be the guy you say he ran over – and he asked me for meds. He has PTSD. Got his in Bosnia. I got mine in Iraq. The military treated us like scabby dugs, threw some pills at us and suggested we fuck off. I'm OK now, but Walter's in denial, thinks he's only depressed.'

Malkie nodded. 'Aye, we found his meds in his cottage. Seraxonine.'

'Ah, that explains it. If you took his supply, he'll not be far from another episode. I told him to turn himself in before he hurts someone.'

Malkie's bullshit detector maxed out, and Robertson's face fell.

'I gave him what I had, alright? But it wasn't much, so he freaked. He smashed a bottle of bloody Cardhu on the wall, then stood there playing with my lighter like he wanted to burn me alive. Have you ever seen what burns can do to a person? I have. It's fucking horrible.'

Yes, mate. I bloody have.

'Are you listening, copper? You need to get him back on his meds, quick.'

He anchored himself to the dread in Robertson's warning. 'What's Cardhu?' He'd heard that name recently.

Bernard took a patient breath. 'Cardhu is a bloody expensive single malt. He brought it with him.'

The High Street shop. Armitage. Damn it, coppers carried police-issue notebooks for a reason.

Bernard drifted off. Malkie waited. 'We all came home fucked up. Walter, me, loads of others. But we kept going back for more. We couldn't hack it here, the way we were treated, but even on the hardest tours, we knew who we were, what we were there for. Nothing here made sense anymore. So, we lied, said we were fine. Bosses were happy to take our word for it and fly us out again. Bastards.'

Robertson fell silent. Malkie gave him time.

'Walter came home worst of us all.' Robertson refocused, seemed to remember Malkie was there. 'But every time I've seen him lose it bad, he always, always tried to withdraw, first. Except one time...'

He tailed off again, as if reluctant to elaborate. 'He knows the damage he can do when he goes AWOL.'

'Absent Without Leave. You mean when he has an episode?'

'Aye. Is it possible someone stepped in front of his car, and he's wiped it from his memory?

'No. Evidence indicates it wasn't accidental, that he was waiting for the man, aimed the car at him.'

Robertson shook his head. 'No way. Walter does everything he can to avoid going AWOL. Keeping it muzzled, he calls it. You know people talk about The Black Dog? Depression?'

Malkie nodded. *Damn right I do, pal.*

'We call PTSD the same thing, The Dog. I've told him but he doesn't listen, swears he's just depressed, but he never does anything that might put him in a bad situation. He doesn't even work nights, too many pissed-up hard men with birds to impress.'

'So, you don't think this sounds like Mr Callahan?'

'Mate, I bloody know it wasn't him. I've known him over thirty years, and he's had my six more times than I can remember. His blackouts always happen after someone's backed him into a corner, given him no choice. Always. Something like you say, he'd at least remember driving into town.'

Malkie studied Robertson's gaze, intense and rock-solid. He found himself more convinced than ever. 'So, you helped out an old mate. I get that. Where's he going to get more meds?'

'No idea. I gave him what I had, but that wasn't much.'

Robertson couldn't help himself. His eyes flicked to the cupboard again. Malkie stepped over to it, made a show of examining the woodwork.

'They don't spend much on sheltered housing, do they?'

He followed Robertson's gaze to an army kitbag.

'Oh look. Some scoundrel has left your wardrobe all messy. Let me tidy up a wee bit for you.'

He lifted the kitbag, found a package of capsules underneath. Hundreds, all filled from the weight of it. He turned and hefted it on one hand.

'Mr Robertson, I suspect you didn't get these on prescription, did you?'

Robertson pointed a furious stump at Malkie. 'I bloody knew there was more.'

'I may have to invite you in for a formal interview.'

Robertson found his voice. 'You can't do that. You need a warrant to poke about in my stuff.'

'Correction, Mr Robertson. You invited me into your property having confirmed my identity and agreed to speak to me voluntarily. Anything I see that concerns me, I'm obliged to check it out. And a large bag of drugs sitting in plain view—'

Bernard exploded. 'But they weren't. They were...' He saw

the smile on Malkie's face and stopped, flopped back into his pillows, closed his eyes. 'Bastard.'

Malkie sat again. He was far from proud of his tactics. He'd never take it any further, but Robertson didn't need to know that.

'So, Mr Robertson. I'd love to know what these are and where you got them.'

The fight drained out of Robertson. Malkie respected the bloke for having any in the first place, living in a dump like this with no limbs.

'A squad-mate of ours used to cut the standard meds with other stuff, much better than the rubbish the army gave us. I came off them soon after I got home, but a few guys stayed on them.'

'Mr Callahan?'

Robertson hesitated. Something significant was coming. 'Aye, he was on Muzzle, but—'

'What's Muzzle?'

Robertson nodded at the bag. 'That's Muzzle. That's the last good batch that ever got made.'

'What do you mean the last good batch?'

Robertson shook his head. 'Doesn't matter. Look, Walter's a solid bloke, but—'

'I can't help him without you, Mr Robertson. And I want to help him.'

'Fifteen years ago, he got selected for special training, the SAS we guessed. He disappeared for a couple of months, then appeared again, RTU'd – Returned to Unit – without any explanation. But he'd changed.'

Malkie nodded at him to continue.

'He never talked about it, and he got stroppy as hell if we asked or took the piss. We think he told Jake, but—'

'Jake Fielding?'

'Aye, but it changed Jake, too. We caught him watching

Walter all the time, and there was something wrong in Walter after that. Still a good guy, but...'

He paused, hunted for the right word, looked troubled when he found it. 'Scary. He was scary.'

'So, what pissed Jake off so much?'

'Jealousy. Before Walter went away Jake was the big man, but after those two months even *he* was scared of Walter, and he didn't like people seeing him scared. That's all I know. You can put those back now and go catch that daft bastard, aye?'

Malkie held up the bag. 'He risked coming back to his cottage. Now I know why.'

'Mate, if Walter's off his meds and hurting, people are going to get damaged.'

Malkie stuffed the bag into his jacket pocket. 'I'll hang on to these. If we can keep this wee chat between us, I won't have to tell my DI where I found them. Or Mr Callahan. Speaking of whom, where is he now?'

Robertson had no fight left in him. 'No idea. He gave me a phone number. That's all I know.'

Malkie stood, clapped his hands together.

'Excellent. Let's start with that, then?'

FORTY-THREE

Callahan jolted awake, soaked in sweat. Daylight blasted through a window. Moisture prickled his face and suffocating heat clogged his throat. He smelled sweat and stale urine, fumbled for his weapon, braced for a firefight, for violence.

Hot and humid, and that stink. Freetown? No, that was long ago.

A man, tied to a chair, knocked sideways onto the floor. Face-down. Motionless. Blood.

And – strangely – music.

Not Freetown. Markham.

He screwed his eyes shut, like a child who hoped that not looking for a second might banish the nightmare.

When he could look again, nothing had changed. A knot of anxiety twisted his guts. *Too far. Again. I'm out of control.*

He watched Markham and prayed to a God he'd never believed in for even the slightest rise and fall of the man's chest.

He clasped his hands behind his head, blinkered himself with his arms. Would it be best for all – himself included – to simply never leave this house alive? How many more might die at his hands? The guy he hit with his car, McGuire, and now Markham. Three men dead.

Markham coughed.

A string of bloody saliva hung from his lips. The one eye that could still open rolled in its socket, vague and glassy.

Callahan sprang to his feet, more horrified than relieved. In the space between one breath and the next, Markham became a bigger problem alive than dead. Callahan knew that even now he couldn't bring himself to finish him, to tie this off cleanly. His brutal treatment of Markham now hemmed him into only one possible future – he was going down and deserved to.

He lurched backwards into the hallway, slammed the door shut, slid down a wall to sit on the parquet flooring. He squeezed his eyes shut, banged his head against the wall. And again. After the decades of ugliness and horror he'd seen and done, was this finally the thing that would break him?

His phone rang, shocked him from his pity party.

'Walter? It's me. Bernard.'

Callahan held his breath, surprised to find comfort in his old friend's voice. He swallowed, choked on his own shame.

'Walter? You there?'

'I'm here, Bernard.'

'You need to get back here. We need to talk.'

'Bad idea, Bernie.' He stared at the kitchen door. 'You don't want me near you right now. I'm *FUBAR*, mate.'

'But...'

He'd never heard Bernard lost for words.

'A copper's been asking me about you, Walter.'

Callahan stood, crossed to a front window, peered out. If the police cornered him here, with Markham like that...

He saw no blue lights, heard no sirens. 'What did they say?'

'That you ran someone over in your car. Like you said.'

He choked on a knot of frustration, unwilling to believe he'd succumbed to *It* so badly after so long, but unable to deny the mounting evidence. *This is all my fault. I let* It *in, again.*

'What did you tell them?'

'I told them no way you did that, mate.'

Walter glanced at the phone as if it might show him Bernard was lying. 'Bollocks.'

'No, the Walter I know never puts himself in a bad situation in the first place. I don't think you did it. You're not weak, not like Norrie, or Markham.'

Yes, mate. I am.

Walter felt ready to fall apart, surrender himself to whatever the future held. Anything but this unending fight. He was beyond tired.

'Bernard, my car was smashed and bloody and parked right outside the cottage. Jake admitted he spiked my whisky, so I don't remember a thing, but I must have done it. You know what'll happen if I go back to prison.'

A wave of fatigue numbed him. How many killings was too many? Where was the line between psychiatric treatment or banged up in a cell for life? Two corpses? Three? More? Self-defence or psychosis – did that make any difference?

'Walter?'

'I'm here. But I'm not coming back.'

'You need to. I found—' Callahan heard another voice in the background.

'Who's there with you? If you've—'

'Hello, Mr Callahan. Please don't hang up. My name is Detective Sergeant Malcolm McCulloch, and I don't think you did it. I mean, I don't think you were completely responsible.'

Walter reeled. Was Bernard stitching him up? He checked outside again.

The man continued. 'I'm not tracing this call. I shouldn't even be here.'

Something clicked in Callahan's mind. 'Are you the guy who was at my house on Monday?'

'Aye, that's me. And my colleague, Detective Constable Stephanie Lang.'

'How are your guts?'

McCulloch chuckled. 'They're fine. I'm well padded.'

'Aye, I noticed.' Callahan smiled. Under other circumstances, he might like this man.

'Mr Callahan, can we talk? Face to face?'

'Certainly. I'll drive over and stick my hands through the letter box so you can cuff me, aye?'

'Not necessary. Despite all the evidence pointing straight at you, I have no trouble believing that fucker Liam Fielding is behind it all. Somehow.'

'That's very unprofessional language, Detective...'

'McCulloch. Malcolm. Malkie to my mates.'

'OK, Detective McCulloch. But I'm not coming to Bernard's place. I'm no idiot.'

'Where, then?'

'I'll call you on Bernard's phone in thirty minutes.' He hung up.

Could that be it? Was he nothing more than a handy nutjob for Liam to hang his mess on? Did Liam do it then swap their cars? But then why did he remember glass and blood and that face screaming at him?

The radio music from behind the kitchen door demanded he face up to his actions, but he could only bear to move forward, away from Markham, away from his latest crime. He picked up his blade, slid it into its scabbard, then left by the front door.

He thrashed the Astra. It complained but got him to Bernard's in fifteen minutes. He parked a street away and recce'd the perimeter of Bernard's block, checked every car and garden for lurking coppers. Through the bedroom window he saw McCulloch beside the bed, holding a mug for Bernard to sip from.

At the front door the key safe hung open, no key. The door looked solid, but the frame was rotten. He confirmed the street was empty, unsheathed his knife, then booted the door in, charged down the hallway and into the bedroom. McCulloch had sat down. Callahan grabbed a handful of his hair, dragged him to his feet, and tucked his blade under his chin.

Bernard yelled at him, 'Oh for fuck's sake, Walter. My bloody front door.'

'Sorry, Bernard, couldn't be helped.'

He kicked the copper behind the knees, forced him to the floor, and spoke in a low, dangerous voice.

'Don't even sneeze.'

He dragged McCulloch to the wall and slammed his back against it.

'You,' – he pointed at Bernard – 'don't move.'

'I had to let him in, Walter. He was threatening to arrest me.'

'It's fine, Bernard. Sorry for earlier. Not myself, today. But the mood I'm in, I'd keep quiet if I were you, mate.'

Bernard opened his mouth again. 'Walter, I found—'

Callahan felt his grip slipping. 'Bernie, please. I'm getting a hell of a headache.'

Bernard looked distraught but closed his mouth and slumped back into his pillows.

Callahan turned to the copper. 'Detective Inspector McCulloch?'

'Sergeant. Detective Sergeant Malcolm McCulloch.'

'Whatever. What did you mean, I'm not completely responsible?'

No answer. He lowered his blade to the man's kneecap but saw no fear widen his eyes. A memory of PC Jen's gasping and bloodied face flashed across his mind. He couldn't risk this.

There would be no leniency for anyone who tortured a copper. More to the point, he didn't want to hurt this man. There was something in him to respect. He sheathed his blade.

The copper sagged with relief. 'When my colleague DC Lang and I met you at Kirknewton, on Monday, I had immediate doubts. When you saw your car, you weren't faking it, your shock was real.'

Was that only two days ago? McCulloch's words echoed the gaps in his own fragmented memories. He still couldn't remember leaving the cottage that night, but the damage to his pool car said otherwise. Was it Liam? He shook his head, screwed his eyes shut, banged the heel of one hand against his temple. Two certainties battered his mind, both demanding to be heard, both contradicting the other. The state of his car proved he'd done it – that and those dreams – but his complete failure to remember anything said he couldn't have. And underneath it all his newly awakened need for violence, his hunger for retribution against someone, anyone.

'Steady, Walter. Stand down, soldier.' Bernard's voice, afraid.

He opened his eyes. The copper stared at him, apprehension in his eyes, but still no fear. He decided to trust the man's strength, his composure, used it to push The Dog down inside himself, muzzle it before he stepped over a line he might never return from.

McCulloch spoke, his voice calm. 'Mr Callahan. I can't say you didn't drive that car, but if you did, I'm positive it was that bastard Liam Fielding put you in it.'

The man's tone pulled Callahan back to his senses, grounded him. He searched the copper's eyes for signs of manipulation, saw nothing. He meant what he said. Despite the evidence.

'But my car? Doesn't make sense. I'm getting a bad, bloody, headache now.'

McCulloch stretched one leg out, grimaced and rubbed his thigh.

'I can't deny you drove that car, but we have proof the victim was known to Fielding. That tells me either he did it, or he put you up to it.'

Callahan snorted. 'Wouldn't surprise me. I hate him and he hates me.'

'Aye, he claims he has psychiatric reports on you, said you're as unstable as they come.'

'Anything else?'

'Amanda Fielding's disappeared. No one knows where she is.'

'Good. She's better off without him. What about Jake? He's turned on me recently.'

McCulloch scoffed. 'Oh, that old bastard will be up to his eyes in it somehow – I think he put Liam up to it in the first place. When did Jake ever get his own hands dirty, right?'

'Aye, good point. So, if I take them both out, I'd be doing you a favour?'

McCulloch's eyes widened. 'No! That's not what I'm saying. I'm saying you come into custody, and we'll nail them together. I promised Helen Reid you'll be treated fairly.'

The mention of Helen twisted a shard of guilt in Callahan's guts, but he reconsidered McCulloch – if the copper had found the LESOC, he was no idiot. And it confirmed that Bernard hadn't screwed him over.

'Who was the guy I'm supposed to have run down?'

'His name is Robin Wilkie.'

Callahan's world turned upside-down. 'Is? He's alive?'

'Aye, he's in a bad way, but stable.'

Realisation slammed into him – he was never looking at murder in the first place. The McGuires were self-defence, but Markham – the Fiscal would push for attempted murder for that.

'So, where's Wilkie now?'

'The Edinburgh Royal Infirmary. With a uniform on the door twenty-four seven.'

'You're a rotten liar, McCulloch. St John's, then.'

McCulloch stared back.

The copper had a point. He could believe Liam was behind whatever happened that night. But if that were true, he couldn't handle doing time knowing that bastard was free and living the good life. Liam had to answer for all of this – Jake too. And if it brought his own end in the process, was that so bad? All through his last tour in Helmand, he'd waded into every firefight without caring a damn if he walked out again. He'd sought death so many times he'd lost count. Now, after eleven years in denial under Jake's conditional charity, had Liam taken even that self-imposed exile from him?

No. You fight. You always fight.

'Not enough. You *prove* to me I didn't do it, and I'll come in.'

McCulloch's lips opened. Then closed, again.

'Thought so.' How could he trust McCulloch when he no longer trusted himself? He needed answers and there was only one place he'd get them. Time to send McCulloch the wrong way and have a final reckoning with Jake and Liam.

He drew his blade again. 'Phone and car keys.'

McCulloch handed them over. Callahan thumbed the phone's wake button, saw a lock screen.

'PIN number?'

McCulloch stayed silent.

Callahan jabbed the point of his knife into the man's kneecap.

'Fuck's sake, man. 1971.' He rubbed his knee.

He unlocked the phone, found Lang in the phonebook, and pressed 'Call'. When she answered, he pressed the speaker button.

'Malkie, where the hell are you? McLeish is raging. Again.'

McCulloch closed his eyes and groaned.

'Detective Constable Lang. This is Walter Callahan. You'll find your colleague at number seven West Pilton Square, in Bathgate.'

He hung up and dropped the phone into McCulloch's lap. 'I think I'll pay Mr Wilkie a visit, see if he can help me sort this all out.'

Outside, Callahan threw the car keys over a wall into a neighbouring back yard. McCulloch watched him from the doorway, clutching at the doorframe like a broken man struggling to stand.

Callahan sat in the Astra for a while, his mind reeling. Wilkie was alive. The McGuires were self-defence. Markham wasn't.

He needed to stop Markham from becoming another casualty.

But first, he ached to see the only person who'd never let him down.

Even if it broke him.

FORTY-FOUR

Malkie didn't bother trying to escape. If the call from Callahan on his phone wasn't bad enough, his car sat outside, and he had no chance of finding the keys in time – the adjacent yard was piled high with junk. He sat with Robertson and waited for a kicking he probably deserved. When Steph walked through the door, her face promised violence, but she did him the favour of not tearing into him in front of Robertson.

'What happened to your lip? Don't bother. I don't want to know.'

She took out her notebook. 'You'll be ATO Bernard Robertson, then?'

Robertson rolled his eyes but nodded. From behind Steph, Malkie looked from Robertson to the open cupboard door and back, let his eyes convey a silent warning.

'Steph, I was—'

She held up one finger over her shoulder but didn't turn to face him.

'Not now. Sir.'

He hated when she did that.

'Mr Robertson, I'm Detective Constable Stephanie Lang. I

was planning to visit you later today. Even though my colleague has already interviewed you, I'll need you to repeat to me what you've told him, please?'

Robertson stared at Malkie, looked like a rabbit caught in a pair of headlights.

Steph slapped her notebook closed. 'Oh, good grief. I'm going to step outside with my colleague for a chat. Will you be alright? Do you need anything?'

Robertson shook his head slowly but kept his mouth shut.

She turned and walked past Malkie without making eye contact.

Malkie gave Robertson one last look to nail the point home, then followed her. Outside, she pulled the door closed, fingered the broken lock as if seeing it for the first time.

Malkie couldn't think of anything that wouldn't sound idiotic.

She turned away from him. Her voice sent a chill deep into his guts. 'We discussed this, didn't we, Malkie?'

Before he could answer, she continued. 'We agreed you'd take some time off, let me handle this.'

He opened his mouth but again wasn't quick enough. 'We agreed you'd stay away from Callahan and the Fieldings and Wilkie. We agreed all that, didn't we, Malkie?'

'Aye, but Steph—'

She turned on him, rattled off questions, her voice rising in volume as she ranted.

'So, why did Dr Freeman from the LESOC call to ask me some bloody hard questions about you, after I'd already interviewed him? And why did a nurse called Colin Prendergast call your desk phone to update you on Wilkie? And how the hell did Callahan know you'd be here tonight?'

Steph had torn chunks out of him on many occasions but the fury in her eyes now was a terrible thing to behold.

She clamped her lips shut, her chest heaving as she struggled to calm herself.

'Steph. All I did was visit the outreach centre that Callahan attended. They gave me Robertson's address. So, all I did was have a chat with his old buddy. Where's the harm in that? Callahan turned up here while I was talking to Robertson. I didn't go to him. He came to me.'

God help me if she knows Fielding and Wilkie are an item.

Her gaze was pure ice. 'Bollocks.'

'Eh?'

'Bollocks. There are loads of ex-services charities across central Scotland and you turned up at LESOC first thing this morning. The one he attended. Lucky guess, aye?'

He stared at her. Admitting he'd spoken to Amanda could lead to McLeish, and Steph wasn't ready to go there, yet.

He scoured his mind but saw no clean way out. 'I can't tell you, Steph.'

Her expression shamed him. Last bridge smoking, flames guttering.

'Are we not pals, Malkie? Don't you trust me? Or do you think I'm not up to handling this case by myself?' She sounded tired. Her tone hurt him more than if she'd stuck Callahan's knife into his gut.

'I'm protecting you, Steph. I need you to believe that.'

'Really, Malkie? There's a limit. I've seen that man's file – he's the worst kind of bad news. If he kills someone and you've withheld information, I'll have to arrest you. Or I'll get McLeish to do it, I don't think I could stomach it.'

Her eyes damned him. Her disappointment stripped him to his battered soul. He ached to confide in her but couldn't. Not without taking her down with him if it all went bad. He allowed his silence to speak for him; she was shut out, powerless to save him from sliding down yet another long and greasy slope to yet another humiliating fuck-up.

She turned away as if she couldn't bear to look at him anymore. 'McLeish wants you at the station first thing in the morning. I've passed on his message, but I'm sure you'll do whatever the hell you want.'

She stopped, spoke over her shoulder. 'Does it never occur to you that your behaviour reflects on me, too? You think I don't have stuff I...' She sounded broken, tired. 'I don't need this, Malkie. Not right now.'

She shook her head, turned away from him again, and walked back towards Robertson's house.

Malkie wanted nothing more than to tell her everything, share his load and beg her to share hers. Her words, her tone, the exhaustion in her posture, all told him she needed a friend too, but for now all he could do was insulate her the best he could from his own mess.

'Steph, you need to put protection on Robin Wilkie. Callahan said he was going to pay him a visit.'

She nearly slammed the door behind her but stopped herself and walked away down the hallway without a backward look.

He headed for the yard to find his keys. They'd landed in clear sight on bare concrete. He could have scarpered after all.

Is this what hitting the bottom feels like?

He doubted Callahan would harm Wilkie, but the Fieldings... Robertson might spill his guts in the face of a full-on Steph, and hand Malkie's arse to McLeish on a plate. And if he lost his job, he'd lose the cabin and the *Goose* and what was left of his dad's chance of happiness.

Aye, this must be what hitting the bottom feels like.

He had to hope Amanda had more he could use, but knew he was kidding himself. Shit was coming his way, and he wanted only to lock himself away on the boat with her. If she was game for a few hours of inappropriate comfort, then to hell with the consequences. Tonight he planned to hide, pretend it wasn't happening until it came looking for him.

He stamped on the accelerator and pointed the car towards the Forth, towards the *Droopy Goose* and Amanda. If she had more to reveal, they both needed it out now. If she didn't, then perhaps he could at least hope for a few hours of blessed denial. He needed sleep, needed to straighten his head out, find a way forward tomorrow.

His phone rang twice but he ignored it. Then a different chime indicated a follow-up text message. He ignored that, too.

When he reached South Queensferry he grabbed his phone and couldn't help himself.

McLeish.

My office. 08:00 tomorrow.

McLeish didn't have the authority to trigger Professional Standards himself, but he'd have no trouble escalating it up the chain. He threw the phone back onto the car seat, slammed the door, and strode towards the *Droopy Goose* like a man on a mission.

He'd had a bellyful of shit today. Time for him, now. Him and Amanda. Whatever that might mean.

He found the boat hatch open, the wooden frame chewed and splintered. Inside, wreckage. Doors hung open. Dishes and books scattered on the floor. The rubbish bin emptied on the carpet.

Both cabins and the toilet were empty.

Blood spattered a worktop.

Amanda's glasses lay on the floor.

But no Amanda.

FORTY-FIVE

Callahan caught the smell of cooking before he reached the tree line. He'd parked in a space off the approach road, couldn't risk driving up to the door.

He checked his watch – a few minutes past 1300 hours. The residents would be lining up for chow in the mess hall, those that could. He remembered one guy – what the hell was his name? No legs, yet he'd spent all his time helping to rehabilitate others. Everyone except Callahan. He'd given up on Callahan minutes into their first meeting, the words 'lost cause' all he could remember from that conversation.

Was he saveable then?

You mean before you tried to kill her?

He braced himself against a tree until the world stopped pitching around him. He needed to see her, despite knowing how much it would hurt.

At the tree line, he crept to the near end of the dining room and dropped to the ground when he spotted her.

Dame Helen Reid. The woman who'd worked the hardest for him and had suffered for it.

Suffered? Nearly died, you animal. Look at her. Remember what you did.

Tears welled and he brushed them away, furious. He had no room to regret what he'd done to her. It would break him.

She fussed and tidied, chatted, helped the inmates to eat. Every person reacted to her the same way. Affection edged with respect. Affection for a woman whose compassion was, for many, the sole remaining constant in their lives. Respect for a benign tyrant who demanded nothing less than full commitment to their own rehabilitation.

Was Bernard right? If he walked in there and asked her to... Might that single gesture of his faith in her be enough to overcome her anger at what he did to her? She never gave up any patient who refused to give up on themselves, but for him, could she feel anything but revulsion?

Brutal memories ambushed him. Late night, cold. Standing on the patio, searching the silence, listening for distant gunfire and artillery, scanning for incendiary flashes lighting up the night sky like far-off fireworks. Wondering if he was happy to see and hear nothing, or if he missed the sights and sounds of his many tours despite the damage they did to him.

Helen appearing beside him, forgetting her own safety rules, trusting him, slipping her arm through his without warning.

Her eyes terrified, pinned down, her fingers clawing at his as they crushed her throat, the broken neck of his beer bottle lifted high, trembling, every nerve in him screaming at him to rip her open.

He'd fled that night, spent the following week expecting his door to be booted in at dawn, hoping it would. Armed coppers if he was lucky. Death By Police, he'd heard it called, a fast and certain end to his hell.

But they never came for him. She never reported it.

Tears came now, refused to be stopped. He hung his head

and damned himself. If he'd ever wondered why Jake and Bernard and too many others had disappointed him throughout his miserable life, he had his answer now – he never deserved any better. One person had shown him unconditional care and commitment, and he'd nearly ripped her throat open.

He shook himself, wiped his tears, rough and furious. To his horror, she stood at a window facing directly towards him. He dropped to the wet leaf litter. She stared in his direction, then turned as if someone had called for her. If she'd seen him, she'd chosen to ignore him. Which was only what he deserved.

He crawled backwards, away from her, away from the one place he'd ever found any peace. When he had trees between him and her, he bolted, scrambled into the Astra and floored it, his vision blurred from tears he couldn't stop.

FORTY-SIX

Malkie found Fielding's Aston at the house, the driver's door open.

He opened the front door without knocking, heard nothing. The kitchen was empty – she must be upstairs.

The Jakey appeared from the back of the house. 'What do you want now, copper? You were told to stay away from me and my boy.'

Malkie suppressed an urge to punch the old bastard. 'I'm off the clock, here on a personal basis.'

Jake sneered. 'Here on a personal basis. What kind of fucking gay talk is that?'

Malkie choked back a stubborn surge of sympathy for Liam. What chance did he have with a father like this? It did nothing to justify his treatment of Amanda, but did it go some way to explain his rotten nature? No. As much as Malkie looked for good in everyone, he doubted either of the Fieldings would ever surprise him in any positive way.

'Where's Amanda?'

Jake's face cracked into a rancid and malicious grin. He

leaned on the doorframe and crossed his ankles. The man's arrogance ate at Malkie's self-control, but his priority was Amanda.

Jake pointed his stick towards the ceiling.

Malkie stepped towards the stairs.

'Liam can't wait for you to try to take her, dickhead.'

He grinned again, his few remaining teeth crooked and yellow.

Malkie hesitated. What was he thinking? Alone, he was no match for the younger Fielding. Jake yelled up the stairs in his hoarse and gravelly old voice.

'Liam. That McFuckup guy wants to see you, again.'

The younger Fielding appeared at the top of the stairs. Malkie started up towards him, intent on doing whatever damage he could to the much stronger man, but Fielding charged down the staircase and slammed a fist into Malkie's gut. Malkie went down, winded. He gagged but refused to give them the satisfaction of puking in front of them.

Fielding stood over him, his breath heaving in and out. 'I got my wife back, McFuckup. Thanks for that.'

Malkie glared up at him.

Liam stood over him, his fist raised. 'What was it you said? Your dad brought you here for the weekends. And that stupid plastic anchor on your keys? There are only five pontoons at Port Edgar, moron. How long do you think it took to find her?'

Malkie groaned. *Another promise broken. I'm so sorry, Amanda.*

He stood, nearly buckled as he straightened. Pain like this might mean something had ruptured.

'I want Amanda. She leaves with me now, or...' He looked at Jake without any attempt to hide an unspoken threat.

Fear flashed across Liam's eyes but disappeared again.

'And what happens when I tell DI McLeish you're harassing me again after you were told to leave us alone? Stop embarrassing yourself. Suspension not enough for you?'

Malkie caught Jake flashing a look at his son, wondered for a second, but more immediate concerns took over.

He knew he'd dealt himself a crap hand, had little he could bluff with. Even a threat to reveal Fielding's sexuality to The Jakey held little value against Malkie's whole career. Hiding a key witness on his own property, withholding case information, interviewing witnesses while removed from the investigation, his recorded assault on Fielding – McLeish would crucify him, and these days more than only his own financial security depended on his salary.

Malkie slumped against the wall, squeezed his fingers into his eyes.

Liam stared at him, incredulous. 'You deaf? Fuck off.'

Malkie was down to his last cards, all or nothing. 'I'm not leaving. First, you explain why you wanted Amanda back. It's not like you actually love her, is it?'

Liam crossed his arms. Malkie couldn't help noticing the thick mass of muscle in those arms, and his guts ached again.

'She's my wife. I had to rescue her.'

'Rescue her? I was protecting her from you, you bloody animal.'

Liam smiled. 'That's not the story she'll tell.'

And there it was. Malkie held a busted flush, and his bluff was called. Game over.

Or was it?

'What if I bring you Callahan?'

Liam grinned. 'Oh, clever wee Pig. Talk to me.'

Malkie loathed himself for even pretending he'd do such a thing, but he had nothing else. Fielding wanted Callahan for something, but what exactly? What was he supposed to have done to Wilkie? Had Callahan driven that car after all?

'I'm interested. You bring him to us. We'll hurt him a bit then turn him over to you. You might even save your shitty wee job.'

Malkie snorted. Even if he meant to actually deliver Callahan, the chances of getting him to the station alive were a long way south of zero. But right now, he needed any measure of damage limitation he could get.

'As long as I get him back breathing and able to talk. I need him in custody, not at the bottom of Cobbinshaw Reservoir.'

Liam held out his hand. Malkie stood, ignored it.

'First I see Amanda, or nothing's happening.'

Liam looked amused. 'Not a good idea, mate. She's a bit emotional. Time of the month, I think.'

Another grin Malkie ached to wipe off his face. 'I see her, or all bets are off.'

Liam frowned, clearly didn't want her to make an appearance. 'She won't be pleased to see you. Not after you told me where to find her.'

'But I bloody didn't...'

Liam grinned, again.

Malkie's guts sank. She'd never trust him again. Whatever he'd hoped might grow between them was knackered now. That hurt more than all the other shite, but he had to see her, even if it meant facing her loathing.

'I see Amanda, then I go find Callahan. That's the deal.'

Liam grinned then stepped past him and headed upstairs.

Malkie massaged his aching belly, noticed Jake watching him. He'd forgotten the old bastard was there.

'Clever wee bitch. Messing you right up, isn't she?'

Are you, Amanda? Have I judged you so wrong? 'Fuck you, Jakey.'

Jake chuckled, set off a coughing fit, and Malkie got a waft of stinking breath he could almost taste. He didn't quite gag but had to turn away.

'Funny. Wouldn't think you had the balls to nick another man's property.' He limped away into the lounge, coughing and hacking and chuckling to himself.

Malkie clamped his hands to his gut, refused to punch a wall.

Amanda appeared at the top of the stairs. She wore fresh bruises, and a split lip. Liam beamed behind her, proud of his handiwork.

The dead look in her eyes changed. All the other shit of the past three days disappeared, eclipsed by the poison radiating from her. Fury, disappointment, loathing, all hammered into him. Liam held her by one arm. She looked ready to tear Malkie apart with her fingernails. He recoiled from the change, barely recognised her. Was he kidding himself from the start? If she could so easily believe Liam's lies, was there ever any genuine affection there at all? And the fury in her eyes. Was she damaged, unhinged even, all along? Was Malkie so blinkered by his own shameful motivations she'd taken him for a mug? He'd been played before, knew too well the consequences of falling for fake tears from the wrong woman.

Liam dragged her away again.

Malkie's eyes burned. Another let-down, another bitter betrayal.

But who betrayed who, Amanda?

FORTY-SEVEN

Callahan returned to Markham's house torn between desolation and fury.

Part of him wanted to curl up in a hole and wait to die, put himself and the thing inside him to sleep for good. Another part craved absolution, permission to go on living, if that was even possible after everything he'd done.

Could Helen forgive him? She hadn't reported his attack, so she'd kept faith he could deal with his issues by himself. If she'd considered him a danger to others, she'd have had no choice but to report it. If he could show her, and himself, that even after his actions of the past few days he could get himself under control, leash The Dog, prove himself worth saving, might she be able to swallow her revulsion to support a psych sentence?

Or should he simply disappear, live the rest of his rotten life hiding. Up north, away from the infestation of CCTV cameras spying on every town and city. A place quiet and isolated and far from any kind of phone or radio or TV signal. Spend his remaining funds sparingly, pick strawberries through the summers. It could work.

It would never work. He could never bring himself to let it work.

He hadn't asked for any of this. He hadn't asked the school system to spit him out an unemployable lout. He hadn't asked the army to send him to shithole after shithole, badly equipped and poorly supported, then deny the damage done to him and too many of his squad-mates. He hadn't asked the Special Forces to let him get so close to the best he could be, only for Markham to snatch it from him.

He'd never asked for any of it. He deserved better. And that meant fighting on.

Everything depended on one merciless fact – he needed meds. He was a walking IED without them. Any chance he had at treatment depended on stabilising himself first.

He braced himself to face the most recent of his failings and entered Markham's kitchen.

Markham lay as before, but his eyes were now open. Open and furious and damning.

Callahan switched off the radio. Near silence settled over the dank air of the kitchen, the only sound Markham's laboured breathing, rattling in his throat.

Why hadn't he tried to escape? Why was he now glaring at him without fear, only hatred?

He dragged Markham and the chair upright. Markham grunted. How much pain had he been suffering? Callahan sat before him, studied him, found his earlier loathing now distant and half-hearted.

'Did you even try to escape?'

Markham shrugged, miserable and broken.

'Why the hell not?'

No answer.

Callahan rested his forehead on the chair back, heaved in a long, deep breath. 'I need your Muzzle, Markham. Or something else. You must have something.'

A defiant gleam appeared in Markham's eyes. 'Fuck you, Callahan. You want to know what I've spent the last three hours doing?'

Callahan, to his own surprise, found he did.

'Trying to find a reason to do just that. Scream for help, try to reach the phone in the hall. And you know why I did nothing?'

Callahan waited.

'Every breath I took was agony. I was spitting out my own blood for half an hour before it stopped coming up. My head feels like there's a bloody vice on my brain. But I couldn't bring myself to give a shit.'

Callahan waited.

'Who the hell do you think you are, you and your precious bloody PTSD? You think it was only grunts like you that came home damaged? You don't think I was hurting? Are you that fucking arrogant?'

Markham closed his eyes and dropped his chin onto his chest. Callahan racked his mind for something to say but came up blank.

'I didn't try to get free because despite the pain you left me in, I hoped that was as bad as it would get while I died, right here on this floor. But you couldn't even get that right, you stupid prick. I don't know how many times I came round and thought "Damn it, still not dead." And every time I did, I remembered what a miserable bloody failure you always were, couldn't even finish me trussed up like this. You're a joke, man.'

Markham's words hammered into Callahan. They shamed him, drove his self-loathing inwards where it hardened into a dense, bitter, lump. Markham was right – the man wanted to die, had probably wanted it for years, and Callahan couldn't even get that right.

And now he had to make sure Markham survived. Wilkie

was alive, and McGuire was self-defence, but Markham's treatment was all on him.

First he needed meds, and for that he'd need to promise Markham the one thing he knew he could never deliver.

'OK, Markham. Tell me where your Muzzle is, and I'll end you. Quick and clean. Right here.'

Markham studied him. Callahan thought him ready to agree, but then his heart sank.

'Seriously, Callahan? You think I'll take the word of a grunt? Yes, I have meds but you're not getting them. And trust me, you won't find them.' He grinned, congealing blood sticking to his lips and teeth.

Markham bit down on The Dog, hungry for Markham's throat. Frustration boiled in him – as much as he itched to give Markham what he wanted, he refused to allow himself to slide any further. Like some pathetic misbehaving schoolchild, he imagined Helen Reid watching him, challenging him to hold on to himself, not to give in to *It*.

He stood, grabbed a tea towel and gagged Markham, then tore the place apart. He started with the bathrooms – five of them for pity's sake – then moved on to closets, cupboards, drawers, under beds, on top of wardrobes. He trashed the garage, sweeping bottles and plastic boxes and tools and gardening gear from shelves. Even as he ridiculed himself for checking inside a huge grand piano in the drawing room, he refused to give up, digging into every hole, space, nook, and cranny big enough to hold a blister pack or a bag of capsules.

When he returned to the kitchen empty-handed he found Markham unconscious. Walter found a pulse, but barely. The man had pissed himself at some point, which led to the realisation that he hadn't drunk anything for four hours. Callahan filled a coffee mug from the kitchen tap, yanked the gag from Markham's mouth, and splashed enough water on his face to wake him. He held the mug to Markham's lips and tilted his head back. Markham coughed and choked but managed to swallow the water.

He stared at Callahan as if reappraising him, and managed, 'Thanks.'

'Where is it, Markham? Is there any, or were you lying?'

Markham's eyes narrowed. His mind worked. Callahan waited.

'Untie me.'

'No chance. Tell me first.'

Markham sighed and nodded towards the hallway.

Callahan headed where Markham had pointed, stopped outside the first door. 'The toilet? I looked there.'

'Look again.'

Callahan opened the door. His first look had been brief, only cupboards and wall cabinets, anywhere he might find some meds. He now studied a wall covered in photos of Markham in uniform. He spotted a vertical empty space that split the otherwise random arrangement in two. A closer look revealed a hairline in the plaster. He placed his hands wide and pushed. After a moment's resistance, the left section swung inwards.

A set of steps descended into darkness. After one more glance at Markham he stepped forward.

He braced one hand out to steady himself on the rough wooden steps but recoiled from a strange texture. Foam rubber. Protruding pyramids, repeated at eight-inch intervals, the reverse side of the door and every wall covered with the stuff. He returned to the hallway and glared at Markham.

'What's the soundproofing for? What the hell is down there?'

Markham pulled an evil grin, and Callahan's hackles rose.

He descended, slow and careful, dreading what he'd find. How damaged was Markham?

At the foot of the stairs another door, this one a solid slab of steel that wouldn't look out of place in a bank vault. He tried the handle, found it locked. He returned to the kitchen, spotted a bunch of keys hanging from a hook beside the outside door.

He took long minutes to find the correct key. As he pushed down on the handle, he heard heavy bolts retract all around the frame. What the hell was in there?

He eased the door open to find more darkness. A fumble on the wall found a switch. He flicked it on. Hard, white light filled the space.

Of all the discoveries Callahan might have feared, a shooting range was the last.

Paper targets, human-shaped, stuck to boards against a wall forty feet away. Each head was plastered with a large photo of the same man, peppered with bullet holes – an officer, but with no rank visible. On a table sat a polished mahogany box. The soundproofing covered every square foot of the walls and ceiling, and he could see no windows or vents. The depth of the staircase suggested the entire room lay below ground level.

Callahan opened the box on the table, found something he'd forgotten about for years since returning home, and his breath froze in his chest.

He lifted it from the moulded velvet base of the box. He'd forgotten how heavy one of these was. A customised 9mm Browning Hi-Power 510, silver-chrome frame and matt-blue slide, a thing of beauty. He ejected the clip, checked the breech was empty, and pulled the trigger. The action felt light, so Markham had also removed the magazine-disconnect. Powder-blue rubber grips with 'JM' embossed on both sides finished off a breathtaking piece of kit.

Oh, the damage we can do with that.

Callahan dropped it into the box as if scalded. That way lay a future he couldn't allow to happen.

He slammed the lid of the box down, backed away as if it might lash out and bite him. It had been an age since he'd handled a firearm, and it scared him how much he'd missed it.

He spotted a cupboard against one wall. Two doors swung outwards to reveal something ridiculous as hell and yet unsurprising: a memorial to Markham.

Army gear laid out like a museum exhibit and more photographs, all showing him in uniform. All but one. The squad footie team, Markham in the goalie's colours. He'd forgotten that day. They allowed Markham to sub for an injured goalie rather than play a grudge match against the locals a man short. Markham surprised them by letting only two shots past and proved himself key to securing the victory. A few of the team managed token words of congratulations, and they couldn't bar him from the team photo, but that was the first, last, and only time he'd ever engaged with the squad on any kind of social level.

That photo hung at the centre of them all. Callahan choked down yet another spark of empathy for the man. He couldn't afford to soften, needed those meds before he lost himself completely.

The cupboard displayed what looked like Markham's entire military life – utility and dress uniforms on tailors' dummies, an army-issue Bergen backpack, boots polished like black mirrors, a wooden first-aid box.

His stomach lurched – could he be that lucky? He lifted the lid, found three white pill bottles hidden under bandages and dressings and medicines. Not daring to hope, he lifted them from the box and read the labels.

Zinc supplements, saffron extract, and St John's wort.

He lifted the box, smashed it on the floor at his feet, and let out a howl of rage and frustration that must have had Markham fearing for his life. Or hoping for death.

When he could breathe again, he climbed the stairs to the kitchen.

'Herbal remedies? Is that it? Where's your fucking meds?' His last words screamed inches from Markham's face.

Markham returned the stare. Not afraid, not intimidated – broken beyond caring.

'Welcome to my world. Do you know what it's like having an executive-level officer for a father, Callahan?'

Callahan sat, rubbed his eyes. His fury drained from him, replaced by exhaustion he feared might kill him by itself.

Markham continued. 'Worst thing about it is the politics. It affects everything. You're not allowed to fail exams. You're not allowed to get fat, or grow your hair, or dress like a scruff. You can't get pissed in public to forget all the bloody rules for a couple of hours. You can't fraternise with grunts.'

He paused until Callahan removed his fingers from his eyes and looked up.

'And you can't register for treatment, or meds, or anything else that might embarrass your perfect, fucking, big-shot, soldier Daddy.'

FORTY-EIGHT

'You'll like this one. Tastes like strawberries and cream.'

Malkie sighed. 'No, Monty. I won't. I never do.'

'Ah, but this one's lovely. You won't even feel it go down. Trust me.' He beamed.

Malkie opened his mouth to protest further but Monty had that look in his eye. The gurning oaf opened a bottle and slopped some into a shot glass. Malkie had to try it. One day he might find something he could stomach, then he could enjoy the same temporary anaesthesia Monty's other customers found in their glasses.

Monty was a Mancunian who'd lived in Paris for three years then left in a hurry with a French wife and a new surname and no explanation. He bought a decent wee bar with a wodge of cash he also never explained. His wife divorced him when he started drinking more booze than he served. With his half of the divorce settlement, he bought this dive on the north-west side of Linlithgow. Malkie first attended the place during door-to-doors following a spate of robberies in the adjacent industrial estate. To his surprise, he found the place felt more comfortable than he'd ever expected of a pub. The clientele was perfect because they were just like him: the bungled and the botched. People who cared nothing for decor or ambience as long as the drink was cheap and Monty threw plenty of lock-ins. Plus, it was only a fifteen-minute stagger back to Malkie's rented digs, should he ever manage to achieve the Unholy Grail of getting completely shit-faced one day.

Malkie loved the place. At first, it made even him feel like an over-achiever, but over time he listened and realised his ignorance. Tommy was a plumber, ran his own thriving business for decades until a bank withdrew his overdraft for no reason. Steven lived with his ancient and poisonous father, who rewarded his care with constant verbal abuse; his only respite was that his dad fell asleep early and slept through the night, allowing Steven to drown his misery in this dump. His parting words at closing time were always a variation on 'Maybe the old bastard has gone and died at last.' Lorraine married young and raised a family of four fine children, then lost them all to a drunk lorry driver. She'd gained a colostomy, lost half her liver and joked that her mission in life was to finish off the other half.

Shit happened to everyone, from fucked-over tradesmen to grieving mothers, to under-achieving police detectives. He recalled a Tom Waits song. Some guy in a bar, spending the facts of his life like small change on strangers. What a fortune he could make, the things he'd seen, if he could be bothered recounting them.

Monty nodded at the shot glass sitting on the scratched and sticky bar. The dark amber liquid looked like every other alcoholic liquid he'd ever tried. It smelled sweet, which was promising; sugar tended to mask the taste of alcohol.

'What is it?'

Monty leaned back under the optics and folded his arms, a smug expression plastered across his beaming, greasy face. 'You'll love it. If you don't, the next one's on me.'

Malkie debated with his better judgment for a few seconds

but as usual, lost. He'd learned to down it in one. Sipping and screwing up his face was a sure way to earn the scorn of his fellow patrons. They watched him now, curious to see if Monty might finally crack it.

The liquid washed across his tongue and down his throat. He got a hit of sweetness, then the bite of the alcohol came through and he coughed.

Lorraine tutted and shook her head in disappointment.

Malkie ignored her. 'That's bloody disgusting.'

Monty grinned. 'Another?'

'Aye.'

Malkie settled in, determined for once to drink himself stupid. The label was in some Eastern European language, completely unreadable.

'Where the hell did you get this?'

'Buddy of mine used to live in Croatia. He gets it from pals he has there. He gets ciggies too, but they're like smoking wet cardboard.

Something tickled at Malkie's mind, but he shut it down. He decided, in the interests of self-preservation, not to give a damn anymore.

Everything he'd done so far had sunk him deeper into shit. At best he could expect a kicking from Professional Standards. At worst, unemployment, maybe even criminal charges. His best – his only? – pal, Steph, was close to disowning him. His dad might not survive if Malkie bankrupted them both and had to sell the boat. He couldn't remember feeling more like wrapping the *Goose*'s anchor-chain around his neck and dropping himself in the Forth.

He heard his mum's voice snap at him in his mind. *'Don't you dare, Malcolm. You do what you can. Always.'*

But I didn't, did I, Mum? I didn't do all I could. I'm fucked if I can remember what, but there was something else I should have done.

His earlier conversation with Steph forced itself into his thoughts. She was right. Giving a man a gun wasn't the same as shooting him with it, so giving your mum a candle didn't mean...

It hit him – another ugly missing scrap of the picture, and further confirmation he'd betrayed his care of duty to her. He wanted to put the candle on the dresser, far from the bed. Safe. She'd insisted – no, she'd demanded – he put it on her bedside table and light it. He'd argued, snapped at her, shouted at his own mum. But she'd pleaded with him, and he did it. He sat the candle right next to her bed. Beside her cocoa. Where it had later proven so easy to knock over. Worse, the ugly, petulant, parting words he growled over his shoulder as he slammed the door on her were the last she ever heard from him. He couldn't remember what they were but he knew they'd been petty. And cruel.

You did something you knew was risky because your mum begged you to. On her birthday. Was that it? Were you nothing more than negligent and petulant with it? As if that's not bad enough?

'Good grief, Malkie. What is it this time? Looks bad even for you, mate.'

Malkie shook himself from his thoughts, tried to smile but couldn't. 'Just the job, Monty. Doing the right thing never seems to be the right thing anymore.'

'Pack it in, then? Get a part-time job. Security or something. Tell you what, I'll give you a lifetime discount, ten per cent off every drink.'

Malkie did smile then, but it faded as life crowded it out again. 'I've really fucked up this time. I made a promise to someone—'

'Aw Christ. Again, Malkie?'

'I know. Not a proper promise this time. More like a gesture she couldn't misinterpret.'

Monty leaned his elbows on the bar and grinned. 'She?'

287

Malkie downed his second shot and grabbed the bottle. 'Aye. She loathes me now. Hates my guts and I deserve it.'

Monty stayed quiet. He specialised in loud-mouthed and insensitive, but even he recognised a man in trouble.

'I stuck my neck out for her, let her think I'd look after her but now she's in worse shit than before she met me.'

He poured another shot and downed it. It tasted as bad as the first two, but then medicine was supposed to taste rotten, wasn't it? His mind drifted as he rotated his empty glass on the bar as pissheads have done since booze was invented. Monty wandered away.

Malkie felt more alone than he would have thought possible, and further from any hope of personal redemption than ever. He grabbed his phone and surprised himself by quick-dialling his dad. He was so tired he could barely think straight, but this might be one thing he could get right, one scrap of self-respect he might yet salvage.

He ended the call in the middle of the first ring – was he doing any more than looking for one more person to lean on? His dad deserved better than that. He dropped the phone on the bar, wished the impact would break the damned thing.

It rang. Dad's name on the display. He'd been too slow to hang up.

'Hi, Dad. How are you feeling?'

Silence for several seconds, then, 'What's wrong, son?'

A sob surged up Malkie's throat and demanded to be vented. He wiped his eyes with his sleeve, managed to keep the tears of self-pity at bay. 'I'm fine, Dad. Work's not great right now.'

More silence as he dredged his mind for more to say.

'Malcolm, you remember the motorbike?'

He did. They'd fixed up a knackered old Triumph Bonneville when he was in his teens. They couldn't afford parts so they bodged what they could, strapped it together, made it work. It looked like a joke, but they got three days' joy out of it before it died, crunching gears and spewing black smoke. Together they pushed it two miles along the A70 and down the lane to the cabin, sore and knackered and happy as pigs in shite. They had the best three days he could remember. 'You said we did the best we could with what we had.'

'Aye. You got that bike running, you can do anything. Do you remember what we called it?'

He marvelled at his dad's ability to say something so corny, so trite, and yet pierce through the stubborn self-loathing to the boy inside who believed there was nothing his dad couldn't do. 'I remember. We called it Lazarus.'

His dad chuckled again, and it lifted Malkie more than he could have believed possible.

'Thanks, old man. I needed a laugh.'

'No problem, youngster. What was it you called for?'

'Nothing important. It can wait.'

Another pause. 'Call me tomorrow?'

Malkie smiled. 'I will, Dad,' and he meant it.

'Love you, son.' And he hung up.

Malkie dropped the phone on the bar again. Someone believed in him, even now. He didn't deserve that, and he wanted more than anything to deserve it.

The phone lay beside the Croatian rotgut and demanded a choice from him. See this through or watch it all go tits-up from inside this bottle? He'd be more than justified – both Steph and McLeish had ordered him to stay away. And now he was head of his family and its sole earner. He chuckled to himself, but it was bitter, filled with acid. The family. The one he'd destroyed, whatever it was he'd done or not done. Why couldn't he remember? Why couldn't he drag the memories into the light, face them, begin to deal with them?

He grabbed the bottle and downed three deep swallows straight from the neck, then braced his hands on the bar and managed to keep it down without puking. Lorraine patted his hand and nodded to herself.

He'd never know if it was Lorraine's hard-earned approval or the pathetic sense of achievement he allowed himself from downing so much booze without gagging, but a flash of clarity burned away his self-indulgence.

He had one last way forward. And not just for Callahan. For himself, too.

He had no intention of turning Callahan over to Fielding, but could he get him to McLeish? Did he want to risk that? Was McLeish in up to his neck with Liam Fielding or just flexing the rules as per his reputation, and playing Fielding for a mug?

Or was it the opposite? Did Liam have something on McLeish and was turning the screws, using an inside contact to ease the pressure on him and his old man? Did McLeish even want Callahan brought in? And Amanda. He'd barely recognised her at the house. Could he still believe she was blameless in all this? Could he have judged her so wrongly? Could he even trust his own judgement anymore?

His head started to pound again. He placed his forehead on the bar surface, ignored the sticky residue of years of half-arsed cleaning. Closed his eyes.

More and more, walking away seemed the best idea. He'd suffer another bruise to his reputation, but what was one more knock to something already in the toilet?

He straightened again and grabbed the bottle. 'Fuck it. For once, I'm following orders.'

Monty turned to him, shook his head, pompous and solemn and condescending. 'That argument has been proved to be bollocks before, mate.'

Malkie scowled at him for talking sense, which was a first.

'I could meet Callahan alone, just to talk, sound him out. That can't hurt, can it?'

Do what you can. Always.

Monty, devoid of any context or frame of reference, formed an opinion, anyway. 'Course not. It's always good to talk.' He plucked the bottle from Malkie's fingers.

Malkie put his hand in his pocket and fingered the bag of Muzzle, then he picked up his mobile and dialled a number he should already have deleted.

FORTY-NINE

Callahan walked Markham to the basement with a box of cold pizza he found in the fridge and bottles of water. He pocketed the Hi-Power and the spare magazines, didn't trust Markham not to use it on himself.

As he locked the steel door, his phone rang. McCulloch again.

'We need to talk.'

'No, we don't, McCulloch.'

'Campbridge Pond. Ten o'clock. Or run and hide. Up to you.' Then he hung up.

The man was no idiot. His words hit home, and Callahan found himself jumping in the Astra and heading for what might be a last chance to salvage something of himself.

He knew the spot from minicab drop-offs nearby. A pond surrounded by dense stands of trees, with a wooden jetty built out into the water. Either a rotten choice or an excellent ambush spot. The trees could hide any number of coppers. He arrived early and settled at the water's edge on the south side of the pond. In a full hour, he saw and heard nothing. No vehicles cruising past, no hushed whispering, no orange glows from cigarettes being lit.

At 2150 hours a car parked on the Murieston Trail, to the north. A man got out, looked around, then walked down the muddy path to the jetty. The copper from Monday. He stood at the water's edge, his head hung low, as if praying.

Callahan breathed in the damp, woody, air, savoured it, wondered whether he'd ever again enjoy the simple pleasure of a walk and...

He shook himself. Worst time to lose focus.

What did McCulloch have? Something on Liam? Something to explain Sunday night? He was starting to believe he really had seen someone's terrified face hit the windscreen. But he still remembered nothing of driving into town or returning to Kirknewton afterwards. Might McCulloch have answers for him?

He crept around to the jetty. He studied the copper for ten minutes, watched for any small nod of his head which might indicate he was wired and talking to hidden colleagues.

The Dog pushed at him. *So, so easy.*

'I'm here.'

The man's head snapped up.

Detective Sergeant McCulloch looked like a heart attack waiting to happen.

'Thanks for coming, Mr Callahan. It's in both our interests, I promise.'

'I'm not coming down there.'

McCulloch held up his hands and trudged towards Callahan.

Callahan stopped him a pace away. 'Arms up.'

He frisked the man, smelled spirits on his breath. When he touched the man's shirtfront, McCulloch grabbed his wrist.

'I'm not wearing a wire.'

Callahan remembered him scratching his chest outside the cottage. He ran the back of his hand down McCulloch's shirt, felt nothing.

With a nod, he directed McCulloch back towards the better-lit road. The Dog growled in his head, demanded he rip the man's throat out, but he ignored it.

'I'm in enough shit to fill that pond, Mr Callahan. I tried to protect Amanda Fielding, tried to hide her from Liam. But I screwed up. She's back at Kirknewton, again, and I'm facing suspension or worse.'

Bad news: Callahan needed her healthy, able to character-testify for him. 'I like Amanda. We never spoke much because Liam was always watching, but she's a nice enough girl.'

'She is. Which is why I need to get her away from Liam, nail him, and clear you. Saving my job might be pushing my luck, though.'

Callahan stopped. 'I don't remember anything from Sunday, so unless you've turned up some solid new evidence, I'm going down for it.'

McCulloch stopped. 'Don't count on it. I think Jake sent you after Robin Wilkie, knowing about your – can I say "*issues*"? I want to get you the help you need, rather than a prison sentence. Your only crime was allowing yourself to be used. And Wilkie's chances are looking better than they did.'

Callahan started walking again, didn't want McCulloch to read his eyes. *He hasn't heard about Mitch McGuire yet.*

'Could Jake or Liam have spiked your drink before sending you after Wilkie? Might explain the gaps in your memory? I understand even acute PTSD sufferers always remember something from a blackout? Forensics found evidence of you and both Fieldings in that car, but I believe you when you say you don't remember anything. And I've promised people I'll help you get help rather than a cell in Addiewell. If that's what you want.'

McCulloch stepped closer. 'Plus, I want to nail that low-life Fielding.'

McCulloch seemed genuine in a way Callahan had missed before. Could he offer a way forward?

At the junction with the main road, McCulloch turned right, towards a housing estate.

Callahan followed but scanned the trees and houses ahead. 'Pretend I'm interested.'

A long, relieved sigh suggested McCulloch had a lot at stake too. 'Mr Callahan, if I involve you, I need to reveal intel I haven't even told my DC. How do I know I can trust you?'

Callahan nodded. 'You can't. And I don't trust you either.'

They walked on, the silence almost companionable. He waited for McCulloch to continue.

'Tell me what you remember from Sunday night. Every small detail. Anything that might explain why you were in your car that night.'

Memories flashed across Callahan's mind – Monday morning, two coppers at his door, the state of his car. The Dog howled at him to gut this guy. What could he gain from reliving the events? He drove the car, he was guilty.

But McCulloch had another theory and Callahan needed to hear it.

'I remember playing poker with Jake and Liam until late, then I must have fallen asleep. And you're right – Jake admitted he'd slipped me something, having a laugh at my expense. Next thing I remember is waking up terrified, like I'd fallen off a cliff, and the TV screen smashed, and that's as much as I remembered before I found you at my door.'

McCulloch didn't miss his choice of words. 'Anything more since then?'

Callahan braced himself. What did he have left to lose?

'I do remember sitting in a car.' He took a breath, braced

himself to cross a line. 'And I remember a collision, and glass smashing, and blood.'

The depth of McCulloch's disappointment was plain. 'But do you remember actually driving?'

'No, but I must have been. I remember blood. And smashed glass. Then I woke up with my car right outside, and in that state.' He left out the face he saw in his dreams, chewing through the glass to get to him.

McCulloch held his hands out. 'OK. I believe you.'

Callahan struggled to believe what he was hearing. A jury might listen to this man. If, together, they could get Amanda to safety, she might testify he did all he could to avoid trouble. Would a few years in a secure psychiatric wing be so bad? A chance worth taking to silence the bloody Dog for good?

'OK, if you can get me into treatment, I'll help you nail Liam. But convince me, swear on your mother's life, anything.'

McCulloch froze, and Callahan saw pain sear the man's eyes. It passed, and they walked on.

McCulloch took several seconds to speak again. 'So, you believe Liam might be culpable somehow? And Jake? You and he go way back, don't you?'

'Aye, but Jake's all over the place recently. Liam's pressuring him to pull out of some big deal he's putting together. Liam's usually up for everything, more of a head case than Jake ever was, but his dad's turning into a recluse. I think he wants to scale down their businesses. Like he wants a quiet life.'

'Aye, I bet he does.'

Callahan caught McCulloch's tone, gestured for him to elaborate.

McCulloch waved a hand, dismissive. 'Did Wilkie have something on both of them? Could Jake have sent you and Liam to Wilkie's place to get something, and it went bad?'

There was more to that question. 'What are you not telling me?'

McCulloch seemed to carefully consider his next words. 'You first, Mr Callahan.' He walked on. 'I don't think I've seen this neighbourhood before. Funny, you live your whole life in one town and still find bits of it you never knew. You familiar with this area at all?'

Callahan studied his surroundings, needed to know what McCulloch was up to. A road running south out of town, lined on one side by trees and farmland, and on the other by detached villas with huge gardens. Affluent, quiet, boring. What the hell was McCulloch up to?

'I've dropped off fares here. Your turn – what are you not telling me about Liam?'

McCulloch turned to look at him. 'Are you positive, Mr Callahan? Look again. Be sure.'

Impatience nearly overcame him, but he looked again. Terraced villas, lights burning behind curtains, hedges and gardens.

Yellow plastic police tape, flapping in a breeze, stretched across the driveway of one nearby house.

After a brief double-take, he trawled his mind, hunted for any memory of this place, anything to tie him to the events of Sunday night. He was relieved to find nothing.

'It was here? It happened here?'

McCulloch nodded. 'On the main road. I think you were here, but you were out of your head. I think you and Liam drove here, and it went bad, but I can't work out why. Or who was driving.'

He couldn't answer, wasn't sure he could handle remembering that night. What if his memory returned and it damned him? He soaked in the scene, absorbed it. None of it was familiar beyond passenger drop-offs. No way he drove along this road and ploughed into someone. And yet, something nagged at him. He walked north, past the junction, towards town. Something whispered to him. *Look again*. Police tape across just one

297

house? Scraps of tape hanging from one lamp post at the road junction. And then he spotted them: tyre tracks burned onto tarmac.

McCulloch's voice made him jump. 'Liam wouldn't hurt Mr Wilkie. Not knowingly. They know each other.'

'Business partners?'

McCulloch locked eyes on him. 'Partners, aye. But not in business.'

It took him a while to work it out. Then his mind rejected it outright. 'No chance. Liam and Wilkie? You mean...'

McCulloch's steady gaze attested to his certainty of the fact.

'You're a bloody liar. Liam is just as bad a homophobe as his dad. What are you really after, McCulloch? And don't insult my intelligence again.' He stepped forward, one hand raised as if to grab McCulloch's throat. The Dog slavered and growled.

McCulloch held his hands up. 'Whoa, man. I'm on your side.' He dug into his jacket pocket and pulled out a bag of capsules.

'Here – proof you can trust me. I found these at Bernard Robertson's place. He said this is the last batch of Muzzle ever made. Said he wanted you to have them but he let you down.'

Callahan felt relief surge through him, electrify him, but he masked his reaction the best he could. 'The last safe batch, he meant.' A pang of guilt soured the rush of adrenaline. *I'm so, so, sorry, Bernie.*

McCulloch frowned. 'What do you mean?'

'Doesn't matter.' He took the package. They did look like Norrie Wallace's Muzzles. After the last three nightmare days, he had what he needed. He could run, hide, sort himself out. Could be two years' supply here. It might be enough. Keep him out of a cell. But why would McCulloch give him the one thing he needed to let him disappear? Were these really Muzzles, or was McCulloch just another liar? But what if he were genuine, the only honest man he'd met since this whole mess began.

Could he mean what he said? Was it worth trusting this man for a chance to get into treatment and, with the right help, bury The Dog for good?

The decision came to him more easily than he expected – he was so tired. 'Talk to me.'

McCulloch's shoulders dropped, and the frown fell from his face, replaced by what looked like desperate relief. Did he have more than professional pride at stake? How personal was this for him?

McCulloch pulled a card from his pocket. 'Name a place and time. I meet you with DC Lang – you remember her from Kirknewton? – and my DI, McLeish. Any place you feel safe. Tell them your version of events. I'm on sick leave, so I'll need both of them onside for this to work, but I'd trust Steph Lang with my life.'

'And McLeish?'

'He's a prick, but I trust Steph.'

He took McCulloch's card and tapped it on his lips as he thought, came up with the perfect place. He'd spot any ambush a mile away.

'I'll call you with a location.' As he walked away, something scratched at his mind, whispered to him.

'Get your lot to look at those skid marks again.'

Malkie recalled the Road Policing report he'd never got around to reading. 'For what?'

'I don't know. Just do it.'

FIFTY

Callahan called with instructions at seven. Malkie showered in record time and arrived at the station minutes before eight.

When Steph arrived, he nearly chickened out. If she were in one of her moods, what he had to say might result in his immediate castration.

But what choice did he have? He wouldn't make it to his own desk without some career drone grassing him up to McLeish. And text or no text, he had no intention of putting himself through that meeting today.

He intercepted Steph at her car, dragged her by the elbow to the rear of the building. When they stopped, she leaned close and sniffed his breath. She glared at him, looked appalled and disappointed.

'What the hell are you doing, Malkie? McLeish is going spare. He offered you sick leave, or he'd call Professional Standards. You won't get a better offer, mate.'

He held his hands up. 'I know. I'm supposed to be meeting him right now, but I can't. Not yet.'

He swallowed, hesitated, and her expression turned dark.

'I met Walter Callahan last night. He and I had a chat.'

She shook her head. 'Are you trying to get yourself charged with obstruction? Have you lost your bloody mind?'

She ran out of words. Her mouth worked but she could find nothing more to say. He'd never seen her so furious.

He lowered his hands but maintained eye contact, waited for her to calm down enough to listen.

'I think Liam Fielding was driving that car. I think Jake fed him a story, some threat to the family business he's putting together, and he sent Liam and Callahan to sort it out. But it turns out Liam already knows Wilkie.' *That's enough for now.* 'Liam didn't realise who he was driving at until it was too late. Hence the two sets of skid marks – one where he accelerated from stationary, the other where he recognised Wilkie and tried to stop. He was pissed, hence his late reaction. Callahan was in the passenger seat, but he was even more pissed, and stoned too, thanks to Jake. That's why he has no recollection of driving. And it explains why Liam looked so messed up that morning. He'd just run down...'

Too much, too soon?

Steph planted one hand on her hip and raised her other forefinger in front of his face. He hated when she did that.

'Hang on. How does Liam know Wilkie, and how do you know that? Did Callahan tell you? And what does that change, anyway? We still have to bring Callahan in. Forensics says he was all over the inside of that car – parked outside his home, by the way – and he has a history of violence and mental issues. It's a no-brainer Malkie, and you know I never settle for easy collars.'

'I know you don't, and that's why you need to hear him out, but not in an interview room. Somewhere neutral.' He took a deep breath. 'And I want you to get McLeish there, too.'

She laughed, loud and sarcastic.

'You're kidding, right? I should drag your sorry arse up there right now, but you want me to – hang on, let me get this right –

you want me to ask the SIO on Wilkie's case to meet the prime suspect in Wilkie's case, but not on the record, and not even in an interview room. Have I got that right, Malkie, because I'm struggling here?'

Her eyes raged. He didn't have long.

'Callahan wants this all sorted, too. I told him if he co-operated, I'd do my best to get him treatment rather than prison.'

She said nothing for long, long seconds. 'You made a deal with him. A deal you didn't clear with McLeish or the Fiscal's Office. A deal you can't guarantee.'

He shrugged. 'I was desperate. I need to bring this guy in the right way. I promised someone.'

She shook her head. 'You promised someone.'

He waited.

'Who did you make this promise to?'

'Helen Reid, at the LESOC. She asked me to get him treatment rather than being banged up.'

Her voice was quiet now, as if mourning the end of her friend's career. 'You can't make promises like that, Malkie. The Fiscal's Office sanctions deals, not us. Our job is to gather evidence, analyse it, then present that evidence to them. Then it's out of our hands. You remember this stuff from basic training?'

Malkie shuffled his feet, stared at them. Her fury and her justified disappointment cut him to his core. 'If I can bring Callahan in voluntarily, and if I'm right that Liam was behind the wheel of that car, then they might go easy on him.'

Steph studied him. 'And you're doing all this just for Callahan, aye?'

His head snapped up. She couldn't know, could she?

'I bloody knew it. You know where Amanda Fielding is, don't you?'

He sighed – no point lying. 'She's at Kirknewton, again. She turned up on my doorstep a couple of days ago, terrified, but refused to come in for protection, so I let her stay on my dad's boat for a while. She refused to let me bring her in, so my only options were to cut her loose and leave her to Liam's mercy or look after her for a couple of days. But Liam found her and took her back to Kirknewton. I saw her yesterday. She's walking into doors again.'

She threw her hands up. 'I'm done, Malkie. There's no saving you, sometimes. I'll try to get McLeish to go easy, but I'm not going down with you, I'm sorry.'

He slumped against the wall. Without her help his career, his life, his remaining self-respect, all would collapse and leave nothing but the worthless core of shit he always feared lay at the centre of him. Could he blame her? She'd stuck her neck out often enough for him before.

'Steph. Please. I need this.' He made no attempt to mask his desperation. After all he'd got so badly wrong, after betraying so many people he'd persuaded to trust him, one more fuck-up might shatter what little will he had left to redeem himself.

She leaned on the wall beside him, folded her arms as if feeling the cold.

'Malkie, what can I do? You've put me in an impossible position. God help me I love you but you're one massive, unstoppable self-implosion.'

The look in her eyes nearly broke him. Steph's stubborn concern, her non-negotiable affection, pushed him to an edge.

Tears welled, but – still – he wiped them away.

Not yet. Earn them.

'I'm a good copper, Steph. I know I screw up, and God knows I don't deserve to call you a friend. But this one's important to me.'

He swallowed, steadied a tremor that threatened to become a full breakdown. 'I let my mum and dad down so badly I'll ever get over it. And now I'm letting Amanda down, and Callahan and Helen Reid. And you. I can't keep disappointing people, Steph. It'll break me.'

'Aw hell, Malkie. McLeish will hammer us both if I go to him with that.'

He needed to come clean. It was the only way to regain her trust, to prove to her that his behaviour made any kind of sense.

'There's more.'

Her eyes snapped back to his, dread in her expression.

'Liam Fielding and Robin Wilkie are partners. Lovers. But that mustn't get out or Amanda is in even more danger.'

He watched her argue with herself. She'd know he wouldn't make such a claim without being certain.

'So he's out of the picture for the attack on Wilkie, then?'

He had to push his next words out, knew how feeble they might sound.

'No. He also as good as admitted to me that Robin's attack was his fault.'

'He admitted? As good as?' The comment hung between them, thick with her doubt.

Malkie shrugged. 'All but. I was there. I saw his eyes. He was telling the truth.'

He was pushing it now, but he had to finish.

'And finally...' He sighed. Her reaction to this could make or break him.

'Amanda saw Liam meeting someone in the trees behind the house, late at night.'

'And?' Her patience was nearly exhausted.

'It was McLeish.'

She threw her arms up, turned away. Not good.

'Think, Steph. Why else did he warn me off them? Why did he let Fielding walk so easily? He's up to something he doesn't want us poking about in.'

This proved too much. 'No, Malkie. She's bloody playing you. Fielding and Wilkie I can believe because I'm guessing you've checked that out. But McLeish, bent? Can you hear how you sound, mate?'

He couldn't deny she could be right. Had Amanda manipulated him from the start? McLeish's name and rank was printed below the photograph on the boat – had she used him to muddy the waters, while keeping Malkie panting after her like some stupid, horny mutt? Did she already know about Liam and Wilkie? Was that why she didn't seem surprised? The whisper he'd been ignoring wouldn't be ignored any longer.

Did she run over Wilkie, to punish Liam?

As if she saw this going through his mind, Steph stepped close and gripped his arms. 'Is that everything? And I mean everything?'

'That's the lot. I promise.'

She came visibly to a decision. 'OK, you stop feeling so bloody sorry for yourself, promise me you'll be straight with me from now on, and I'll persuade McLeish to meet Callahan. But I'm saying nothing about Amanda Fielding's story. And bring her in, for pity's sake. How many times, Malkie? You can't protect everyone. I'll tell McLeish there's some connection between Liam and Wilkie we're still working on.'

He nearly lost it. One last chance to save himself from his own total inadequacy. If this went bad, McLeish wouldn't have to sack him – he'd quit.

'Thanks, Steph.' He held out his baton, warrant card, and cuffs. 'Can you take these? I don't want them on me.'

'Nope. You're on leave, not suspended. You're still a copper, old man.' She walked away without another word, leaving him to wonder if he'd made things better or much, much, worse.

FIFTY-ONE

Malkie hated sports clubs. He didn't resent fitness addicts, but they did tend to remind him of everything he wasn't.

He found the bench Callahan had described, at the north side of the football pitches. He could see why Callahan had chosen the spot: wide open, trees on three sides, open scrubland and a factory to the north. If he suspected trouble, he had plenty of exits to choose from.

Malkie sat, stretched his arms along the backrest of the bench. He tried to relax, soak up the sounds floating across the rarefied winter air from a football game: instructions barked, insults yelled, cheers and jeers from fans dotted around the pitch. A girl in a duffel coat walked two Rhodesian Ridgebacks with tennis balls clutched in their slavering mouths. Two men in bicep-flattering vest tops threw a frisbee on an adjacent empty pitch, neither putting much effort into it. A young couple occupied another nearby bench, neither happy with the other judging by the way they sat in silence, sunk into their coats in the freezing air.

Being a bachelor isn't all bad. Especially when he tended to attract disaster-zones like Sandra Morton.

He closed his eyes, let his mind wander. He saw his dad, eyes bright and alive, his glass ever full. He saw Amanda stretched out in the *Droopy Goose*'s cabin, her eyes dreamy, her complexion glowing and free of bruises. He saw himself at work, the corridors of the station no longer a daily walk of discomfort.

Could he pull this off, bring Callahan in safely, keep one promise and redeem a scrap of himself after failing his mum with such appalling consequences? Fix his car crash of a life and sleep at peace again, without waking soaked in his own sweat, hands clawing at his scarred chest, tasting ashes in his throat?

'McCulloch. Wake up.'

McLeish stood, arms folded across his chest, his posture a threat of much shit to come. Steph stood to one side, hands in her trouser pockets, a warning in her eyes.

'DI McLeish. Thanks for coming. Appreciate it.'

He offered Steph a grateful nod. She rolled her eyes.

McLeish's expression darkened. 'Get to the point, McCulloch.'

Malkie realised, only now, that he'd put no thought into how to handle this. He hadn't dared to believe he'd get this far, but he should have prepared for it.

'OK, McCulloch, I'll start. You're on mandatory leave as of yesterday. If I find you within spitting distance of the Wilkie case, I'll drag you to Professional Standards so fast your fucking nose will bleed. Got it?'

McLeish rarely swore, considered it beneath a man on his obviously stratospheric career trajectory. He had to be seriously pissed off to use Language.

Malkie slid to one end of the bench. 'Sit down, McLeish. What I have to say is worth hearing.'

McLeish muttered more Language under his breath but sat.

Steph remained on her feet, her eyes scanning the playing fields.

'Fine. I'm sitting. Where's Callahan?'

Malkie checked his watch – fifteen minutes to go. 'Noon. He'll be here, and I want you to listen to him. And before you ask, *he* came to me.' Another lie, but a necessary one. 'I persuaded Callahan to meet you because I think there's more to the Wilkie case than even he knows, and I want us to work together to find out what happened that night.'

Ask him why – if – he's been meeting Fielding junior.

'How is Mr Wilkie by the way? I'm guessing I'm not allowed near him, either?'

McLeish's eyes confirmed his answer.

Steph spoke. 'He's stable. Doctors think he'll survive, but in what state...'

'That might help, I suppose,' Malkie muttered.

McLeish's expression demanded to know what he meant.

'Homicide will get Callahan fifteen years in Addiewell, and with his violence issues he'll never get out. Attempted with diminished responsibility, though – that might get him a psych order. The man is screwed up, PTSD from too many tours in Iraq and Afghanistan. He admits he does remember sitting in that car but he still can't believe he was driving.'

He breathed. Make or break time. 'I think he wants to come in. I think he wants help. I suspect he's only accidentally culpable at worst.'

McLeish studied him. 'Go on.'

'I believe him. I think Liam Fielding was at the wheel and I've found out he already knew Wilkie.'

Did Amanda know Wilkie, too? Could I be so wrong?

'I think he and Callahan went there on Jake's orders, and Liam didn't recognise Wilkie at first. He slammed the brakes on but too late. Hence, two sets of skid marks.'

Get your lot to look at those skid marks again – what had Callahan noticed?

McLeish waited. Steph waited. McLeish didn't disappoint.

'McCulloch, you've had it in for Liam Fielding ever since that bloody nightclub incident. I agree the man's a shitbag, but where's your evidence? Forensics found prints from both Fieldings and Callahan and partials from three others they can't match, but the car was parked outside Callahan's house, and he has a reputation for violence. Callahan drove that car. Callahan ran down Wilkie. He's in a cell today whether you like it or not.'

Steph glared at McLeish. What assurances had McLeish given her that she now doubted? Malkie stood, scanned the area for any face he might know from the station. McLeish stared at him, a defiant gleam in his eye.

'What have you done, McLeish? I promised he'd meet me and Steph and you, no one else. What have you done?'

'Sit down, McCulloch. I would imagine he's watching us now.'

Malkie scanned the playing fields again, saw no one he recognised. If he bailed out now he went back to having nothing and Callahan would disappear. This crap plan was all he had.

He sat. All three waited in tense silence until Steph said, 'Incoming.'

Callahan approached from the south, across the empty pitch. He walked like a man fearing sniper sights on him. Twice, he turned and walked backwards.

He stopped ten feet away. 'You must be DI McLeish and DC Lang.'

McLeish stood, held out his hand. Callahan stared at it as if it were dipped in shit.

Callahan studied McLeish. 'You're chasing the wrong man. If I drove that car, I'd remember. And I don't.'

Malkie's stomach sank. *Oh well done. That should do the trick.*

Callahan hesitated, glanced at Malkie, made a decision. 'I want to get myself committed. I need help.'

McLeish nodded as if considering his words. 'OK, we can discuss that. First, an item of Liam Fielding's property was found in Mr Wilkie's possession – do you know what that was?'

Callahan frowned. 'No idea. I told you, I never met the man. What was it?'

'I'll discuss that only under caution.'

Callahan's face darkened. Malkie needed to act to keep him hooked.

'It was a memory card. But we can't get into it.'

Both Steph and McLeish shot him disbelieving looks.

Callahan considered this for a moment, then shook his head. 'Nothing to do with me.'

McLeish's eyes hardened. 'OK, so tell me how you're so sure you weren't driving the car that struck Mr Wilkie.'

Callahan's shoulders sagged, and he rubbed his eyes with his fingers. He looked exhausted.

'I've suffered from depression and anxiety since...' He shook his head, as if arguing with himself, then looked Malkie in the eyes. 'No. Not depression. I have PTSD, don't I?'

McLeish opened his mouth, but Malkie shut him up with a glance.

'I was given medication and left to fend for myself. I've spent the last eleven years learning to control my symptoms. I stay away from people. I avoid stress. I don't even watch war films on TV. But sometimes people get in my face, push me too far.'

Malkie recalled Derek Woodburn's gleeful storytelling. 'Like Frankie from the cab office.'

Callahan looked at him. 'Aye, like Frankie. You spoke to Woodburn?'

Malkie nodded.

'Every time I lose my rag, I end up hospitalising people. Once I get started I can't stop. But I've never killed a civilian.'

He scowled, shook his head as if dislodging a bad memory.

McLeish raised a forefinger. 'So, let me get this right. You can't have run down Mr Wilkie because you have a violent nature and a short temper, and you suffer blackouts during which you lose control of your actions? Help me here – how does that help your case?'

'Because, DI McLeish, I always remember the before and after of those incidents. I always remember what started them and I always remember the fallout from them. It's often me who calls an ambulance. And I've always – *always* – tried to defuse trouble before it goes too far. I've never picked a fight with anyone in my life. Not once.'

He spread his hands to emphasise his candour. 'If I had run down Mr Wilkie in that car, I'd remember driving beforehand even if I'd then blacked out. But I remember nothing. And I think I know why.'

They waited. Steph looked troubled.

'Jake spiked my drink. Your lab should find something in my whisky glass if they took it.'

He held his hands out as if, having unburdened himself, he was ready to accept the consequences.

'You need to section me, and I won't resist.' He sounded broken.

Malkie wanted to offer him a smile of reassurance, but Callahan stared at the ground.

McLeish paced a few yards, pondering. Steph stared at Callahan. She looked confused. Perhaps she also believed him now. Malkie might yet manage to haul his arse out of the fire, if nothing else went wrong.

McLeish stopped pacing. 'OK, come in. We'll re-examine the forensics, check that glass. We'll get you a doctor. And I'll bring in the Fieldings, see what they say. Acceptable?'

Warning bells sounded in Malkie's head. Why would McLeish bring the Fieldings in if it might expose his connection to Liam? Unless there was no connection, after all? *Did you make it up, Amanda? Did you see that photo and spin me a story I was too happy not to question?*

Malkie stretched to ease the tension knotting his shoulder. He stepped a few paces away and spotted them. The frisbee chuckers wandering across the pitch behind Callahan. The unhappy couple now on foot and walking towards him. Two spectators facing his way, eyes locked on Callahan, despite a flurry of action on the pitch behind them.

Callahan noticed Malkie's reaction. He scanned the scene and spotted them as quickly. He turned on Malkie, furious.

Malkie tried to pre-empt the inevitable. 'I had no idea. I swear, man. You have to believe me.'

Callahan sneered at him then took off. He aimed halfway between the frisbee pair and the unhappy couple. He dummied left, then switched right so quickly he left all four clutching at nothing. Taser wires lashed out but fell, slack and tangled, to the grass. He ran west, crossed a footbridge over the main road through the town. The plainclothes coppers ran after him, but it was clear he would outpace them, just as he'd escaped Steph in Kirknewton.

McLeish pulled his radio from his pocket and barked orders, but his man was long gone.

Malkie lost it. The slap of betrayal in Callahan's expression stung him to the core. Another promise broken.

'You. Fucking. Idiot.' His words built to fury, the last spat directly into McLeish's face.

McLeish returned the stare, didn't flinch. 'Detective Sergeant McCulloch, you are on mandatory leave, effective yesterday. You will not speak to anyone involved in the Wilkie case, or the Fielding family. Have I made myself clear?'

Malkie brought his breathing under control, with difficulty.

'And will you be taking a more direct lead in the case? Any more late-night house calls to Kirknewton? Sir?'

Malkie saw a flash of fear in McLeish's eyes, which confirmed at least one of Amanda's claims. McLeish blinked, swallowed, then defiance returned to his eyes. Malkie ached to push for an answer, in front of Steph, but he couldn't count on the man buckling.

The plainclothes coppers reappeared, shaking their heads and breathing hard.

Malkie turned away, the fight draining from him. His one chance to save something from this shambles had just sprinted away to who knew where.

And he'd broken yet another promise.

'We had him, McLeish. He wanted to come in. If he hurts one other person, including himself, I'll see you held personally responsible.' He fixed McLeish's eyes with his own. 'Now, have *I* made myself clear?'

McLeish turned and strode away.

Malkie turned to Steph. 'He's as big a prick as I ever was.'

'Aye, but he's a Detective Inspector Prick, Malkie.'

She gave his arm a squeeze and headed after McLeish.

FIFTY-TWO

'What the hell did you expect? You can't trust any bastard these days, let alone another grunt. You were set up, you idiot.'

Callahan stared at Markham. They sat on the floor of the basement, backs against a wall. The pizza lay untouched but two of the water bottles lay empty. Markham had cleaned himself up, washed off the worst of the blood, but he winced when he moved. Had to have bruised ribs. If they were broken, he'd struggle to even sit up. No need to call an ambulance yet.

The depth of Markham's cynicism offended Callahan. Even during his lowest and darkest times, he'd fought on. Even when he failed to run himself to death high on the Pentlands through furious, gale-lashed nights, he took it as evidence that deep in the core of him, he wasn't ready to check out quite yet.

'Bollocks. I have people I can trust.' As he said it, he doubted his own words, but he refused to join the man's pity party.

Markham sneered at him. 'Who? Jacob Fielding? You're deluded, man.'

Callahan could find no words, no defence of the man that would ring true in his own ears. If the copper, McCulloch, was even half right, then Jake was neck-deep in this whole mess, somehow.

He came up with one name he believed could refute Markham's pessimism. 'Bernard Robertson. He's a good bloke.'

Markham thought for a second, then ugly recognition crept into his eyes. 'That bomb-disposal clown who got himself blown up because he didn't know when to stop? Fucking amateur deserved what he got.'

Callahan launched himself forward, forced Markham to the floor, raised his fist to wipe the ugly sneer from the man's face. The Dog howled, hungry for violence.

'Deserved it? You knew he needed time off, but you kept sending him out there. It was your fault, Markham. Yours...'

Something in Markham's expression stopped him. Disbelief, but laced with an appalled smugness. 'You don't know, do you? Even *he's* been lying to you.'

Callahan released him, sat back, squeezed his fingers in his eyes, wasn't sure he could bear to hear what might come out of Markham's mouth.

'Be careful. Be really, bloody, careful, Markham.'

Don't listen to him. Kill him.

Markham sat up with a grunt, clutched his ribs. 'You sad, sad, bastard, Callahan. You really don't know, do you?'

Callahan stared at him, promised more violence if Markham didn't get to the point.

'When Robertson asked me for R&R I granted it. Immediately. I signed him off for a week, but when that call came in, he couldn't help himself. Couldn't pass up another chance to be the big man.'

No. Even Bernard?

'He wouldn't lie to me like that.'

Markham's eyes remained rock-solid and unblinking.

Callahan lowered his head between his knees, screwed his eyes shut, willed his sorry life to end, there and then. One sudden, massive cardiac and he could go out like a light. When he looked up again, Markham's eyes had softened.

'None of you gave me a chance, did you? I was the toff with the silver stick up his arse, a Rupert, no use to anyone. You think I wanted to be there any more than you did? You think I was sleeping easy at nights, knowing a mortar shell could come over that fence any time? Do you think I enjoyed sending you poor bastards out every day and praying the same number would come back? Do you even realise how easy you lot had it? Yes, Callahan. Easy. You followed orders that could mean any one of you going home broken or in a bag, but I was the one that had to give those orders. I knew what it was like out there, but I had to keep sending you all into it.'

He stopped, shrank into himself. When he spoke again, his voice was broken and heartsick. 'Don't you think I fancied a few beers and a laugh some of those nights, a scrap of normal R&R instead of sitting alone in my tent watching shitty rip-off DVDs and listening to you lot laughing and drinking? Did it never, even once, occur to you that I would have joined in if I knew how?'

He stopped again. His eyes brimmed and spilled over. He didn't bother to wipe them away.

Callahan refused to feel sorry for the man but couldn't help re-appraising him. He was right – they'd pegged him as a soft, entitled waste of space from day one.

But the bastard had pulled him from Special Forces selection, his biggest ever chance to change his life, and that was something he could never see past.

'Is that why you had me RTU'd? Because we wouldn't let you play with us?'

Markham's face took on a look of weariness that Callahan thought couldn't get any worse.

'You were returned to unit because I was paid to do it. It was Jacob Fielding who got you RTU'd, you idiot.'

FIFTY-THREE

Malkie found his dad's hospital bed empty. His mind reeled. Recriminations hammered at his already battered conscience. Absent again, just when...

When what?

Common sense asserted itself. His dad's crossword book lay on the table. If the worst had happened, the staff would be clearing it out for the next patient. He found him in the day room, playing dominoes with a young lad. He stopped in the doorway, his breath stolen by the sight of the old man's smile, his eyes bright again. Malkie forced himself to step into the room. His dad spotted him and grinned.

'Malcolm. They say I can get out soon.'

He stood up from his wheelchair with care, tested his legs, then gathered his son into a desperate hug. Malkie tried to pull away, refused to accept comfort he didn't yet deserve, but his dad held on to him. He heard muffled weeping on his shoulder. His dad stepped away, wiped his eyes on a pyjama sleeve.

'How are you, son?'

Malkie nearly lost it. His dad never wasted breath on platitudes. He'd want an answer. Malkie could find no words. If he started, he might not stop, and the day room was too public a place to confess his many failures.

The lad stood. 'You can finish gubbing me later, Mr McCulloch. I'll go and have another crack at nurse Sophie. I think I'm wearing her down, you know?'

Malkie's dad grinned and the boy left, closed the door behind him. They sat. He waited, patient as only a parent can be.

Malkie told him everything, left nothing out. When he finished, he sagged in his chair, exhausted. The strain of unburdening everything had left him drained.

His dad considered the tale for long seconds, then smiled. 'I wouldn't expect anything less, son. I'm proud of you.'

Malkie nearly sobbed with relief. In less than a dozen words, the man who knew him better than anybody had taken his confession and absolved him. He hung his head, but more in relief than in the shame he'd become accustomed to.

'Son, ever since you joined the force, you've struggled with the way the job's changing. You used to enjoy catching bad guys, but all you do now is moan about paperwork, about how hard it was getting to do the right thing. When that woman...'

'Amanda.'

'Aye, when she knocked on your door what else could you do if she was too scared to go to the station? Let her walk away on her own? I'm sure you had your doubts, but what if you'd refused to help and she'd got hurt? I've got no idea if what you did was illegal or unprofessional but it was right. Anything else would have risked letting that woman down so, so badly, Malcolm. And without solid proof she was guilty of anything, what other choice did you have?'

Malkie allowed this to sink in, forced himself to listen to a man wiser than he'd ever be. 'Thanks, Dad. That does help, but I'm still in a shitstorm of a mess, though.'

'No problem, son, but less of that bloody language, OK?'

Dad laughed, and Malkie laughed, and the damning voice inside him backed off.

They sat in silence for a while. Malkie could see his dad had something more to say but gave him time. Malkie's phone rang. Steph's name on the screen. He sighed.

'Is it work, son? Has that stupid man you work for suspended you?'

'Not yet. Takes a lot of forms to get someone suspended, and it has to come from way further up the command structure from him. No, I'm just on mandatory leave. Again.'

'So, ignore it. You're on leave.'

He wanted to, but after letting Steph down badly, the least he owed her was to answer her calls.

'Steph. McLeish said I'm not allowed to talk to you.'

'Oh, shut up, you idiot. I said I'd keep you informed. McLeish has every spare officer in J Division hunting for Callahan. He knows he messed up today. He's pulling people off other cases, it's like a bloody war room here.'

'I thought McLeish was smarter, Steph, even him. Callahan's a fit man – we saw that on Monday morning. And he's had military training. There was no chance of ambushing him in a place like that, probably why he chose it. I'm glad no one got a taser on him. McLeish pulled that stunt and he'll take the shit for it if someone else gets hurt.'

'Aye, I made sure it all went in the case notes and McLeish knows it. He's trying to dig himself out of a big hole full of Stupid. He'll try to hang it all on you, though.'

'He can try. Not sure I care anymore, Steph.'

Neither spoke for a few seconds. During the silence, his phone buzzed and his screen announced a text message from an unknown number.

'Steph, give me two seconds.' He couldn't keep a tremor from his words.

He opened the text, and his stomach sank.

He returned the phone to his ear. 'You won't believe this – I got a message from Callahan. Says he has no issue with me and warned me to stay away. So, no worries there, right?'

Had he decided to disappear? Had Malkie's unwitting betrayal pushed the man too far? Should he have left it to Steph and McLeish?

Steph interrupted his internal flogging. 'What does Amanda think McLeish is up to with Fielding? I was struggling to believe her until I saw McLeish's reaction to your "house call" comment today. Now I can't stop thinking about it.'

Malkie hesitated. Could he cause much more damage than he already had? 'Amanda thinks he has something to do with this new deal Liam's putting together. She recognised him from a newspaper clipping on my dad's boat.'

'That stupid boy band thing? Malkie, a million people read that story. But you believe her?'

'Aye, I do. She's positive it's him. No doubt in her mind at all, and I'd bet your pension her reaction was genuine.'

'And when did she see McLeish at Kirknewton?'

'Couple of times, always after dark. She remembers because Liam and Jake had a massive argument one night. Amanda heard Liam sneak out hours later. She followed him to the trees behind the house. Liam met McLeish in a lane on the other side of the trees. She got close enough to watch, but not to hear what they talked about. But they were at it for more than twenty minutes, and it was intense.'

Steph sighed. 'But McLeish, bent? Stupid, maybe, but on the take? I can't see it, Malkie. But it explains his reaction to your wee poke.'

'Yep. I wanted to ask him, was waiting for the right time. I know I should have told you this morning, but how would you have reacted without seeing McLeish's behaviour today?'

'Aye, fair point. And when the wrong time arrived, today,

you exhibited uncharacteristic good judgement and didn't push it.'

'Patronising as ever, but aye, fair summary.'

She was quiet for a moment. It was a lot to digest. 'OK, you stay away. Go mend your roof or something. I need to think about this.'

She hung up in the middle of his attempt to thank her.

His dad stared at him, not happy. 'Should I be worried, Malcolm?'

Malkie braced himself. If his dad was anywhere near being discharged, he needed to know what waited for him.

'Dad, about the house. The insurance—'

'I know, Malcolm. I know. You youngsters do underestimate us wrinklies, don't you?'

Malkie closed his eyes, squeezed them with his fingers as relief threatened to break him.

Not yet.

His dad spoke into the awkward silence.

'We'll manage, son. You and me, we'll manage. We have the cabin. But...'

Malkie looked at him, dreaded what lay behind his dad's ominous tone.

'There's something you need to know too, son.'

FIFTY-FOUR

'Is it true, Jake?'

The phone line went silent. Scared? No, stubborn.

'Is what true, Walter?'

Callahan sighed. 'Did you pay James Markham to have me RTU'd from Special Forces selection?'

Jake couldn't hide an intake of breath. 'Who told you that? Was it that prick Robertson? Fuck's sake man, you—'

'Markham told me. Is it true?'

Callahan heard him swallow.

Tell me it's not true, Jake. Tell me Markham lied. Let me walk away.

'I've got sixteen men out here, Walter. Don't you come near me.'

Callahan's stomach sank.

'No. If they know it's me that's coming you can count on five or six, at best.'

'Sixteen, you psycho bastard. You come out here you're fucking dead meat.'

Walter waited, wished he could see Jake sweat.

'So, Sunday night. Anything to tell me, mate?'

Anger edged Jake's voice now. 'Christ, Walter. Not this shite again. It was your car, and you're a fucking psycho. That was all you. You're not hanging that on me.'

Callahan's world pitched around him. Jake's conviction sounded solid. If the old sod really knew nothing, that dumped full culpability for Callahan's actions on himself. But even if it was Liam all along, Jake had to know something.

Callahan took long seconds to stop his stomach from turning over.

'You remember Markham's Browning? The Hi-Power?'

'Fuck off, you're bluffing.'

'I'm coming home, Jake.' For once in Callahan's life, the perfect punchline came to him when he needed it to. 'Put the kettle on.'

FIFTY-FIVE

'Cancer?'

'I'm sorry, son. She swore me to silence. I've been trying to tell you since... But you weren't answering my messages.'

Cancer. 'Fuck's sake, Dad. How long did you know?'

'Only two months before that night. Apart from the exhaustion and weight loss, she hid her symptoms from everyone except me. She made me swear not to tell you.'

Malkie's throat constricted, thick with grief. This was too much. Cancer happened to other people, people on TV programmes, not to his mum. She'd known and yet...

'That's why she wanted that damned candle beside her bed.' His voice broke as he remembered his last, cruel words to her. 'She knew it was the last birthday present she'd ever get from me, didn't she?'

Tears spilled from his dad's eyes, and Malkie felt them pull at his own, tempt him into a breakdown he now deserved even less.

Malkie surged to his feet and his chair fell over backwards. He crossed to a window, turned his back on the suddenly suffocating room, forced his gaze out and away from his dad's grief.

What else is there? How much more terribly did I really let her down? There's more. God help me, I know there's more.

His phone rang, and he jumped, ripped from his self-shaming. He turned to his dad, who smiled and nodded at him to answer.

The display flashed Steph's name at him, and he realised she might be the one person, apart from his dad, from whom he might draw some comfort, perhaps a scrap of solidity and reliability to anchor himself to. He felt the pull of self-pity and a need for solitude, but he rejected it – his dad deserved to see him fight. For his self-respect, and to be a man they could both rely on into an uncertain future.

'Steph?'

'Aye. Need you, boss. It's McLeish.' She spoke in a hushed voice, which hooked his curiosity despite the current circumstances.

'OK, I'm here, Steph. What's that idiot done now? If he's punishing you for my screw-ups, I'll resign before I see you get a kicking you don't deserve.'

'I know you would. But it's not that. Something's going on. Something dodgy. He was on his way out the door, but he got a call. He sat back at his desk, didn't even take his coat off, looked massively pissed off. When he saw me watching him, he grabbed some papers and pretended he was studying them. That man is the worst actor in history.'

Despite his dad's revelation and his own fraying state of mind, this grabbed Malkie's attention. What the hell could make McLeish want to hide in his office? After today's shambles, he should have been out of there like shit off a hot shovel. As he considered, Malkie turned to his dad, caught him wiping his eyes on the back of his hand. Malkie choked, and shame filled him. Even now he clutched at his job for distraction, any excuse to turn from his car crash of a life when he should be facing it head on. He cast a look that promised he'd end the conversation, but his dad shook his head and gestured to him to continue.

'Malkie, you there?' Steph, still whispering, but urgent now.

His dad nodded at the phone, tears soaking his cheeks but pride bright in his eyes.

'I'm here. Was it his desk phone, or his work mobile?'

'Neither. Looked like his personal mobile.'

'Bollocks, means it won't be logged.'

He could almost hear Steph's brain working. He'd given her things to consider that were not normal – or completely ethical – in their job. 'Is he there now?'

A pause, probably her taking another look at him without being too obvious.

'Aye. Funny thing – he keeps checking his watch and his phone. The bastard's waiting for something.'

Steph using Language again – a bad sign.

'So, let me get this straight. He's about to leave but gets a call, then sits back down and pretends to be busy, and now he's waiting for something.'

'Aye. Wait, he's logging on. Two minutes – I've got an idea.'

She was silent for less than a minute, but the wait had Malkie grinding his teeth. He heard her fingers on her keyboard, but nothing more.

'The timestamps on our case files show he's in the Wilkie interview notes. Hang on...'

Malkie swore under his breath. He needed to let Steph do her thing – God knows he was lucky she was still talking to him – but the waiting was doing his head in.

Steph sounded intrigued. 'He's adding queries to our notes. Only minor stuff, but it's weird...' She paused, as if reading.

'Well?' He couldn't keep the irritation out of his voice.

'His comments are rubbish. I mean, they're relevant but nothing that can't wait.'

The penny dropped. Malkie grinned. 'So, what do you think?' He wanted her to reach the answer for herself.

Silence on the line – she might have arrived at the same conclusions he had but was struggling to articulate it.

'Amanda Fielding was telling the truth – he's involved. He's logging an audit trail of his presence here, in his office. He's giving himself a bloody alibi.'

'Aye, I think so.'

'But an alibi for what? Why is he hiding here if he's got a stake in this?'

Malkie had no idea either. Was he afraid Callahan would come for him? Or was he bent as a six-pound note and neck-deep in the Fieldings and their businesses?

And then it hit him, and he wished it hadn't. Callahan's text message. *Stay away.*

'Aw hell, Callahan's going after the Fieldings. That text he sent me – he was warning me to stay away from Kirknewton. And I'll bet my pension McLeish's call was Liam asking for help. But McLeish is washing his hands of the whole mess.'

Could he flush McLeish out, force him to reveal his involvement? 'I've got an idea. Don't hang up but watch him.'

He pulled his personal phone from his pocket, speed-dialled McLeish's work mobile and switched it to speaker so Steph could listen. When McLeish answered, he didn't speak right away, gave him time to stew.

'What do you want McCulloch?' Tension in his voice now.

'I've had a message from Walter Callahan.' He waited.

Eventually McLeish asked, 'And?'

'He told me he saw you at Kirknewton, talking to Liam Fielding, long after bedtime, a couple of weeks ago.'

Why the hell am I still protecting Amanda?

Silence.

'Well? Sir?'

More silence. A good sign.

327

'What's going on, McLeish? And don't give me any more shite because I've had a gutful of it from you.'

McLeish didn't go off on one, which confirmed Malkie was onto something.

'Did you have anything to do with Robin Wilkie's hit-and-run?'

'Of course I bloody didn't. You want to make accusations like that you file them formally, and we'll see how management reacts, with your record.'

'Who did then? Tell me how you're involved with the Fieldings. We both know I'll find out eventually.'

McLeish was silent for so long Malkie nearly repeated his question. When he did speak again, he sounded like he was pulling his own teeth. 'Liam Fielding is one of my informants. Has been for months.'

Both Fieldings would rather have their fingernails pulled out than get chummy with the Pigs, but in the current circumstances it made a strange kind of sense. 'Months. Around the same time your big secret operation kicked off? The one you don't talk about?'

'You don't need to know. Operational reasons. I strongly suggest you leave it at that, McCulloch.'

Malkie hesitated. Could he make him crack over the phone? Was he afraid of the Fieldings, or was he personally invested? Was he up to his neck in business with them, or only slightly bent but afraid exposure would damage his precious career? Time to push his buttons.

'Fine. Don't tell me. But whatever happens next is on your head.'

When McLeish spoke again, his voice was low and wary. 'Where are you, McCulloch?'

He had him. 'Doesn't matter, but Callahan told me to stay away from Kirknewton tonight. Sounds bad to me.'

More silence. Malkie waited. McLeish hung up.

Malkie picked up his personal mobile and listened. He heard Steph's voice, faint and muffled – she had her hand over the mouthpiece. After a few seconds, her voice came through more clearly.

'He's just charged out of here looking really rather stressed. I asked if we had a shout, if he needed support, but he ignored me. He even blanked Pammy Ballantyne.'

'He's going to Kirknewton, Steph.'

'So, what do we do now? Back him up? Pull some uniforms in? Callahan's dangerous – do we need to call out an ARU?'

She had a point, but an armed response would need McLeish's sign-off as acting DCI in Spalding's absence. Plus, he'd promised Dame Helen Reid that Callahan would get the treatment he needed, and that didn't include a couple of lead slugs in his chest. But if he left it to Steph and Callahan made no show of himself, she'd suffer, professionally.

'Steph, I'm with my dad. I'm going to stay...' He stopped. His dad was grinning and waving him to go. 'Change of plan. I'm going out there, see if I can talk Callahan down. I'd appreciate your support, but I know I'm asking a lot. Callahan's completely off-reservation now, and fuck knows what McLeish is playing at.'

She was silent for a few seconds. He couldn't blame her; this was completely off-protocol.

'Aw hell, Malkie, I can't let you go out there on your own.'

He waited, dreading and hoping, for what might come next.

'Where's your head, Malkie?'

'What? On my bloody neck. What do you mean?'

'Tell me you're ready for this. McLeish, Callahan, the Fieldings?' She paused for a second. 'Amanda Fielding?'

Amanda.

How many unfortunates had he left damaged and disappointed as he blundered through his supposedly adult life? Amanda, his mum, his dad, Callahan, even Steph. Was even toxic wee Sandra Morton partly his fault? Did his own hormonal, teenage weakness inflict his stupidity on her, as well as himself?

'Malkie? I need to know. It matters, mate.'

Of course it mattered. She was offering to risk so much, he needed to prove himself equal to it. For Steph and for every other name on his growing list.

'It's where it needs to be, Steph. I'm sure, now.'

A longer pause than he liked, then, 'You at St John's, aye? Pick you up at the main entrance?'

'Aye. Thanks.' He hoped even a fraction of his gratitude got through to her. Against all the odds, he had one more chance to fix this. He didn't deserve her.

He pocketed his phone, crossed to his dad, stood him up, and hugged him as if he might never see him again.

FIFTY-SIX

They arrived at Kirknewton after dark. Only now did Malkie realise he felt no urge to head for the cabin, a fact he hoped he wouldn't regret later.

Two massive men stood in the middle of the open gateway, feet spread, arms braced by their sides. Each wore a winter jacket open to their belt lines, but showed no clear sign they were carrying, so still no justification for going around McLeish to call out an armed response.

Steph rested a hand on his arm. 'Let's sort this bloody mess out shall we, boss?'

He smiled, felt something he'd missed – a purpose worth getting bloodied for. This he could do. Here he could make a difference.

They headed towards the house.

Silver puffs of breath, long and steady and assured, rose from the two goons silhouetted under security lights spaced along the front of the house. He stayed back, allowed Steph to approach them – she did her own particular brand of menacing that he could never hope to emulate. She approached the man on the left and stared up into his face, a foot above hers. He didn't move. A flash of her warrant card, then she spoke, her words low and dangerous. 'Step aside, or I'll arrest you for obstructing a police officer. It will hurt.'

The man glanced at his associate, who shrugged. Neither spoke, but they moved apart.

'Wise.' She stepped between and past them.

Malkie stepped forward. 'Wise move, lads. She's small but bloody lethal if you get on her bad side.'

He grinned at them, then followed Steph. A soft beep sounded from behind, and a low voice said something about two Pigs.

Two more men stood either side of the front door. They closed up as Steph approached them. Malkie sauntered along behind her, enjoying the show. She stopped, sighed, held her warrant card up again as if bored. One of them took it from her, peered at it, turned it over, held it up to a security light as if checking for a forgery. He handed it back to her. 'Warrant.'

Steph folded her arms. 'Tell both Mr Fieldings that Detective Sergeant Malcolm McCulloch and Detective Constable Stephanie Lang want a word.'

One of them thumbed the doorbell and waited for a buzz. 'Couple of Pigs at the door. That McFuckup guy and a female.'

A voice replied, crackly with static. 'Let them in.'

The man beamed a grin at McCulloch and pushed the front door inwards. He left barely enough space between himself and goon number two for Steph to squeeze through, let alone Malkie. It was like stepping sideways into a cleft in a rock face.

As he passed between them Malkie sniffed the air. 'Out of deodorant, boys?' He slammed the door behind him as they turned to come after him.

Steph shook her head. 'You can't help yourself, can you?'

He opened his mouth to respond, but Liam Fielding appeared from the lounge at the far end of the hallway.

'Where's McLeish? I sent for the organ grinder, not his fuckin' monkeys.'

Malkie spoke before Steph could. 'You *sent* for DI McLeish?'

Liam studied Malkie. 'I asked McLeish for help. We think Callahan's coming after us. We need protection.'

Malkie smiled. 'Big bad Liam Fielding needs protection from one man?'

'Aye. He's a bloody psycho.'

'Yes, so you've said before. But he's just one man. Why all the muscle? And why didn't you call 999? Why McLeish? Why only him?'

Liam swallowed. He glanced over his shoulder, towards the lounge. Jake appeared in the doorway.

'Aw, for fuck's sake. You two again?'

'Good evening, Jakey. We got wind that Mr Callahan might come here tonight. Thought we should check you're both OK.'

Jake flapped a scornful hand at him. 'We'll deal with him just fine. He's in for a shock when he gets here.'

'Can't do that. You've just verbally confirmed that you expect him to make an appearance tonight and that he intends harm to you and your family. We're obligated to remain here now. For your own protection, you understand.'

Jake's eyes narrowed. Malkie watched his feral little brain work. He licked his lips like a nervous dog. 'Fine, but you wait outside. You've not got a warrant, have you? No, I didn't think so. Go sit in your car. If you need a piss, there's plenty of trees out there.'

Malkie considered fronting it out, but Jake was right. Without a warrant, they couldn't stay inside without permission. As he turned to leave, Amanda appeared from the lounge and stomped towards him, new bruises on her face, one eye bloodshot. She supported her left arm with her right and winced as she walked.

Rage boiled up in Malkie. Callahan, Wilkie, and McLeish faded into murky grey at the back of his mind, blown into irrelevance by a searing blast of hate for both Fieldings.

Before he could open his mouth, Amanda slapped him, an almighty blow that rattled his jaw and left his cheek burning more with shame than pain. She glared at him, cold hate in her eyes. Malkie reeled. Gone was the terrified and vulnerable woman he'd comforted so recently, replaced by – by what? The fury in her eyes confirmed the truth of the vicious temper he'd refused to believe existed. With a disgusted look at him and both Fieldings, she pushed past them and sat on the stairs. She heaved in one anguished breath but instead of the breakdown Malkie expected, she sat in calm silence, with nothing but cold, hard hate in her eyes.

Jake grinned. Liam grinned. Steph looked embarrassed.

Aw hell, Amanda. Not you. Please, not you. The SOCO report, the car, the partial prints, probably female. Your record, all that violence. Could I have been so wrong about you?

'Out. Both of you.' Liam shoved Malkie towards the door.

Malkie turned on him. 'I'm not leaving here without Amanda.'

Amanda sneered at him, her disgust plain.

He felt Steph's hand on his arm, firm but gentle.

Liam leaned even closer. 'Fuck. Off. McCulloch.' He punctuated each word with a finger-stab into Malkie's chest. 'We don't want you here. My wife doesn't want you here. So. Fuck. Right. Off.'

Malkie landed a solid head-butt. Fielding staggered back, clutching the bridge of his nose.

'You're fucking dead, McCulloch.' Liam sprang at him. Somehow Steph appeared between them. She barely moved, but Liam seemed to slide off as her left arm swept his hands sideways and her right foot slammed into his groin. Liam went down gasping for air.

Steph stepped forward, stood over him, her fists raised, her breathing fast and hard. Malkie took hold of her arms, enough to remind her he could pull her back, if necessary. She turned to him, and Malkie recoiled from the fury in her eyes, barely recognised her. She calmed herself with an obvious effort and stepped behind Malkie.

What the fuck, Steph? Where did that come from? This isn't you.

A voice barked an order from the front door. 'McCulloch. Stand down, or I'll arrest you myself.'

They all turned. Liam rose to his knees. McLeish stood in the doorway, his hands braced on the doorframe, his face dark and dangerous. His tie, normally a perfect Windsor knot, hung loose three inches below his chin, his top shirt buttons open.

Malkie opened his mouth to rip into McLeish, but a gunshot sounded outside, then another, then screams of the like Malkie prayed he'd never hear again.

FIFTY-SEVEN

Callahan had parked the car on the Lanark Road and double-timed it to the gates. When he spotted the first guards, he was breathing hard but felt more alive than he had for years. Anyone between him and Jake knew the score, and so was a legitimate target. He and the damned Dog could enjoy themselves with a clear conscience.

He spotted them in seconds – complacent, leaning against trees, smoking, the glow of their cigarettes visible from a hundred yards away in the dark. Amateurs.

The Dog raged, demanded violence, hungered to hurt them. But he had it muzzled now, locked behind a cold and hard need to acquit himself the best he could on what might be his last mission. It burned inside him, but he channelled it, used it to razor-focus his awareness on the task – solo, no backup, no support, no medics, the ultimate test of his skills and his courage.

He took both men down in seconds without firing a shot or drawing his steel, then stood over them as they lay trussed and winded and grunting on the muddy ground.

The Dog growled. *Finish them. Use the steel.*

Callahan snarled back, a wordless and bestial warning.

When both men had their eyes locked on him, their breathing fast and laboured, he drew the Hi-Power and blew away one kneecap on each man.

The noise battered at him and set off a low whine in his ears. The muzzle flash lit up the dark, tangled mass of tree branches around him. He'd missed this more than he'd realised.

He let both men scream loud and long before bending to silence them.

FIFTY-EIGHT

The goons from outside rushed inside, pistols in hand, and barged McLeish into the hall. They slammed the door shut behind them and peered through the glass blocks on either side.

'It's him. He's bloody armed, Mr Fielding,'

Jake screamed at them. 'Christ's sake, so what? Get out there, you fucking cowards. Kill that bastard.' Then he stumbled up the staircase. The two apes returned outside, neither looking happy about it.

Liam, grunting in pain, followed Jake, dragged Amanda after him. Malkie glanced at Steph. *Callahan's bloody armed. We couldn't know, could we?* He turned to McLeish. 'Sounds like Callahan's got a gun from somewhere. Now might be a good time to call for some shooters of our own? Sir?'

McLeish glared at him. 'Don't push your luck, McCulloch. You've got a shitload of explaining to do, pal.'

'As do you, sir. As do you. Now, shall we?'

McLeish swallowed, and the defiance drained from his expression, replaced with a look of sick dread. Malkie stepped past McLeish and up the stairs. At the top, he spotted Liam push Amanda through a doorway and managed to wedge his foot in the opening before it closed.

When Steph and McLeish piled inside too, Malkie closed the door. The woodwork around the lock was wrecked. Liam waved his hand at it, dismissed it. 'Don't ask. Dad, get through to my room.'

Jake glared at him. 'Don't tell me what to do, boy.' His voice was a low and dangerous growl.

Liam stared at him over a handkerchief pressed to the bridge of his nose. 'Seriously, Dad?'

Jake sat on his bed, dropped his stick on the floor and folded his arms, defiance in his eyes. Liam sighed then dragged a dresser across the inside of the ruined door.

Malkie turned to McLeish. 'So. Sir?'

McLeish held his hands out. 'What?'

'Callahan? Gun? Maybe call out our AFOs? Just a suggestion, sir.'

Jake tore his furious eyes from his son. 'What's an AFO? I don't speak Pig, just English.'

Malkie turned on him. He'd had a bellyful of them all. 'Authorised Firearms Officers, you idiot. Big fuck-off police officers with big fuck-off guns.' He turned on McLeish again. 'Might be useful, right now.' He noticed Liam shoot the man an incredulous look as well.

'I'm warning you, McCulloch...' He pulled his mobile from his jacket pocket and walked to the window, his eyes on the display held above his shoulder.

'I'm sure you are, sir. I'd stay away from the window, though.'

McLeish stepped to the side and leaned against a wall. Steph flashed Malkie a warning look – not the best time to push his supposedly superior officer's buttons.

Liam took up position on the other side of the window, behind the opened curtain, and peered out into the darkness.

The lawn glowed a brilliant green under the roof-line security lights. He blew his nose into his handkerchief, and Malkie was sorry to see no blood.

Malkie crossed the room to Amanda. 'Are you OK?' His question sounded trite as soon as the words left his mouth.

She raised her swollen face to him, venom and sorrow and confusion in her eyes. 'Why, Malkie?'

Her pain, her grief at his betrayal, drained the anger from him. He looked at Liam, who shrugged and grinned, then returned his attention to the lawns and the cottage.

Amanda's eyes filled, and she swallowed. 'You didn't tell him, did you?'

Malkie touched her cheek, held his fingers there. 'I'm sorry you believed I would. No, I didn't tell him.'

She lowered her head, pulled away from his hand, stared at the floor.

Malkie's own shame threatened to choke him. *Aye, like you never suspected the worst of her, you hypocrite.*

'You two belong in a fuckin' Meg Ryan movie.' Jake stood and stepped to the window. 'Any sign of that bastard?'

Liam shook his head but kept his eyes on the lawns and his hand on his balls.

McLeish snapped his phone closed. 'AFOs ETA fifteen minutes.'

With difficulty Malkie turned from Amanda to the three other men in the room.

'You clowns have until the AFOs get here or until Callahan comes through that door to tell me what the hell's been going on. If I get all the facts, maybe I can talk him down, stop him from ending all of you. Maybe. But of course, after that shambles at the sports centre today, he's not going to be a very trusting soul, is he?'

He faced McLeish. 'Why were you meeting him' – he pointed at Liam – 'out there in the dead of night?'

He turned to Liam. 'Why was there a memory card with your prints all over it in Robin Wilkie's safe?'

He opened his mouth to tell Jake to keep it shut, but Jake's eyes were locked on his son, and furious. His voice dripped with menace. 'Aye, what did you and this prick have to talk about that you couldn't share with me?' He stepped in front of his son, nose-to-nose. 'Well, boy? Tell your old dad what you and the Filth and that wee arse-bandit Wilkie were up to, eh?'

Liam's eyes snapped up. 'How do you know Robin's gay?'

Jake's eyes narrowed, and his mouth twisted into an ugly, yellow-toothed sneer. 'So, it's Robin now, is it? How about you tell us how *you* know he's gay?'

As father and son stared murder at each other, another gunshot rang out and something thumped into the stonework outside the window. Everyone dropped to the floor. Steph jumped to the door and flicked off the light switch.

All went quiet.

Liam crept back to the window and inched up to peer over the sill.

Another deafening crack and the security light outside the window went dark.

FIFTY-NINE

Callahan worked his way around the tree line to the shadows behind the cottage. The range to the foot-wide security lights along the roofline of the main house was pushing it for a Hi-Power, but he couldn't risk stepping onto the floodlit lawn. He braced his wrists on his rolled-up jacket and took out the light outside Jake's bedroom with his second shot. One blinding light on the roofline turned to black, and the lights inside the room went dark. His guess had been bang-on. Jake had retreated to his room like a frightened wee laddie.

'You should be scared, Jake.'

He re-sighted on the window and let one more go. The glass exploded into the darkened room. He sprinted back to the garage.

Behind the main house, he dropped into shadowed flowerbeds and watched. Two men ran, crouched low, weaving from side to side. They held their hands together in front of them, clamped on the butts of pistols.

These were not Jake's usual boys. These guys were armed and knew how to move. Time to up his game if he was to fulfil his last – and most personal – mission.

He left them to chase his shadow and crept to the front of the house. Two more men crouched in the undergrowth, scanning the length of the gravel drive.

He backed into the trees and crept in a wide arc to approach from their six. Both went down quickly with slugs to one knee, and both obliged by screaming as loud and terrified as the first two. The Dog hungered to finish them, but Callahan wanted Jake to hear him coming.

He backed up five yards into the trees and waited. The men who had headed for the cottage returned and he took them both down as they examined the men on the ground. Two more kneecaps destroyed, two more screams, then he silenced all four and sprinted to the house.

Through a grimy window he saw the garage, dark and empty, the floor piled with sacks of lawn treatment and seed. He smothered a pane of glass with his jacket and jabbed the pommel of his knife through it. When no one came to investigate after sixty seconds, he unlocked the frame, slid it up, and climbed through.

He stopped to listen, to calm his thoughts and settle The Dog for the final push to his primary targets.

SIXTY

When a third shot blew the window in and sprayed the room with glass, Amanda cried out and crossed the room to Malkie, took his hand and hid behind him. Liam's eyes burned at them both in the dark.

Steph took Amanda by the shoulders and pulled her towards the side of the room away from the window. She sat her down on the carpet, against the wall, and joined her. Amanda pulled her legs up in front of her, hugged them and lowered her face onto her knees.

Malkie nodded a silent thank you to Steph, then turned back to the Fieldings and McLeish. 'You lot' – he glared at McLeish – 'all of you, need to level with me. When Callahan comes through that door, if I can't reason with him, he might kill all of us.'

Liam stared at his father. 'You know about me and Robin, don't you?'

'I don't know fuck all. If you and that pervert know each other, I don't want to hear it. Christ, Liam. You've got queer mates now?'

'How do you know he's gay, Dad?'

Jake flapped one scornful hand and sat in a chair beside the bed. 'Doesn't matter how I know. I wish I bloody didn't.'

'Why, Dad? You ashamed of me?'

'Of course I'm ashamed. A bloody queer trying to turn my son? You're better than that.'

Amanda laughed. All eyes turned to her. She pointed at both of them and howled with glee.

'Daddy knew all along? This is brilliant. Did you know about that bloody holiday too, Jake? I never saw your precious son because he was too busy doing the dirty with Wilkie. Or was he doing you, Liam? Why don't you tell us all, eh?'

Malkie wept inside at her words, as ugly as anything he'd heard from Liam or Jake. *You too, Amanda?*

She looked from father to son and back again, loathing and hatred burning in her eyes. 'You two deserve each other.'

She went quiet again, laid her head back against the wall and closed her eyes.

Liam took a step towards her, his eyes wet and red with shame, or fury, or both. Malkie stepped in front of him with an expression that promised violence. 'You've hurt her all you're going to. Back the fuck off.'

Steph stood, her eyes blazing, and Liam did as Malkie had ordered.

Malkie turned to McLeish. 'So, your late-night dates with Liam under the stars?'

McLeish stared at Malkie, then seemed to catch up with the conversation. 'Me? Gay? Fuck you, McCulloch.'

Malkie's temper spilled over. 'Fuck's sake. Is anyone here not a bloody bigot?'

Amanda looked down at the floor, couldn't hold Malkie's gaze. Jake jumped to his feet and grabbed his son by the front of his T-shirt. 'A poof and a Pig, Liam? What the fuck is happening to you?'

Liam exploded, threw his arms up and out. The old man fell

345

backwards against the bed, collapsed on the floor, started coughing and wheezing. Liam loomed over his father. 'You know what, Dad? Robin didn't turn me, and he hasn't made me soft. I'm the same man I always was. I'm just sick of you and your greed. How much money is enough, Dad? How much?'

He screamed his last words. Spit flew into Jake's face. The old man cowered, his eyes furious and appalled at the same time. His own son...

The rage drained out of Liam. 'When do we stop, Dad? When can we just...'

He backed away, glanced out the window, stepped to the side again. He folded his arms against the wall and rested his forehead on them.

Jake wheezed and grunted and glared poison at his son.

No one spoke.

Amanda watched Malkie. Steph watched Malkie.

Malkie stared at McLeish and the penny dropped.

'I get it. McLeish, you've excelled yourself this time, you idiot.'

SIXTY-ONE

Callahan eased open the internal door to the kitchen. Jake hadn't even secured his inner perimeter. Bloody amateur deserved to die.

Two more men lurked behind the breakfast bar, facing the hallway, their backs to him. They leaned on the counter, legs spread, feet planted, fingers resting on shotgun triggers, barrels trained on the inside of the front door.

Too easy to be satisfying. He hoped Liam and Jake would be more of a challenge than these clowns.

He crept through and eased the door closed behind him. The Dog demanded he do these ones up close and bloody, and this time he gave in to it. The men, focused on the front door, didn't hear him until he severed the tendons at the backs of their ankles, all four in two fast, fluid slashes. They dropped, screaming and clutching their feet. Their eyes bulged at the sight of him standing over them with six inches of gleaming steel blade held lightly in one hand.

'Amateurs.'

He kicked their guns away and let them howl like the others. One sobbed and pissed himself.

He waited. The men screeched their agony. No more reinforcements appeared. He stopped their screaming and hoped the silence would shred Jake's nerves nicely.

He stood at the foot of the stairs and called out.

'Jake, you up there? Time for a reckoning, mate.'

The Dog slavered and snarled, and Callahan surrendered himself to *It* at last. He let rage fill him, carry him up the stairs, towards the carnage *It* had waited so long to inflict on his tormentors.

One last push, his final mission. No longer capable of caring if he survived the night, he surrendered to his rage.

SIXTY-TWO

'I already know the big secret business deal was yours all along, wasn't it, Jake? Now I know Laurel and Hardy here were working together to stop it.'

Neither the younger Fielding nor McLeish said a word, but the absence of a denial said enough.

Malkie continued, thinking aloud. He crossed the room to Steph. He always thought better with her to bounce ideas off.

'So, Liam helps McLeish scupper Jake's big new deal.' Derek Woodburn's TV, the news article, sprang to mind. 'Of course – that stabbing in a Glasgow dockyard. What is it, Jake? Booze? Drugs? Wee girls? Smokes? Ah, cigarettes, then. So, D F Browne is Diane Brown, Customs & Excise. She won't be happy about this mess, will she, sir?'

McLeish glared at him but said nothing.

'And why does big, bad Liam Fielding want the deal stopped? Quiet life? Bit of privacy?'

Liam opened his mouth, but more screams sounded from downstairs, and these rang out for long, long seconds.

Callahan was inside the house.

His voice sounded from downstairs. 'Jake, you up there? Time for a reckoning, mate.'

For the first time Malkie could remember, Jake Fielding showed fear. The screams had been bad enough. Even his own son's fury hadn't broken him. But Callahan's voice – calm and chilling, even casual, calling him by name – seemed to snap something in the man. All dignity left him. He shook. His eyes whipped from Liam to Malkie and ended up on McLeish.

Steph stood, started hauling more furniture to the door.

Jake shuffled backwards and forwards along the length of the bed, his eyes darting between the bedroom door and the smashed window.

McLeish crossed to help Steph. 'AFOs should be here soon.'

Jake stared at him, furious. 'Why the fuck didn't you bring them with you?'

McLeish clamped his lips shut for a second and spread his fingers at his side. Sweat beaded his forehead. 'Nobody told me Callahan was armed, did they?'

The door slammed in its frame.

And again.

Jake retreated to the farthest corner, under the window, and slid down the wall, his eyes locked on the door.

Malkie snapped at him. 'Jake, look at me.'

Jake looked up. Defiance battled with fear in his eyes and lost. 'How dangerous is he when he's like this? Can he be reasoned with?' Malkie asked.

Jake stared back, his face white.

Malkie could squeeze just one word past a lump of dread clogging his throat. 'Fuck.'

Callahan slammed into the door again. The frame splintered, and even the heavy sideboard moved an inch away from the wall.

Liam stuck his head out the window and yelled. 'Every man still standing, get in here. He's in the house.'

The slamming on the door stopped. Callahan's voice sounded from the other side.

'That you, Liam? Sorry about your mate. I still can't remember doing it, but if the *Polis*

say I did it, I must have, right? I hope he pulls through, aye?'

Liam stared at Malkie in disbelief, his mouth hanging open.

'Having said that, I'm coming in there and I'm going to gut both of you, OK?'

He slammed into the door again. The wooden panels cracked. How could such a wiry wee shite put so much force into those blows?

Jake hung his head.

Steph leaned her weight against the sideboard. Her wee body wouldn't add much but she did what she could, as ever. She lurched backwards every few seconds as Callahan battered the door.

Malkie had minutes, if that.

'OK, so he' – Malkie pointed at Liam – 'wants Jake's deal stopped. Because he wants a low profile in case other mouth-breathers find out he's not as hard as he pretends he is?'

Liam glared at him, and again Malkie took his silence as a tacit admission.

'He finds out McLeish is investigating and approaches him, offers to turn grass. Spoil the deal in return for an easy sentence for his dad and the quiet life he wants.'

At this, Jake looked at his son. If Malkie expected anger at his betrayal, he didn't get it. The old man looked broken and bitter, like nothing could hurt him anymore.

Callahan slammed into the door again, and the point of a knife punched through the wood. If he could poke a hole in the door he wouldn't need to get into the room – he only needed space for a gun barrel.

Malkie forced himself to refocus. 'So, was Wilkie run down

because he knew about the deal? McLeish, did you have anything to do with that?'

'No, I did not.'

Another slam on the door and even more steel penetrated.

Steph spoke now. 'You were very quick to declare Wilkie's RTC as accidental, sir. Even when I showed you those tyre marks.'

McLeish looked cornered. He deflated, held his hands out as if begging for a break. 'I didn't want Liam getting dragged into another investigation just because it was one of his family's cars. He told me he had nothing to do with it, swore it was all Callahan.'

Malkie gaped at him. 'And you just took his word for it? Enough to order me to lay off them both? And that's why you let him walk after we found his prints all over that memory card?'

He turned to Liam. 'And what the hell was on that memory card? Might as well tell us now.'

Liam sagged, beaten. 'Insurance. For me and Robin. Recordings of conversations with him.' He nodded at McLeish. 'And phone calls he made' – he jabbed a thumb over his shoulder at Jake – 'to the guys he's getting the smokes from.'

'But you were in the car, though. With Callahan, right?' Malkie felt his grip on the facts slide. Was it all about to fall apart? A sick lump formed in his guts.

'How many times, McCulloch? No, I bloody wasn't.'

'So, you didn't drive at him by mistake. Did you order him run over without knowing it was him? Was he run over because he was holding that memory card for you? Did you drag him into this whole sorry mess and that's why you looked so bad on Monday morning?'

Liam nodded. 'My guess is that stupid old fucker' – he pointed at Jake – 'found out about it and sent that psycho' – he pointed at the door – 'to get it back. And as usual, Callahan went too far.' Moisture leaked from his eyes. He turned away, wiped his sleeve across his face.

Malkie swallowed bile. 'You weren't lying. You were never in that car, were you?'

But Malkie already knew. His worst fear was confirmed. He'd had it wrong from the start. He stared at the door and dread flooded him.

Was it you all along, Callahan? Was I so wrong?

Another impact on the door. A chunk of wood broke free and dropped into the room. Callahan peered through.

'McCulloch? I told you to stay away – I didn't come for you. Just those two bastards.' He noticed McLeish. 'Maybe that piece of shite, too.'

McLeish's face drained to a sickly grey.

Callahan turned to his left, towards the staircase. 'Hang on a minute...' He fired four more shots down the hallway then his hand appeared through the hole in the door, the gun clutched in his fingers. Malkie noticed the empty breech sticking out the back of the gun and Callahan withdrew his hand.

Malkie stepped forward, blocked Callahan's line of sight into the room.

'Mr Callahan, Walter, please? We can fix this.'

'Fix it? McCulloch, I like you but you're talking shite now.'

Malkie watched Callahan eject the magazine and insert another, then aim straight at his head. He nearly pissed himself but stood his ground. Callahan adjusted his aim, braced his gun hand with the other. Did he mean to shoot past him? At Jake? He wouldn't risk that, would he?

He watched Callahan's finger tighten on the trigger. He half expected to see his life flash before him, but instead saw his dad's life fall apart without him. *Good job, mate. One last disappointment, one last shameful betrayal, before lights out.*

He closed his eyes and waited for...

'Damn it, McCulloch, I'm not here for you.' Callahan slammed the gun against the door, furious.

Malkie heaved in a breath.

McLeish ran to the window. 'Where are those bloody AFOs?' He grabbed one end of a chest of drawers. 'McCulloch, get the other end.'

Malkie stayed put in front of Jake, terrified but damned if he'd let Callahan ruin his own life any further. He'd made promises.

Liam, his eyes red and glassy, joined McLeish, and they heaved the furniture to the door. Callahan fired again, high and wild, into the ceiling. 'Oh, for God's sake. I'm coming in there and people are going to die. Stop wasting my time.'

He fired another two shots.

Sirens wailed in the distance.

A half dozen more shots into the thicker wood between the panels, then three blows with the pistol butt. Both top panels and the central supporting wood gave way and fell into the room. He pushed in the top-most furniture and clambered through the gap. Liam grabbed for the gun, but Callahan fired wild at him. He missed but kept coming.

Jake crawled across the floor to the window, looked down at the lawn below, seemed to agonise beyond any common sense, then slumped back against the wall. Liam stood with his hands by his sides, violence in his eyes. McLeish listened at the window, flexing and clenching his fingers. Steph pushed Amanda to sit in the corner of the room and crouched to shield her.

Malkie stood his ground and braced himself for the mother of all difficult conversations. Yet again, lives depended on him. Yet again he'd made promises he feared he'd fail to keep.

One more failure, one more broken promise, might break him beyond all hope of redemption.

SIXTY-THREE

Malkie's guts churned as Callahan climbed over the remaining furniture into the room and stood, his breath heaving, his eyes wild, his hands shaking.

Callahan stared at Jake, his fingers clutching and loosening on the butt of the pistol.

'By my reckoning I have three rounds left. One for you, Jake. One for you, Liam. And a spare.'

Malkie's mind flashed on the worst and most final reason Callahan would reserve one round, and he was certain it wasn't for McLeish.

Jake stood. 'I'm not scared of you, Walter.' The tremor in the old man's voice betrayed his lie.

'Oh, you were always scared of me. You were just too stupid to know it.'

Liam stepped forward. 'Don't talk to him like that.'

Callahan's eyes widened. 'Really, Liam? After what he's done to you? You still defend him?'

'What he's done? You did this. You always go too bloody far, you fucking maniac.'

Liam's rage hammered into Callahan, who seemed to reel from it. Malkie prepared himself for the worst.

Callahan frowned. His eyes glazed over as if drawn to some troubling memory. He shook his head. 'I...' For a moment he was gone, drifting, lost, but he snapped back to the present when Malkie tensed to make a move.

'I couldn't have...' He swallowed, rubbed the heel of his hand across his eyes, left them red and raw. 'I'd remember. I always remember. Christ, why can't I remember?' His last words became a scream, an outburst of frustration and fury that shook Malkie to his core. Malkie saw again, in his mind, the look on Callahan's face when he'd first seen the damage to the car. No way this man was driving that night. Despite all the evidence, despite the conviction in Liam's earlier claim, he'd stake everything on it. He was missing something, and lives hung in the balance while he failed completely to see through the fog to the answer.

'Walter, I believe you.' *Just wish I knew why.*

Callahan stared at him. His eyes were glassy and bloodshot, desperate. He stepped backwards, turned half to one side, muttered to himself, wrapped his arms in front of him as if his heart were shattering. He banged the heel of his hand on his forehead, screamed at himself. 'Shut up. This is all your fault. I never wanted this.'

Malkie stepped forward, his hands out to the side, palms up, pleading.

Callahan recoiled. 'Stand down, McCulloch. It'll make me hurt you.'

Malkie retreated.

Callahan backed up a step, the pistol waving at the four men. The barrel shook. Steph moved behind Malkie, towards the far side of Callahan, but Malkie glared at her over his shoulder. She scowled and shook her head, but sat beside Amanda again. From outside, the sound of sirens rose to a crescendo then cut off. Malkie heard wheels brake hard on gravel. He saw blue flashes on the trees surrounding the lawn and heard van doors slide open. He had minutes to talk him down, minutes to save a life, minutes to keep too many promises.

Something about the sound of tyres on the gravel whispered in his mind. Tyres... Skid marks...

'Walter, that's an Armed Response Unit. They'll be coming up those stairs any minute. They don't hesitate. The slightest move against one of us, and they'll put you down, and neither of these fuckers is worth that.'

Callahan looked at him. Malkie's heart lurched in his chest. The rabid animal had gone, replaced by a broken and tormented man, bewildered and hurting.

Callahan's eyes pleaded with Malkie. 'Was it me in that car? Is that why I remember blood? And broken glass? And God forbid me, that poor man's face.'

Was that a confession? Did Callahan believe he did it, after all? Where else could such graphic memories have come from?

But the voice in Malkie's head hissed at him again, insistent. There are two front seats in any car. And what was it Callahan said? *'Get your lot to check those skid marks again.'* And seconds ago, about Jake – *'after what he's done?'* The skid marks. Two sets. One from hard acceleration. The other from braking. The second set, closer to the impact point, two solid lines of burnt rubber.

From the hallway, the sound of boots on the stairs.

Two lines... Solid lines, no gaps... The wheels locked... On a 2010 Astra...

The tyres... The damned tyres...

More boots on the hallway floor, but slow now, cautious. AFOs. He had only seconds...

Two solid lines. No gaps.

The brakes. No gaps.

No ABS.

'It was the handbrake.' Everyone stared at Malkie, even Callahan.

In the space between one breath and the next, the truth battered into him, fully formed and making perfect sense, and he cursed himself for his own damned stupidity.

'Walter, listen to me. You were in that car, but you weren't driving. Isn't that right, Jake?'

Jake stared at him, defiance blazing in his eyes. 'You're reaching, Pig.'

Liam turned to his father, Callahan forgotten. 'Was it you, Dad? Would you kill someone I care about that much?'

Jake snapped, raged, his face scarlet, his eyes wild. 'Don't you say that. Don't you fucking say that. You're not gay. My son is not a poof. That pervert, all over you like...'

Liam shook his head, his eyes desolate with grief. 'Why, Dad? What did he do to you?'

'He fucking corrupted you, son. I only followed you to find out who was messing you up. Your head's been up your arse for months. But we can fix this. We can get you help, boy.'

Jake looked to everyone in turn, his eyes desperate for validation, cowered when he found nothing but loathing.

He pleaded with his son. 'I thought you had another woman. I just wanted to warn her off you. Fuck's sake, son, I saw him kiss you. A man. It's disgusting, Liam. You're not one of them. I know you're not.'

He cowered back against the wall, his head down, his voice trailing away to a miserable mutter.

From the hallway, a woman's voice called, 'Detective Inspector McLeish?' Her face appeared for a second, scanning the room.

McLeish's eyes lit up. 'Yes. Three officers, three civilians, one assailant armed with a semi-automatic handgun, middle of room, your left. Be advised, officer in your firing line.'

Callahan seemed not to hear McLeish's eager shout. He stared at Jake, disbelief and betrayal etched on his face.

Malkie stepped between the two men. 'Give me the gun, mate. Those guys don't give second chances.'

Callahan looked at him, his eyes lost and bewildered, his lips a thin, hard, trembling line. 'It wasn't me?'

'No, Walter, it was never you. It was Jake, and I'm sorry I've been blind to it until now. He's nothing but a bigoted old man and he isn't worth losing your life for, is he?'

Callahan looked over Malkie's shoulder at Jake. 'You put me through all that. You let me think I'd killed that man. You let me think I was losing it again.'

He moved to step forward, but Malkie stood firm.

The woman's voice bellowed from the door, 'Armed police officer. Drop the weapon and get on the floor. I won't ask again.' Her rifle barrel poked through the hole in the door.

Malkie suppressed his instinct to move. Callahan looked desperate enough to go right through him to get to Jake, but as long as the AFOs held fire for fear of hitting Malkie in the gloom of the darkened room, he had a chance. Classic Malkie – fucking everything up again, but he knew he couldn't do anything else.

He placed his hands on Callahan's shoulders. 'Walter, stand down, man. You didn't do it. You were in the passenger seat. You pulled the handbrake. You saved Wilkie's life, mate.'

Malkie edged his hands down to Callahan's elbows.

From the door, the voice now a low, urgent, order: 'Sir, step away from the suspect.'

Callahan blinked. His shoulders sagged, but the gun stayed at chest height between them, shaking. His eyes welled up and spilled over, four days of hell he could contain no longer.

'I didn't kill him?'

Malkie's hands gripped Callahan's forearms. 'You saved his

life, Walter. He'd have died on the spot if you hadn't slowed the car down.'

McLeish growled, 'Move, McCulloch. That's an order.'

Malkie's fingers moved down to Callahan's wrists, gentle but firm. He searched the man's desperate and miserable eyes for any sign he'd got through, found a glimmer of a connection, a scrap of trust all but extinguished, and he willed it to spark into life.

'I told Helen Reid I'd bring you back to her. Don't make me break that promise, OK?'

'Helen asked you to help me? She doesn't hate me?' His fingers relaxed. The barrel of the gun dropped an inch. A fond smile touched his lips as tears spilled from his eyes.

Malkie shook his head and smiled back. 'Hate you? No, mate. She—'

McLeish barrelled into Malkie and tackled him to the floor. A deafening crack exploded from the doorway, and a round took Callahan in the back of one shoulder. The impact spun him around and two more shots slammed into his chest. Crimson starbursts erupted under his shirt as he flew backwards into Jake's arms.

Malkie screamed at the AFO. 'Stop shooting, stop fucking shooting.'

Jake dropped Callahan and recoiled. He fell back against the wall and slid to the floor. He raised his hands in front of himself, his fingers thick with Walter's blood, and stared at them, looked bewildered and appalled.

Malkie dived over and lifted Callahan, cradled him. The same as he did for the poor man in the nightclub. The one he never did go back to check on.

'I'm sorry Walter. You hear me? I'm sorry, mate.'

Callahan gagged and spat a gob of blood at Jake. He grabbed Malkie's coat lapel, pulled him down, face-to-face. 'Markham. Basement.'

He frowned, coughed, choked on more of his own blood.

Malkie looked away. As much as Callahan deserved to know one last true friend, he couldn't bear to meet his broken and bewildered eyes, and he knew he'd always hate himself for that.

Callahan went slack. When Malkie forced himself to look again, the light had left Walter Callahan's eyes.

SIXTY-FOUR

Water slapped on the hull of the *Droopy Goose*. Dad snored. Malkie stared at Steph in disbelief.

'Not one?'

'Nobody told you?'

'Nope. I'm on leave again, remember? Two weeks and McLeish has told me nothing. I'm keeping out of it, can't stomach any more of this one.'

'Fair point. No. Not a single one.'

Malkie scowled. 'Nae justice.'

Steph shook her head as if not quite believing it herself. 'All of them knee-capped but alive. Every one of them trussed and gagged and with tourniquets tied off above their knees. They'll walk funny for the rest of their rotten lives, but not one of them dead. Walter Callahan was a hell of a man, right enough.'

'Aye. He never wanted to kill anyone, but he ends up in the ground. That's a whole new kind of fucked-up, Steph. The wrong man got those bullets; should have been The Jakey, or his rotten son. I should have let you loose on Liam at their house. By the way, what the hell was that about? I thought you were going to kill him with your wee bare hands.

I've never seen you like that before. Where did that come from?'

Steph looked about to give him something, but then nodded toward Malkie's dad, asleep. 'Time and place, Malkie?' It was both a request and a refusal, so he added it to his mental *to be continued* list.

OK, Steph. Later. I promise.

Steph waved the subject away as if not worth talking about. 'How was the funeral?'

Malkie sighed. He'd dreaded today, and now he dreaded being asked about it.

'Disgraceful. Poor bastard deserved better. Lovely wee private cemetery at the LESOC but the turnout was pitiful. Me, Bernard Robertson, and Helen Reid. That Markham bloke that Robertson helped us find. I asked him how he was and he said "I'll live" but he didn't sound happy about it, weirdo. And a scruffy wee toerag called Norrie. Junkie, I think. Robertson glared at me all the way through and wouldn't speak to me. Helen Reid said she was sure I did my best but didn't bother to hide her disappointment.'

He looked at Steph, his eyes red-rimmed and raw. 'What the hell else could I have done, Steph?'

He should have known better than to ask her questions like that – he never liked the answers.

She shrugged. 'Maybe if you'd brought Amanda in right at the start—'

Malkie's arm lashed out and his coffee mug smashed into the galley sink. His dad sat bolt upright, confused, his eyes bleary, his thin white hair standing on end. 'What...?'

Malkie felt a stab of guilt at the sight of his dad's paper-thin skin and knotty fingers, his eyes bewildered and confused. 'Sorry, Dad. Just me being clumsy.'

His dad rubbed his eyes and yawned. He picked up the bottle from the table.

'Where did you say Monty got this? Tastes like cough mixture.'

Malkie laughed.

Dad smiled. 'That's a good sound to hear, Malcolm. I'm going to bed.' He patted the inside of the *Droopy Goose*'s hull with his hand. 'We'll carry on patching things up tomorrow, aye? Maybe go see the cabin.'

He shuffled away, forward.

Malkie pictured the cabin, huddled at the foot of the Pentland Hills that loomed over the flat, green expanse of West Lothian. His refuge from a youth ruined by vicious wee Sandra Morton and her disgrace of a family. He wondered if Sandra had really forgiven him with the passing of the years, but he doubted it. More likely she feared the fallout if one of her brothers was stupid enough to kill a copper.

He found Steph failing to hide a grin, a twinkle in her eyes.

'What?'

'Nothing, Malcolm.'

'Ha bloody ha. Shut it, Stephanie.'

She punched him on the arm. 'I've warned you about that.'

'Aye, well...'

Malkie slumped in his seat. Fatigue pulled at him, but his mind wouldn't rest.

'I'm sorry, Steph. You know, for...'

She gripped his arm in one hand until he had to look at her.

'I can see, now, why you did what you did, but... Never again, OK? At least try?'

Malkie nodded, but his relief at her forgiveness did nothing to salve his shame. He stood to find another mug. All the coffee he'd been guzzling explained why he couldn't stop his mind from eating at itself.

'Pammy Ballantyne asked me how you are.'

Malkie turned to her, disbelieving. 'Meaning she wants to

know if I'll help Management crucify her boss? Slimy wee cow's realised she backed the wrong horse, hasn't she?'

Steph chuckled. 'Aye, that's the impression I got. McLeish is worried. Aren't you?'

Malkie leaned his backside on the galley counter, chewed this over for a second.

'No. I spoke to a few witlesses when I shouldn't have and lost my temper with a mouth-breather. That's all.'

Steph tutted at 'witlesses' but let it go.

'He never formally suspended me, so all I did was disobey a superior officer who's since demonstrated he's more of a liability than I ever was. Bringing Amanda in earlier wouldn't have changed Callahan's actions. But if McLeish hadn't chased him off that day... No, he's got more to worry about than I do. All I did was protect the abused and terrified wife of a Person of Interest, not even a formal suspect. And only for a couple of nights. And maybe I forgot to update you about a couple of minor details.'

She gave him a look that promised violence if he pushed his luck.

'But McLeish? He was holding unsanctioned meetings with a known career criminal and withholding evidence from a Gartcosh Customs and Excise task force. I think it'll get handled on the quiet, if only to stop their big case from collapsing. I got a call from Whitton, though. Warned me what another fiasco like this might do to my career. Then he helpfully suggested I keep my gob shut, help them gloss over the whole clusterfuck. Although he might not have used those exact words.'

'Detective Superintendent James Whitton?'

'Aye. So, that's me done for if I'm on his radar now.'

Steph giggled, a musical chuckle more feminine than he was used to hearing from her.

'So, was it ciggies after all?'

She nodded. 'With booze planned for the future. The Jakey had big ambitions.'

Malkie's turn to laugh. 'Aye, but now he'll be scared shitless some Balkan brute with a porn star moustache and a garrotte comes looking for him; he's screwed up a lucrative smuggling route. And he won't find any welcome at home; Liam's disowned him and changed the locks.'

Steph frowned. 'It's not enough, though, is it? He'll not even do time for Wilkie.'

Malkie sighed. 'Let me guess – Jake's bedroom confession is inadmissible, made under duress and without a formal caution? And that weasel Simon Fraser will make sure nothing sticks to him, not with all the forensic evidence pointing right at Callahan, who can't defend himself now.'

She nodded. 'Correct. You could make a good copper, mate. The lab found traces of Ketamine in Callahan's whisky glass – like he said they would – but Jake's denying any knowledge of it. The Fiscal's doubtful it'll make it to court even though Fielding junior handed over everything he had on his dad's new business venture. McLeish took it all to the Task Force, hoped he could repair the damage, but he got a "Thanks – we'll call you." Struan Spalding's been asked to come back to work early but part-time, so McLeish is back at a desk and further from DCI than ever. I suspect you're off his good-guy list for life. Which will hurt, obviously.'

He sat beside her. Something dug into his backside. Amanda's spectacles case. His mood fell. How long since she sat on this couch, huddled into him, fragile and trusting? At least until he allowed himself to believe the worst of her. Shame flooded him. The fact that nothing happened would never excuse him for wanting it to.

Steph's voice was the softest he'd ever heard it. 'Amanda's?'

He held it up in his fingers and smiled. 'Aye. I'm happy she got out OK. Fielding junior agreed to divorce her in three seconds flat when I told him how careless my mouth can be. He's converting the whole place for wheelchair access, for when Wilkie gets out of hospital. Which he will, thanks to Callahan.'

He put the case on the table, left his fingers resting on it.

'Malkie...'

'I know. Nothing was ever going to come of it. Not after finding out her pal Marjorie is a six-foot-seven barman called Anton.'

Steph rubbed his arm, but the gleam in her eye said she found the whole thing hilarious. 'Are those flowers from her?'

Malkie grimaced. 'Aye.'

Steph picked up a white card beside the vase.

*Malkie. Thanks, and sorry. I was desperate. Your friend,
Amanda. Xxx*

'Nice. Kisses, even.' She said it with sincerity, which meant she was taking the piss.

'Oh, sod off.'

She laughed. 'Ach, you're a precious wee soul, Malkie.' She stood, grabbed her jacket. 'Time for bed. I've still got shed loads of paperwork to do thanks to you and McLeish. Callahan's body only got released so quick because they couldn't find a next of kin for the poor guy. Oh, and Robbie McGuire's reported his brother missing, says Jake Fielding's behind it, so we might get to nail that animal for something, after all.'

She put one foot on the bottom step of the deck ladder, then turned back. 'Oh, I nearly forgot. That guy at The Libertine you asked me to check on? His name is Davey Hutson, or Luscious Letitia on Friday and Saturday nights. He's fine, made a full recovery, and he remembers you. He sends kisses.' She grinned, loving the look on Malkie's face.

'You going to be OK, old man? Do I need to worry?'

367

He gave her a small smile of affection. 'I'm fine. Now piss off before I get all misty-eyed.'

'Arse.' She grinned, then climbed out into the night.

After one hundred and ninety-two days of refusing himself any kind of comfort, he allowed himself to cry. Quiet, miserable tears he could believe – at long last – he might deserve. He'd saved one poor woman from a brutal and abusive life and helped two tormented men escape their different personal hells. But was it enough?

The massive, mum-shaped hole in him ached. He promised her one day he'd find the courage to look back to that night, to banish the guilt he clung to like a penitent's scourge. He'd not rest until he remembered how else he'd failed her, what final sin of his let her die alone and terrified. He doubted he'd ever believe himself completely blameless in her death. Until then, if he could at least believe she'd approve of his recent actions, he'd lift his head and find the courage to look forward again.

He stepped out onto the deck, heard Steph's car drive off. The calm of the marina settled around him, the night air icy. A salty breeze blew in off the Firth of Forth. Rigging lines flapped and smacked against masts. A lone gull called, seeking a roost for the night. He sipped his coffee and watched lights twinkle across the mass of black water from homes in North Queensferry. Homes full of people. Good people. The best of people under constant threat from the worst.

What he did mattered, didn't it? Made a difference?

We do what we can, as his mum used to say.

A LETTER FROM THE AUTHOR

I hope you enjoyed this, my debut book, and I hope you found yourself rooting for Malkie's constant fight to see some good in everyone, even the most irredeemable of us. If you'd like to hear about all my Storm Publishing releases, you can sign up here to my newsletter.

www.stormpublishing.co/doug-sinclair

Can I ask you to be kind enough to leave a review of this book on Amazon? Let me know what you liked and what you didn't like, what resonated with you and what really didn't. I need to know so I can grow as a writer and help Malkie be a better man.

One of the questions most often asked of authors is 'Where do you get your ideas from?' I don't always know where my specific ideas come from, but I know why I write. Why I have to write. To paraphrase something very damaging someone used to say to me, 'For an intelligent species we can be very stupid, sometimes', and even into adulthood, I find myself confused and dismayed by the depths to which human behaviour can sink. I believe crime fiction is the single best medium to explore social issues, particularly how circumstance can drive even the best of us to commit the most horrific deeds.

Please check out my website at www.dougsinclair.co.uk for information on forthcoming books and some free short stories, some of which were written decades ago and languished in a drawer until I dusted them off and decided to believe in them. I write an occasional blog, too, where you can get to know me a wee bit better.

You can connect with me on Facebook or X, and I'd love to hear your comments – the good, the bad, and the ridiculous.

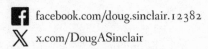

facebook.com/doug.sinclair.12382

x.com/DougASinclair

ACKNOWLEDGEMENTS

This book could easily have not happened. My amazing wife, Maaike, is by far the primary reason it did.

I spent the first fifty years of my life suffering undiagnosed depression and convinced nothing I might ever write could be any good, however much I dreamed of doing so. Maaike made me get help, and probably saved my life. Only then could I start the long fight to build some self-belief where none had existed before.

The crime fiction tribe is amazing. There's no competition between authors, everyone wants everyone else to succeed. 'All about sending the elevator back down', as someone told me. I've been supported on my journey to publication by too many people to list you all. If I missed anyone who deserves a mention, please accept my abject apologies.

First thanks go to my wife Maaike, and my mum, both of whom believed in me when I couldn't, and to Donna, my ever-supportive sister-in-law and beta reader.

Thanks to Gordon Brown who asked me one day, 'What the hell is happening with your book?' then read it and passed it to my now-agent the lovely Kevin Pocklington of The North Literary Agency, who found it a home with the excellent Storm Publishing. I'm grateful to Oliver Rhodes and Claire Bord for taking a punt on me.

As for my incredible editor, Kate Smith, where do I start? I'm in awe of her talents. Many writers dread edits, hate seeing all that red ink. I love edits. I get too close to my books and stop seeing them straight. Kate 'gets' Malkie and she improved this book immeasurably while never once sparking a full-on bun-fight. Thanks, Kate – you're a wonder.

Thanks to all who supported and advised me, and kicked my arse when I needed it. Craig Robertson, Caro Ramsay, Douglas Skelton, Mark Leggatt, Neil Broadfoot, Gordon Brown, Michael Malone, Carla Kovach, Zoe Sharp, Alex Gray, Graham Smith, Alison Belsham, Noelle Holten, Sharon Bairden, Jacky Collins, Kelly Lacey, Suze Bickerton, Gail Williams – thank you for repeatedly reminding me I *can* do this writing lark.

The Twisted Sisters of Dumfries – Irene, Fiona, Linda, Anne, Jackie, Hayley – thank you for letting me join your gang and being there for me.

Andy & Al, Rich, Dave T, Meesh, Wendy – thank you for your patience and for keeping your sarcasm to a minimum.

Eleanor, Fergus, Rosie, Lorne, Kathy, Henbo, Joss – thank you for sticking with me when I made it so difficult, sometimes. Love you more than all the garlicky scrambled eggs in the known universe.

Made in United States
Orlando, FL
24 March 2024

45121844R00225